Shadow Family

a novel

Also by Wayne Caldwell:

Novels

Cataloochee (2007)
Requiem by Fire (2010; reissued 2020)

Poetry

Woodsmoke (2021)
River Road (2024)

Shadow Family

a novel

Wayne Caldwell

LAKE DALLAS, TEXAS

Requests for permission to reprint or reuse material
from this work should be sent to:

Permissions
Madville Publishing
PO Box 358
Lake Dallas, TX 75065

Cover design: Jacqueline and Kimberly Davis
Author photo: Mary Caldwell

ISBN: 978-1-963695-13-7 paperback
978-1-963695-14-4 ebook

Library of Congress Control Number: 2024946133

For

Peggy Jo

who gave me up—

and for

Troy and Ruby

who took me as an infant

and made me feel most welcome in this world

For unto us a child is born,
Unto us a son is given...
—Isaiah 9.6a

With hope we tell our own stories—to make sense both of our walk in darkness and our glimpses of great light. Our voices, seeking ground for being, call out to kin and stranger—and who really knows the difference?

Following are three voices, bound—whether known or not—by chance and blood and ineffable grace.

I

April Fool

Priscilla Ruth Lance

Want to know who I am? Couldn't answer that with a kabillion words. But I can sure say who I *was*. Maybe that will help with the first question—then maybe we'll both know.

I was a blonde-headed, gum-chewing high school senior living in a mountain settlement near Asheville. I really wasn't a bad girl. Didn't smoke. Didn't drink. No beauty, but not bad-looking. Technically a virgin. Engaged to a sailor who didn't cuss. My world was school, Friday night football, square dancing, church, ice cream and ginger ale. A long and happy life ahead.

Then...

Oh, phooey, this is tip-of-the-iceberg stuff. Miss Harrell, my English teacher, said, "If you start at the beginning and leave nothing out you'll have something worth telling. That's how the Bible works, you know." So here goes.

I was born April 1, 1930. Yes, I know, "there's a big old bug in your hair" or "I got you a nifty present this year," then comes "April Fool!" Enough to ruin a little girl. At least it wasn't as bad as being a Christmas baby.

My mother, Wanda, called me her "little April fool" when in a good humor, and "Priscilla Ruth Lance" when she meant business. My father, Walker, mostly called me "Sweetheart," although he said if he'd known the Depression was coming he'd not have come near Wanda the July before I happened along. Makes a girl feel wanted.

Walker Lance and Wanda McKinney first met at the Crawford Baptist Church as Cradle Roll babies. Afterward, except for Walker's army hitch, they were never—at least that I know of—apart. In a wedding picture he stands with suit jacket slung over his left shoulder, right arm around Wanda, his brown hair almost long enough to curl. His arms seem ready to split his sleeves—he became a body builder in the service and did calisthenics daily until his heart exploded at fifty-five—and he grins like he'd bagged Wanda on some safari. Her smile says she enjoyed being a blue-eyed, blonde, busty trophy.

Crawford, North Carolina wasn't really a town or even much of a village, and I hear it's been bypassed by DOT and swallowed by development. Back then it was a lively enough mountain crossroads, and if you needed more excitement you caught a bus to Asheville or the Southern Railway to wherever. Three creeks converged under twin bridges, and what we called Main Street—a mere gravel road—ran between water and train tracks. Our one-story post office was veneered with creek rock, and next door—close enough to look glued on—sat a clapboard barber shop, lunchroom, and general store. North of Main Street our school was dug into the hillside on top of which the Baptist church kept watch over the settlement, just as the Methodist church protected our southern flank.

Crawford's biggest house, with enough porch to hold a square dance, belonged to our doctor, who, a decade before I arrived, gave up horse and buggy in favor of a Ford. Two years before I was born, a clutch of rambling boarding houses for workers in the new textile mill a mile or two away had sprouted like a string of mushrooms. The unrighteous among these men frequented the Crawford Springs, a white building with a second-story overhang like a beer belly. Poolroom downstairs, Lord knows what upstairs. Nice people, Wanda said, didn't go there.

We lived in what I thought was a big house—a story and a half with a full front porch, brick columns at either end. As an adult I learned it was a bungalow, a word my little girl's imagination had figured to be a house for rabbits. When I graduated to Nancy Drew I thought a bungalow was a kind of shack. Whatever, our place was comfortable, full of reassuring groans and creaks, corners to hide in, and the weekly perfume of fresh pound cake.

We didn't suffer during the Depression like some did. Walker, a fine builder, worked for the few people who had money, repairing stuff, adding rooms and such. He was frequently out of state. We raised chickens for eggs and meat. Down the road the Birdsongs kept hogs and a milk cow. Mrs. Birdsong, a flat-faced woman, always wore an apron—I never saw Mr. Birdsong in anything but overalls. She didn't look Cherokee but he sure did, dark-complected, nose like a tomahawk. They sold milk and butter, and every fall my father went shares with Mr. Birdsong on a hog, so we ate sausage and bacon and ham. And, like everyone, we tended a kitchen garden. As my mother said, people didn't know they were poor.

Many girls had two dresses, one for school, one for church, but I had several, none made from feed sacks, and always got a new dress and shoes for Easter. Walker, who owned one Sunday suit worn twice a year, groused about spending on "just clothes," but Wanda said they were not luxuries. "We have to hold our heads up. Priscilla Ruth, never look or sound *common*," a disdainful word I inherited from her. I even frowned on common denominators in arithmetic.

We played with found stuff or things we coaxed parents into making. Summer Saturdays, boys on Main Street walked on stilts, rode in wagons pulled by fair-sized dogs, played stickball or hoops. We girls either covered cornshuck dolls with little quilts in perambulators handed down from our own babyhood, or carried our "babies" papoose-style. We held tea parties with imaginary guests and played dress-up in our mamas' high heels. When it snowed we gathered at the top of Main Street with pieces of roofing tin or cardboard to slide down to the railroad, where adults tended a bonfire and served hot chocolate and oatmeal cookies.

The spring I turned six, one neighbor's father, a plumber, built a swing set from leftover galvanized pipe. For a season his yard was our world's center, from which came no telling how many skinned knees and turned ankles. We kids were in heaven.

Walker, not to be outdone, built a two-story ten-room dollhouse complete with scale-model furniture and appliances. It wasn't fancy like the Biltmore House but every girl around brought dolls to visit. Wanda never complained about kids tramping through her house but let Walker know she didn't appreciate my house having a more modern kitchen than hers.

For a time, we had cats. Wanda fed stray kitties outside and watched them carefully, like they competed for an in-house spot. Walker tolerated one indoor cat at a time.

People began to dump cats at our house. Sometimes we'd have three, go to the store, and return to find five. The summer I was four, Walker, gone two months, came home to find a dozen lollygagging around. That night we had only one indoor pussycat, a calico named Blossom, while a German shepherd, Kaiser Bill, ill-disposed toward felines, patrolled our yard.

I've always loved to dance. Wanda said in her womb I jitterbugged one day, waltzed the next. When I was a baby she'd hold me up while I danced in her lap or on a tabletop. I'd sway like a little heathen to the radio. I'd dance with baby dolls, or Blossom the cat, who'd flatten her ears and hiss but never bite me. Maybe she should have.

When I discovered tap dancing I put thumbtacks in shoe heels and toes and drove Wanda nuts. I didn't need music—I always had a soundtrack in my little head.

The problem was, we were Baptists, so I never danced in public. We couldn't even play Ring Around the Rosie at church picnics. This wasn't a big deal when I was little—except Wanda had to keep a close eye lest I forget and break out in a dance—but caused fireworks as I grew older.

Until I started school our routines revolved around radio soap operas and church. I cannot smell grilled cheese or tomato soup without picturing our kitchen, me and my little sister Grace on one side of the counter, Wanda on the other, sitting on backless stools, eating soup and sandwich.

Come hell or high water we parked there at twelve-thirty for what she called "my story."

"Time now for 'The Romance of Helen Trent,' the real-life drama of Helen Trent, who, when life mocks her, breaks her hopes, dashes her against the rocks of despair, fights back bravely, successfully, to prove what so many women long to prove in their own lives, that because a woman is thirty-five or more, romance in life need not be over..." (The sponsor, Kolynos Dental Cream, promised to rid us of Bacterial Mouth.)

For fifteen minutes Wanda listened to Helen pursue happiness in the person of Gil Whitney—or some other attractive man dressed to the nines, even to pocket pouf. We said not a word. If the kitchen had caught fire I suppose she would have saved us along with the radio, but if the phone rang or a Jehovah's Witness knocked? Forget it.

I have tried to fathom what my mother, then in her mid-twenties, heard in Helen's search—whether Wanda wanted steamy romance or was simply afraid of going over the hill. She kept up with Helen's story for decades.

I loved Sundays. I enjoyed dressing up for church, for one thing, and the Asheville paper ran color comics. I'd lie in the floor with the paper, taking in Dick Tracy's axe-blade chin or the Katzenjammer Kids' wild hair. The first word Walker taught me to read was Little Orphan Annie's dog Sandy's "Arf." I didn't much like *Life with Father*, for I thought Maggie with her rolling pin was mean and Jiggs was dumb. Mutt and Jeff were just silly. But I really liked Blondie—she looked like my mother.

Church bound us to its schedule. "Us" didn't include Walker. "I hear about Jesus Christmas and Easter," he said, "and that's plenty. The rest just gets Him from one place to another." But Wanda, Grace, and I showed up Sunday morning, Sunday night, Wednesday night, every revival meeting, Bible school session, you name it.

Oh, I liked when the preacher talked about Jesus suffering little children and finding lost lambs, but when he droned about weird Old Testament stuff I made a lap desk out of a hymn book and grabbed a blunt yellow pencil from the pew rack. I shaded in the letters in the mimeographed bulletin, starting with vowels, then b's, d's, and so on. Teachers talked about "taking pains" with our work, so while the preacher droned I took pains to be neat and wondered why it didn't hurt.

Our little church believed in baptism by immersion, the priesthood of the believer, missions, and dinner on the ground. We did not believe in drinking, dancing, or "frolicking." No "mixed" Sunday School classes—as in men and women together. (In those days Black and white never dared think to worship together.)

Before I was born, my mother started a Sunday School class for women her age, called "The Ruth Class." One member cross-stitched a sampler to hang on their classroom door: "Whither Thou Goest," as if Ruth following her mother-in-law was like obeying Jesus' "Go ye therefore into all nations." I wouldn't be surprised if they figured Lottie Moon, a Baptist saint, had said "Whither thou goest" to God. Actually, she probably did.

These women were thick as thieves. Over the years, on Promotion Day no one "moved up" because age, marital status, or beliefs changed. They worked and played together, baking, canning, stringing beans, quilting, and, as times got better, shopping. They played no cards but sometimes watched a Saturday matinee. If one took sick, child care was shared. During the war they made bandages and knitted sweaters for soldiers. Girlfriends in the best sense of the word, they stuck together through whatever life threw at them—babies, sicknesses, deaths.

Even one divorce. Her husband just up and left. You know how hens will peck a weak sister to death? Well, not the Ruth Class. The Sunday after her no-count husband took off, three carloads showed up at their bereft sister's house to find her in curlers and housecoat. They brought a coconut cake, two Thermoses of coffee, and Bibles. She hurriedly dressed, they cried a bunch, had class, and the next Sunday she was back in church. A shining moment.

The preacher, deacons, and Sunday School Superintendent thought men ran the church. These women knew better. They taught Bible School, supervised nursery workers, and designated who brought potato salad or ham or pound cake to the bereaved. And as they became more prosperous (and generally broader across the beam), they, like my mother, were keenly aware of How Things Looked. It was never spoken of, but their divorced sister never kept the nursery or filled communion cups with grape juice.

When I was in fourth grade my Sunday School room looked out on a corner of the graveyard. Carved on one nearly hundred-year-old stone, for a woman named Susannah, was "She hath done what she could." Every week I stared at her headstone, wondering why that was so important. Later I learned it came from the red letter part of Mark, where Jesus excuses a sinner for anointing his feet. Our preacher said she was Mary Magdalene, a common whore. (I didn't know what a whore was but if she was common, well…) Why would Susannah want that on her headstone? Adults, even dead ones, confused me.

Vacation Bible School happened every July. Every morning for two weeks we marched into the sanctuary behind the Christian flag and stood while some holier-than-thou kid placed the flag in its stanchion. (Did it a few times myself.) Then, in as much unison as kids can muster, we yelled "I pledge allegiance to the Christian flag, and to the gospel for which it stands…"

Bible School was Kool-Aid. Big icy pitchers of it, grape my favorite. We pretended it was wine that gave us the blind staggers, until our teacher put a stop to that. We also had God's plenty of cookies—raisin, oatmeal, chocolate chip. One year a little boy, not the child of a member, showed up the second morning with a sign pinned to his overalls—"Please don't feed me sugar—it makes me mean." We made sure he got an overdose that afternoon. He never came back. It's what happens when you mix Jesus and sugar.

Our preacher, Mr. Brown, was not what you'd call charismatic. About five-and-a-half feet tall, he was really nearsighted and wore round horn-rimmed glasses. During the week Mr. Brown had sold cars until the Depression hit, after which he worked at a bakery in Asheville. He'd get up at two in the morning and go to town, bake until done, then come home, tend to animals and garden, and read his Bible.

He said God called him to preach at sixteen, but like Jonah he high-tailed it and joined the Navy. Instead of having Mr. Brown thrown over-board, God, not to be ignored, arranged for him to preach Saturdays to anyone on the base who might be interested.

When he returned to Crawford, the church, having recently run off a pastor—something about a woman or money or both—hired him on trial. They liked him, soon ordained him, and after a decade the church had grown.

He was not one to scare hell out of you in a sermon but he sure slipped up on you. He'd go on about Jesus and the woman at the well, said Jesus told her she had had five husbands. Then Reverend Brown would slide into the part of the story John left out, about her pitiful children who had nobody to tell them about hell, and next thing you knew here'd slink some snotty-nosed nine-year-old down the aisle seeking baptism before time ran out.

The summer I was ten, Reverend Brown preached about the Prodigal Son. I didn't think that had to do with me, so I studied mockingbirds and blue jays out the open window. I wore a white dress with an itchy collar. I'd doodled on the bulletin and even reverted to filling in letters, when Reverend Brown said not just boys were prodigals. No sir, there could be prodigal daughters! Wanda's business look nudged me.

He said he'd been to Asheville, and to Raleigh, and, once even to Charlotte, where young women entered cesspools of temptation called dance halls, to be embraced in the arms of young men they had never seen before. It was but a step from dancing to entering the broad road to ruin. And ruined women either played the harlot or wandered the streets with tattered clothes and dirty faces and babes in their arms, hungry, cold. Straight out of Dickens.

Reverend Brown asked who was ready to accept Jesus as her (I swear, he said "her") personal savior, and as we began to sing "Just As I Am" Wanda arched an eyebrow at me. I didn't know what a harlot was but to be safe I slipped from the pew and tiptoed down the aisle. I was the only one that day, although we sang all forty verses and started over like we'd sing until the piano lady fell off her bench.

He patted my head. "In the name of Jesus Christ we welcome our sister Priscilla into the arms of His church. She will be baptized, to the glory of God, hallelujah. She's the namesake of Paul's co-worker in Corinth, so will be a tireless laborer for the Lord. Sister, welcome!"

His breath would have knocked a parrot from its perch. I was surprised my dress didn't wither like a cut flower in the sun. But there I was, nowhere to hide, nothing to do except try not to breathe through my nose. After worship everyone congratulated me as a beaming Wanda stood beside, calling it the happiest day of her life.

Several girls walked the aisle that summer, the year before the war started—or, I should say, before Pearl Harbor shoved America into it. I'd like to say we sensed impending doom, but we were ten or eleven. Wanda called us her "chickadees," and that was about right. We noisily flitted after food and attention—none of us felt bound for trouble.

That summer one boy gave his life to Jesus, a quiet kid named Patrick Allen, who, I learned later, already had his eye on me. But boys were as far from my mind as the abominable snowman. Maybe farther.

G.A. stands for Girls' Auxiliary, the more or less teenage arm of the Women's Missionary Union. Little girls started in Sunbeams and graduated to G.A.s as the years advanced. As we piled up verses we became Ladies in Waiting, where most of us remained. The distant (and pushed-for) goal was Queen, which meant you memorized half the Bible and prayed for real live missionaries.

Coronations were big deals for girls in no danger of becoming

Homecoming Queen or even homeroom secretary. It might be their only time to dress like a beauty contestant (we didn't have proms back then) and march down a long aisle, followed by Ladies in Waiting and Maidens and such, to be fussed over by everyone.

Diana Turnipseed, bless her heart, in ninth grade weighed a good two hundred pounds. Her coronation dress took a ton of white organdy, and, as my mother so delicately put it, the Turnipseeds didn't have a pot to pee in. Her father was an odd job man and her mother suffered from some heart condition—we forever left food baskets on their doorstep.

Diana could say the begats backward and forward, and knew her times tables before any of us. So when she made Queen, Wanda rolled her eyes, said to the Ruthians, "Girls, you know what we have to do," and took up money for fabric. She sewed Diana's dress herself.

One Wednesday I leaned on the doorframe when Wanda brought in a basket of folded laundry. "Mama, I don't want to go to church tonight."

"Don't be ridiculous."

"I'm not," I said. "I just don't want to go."

She swooshed by me and began to put clothes away. "Of course you do, dear." She opened various dresser drawers, sighed, checked herself in the mirror, then gave me her business face. "Priscilla Ruth Lance, you're going, and that's that."

I stuck out my lip. "Mama, I'm too old for that stuff."

She put her hand on my shoulder. Firmly. "Darling, nobody gets too old for church. Besides, if a girl stays in church, she keeps away from bad influences."

"Like what?"

She sat on my bed and gazed out the window.

"They are legion. Most have to do with boys. Men. Who dance, and don't go to church."

"But Mama, it says in Ecclesiastes there's a time to dance."

"Hmp. Do you remember the story of the Ten Commandments?"

"Sure."

"So you remember Moses came down the mountain and broke the tablets on the rocks?"

"So?"

"So? Don't you remember why?"

"The golden calf."

"Child, the people were dancing!"

You couldn't win.

"How do you know all these bad—what did you call them, influences?"

She stroked my arm and looked me in the eye.

"Honey, your old mother's been around a time or two. And, by the way, I used to dance, myself. Just trust me. I know what I'm talking about."

"So I still can't dance, and have to go to church."

"You bet. It's for your own good. Besides, how would it look for the daughter of the Ruth Class's leader not to be a Queen?" She left, humming "Bringing in the Sheaves."

At my coronation, my white dress and her yellow one made us look like an old-timey two-tone frilly daffodil. Her class congratulated us and said how pretty and smart I was and how one day I'd be a fine Christian mother like the woman in Proverbs thirty-one.

I guess my unruly streak started the summer I was twelve. Grace and I had shared a bedroom downstairs, but my father, home for an un-heard-of six-week stretch, decided to finish out our bungalow's upstairs, so in August I moved into my own bedroom!

I loved it. At the head of the stairs, it was long and narrow, and filled nearly the whole width of the house. I had a closet with a full-length door mirror, and a white vanity, twin bed, and chest of drawers to match. Walker had put in a bathroom at Mr. Sluder's store in Asheville in trade for it. In one corner I kept my big dollhouse.

Its first-night smell—turpentine, paint, bright nails, and varnish—gave me a headache, so I knelt by the open dormer window and took in random scents of the neighborhood—cows, pigs, a faint skunk, a far-off rainstorm mixed with woodsmoke from our neighbor, who was still up canning beans or tomatoes or something. I heard dogs and the train at the Turnpike crossing and about a million jarflies buzzing in the trees.

About midnight this crazy mockingbird down the road went through every song she knew, robin to thrush to bluebird to train whistle. I lay watching the ceiling, clutching my ratty old teddy bear, wondering why I was lucky enough to have such a serenade.

The next morning Wanda said she'd shut her window so she could sleep. "Last time I heard such a performance was the night before my father died," she said, which about scared the pants off me. I felt better when after a week Walker was still alive and our old, sick neighbor had died. But then I felt ashamed I'd prayed for another man's death. You can't win.

1945 was a watershed year for Wanda's carefree chickadees. The war had knocked most of the foolishness out of us. There was rationing and shortages and, much worse, every now and then someone we knew became a Blue Star Mother, which meant a friend had lost a big brother or uncle or cousin. Then on April 12 President Roosevelt, the only president we had ever known, died down in Georgia. How could that be? A persistent and reassuring bell, suddenly silent. We didn't decorate our kitchen walls with Jesus and FDR like the Turnipseeds, but we did think him a great man. Now he was gone, while war threatened to last forever.

But come August our world changed so rapidly that, as the hymn says, I scarce could take it in. On the one hand, Monday the sixth we bombed Hiroshima, Thursday the ninth we bombed Nagasaki, and the Japanese surrendered on the fifteenth. On the other hand, Wanda and Grace and I became Methodists on the nineteenth.

I never figured out exactly why. Probably Wanda had said or done something un-take-back-able, which gave her no choice but to leave Crawford Baptist. She was close-mouthed as a giant clam about it. But that Sunday we joined Foster Memorial Methodist Church, where we were warmly welcomed. Grace and I knew lots of kids there, so after the service there was general rejoicing at the communion rail, behind which stained glass glowed. We hugged our friends and giggled. We were invited to join Sunday School classes and to attend next Sunday's picnic. Wanda said she'd fix a plate of deviled eggs and bake a pound cake and, I don't know, it was all liberating. Wanda seemed relieved. At least she smiled for the first time in a week or two.

A week later a new friend from church invited me to try out for her dance team, and Wanda said yes! Life suddenly seemed good again. The dreary jackboots of war had been replaced by dancing shoes. I even felt ready for high school.

Crawford had two school buildings—an ancient clapboard affair that until the late thirties housed every grade—and the "new" brick building—erected when I was eight—that became our high school. The old school had been un-maintained, except for paint every decade. The floors creaked and the window glass was as wavy as funhouse mirrors. All we used in it was the gymnasium—the rest of the building was off-limits. It was pretty creepy—desks stacked like they awaited long-dead students.

About the time I went to high school I started "filling out." I'm sure Walker thought about chaining me to our basement wall. Wanda was less strict, although that's relative. At least she encouraged me to look my best. She had always said I mustn't slouch, and hold my head up. When I heeded that part of her advice I felt pretty. Plus she let me use nail polish. My tastes there tended toward bright red.

Boys who sat in front of me tended to drop pencils, hoping when they bent over to pick them up to look up my dress. One afternoon in Mr. Thompson's class, Jerry—this oaf who enjoyed picking on younger kids—dropped his pencil and grinned. I ignored him. When he did it again I crossed and uncrossed my legs, slowly. Gasping, he fell into the aisle, like he was having a heart attack or something.

Mr. Thompson had a long black paddle with holes in it. Without complaining, Jerry took seven whacks from it, after which Mr. Thompson gave me something between a smile and a smirk. Sister Priscilla, she lay low.

Mr. Thompson taught math and science, was tall like a new pencil, and wore his salt-and-pepper hair short. Until the first grades came out, we girls liked him—the boys mostly didn't. I wouldn't say he was dreamy but he wasn't hard to look at. And smart? He made girls who had never missed As in math cry like their mamas had just died. Decorating sorry homework with construction paper flowers didn't cut it. He'd fail you in a heartbeat.

He'd played college baseball and could zing a piece of chalk across your desktop with the best of them. He might be writing an equation on the board while someone passed a note or whispered to a neighbor. He'd wheel around without looking, hurl the chalk, and never hit a wrong target.

Our English teacher, Miss Laura Harrell, was born in east Tennessee. Educated at Carson-Newman College, she threw erasers instead of chalk. Year round she wore tweed skirts, satiny blouses, and cameo pins. Soaking wet, she might have weighed ninety-five. She smelled of Camels, coffee, and lilacs, the last, I guess, in honor of Walt Whitman.

Her mind made hard-to-follow leaps—we might begin with Keats and end up with "Casey At the Bat." I loved that class.

When we acted up she had two ways to get our attention. Throwing erasers—she was as accurate as Mr. Thompson—or ringing a handbell kept on the corner of her desk. It was brass, maybe three inches high, with a walnut handle. Around the bell's outer edge marched a line of what we thought were acorns until she set us straight.

"These are pomegranates. Now, who knows about them?"

Silence.

"I thought teenagers knew everything."

Scraping of feet and clearing of throats.

"Well, let's try another tack. Are there pomegranates in the Bible?"

Diana Turnipseed, looking confident, raised her hand.

"'And beneath upon the hem of it thou shalt make pomegranates of blue, and of purple, and of scarlet, round about the hem thereof; and bells of gold between them round about.' Exodus, the twenty-eighth chapter, verse thirty-three."

"Miss Turnipseed, I *am* impressed. Can you tell me what hem you're talking about?"

"Aaron's robe, Miss Harrell."

"And who was Aaron?"

"Moses's brother—the first high priest of Israel."

"Anybody know these lines?" On the blackboard she wrote in her beautiful hand:

> Holiness on the head,
> Light and reflection on the breast,
> Harmonious bells below raising the dead
> To lead them unto life and rest,
> Thus are true Aarons drest.

More silence.

"George Herbert wrote this. A poem called 'Aaron.' Herbert was a friend of John Donne, about whom we talked yesterday. Remember? The poet and priest who tried out his coffin?" She smiled. "Notice how the lines are shaped like a bell, and the middle line, which changes the image from light to sound, is the clapper."

Pat Allen raised his hand. "Miss Harrell, a bell can't ring on its side."

"Mister Allen, you *are* a literalist, aren't you?" From behind his desk she rolled her eyes and tapped his noggin with a piece of chalk. "Poetry requires imagination, sir. Now, has anyone ever seen a pomegranate?"

Fruit, to us, was strawberries in spring, plums and cherries in summer, apples and grapes in the fall, maybe an orange in a Christmas stocking. If we were trying to be funny, we might call eggs "hen fruit."

On the blackboard she drew a circle filled with smaller circles. "This is what it looks like inside. Tons of seeds. You can see why it was a symbol of fecundity. Define 'fecundity.'"

No takers.

"Know what a cornucopia is?"

A few of us nodded. "It's the horn of plenty," Diana said.

"Very good—that's our emblem of fecundity, which is to say, plenty, fertility, the bounty of harvest. We symbolize it with a horn—ancient Hebrews used a pomegranate."

From there she jumped to *Paradise Lost*, saying "the fruit of that forbidden tree" might have been a pomegranate, not an apple. (Many of us knew that poem's first page pretty well. When we overstepped our bounds, instead of making us write "I will not cut up in class" five hundred times, she made us diagram its first sentence, which ran to about a million lines.)

I only had to do that once—and thought I was going to die before it was over. I'd begun to let Pat Allen carry my books between classes—and he might have been a literalist but he could flat diagram a sentence. See, that passage doesn't have a verb until way later than it should. When I moaned to Pat, he laughed. "I'll show you how to read that stuff," he said, and did, and soon we became serious about each other. You might say Miss Harrell brought us together.

I had known Pat forever but early on he was just a jug-eared kid, part of my life's furniture. In our community Christmas pageants he was a shepherd, never wise man or Joseph. I was an angel, training to be the Virgin Mary.

The only only child in Crawford, he and his mother lived in a three-room shack dug into the hill behind the post office, close enough to the creek you could toss rocks into it from the porch. His father had died in some mysterious incident involving alcohol. His mother took in washing and sewed for people until the textile mill opened. Then she landed a shift job in the reeling department and farmed Pat out to his aunt until she made permanent day shift. She earned ten or twelve dollars a week, which back then kept two people up pretty well.

When Pat's face caught up with his ears he wasn't bad-looking. I thought he'd never flirt with me—every other boy in creation did—so one day—this was right before the *Paradise Lost* encounter—I walked up to him at the water fountain. He looked up sideways like he was a deer and I was a panther. I honestly thought he was going to run through the wall like in the cartoons. His face went through about a hundred expressions before he smiled. "Hi," he said.

I nodded. "Hi."

His eyes stayed on my chest long enough for me to clear my throat, which made him blush like I'd caught him robbing the offering plate. "Hi," he said.

"Is that all you can say?"

"Well, no, I mean, gosh, it's just, well… can I walk you home this afternoon?"

"I'd like that."

"Really? You mean it?"

I touched his arm. He looked at my hand, then met my eyes with a look of joy—or gratitude—like he wanted to take my hand but was afraid I'd disappear or something. He finally touched my fingertips. "Gee… thanks."

We were soon a couple.

Walker was a legend among Crawford boys. To be alone with me—or as alone as you could get in such a place—a boy had to pass muster, which involved a billion questions, a similar number of threats, and an invasive grilling after he brought me home.

Pat was not shy with him. The Sunday after the water fountain he told my father he planned to make something out of himself. He didn't want to stay in Crawford forever, he wanted to join the Navy, see the world, learn a trade, all that stuff. That was right up Walker's alley, for the service had taught him the benefits of discipline, fresh air, and exercise. They hit it off nicely. Of course, Walker told Pat if he found out the boy had tried anything with me he'd find his head separated from his shoulders. But Pat pushed honorable intentions, and even gave a speech about marriage's sanctity. Walker somehow took Pat at his word. They not only got along, they decided to trout fish the next weekend. People said, approvingly, that because Walker hadn't killed him, we would certainly marry in the fullness of time.

Pat was six feet tall, maybe a hundred and seventy-five pounds, with shoulders a girl might hang onto in a windstorm. His short, brown hair turned nearly blond in summer. His brown eyes could go from thoughtful to mischievous within a second, and his smile was marred only by a tooth broken when he was a boy.

The only disappointing things about Pat were his two left feet. He was a terrible dancer not interested in learning. He could carry a football and shoot a basketball but saw no sense in square dancing, not even when I showed him trophies were to be won.

I couldn't even make him jealous enough to learn, because my Crawford Cut-Ups partner, Allan Miller, a prince of a dancer, was—well, not much to look at. Walker said he was ugly as a mud fence, which suited Papa just fine. I danced with Allan all through high school without, as they say, incident.

So Pat and I were the basketball player and the cheerleader. I sure didn't mind decorating his arm, and people said we'd make good-looking babies one day.

I didn't know beans about that. My birds and bees came from girl talk, and a very short session in health class. Oh, and right after my first monthly, Wanda—who never said a word to me about sex except "Don't"—left a toad-colored five-hundred-page book on my bed that, I suppose, she thought would tell me everything.

I opened *Modern Eugenics* to find drawings instead of anatomical photographs. Dark, ominous sketches. The one of female organs made me think the Phantom of the Opera lived inside me, and I was pretty sure my outer parts down there didn't look like a vampire bat. Boys? Monsters inside them, too, but not a single drawing of their privates. The description of a penis sounded right nasty and I wondered why anyone would want to see one, much less anything else. For all the good it did, Wanda might as well have given me a *National Geographic*.

The book was full of advice I should have paid attention to. Diet and exercise. Self-control's virtues, self-indulgence's evils. A long section about how to attract, catch, and keep a decent man. And lots about treating women's diseases. (Regular bathing seemed to be a cure-all.) Really, except for the few times it spoke directly about sex, a boring book.

When Pat and I started courting, had we had time and place we would have figured the sex stuff out. Except Crawford afforded no privacy unless you had a car. Pat's mother didn't drive—not many women did—nor did Wanda. Not that she would have lent it out. You might think we'd sneak into the woods, but let one busybody see us and the party line would hum like a telegraph wire.

So we usually spent Friday or Saturday evenings, when there were no ball games, by the radio, with Wanda, checkers or Monopoly, cake or pie, hot chocolate or lemonade. Pretty darn boring, not to mention frustrating to hormony teenagers.

One evening Pat asked if I wanted to take a walk.

"Where to?"

"The top of the hill," he said, and winked.

Wanda gave us her business look. "Don't be long," she said. "Be careful."

Warm night, moon halfway to full, not yet katydid season, still plenty of buzzing jarflies. The sharp odor of burning trash lingered like a run-over skunk. We walked up the hill hand in hand, not saying much, glad to be outside. "Okay, Priscilla, I got a surprise," Pat said. "Stay here a second." He ducked behind a tree and reappeared with something rolled under his arm.

"What in the world?"

"It's a quilt. We're going to church."

"Is that some kind of prayer cloth?"

"I'm praying you'll let me kiss you."

"But there's no window shades—we can't turn the lights on."

"Not planning to." He showed me a small flashlight.

"What's that for?"

"To see the ladder with."

"What ladder?"

"To the belfry."

"You're nuts."

In the vestibule hung a rope pulled by a deacon every Sunday at ten forty-five. Beside it was a ladder I had never thought to climb, but here we were, he heading up holding flashlight in mouth, me watching his backside, thinking this might be fun. But halfway up I froze. "I can't go any higher."

"Sure you can," he whispered, reaching out. "Here, come on."

He pulled me up and spread the quilt in a corner. I was glad, because the splintery floor was littered with walnut shells and squirrel sign. Bird poo. And enough spider webs to decorate a Dracula movie.

The place was maybe ten by ten. In the center a bell about the size of a bushel basket hung from a wooden frame that reminded me of Walker's sawhorses. Heck, I thought, he might have built it. Pat put his arm around me. "See, that wasn't so bad," he said, and opened the louvers.

The only bright light was the yellow bulb down at the Crawford Springs. Past it, about fifteen miles east, Asheville glowed. "That's Dr. Grove's Inn," he said, pointing to lights on the mountain overlooking town. South was dark as a cow's fourth stomach—so was west, until the cyclops light of an eastbound locomotive poked through. Moonlight washed the church's metal roof and an occasional lightning bug winked from a tree like a leftover Christmas light.

"We're alone," I said. "Can you believe it?"

For answer he gave me a long, wet kiss that by its end threatened to grind enamel off our teeth. We quickly adjusted our bodies to the close walls and each other. When a hand invaded my blouse I turned to him and stretched my legs like a cat waking up in a sunbeam and either I kicked the bell or my feet got tangled in the rope but anyway the dang bell gave one eardrum-shattering clang like the voice of God saying "Gotcha!"

I scurried down that ladder faster than a squirrel. As porch lights glared all over Crawford, we bee-lined to the old schoolhouse and crawled under the wooden bleachers, where Pat covered us with quilt, spiderwebs, lint, dirt, and all.

A fair-sized crowd gathered, from which I expected to hear Wanda's voice any second. I heard "Fire?" and "Who?" and "Maybe some kids" and "Check school."

You bet I began to pray without ceasing. When somebody cut the lights on, we heard people walking and I just knew if a flashlight threw a beam on us they would see footprints and maybe even my feet sticking out. But, finally, people left and lights went off and we began to breathe again. Pat started to laugh.

"What's so darn funny?"

"We were bats in a belfry." He rolled on top of me. "Now, where were we?"

"Not now," I said. "It's filthy under here."

As I tried to comb the dirt out of my hair he brushed my clothes— helpfully at first but that shaded into having some fun. We finally turned each other loose and started down the hill. He hid the quilt and kissed me goodnight on our porch, a gentle kiss that I leaned into like some tramp. I really wanted to stay out, but Wanda waited in the front room.

She looked me over as I prayed the cobwebs were gone. "What was the commotion?"

"Something must have gone kaflooey with the bell," I said. "I bet a bat flew into it."

"So you two didn't ring it?"

"Why would we do that?"

She laid her dog-eared *Good Housekeeping* on the table and stood. "I'm going to bed, April Fool. You need your rest, too. Tomorrow's Sunday."

My last prayer that night was thanks to God we hadn't been caught. Then I lay awake a long time wishing I hadn't kicked that fool bell.

Although Pat and I dated two years, somehow I remained a virgin, less a matter of my "honor" than rotten luck. We had been interrupted by anything from a jangling telephone to automobile headlights flooding a dark room. Worst was the night he borrowed a car—parked it past the top of the hill so we could high-tail it to a deserted stretch of road with lots of turnouts. We had lied enough about what we were doing to send us both to hell for a fair stretch.

Finally, there we were, in the backseat, windows down, warm night tinged with honeysuckle, necking like movie stars. You ever been ready to shed a bunch of clothes when a screech owl goes off thirty feet away? Don't see how something smaller than an alarm clock can make so much racket. Let me tell you, it takes you right out of the mood. Enough to make you think about getting married so you won't have to sneak around.

Pat brought it up every now and then, but didn't press it, until basketball season was underway. Crawford High didn't have much of a basketball team. Oh, Pat was the star and I cheered my heart out but, with the possible exception of Mike Hyatt, who was as dumb as he was tall, we knew we weren't much. We won a few games against schools our size—but town schools creamed us.

I met Pat after the Flat Creek game, which we would have sent into overtime if our last shot hadn't missed everything except the floor. He smelled of soap and shampoo and didn't seem upset over the loss.

It was warm for February—I wore a light coat over my uniform (bulky sweater with a deep blue C on the front, blue-and-white pleated wool skirt, bobby socks, white shoes) and he wore a letter jacket over jeans and shirt. Mister and Miss School Spirit, holding hands, walking home, not saying much.

Pat slowed a bit and squeezed my hand. "Priss, I got something to ask."

"What's that, honey?"

"Not now. Wait till we get to your house."

"Oh, you can't do that. You've got my curiosity. What is it?"

He took both my hands and looked nervously into my eyes. I was almost afraid he was about to say there was someone else. But he finally smiled. "Will you marry me?"

We were, in my mind, fated to marry. I hugged him tight. "Oh, Pat, yes, yes. I love you."

He might have carried me home for all I remember. Next thing I knew I sat on our front porch as he knelt and fished around in his satchel. "Here," he said. "It isn't a diamond but it's the best I can do."

He placed a silvery ring in my palm.

"Oh, it's beautiful. It's old, isn't it?"

He nodded. "It's white gold. See how thin it is there? My grand-mother about wore it through."

"It belonged to your grandmother?"

"Actually, to her mother before her. My great-grandfather was in the Civil War. Story was, he found it at Fredricksburg and brought it to his wife. Then it passed to my grandmother, then my mother. She said to give it to you."

"So your great-grandfather found it, what, eighty years ago or more." I turned it over and over. It wasn't flashy under the porch light but it looked mysterious, rich. "Wow. I wouldn't dare wear it—I'd lose it."

"You could put it on your necklace with the heart."

"Great idea. Did he find it on the ground or somewhere?"

"Family story has no details. It's too little for a man, so he probably didn't cut it off some dead Yankee's finger."

"Ugh, Patrick, don't even think of such things. Of course he found it on the ground."

"I've imagined he runs across a leather pouch after a battle. He shoves it in his pocket, remembers it later around a campfire. He finds the ring, a love letter, a hank of red hair, a picture. It about makes him cry. He throws all in the fire except the ring."

"Miss Harrell's wrong. You *do* have imagination."

"Well, I certainly can imagine us married."

"When did you have in mind?"

"April? May?"

"Silly, Mama'd never let us before I graduate."

"She's right inside. We could ask."

"The one you have to ask is Daddy. Give me tomorrow to get them used to having an engaged daughter. Then you can talk to him Sunday."

"You sure we'll have to wait that long?"

"Sunday's not far away."

"No, I mean until you graduate. That's a year and a half."

"Are you worried I might fall for someone else?"

"No, silly, I just want you so bad I don't know what to do."

"We'll have to wait. Besides, I want to go to business school, remember?"

Sunday, when Pat came for dinner, Walker gave his blessing but he and Wanda put their feet down. I would finish high school first.

"Son," Walker said, "it gets mighty lonesome on the ocean, and a man's thoughts go all kinds of strange directions. He wants his girl not to stray while he's gone, right, Wanda Jean?"

Mama looked straight at me. "She wouldn't dare. Right, Priscilla Ruth?"

I turned about the shade of a radish. "Mama, of course not. We're engaged."

"Pat, don't worry. If she looks like she wants to play stray cat, I'll lock her up till you get home," said Walker.

Pat was a year ahead of me, Crawford class of '48, no big deal when we met. I was envied by some classmates for seeing an upperclassman. But when 1948 rolled around I realized he'd soon be on a ship somewhere. He didn't much want to talk about it—nor did I.

One afternoon he said he couldn't walk me home the next day. "I've got an appointment with a recruiter."

I felt like someone had doused me with ice water. "You're serious?"

"Afraid so. That bother you?"

I stuck out my lower lip but shook my head. "You've got your heart set on this, Pat. I couldn't stand in your way."

The next afternoon I walked home, alone, eyes full of tears. Part of me wanted to tell him to stay, work at the plant, marry me, settle down. But another part was interested in business college, then being a private secretary, or working in a bank. School would fill the time while Pat was gone, and a degree would one day give me a leg up on other girls. I wouldn't mind working a while before babies.

His senior year seemed to last three days. When I watched this handsome boy in black robe and gold-tasseled mortarboard walk across the stage I was both proud and profoundly sad—and meant to give him a special present that night. My body. If we could connive a way. He'd be on a train the next day. I didn't think it a bad sign that he sneezed as he took his diploma.

Of course, he spent that night in bed, not with me but with sore throat, runny nose, and a flannel poultice greased with Vicks Vapo-Rub.

He phoned before bedtime—between coughs and sneezes we vowed eternal love.

"Priss, I'll miss you so bad."

"Me too, Pat. Promise me you'll be true."

"I will, no matter what. You got to promise the same thing."

"You're the only boy for me."

Next morning I met him and his mother at the train. (We didn't have a station, just a wooden platform with a block-lettered sign that said "Crawford.") If it had been the movies we would have said good-bye in lots of fog and drizzle, but it was a warm, cheery day—unless you and a loved one were parting.

His mother hugged him. "Pat, say good-bye to your girl," she said.

I couldn't quit kissing him.

"You'll catch this cold."

"I don't care. I just want to hold you as long as I can."

"It'll be no time before I'm home on leave."

"I can't wait."

As the train pulled away, his mother and I waved handkerchiefs and bawled like babies, just like in the movies. I went home and cried most of the day.

Caught his cold, too. But that didn't matter. I'd figured to be miserable for two years anyway.

Wanda, a teetotaler, kept a medicinal bottle of Seven Crown. Cough syrup she made by soaking horehound candy in it. A cold demanded a dose of tea. Water, whiskey, in equal parts, flavored with brown sugar and lemon juice. You drank it as hot and fast as you could stand, then immediately piled under about fifty quilts. The idea was to sweat out the cold, which worked when Grace and I were little.

When Pat left all it did was make me itch for him. I went to sleep crying and sniffling and feeling about as sorry for myself as a cat with a broken tail.

In August I decided I wanted a part-time job. Life without Pat left me with time on my hands, and I needed something of my own to do.

I asked Wanda one morning when she was putting up pickled peppers. "Need some help?" I asked, coming into the kitchen fresh from the tub.

"Sure, April Fool, get a knife and have a seat. But be careful—banana peppers are a little hot this year."

Walker loved peppers, and so did Pat, the hotter the better. I wouldn't eat one for five dollars, but I had to admit they smelled good as we cut them into strips.

We made small talk about weather and such. She interrupted with "Oh, Lord, that burns," having absentmindedly rubbed the corner of her eye with a finger. I waited for her to quit crying before I mentioned I was thinking about a part-time job.

"Don't be silly," she said. "You're as busy as a one-armed paperhanger. Can you juggle school, church, cheerleading, dancing, and a job?"

"I'll manage, Mama. I really want some new shoes and a winter coat."

She blew her nose and went to the sink to wash her hands. "What would your father say?"

"I think he'd like me working for my clothes for a change." Peppery fumes made my eyes water. You'd have thought we were mourning some run-over favorite cat.

"What about that nice Pete Allen?" Wanda was never good at names.

"It's Pat, Mama, and he'd think it was fine."

"Is anybody in Crawford hiring?" She took up her knife, and, best she could with reddened eyes, gave me her business look.

"There's a job in Asheville—at the dime store on Patton. They want a girl Saturdays and maybe one afternoon a week. I can handle that."

She cut off the top of a pepper, sliced it down the middle, and raked the seeds into a pan. Slowly, like she was thinking, a thunderstorm brewing in her head. Then, quickly, it passed. "I suppose you're old enough to know what you're doing." That nearly bowled me over. I had figured she would make me ask my father, which would get me about as far as the front porch. So after a simple "Thank you," we finished that run of peppers and I washed my hands. Twice.

The next Saturday I started at the S. H. Kress Company, which everyone called Kresses. A beautiful old building, four stories in kind of an off-white terra cotta fronting on Patton. You entered the basement from College Street. Inside, high ceilings, wide aisles, lunch counter downstairs. On the main, a row of columns down the middle, three thin, two thick, each capped with molding that looked like a row of boiled eggs. They put me at the counter in front of the second large column, selling redskin peanuts and orange-slice candy.

I was kinda nervous but felt pretty. I wore my good yellow dress that buttoned up the front and a black patent belt and matching heels. My earrings were little red carnations that matched my nails perfectly. Ready to put my best foot forward, so to speak.

I had a busy day and met the nicest people. Went home tired and sore-footed, but figured once I wore sensible shoes I'd handle whatever came my way.

One Saturday a man walked up and winked. A few years older than I, he was dressed, as they say, to beat the band. Tailored tan-and-brown jacket, ecru shirt and pocket pouf, brown trousers to coordinate with the crosshatch in his jacket. Holding a tan fedora. A red and blue striped tie matched both a carnation on his lapel and two smiling blue eyes. If eyes can be said to swagger, his did.

Instead of "gimme a nickel's worth of peanuts," like I was used to hearing, "That sure is a pretty dress" fell like silver dollars from his mouth. Right then I should have sicced my manager on him. My boss, six-three, an ex-football player, didn't put up with foolishness.

But I didn't.

I kinda couldn't help it. He was so—handsome. A couple of inches taller than Pat, perfect teeth, nice lips, square jaw. Like no one I'd ever seen except in movies. You could tell he was used to getting his way.

Like a birdbrain I said "What can I do for you?"

"Let's go dancing, darling."

"I meant what can I sell you," I said. My face felt like our Warm Morning heater.

"Well, I'll take a nickel's worth of jellybeans," he said, so I weighed them up, scooped them into a bag, and handed them over. He gave me a dime and winked again. "Keep the change, sweetheart. Now, what about that dance? They got a good band out at Recreation Park."

I put the dime in the register, took out a nickel for my pocket, and shook my head. "I don't go out with people I don't know from Adam's house cat. Besides, I'm engaged."

"I'm Dick Snipes." He stuck out his hand. "What's yours?"

I looked at that hand like I knew better but had to take it anyway. Like God was giving a test and I was sure enough about to fail.

He didn't shake my hand as much as engulf it, and the next thing I knew he'd laid his jellybeans on the counter and held my hand in both of his. "You still haven't told your name."

"Priscilla. Priscilla Lance. I'm engaged."

"You said that before." He didn't let my hand go. "I don't feel a ring."

"Pat hasn't got the money for it yet. But he gave me this. It was in his family." I pulled Pat's great-grandmother's ring from my dress front.

"If I lived where that does, man, I'd be in clover. Your lucky bird live around here?"

"He's off in the Navy."

"Well, then we can go dancing."

"No, I can't. You better go now," I said, and recovered my hand. To control it. For in truth, it liked where it was. I could imagine his steady, hairy hands on me. They say idle hands are Satan's workshop. Well. The Devil has plenty of use for busy ones too.

An older couple eyed the peanut brittle so I looked at Dick Snipes like I had to go.

"See you tomorrow," he said, smiling, picking up his candy.

"Tomorrow's Sunday."

"So tell me where you live. I got a nice car."

"I have to go now," I said, turning toward my customers.

"See you," he said, and looked me over, his eyes tongues licking every square inch of me, enough to make a girl tingly nervous. When I finished with my peanut brittle people he was gone.

He left a trace on my hand, a scent not fruity or spicy or alcoholy like most men's smell-good. I should have gone to the Ladies to scrub it off but all afternoon I caught my hand sneaking to my nose.

That night I wrote two extra pages to Pat and read my Sunday School lesson twice and for good measure read the Sermon on the Mount out loud once and the part about cutting off my hand and plucking out my eye twice. After I said my prayers and turned out the light I felt I had looked Satan in the face and if not beaten him at least stood my ground.

But I woke sweaty from a dream in which Dick and I were about to, well, you know. It scared me. I'd seldom dreamed about Pat that way and here I was, giving myself to someone I'd seen all of five minutes, if that.

Next day at church I prayed a lot, not just in preaching but at MYF too. Lead me not into temptation. Deliver me from evil. Jesus keep me safe.

Of course Monday afternoon, like a stray dog you feed, he showed back up. As cool and calm as they come, he pretended to look at stuff up front, sunglasses, lotions, picture postcards. My stomach knotted like when I went to the board in math class without knowing how to work the equation.

He wore a seersucker suit, gray and white, with a solid navy tie. Black shoes you could see yourself in. His gray fedora had a navy band. Pat owned only one suit and necktie. How large was this man's closet?

Between customers he sidled up to the counter. "Ready to trip the light tonight?"

I said I had to work until six, then supper and homework.

"Can I take you home, then?"

I shook my head.

"What about Saturday? Surely a swell-looking girl like you don't sit home with mommy and daddy on Saturday night."

"I told you I'm engaged," I whispered. "Now please leave."

He reached for my hand. "I can't. You're just too sexy-looking."

My boss might be big but he's also quiet. He came up behind Dick and said "Listen, Buster, either buy something or hit the pavement."

Dick turned slowly, looked up, and with no clouds in his voice said "You and whose army's going to make me?"

"Oh, a smart mouth, huh?"

"Just a Marine who's whipped bigger jerks than you."

"Want to go settle this?"

"Suits me. Priscilla, I'll see you in a minute," Dick said. They walked down the stairs like they were off to the lunch counter for a BLT.

Dick came back dusting his hat, but otherwise no worse for the wear. "I knocked some sense into that overgrown rascal's head, so you owe me a dance. How about Saturday?"

"I'm not going out with you."

"Wanna bet?" When he put his hat on and smiled, a chill scurried up my spine.

"I don't bet."

"We'll see about that. When do you get off Saturday?"

"We close at six."

"We'll get a bite, then head to Rec Park." With that he was gone. Leather heels on marble floors gave up a beat my heart kept up all afternoon.

Saturday morning I padded into the kitchen and sat at the table. "Want some breakfast?" asked Wanda.

"I couldn't eat anything, Mama."

"You don't look sick."

"It's my tummy. Nothing bad, I just need to rest." It was a pretty morning—sunlight glanced off the chrome table edges like the border of a neon sign.

"What are you trying to get out of?"

"Nothing, Mama. I just don't feel great."

"You felt good enough to go to the game last night."

"Maybe it was that hot dog I ate."

"I made you a good supper, then you ate an old hot dog that no telling whose fingers had been on it? Serves you right. You better go back to bed." Which I did.

The next Saturday Dick waited for my manager to go to lunch, then walked in like a big dog and gave me a red rose in a green bud vase. "For the counter," he said. "Except all your customers will think you're better-looking. Gotta run. I'll be back for you at six." The seersucker suit again, this time with a silver silk tie.

"Tonight's a church meeting." A lie, but the best I could do on the spur of the moment.

"How about next Saturday?"

I shook my head.

"I got plenty of Saturdays," he said. "Face it, kiddo. We're inevitable."

This went on all through September. I bounced between annoyed and flattered. I liked the attention, but I kept asking who am I anyway? Daytime I was Pat's fiancée, a student, a candy clerk, a Sunday School pupil. Miss Respectability. By night my body wrestled with my conscience. Miss Priscilla Ruth Lance, yearning girl, vs. Mrs. Patrick Allen to be. Mother Eve, so to speak, the serpent nearby.

Early in October I stared at Dick. "If I go to a dance with you, then will you let me alone?"

"Darling, if I take you out once you'll Dear John your buddy, I guarantee."

"We'll see about that."

Famous last words.

I told Wanda I was going to a movie with my friend Maxine, who picked me up and let me off in front of the Imperial Theater, where Dick leaned against his double-parked sedan like he dared police to give him a ticket. We rode around a while in his blue car, a Buick with a backseat big enough for an extended family. When it started to rain I said "I don't know a thing about you." He lit a cigarette, turned on the wipers, and patted the seat beside him. "Scoot over, sweetheart, I don't bite." I moved maybe two inches and looked out the windshield.

"Well, let's see," he said. "I'm twenty-three going on forty. From down around Fayetteville. Little town called White Oak. Peanut capital of the world, or some crap like that. Good place to get out of. Where my mother was born—I guess she'll stay until she dies. My old man was a no-count army sergeant who knocked her up, then cut out on her. He's over at Bragg, I guess. Because he was army, I joined the Marines. At fifteen, mind you. Killed my share of Japs before I could drive a car legal. I wouldn't even start to count those yellow sapsuckers. I was a machine gunner, see, on Saipan, and by Iwo I ran a flamethrower. You wouldn't believe the stink coming out of those caves. Men in there burning to a crisp."

When he looked at me I didn't move toward him. He tossed his cigarette out the vent window and watched sparks fly in his rearview mirror. "Always wanted to live in the mountains. Came up here, got a job with the railroad. Worked my way to brakeman. Pays good, but I'm tired of those boring old tracks. I'm now at the junior college on the GI Bill. Play a little baseball for them. Shortstop. Pretty good at it, if I do say so. Good hands."

He laughed and pulled a can of beer from under the seat. "Darling, open this for me."

"I don't know how."

"Aw, you got to be kidding." He pulled over and showed me how to use a church key. "Think you can do it now?"

"I'd rather not. That stuff stinks."

"Suit yourself," he said, pulled the Buick back on the road, and gulped half that beer. "You're welcome to a few."

We ended up at Rec Park. I hadn't been in years, back when Walker and Wanda took me and Grace. We loved it—merry-go-round, bumper cars, Ferris wheel. And a green and chrome scaled-down diesel train on a track winding around the perimeter—it went through a tunnel and everything. Oh, and a swimming pool. After dark you saw clouds of insects in arc lights and it was like all was well. In this one little place there was no death, no sorrow, no pain. Just fun.

Well, that worked for a kid, but now here I was, an engaged woman going dancing with a guy I barely knew. I had managed to convince myself this wasn't really a date—once would do it—and Pat would never know. I might as well have wished myself a kingdom while I was at it.

Dick pulled the Buick into the gravel parking lot and opened my door, blue eyes smiling in the rain. He unfurled an umbrella and held it with his left hand and put his other arm around my shoulders as we walked on wet gravel, bottle caps, and cigarette butts. I was nervous but halfway up the hill boisterous music bounced into my brain and, quick as flipping a light switch, I wanted to dance.

As we came in from the drizzle a policeman, hands clasped behind his back, eyed us as if to say *no funny business in here, buster*. While Dick hung our stuff up I looked around, relieved not to recognize anyone. It hadn't occurred to me I might need to answer someone from school sidling up with *Well, Priscilla, you engaged girl, you, who's your handsome friend?*

The band, eight skinny men in white shirts and string ties, looked like square-dance guys with the wrong instruments—a piano, drum set, two guitars, an upright bass, a sax and clarinet and trumpet. But they were good—they played Sinatra and Glenn Miller and Eddy Arnold, fun music, easy to trip to.

And, wow, could Dick ever dance! His body knew exactly when to do what, my feet soon trusted his, and we were smooth as malted milk. When our bodies met it was on purpose, his purpose, accompanied by a flirty smile, which, I expect, I returned.

It was muggy and smoky—my upper lip was sweaty. After a half hour or so we took a break. I sat beside the south wall while he went for a smoke. Men walked out and returned, wiping mouths with backs of hands, suddenly bright-eyed like Walker after a trip to his truck.

Dick and I danced another hour or so. Seemed like ten minutes. But I needed to be home soon so whispered for him to take me back to Maxine's. He nodded, gave me a squeeze, and we left. He asked for another Schlitz, which I opened. He tipped it toward me, drained it, and tossed it out the window, all in one motion. He turned up the radio and grinned. We didn't say much on the way back and he didn't try to kiss me goodnight.

Because of that, or maybe in spite of it, I said I'd go out with him again. To tell the truth, I liked him... Pat was gone... I was lonesome. And Dick's hands in mine and on my back stirred me up. I was a mess, head and heart too full to get to sleep. Sometime in the middle of the night I got up and absently put Pat's great-grandmother's ring in my little cedar box.

Next Saturday we pulled the same stunt on Wanda, except Dick headed south on Hendersonville Road.

"Where are you going?"

"There's a joint out here where we can let our hair down. It's early, but if they start playing on time we can dance a while, then maybe have a little fun."

"I think it's fun to dance."

He grinned and pulled me close to him.

"You and me, lady, we've just started to have fun."

He pulled in beside a squarish concrete-block building that between the wars might have been painted white. In one corner of the parking lot a Coca-Cola sign listed from a bent metal pole. The kind of place you'd drive by a hundred times and never see.

"Saturday nights this dive gets to jumping," said Dick as he opened my door. We walked past cars with squirrel tails on radio antennas, a couple of motorcycles, and a rusted-out stake-bed truck. "The band's loud, but they're good. Fishbone, the drummer, was in service with me. He's nuts."

Inside, I was nearly knocked down by the—ripe is a kind word for it—smell of sweat and stale beer and smoke and an overlay that told me I didn't dare use a restroom.

Dick got a Schlitz and a Coke, and we wandered to the corner where the band was setting up—two guitars and a bass, all electric, and a complicated drum set with two cymbal stands. A microphone peered at the bass drum like a curious bird.

Dick and Fishbone shook hands like they hadn't seen each other in decades.

"So, man, who's the doll?"

"Son, this is Priscilla. She's a great dancer."

"If you dance half as good as you look, girl, we'll need to lay down a heavy line."

They began with a kind of hopped-up foxtrot tune, then drifted into "The Tennessee Waltz," which gave Dick and I permission to touch for a while. We were learning the feel of each other, for me, an achy thrill—kind of scary, but somehow I didn't much care, as long as things didn't get out of hand.

After a while I couldn't tell what the band played but it sure wasn't off the radio. Even slow tunes had complicated beats and, Lord, Dick could dance to it all. After a while we were the only couple on the floor, doing a kind of lindy hop, Dick leading both me and the band in a wild ride. Everyone else cheered us on. Even drunks paid attention. We were hot together and he kept looking like come on, girl, make me proud, come on girl, let's show these people how it's done, come on... I let him twirl me and dip me and toss me around. I loved it.

They finished with a slow song. Dick held me close, hand in the middle of my back.

"Let's get some fresh air."

He pulled back and smiled at me.

"Sure, kid, I know where the freshest in town is."

As we left, Dick and Fishbone exchanged a thumbs up and outside it was dark enough to see a big star low in the west.

"Nice night."

"Priss, you ain't seen nothing yet. We're going up the mountain."

"Where?" I asked, a little catch in my throat.

"I know a place we can be by ourselves, darling."

"I don't know, Dick."

"I promise I won't do a thing you don't want me to."

He drove back into town and headed up the mountain past some old castle-looking building. After several twisty miles he pulled up to a pair of stone columns. He got out and unlocked or anyway undid the chain and drove up to a perfectly rectangular stone house squatted like a fortress on top of the ridge.

"Who lives here?"

"Some Flor-idiot spends summers here. I know a guy looks after it when he's not around. We'll be fine. Let's take a little walk."

It was a plateau, kind of, with a view in three directions. At the eastern edge we had a perfect view of the strip where people congregated at the drive-ins just outside the tunnel. Lights shone from the motel and cars reminded me of lightning bugs. From the west we saw northbound traffic and winking mountaintop lights. The moon wasn't up yet, so the Milky Way looked like a sash across the sky's belly.

He spread a blanket and hauled out a metal cooler full of Schlitz and Coca-Colas from the trunk. "Beer or whiskey?"

"I beg your pardon?"

"Well, you said beer stinks, so I brought some Seagram's Seven. It'll go good with Coke."

"Dick, I don't drink."

"Why not?"

"It's nasty."

"You dance like a hellcat, then turn your pretty nose up at a little drink." He opened a Coke, drank a swallow or two, then filled it from a brown bottle. He shook it gently and handed it to me. "Bottoms up," he said, toasting me with a can of Schlitz.

"You know, that doesn't taste like cold medicine," I said.

He chuckled. "You're a funny girl, you know it?" He folded his jacket and laid it carefully in the front seat. He sat on the blanket and patted it. "Come on, babe, I ain't poison."

I sat beside him and slowly finished my drink. He opened another beer. "How long's your boy been gone?"

"You mean Pat? Since June."

"Bet you'd like a little loving, then."

"Dick, I couldn't betray him."

"Darling, you already have." He leaned over and kissed me and, well, I kissed him back, and, I don't know, I shouldn't have let him in my blouse but I somehow kept it and my slip and brassiere on and I didn't let his hand under my skirt. But he rubbed every square inch of my bottom anyway.

Something—guilt, or fear, or more likely a vision of Wanda waiting up for me made me come up for air. "What time is it?"

"Who cares?"

"I do. If I'm not home by eleven I'll get killed." I didn't know how else to get off that mountain and out to Crawford before dawn.

"Damn, girl, it's a quarter till," he said. As we rushed to the car the moon peeked over the mountain and somehow I was glad it hadn't seen us.

I was home by a quarter after. I never want another ride like that. I didn't throw up but maybe should have.

"See you next Saturday?" It really wasn't a question.

Mama was still up, Bible in her lap, pretending she'd been asleep. "Priscilla Ruth Lance, where in creation have you been?"

"Just riding around with Maxine."

"That would explain half your blouse-tail hanging out."

"Mama, this isn't at all how it looks."

"How stupid do you think I am? That car that gunned away from here wasn't Maxine's, and you smell like a brewery. You've been cheating on Pete Allen with some low-morals boy. That won't happen again. Now go to bed."

But Satan most always finds a way.

The next Saturday, October 23, 1948, Dick picked me up after work. It was still warm, at least at first, dark too, the moon nearly new, no clouds. Crickets sang in the grass and we stretched out under the stars and didn't say much. Like we knew what was about to happen. A thing, I thought, I might as well put behind me.

He drank two or three beers and I sipped a Coke and Seagram's. Once past that first little shudder I liked the taste but especially liked how it didn't settle in my stomach but crept down into my legs like some comforting friend. I was lying on my back watching stars wheel ever so slowly when Dick whispered in my ear "Priscilla, I got to have you" and put a hand on my breast and, I don't know, all of a sudden we didn't have any clothes on to speak of and, well, there's not much to say except I loved him like I'd been a fallen woman for decades.

After midnight we fogged up that blue car's windows something awful. Dick found some far-off station playing music I'd never heard before, "colored music" he said, boisterous, spirited stuff. It seemed to go perfectly with our forbidden lovemaking. Like we were dancing in the dark.

We ate breakfast at a diner, and I was ravenous. Eggs, toast, potatoes, ham, the works. After a while he lit a cigarette and watched me eat. "Baby," he finally said, "I'll not be back for a while. I haven't studied a lick for midterms."

Dread crawled into my chest like some feral thing. "So you'd love me and leave me?"

"Darling, after tonight you think I can do without you? Don't be stupid. It's just a couple of weekends."

Getting back home at three in the morning involved, I'm sure, lies and the good fortune that Wanda could sleep through a hurricane.

I could almost hear my belly change, like when a roller coaster meshes at the bottom and gears bring it slowly back up top. Except now I wouldn't get the downhill thrill.

I forget what lie got me out of the house twice in November, but I had missed my late October period and was hell-bent on seeing him. November twentieth I was eager to love him for I hoped that might start my ball rolling, so to speak.

"Baby, you look swell," he said as I got into the Buick. "I love that dress on you."

"You aren't so bad yourself." He wore a tweed suit under a black wool overcoat that made him look like some movie mobster.

"Wanna go dancing?"

"I'd rather be alone with you."

"Suit yourself." We found a deserted country turnout—I prayed it was too cold out for screech owls—and fogged the windows again.

When midweek nothing had happened I figured I had to tell him. To give him a chance to Do the Right Thing. To make me an Honest Woman. But what if he did, what about Pat? I'd deal with that as needed.

Saturday November twenty-seventh was cold, one of those nights when you know real winter's just offstage. We met after work at a café on the square. Theaters wouldn't break between movies for another thirty minutes, so the place was fairly empty. The Greek proprietor stood behind the counter smoking and talking with two men drinking coffee. Commemorative plates lined each wall on high moldings, and radiators knocked like someone in the basement wanted out. In the kitchen a radio played shadowy music. "Tennessee Waltz." Again.

I ordered a vanilla milkshake. "That all you want, darling? Me, I'm starved, myself."

"I couldn't eat. You go ahead."

He ordered a cheeseburger platter and a cherry Coke. "You sure? You need your stamina."

"Not tonight, Dick." Suddenly I noticed he wore the suit I saw him in back in August. Or was this a winter version?

"Why, darling? You getting tired of me?"

The waitress brought his Coke and my milkshake. "Y'all want some ice water too?"

"No, thanks," Dick said.

"I do, please."

"Coming right up."

I took out my compact and freshened my lipstick, waiting for her return. When she left the water—in a conical paper cup stuck in a stainless steel holder—I took a sip and looked him in the eye. "Dick, I'm going to have a baby."

For a fleeting second his eyes reminded me of a boar's at a hog killing, just before its legs buckle. Then he began to look everywhere except at me, fingers drumming on the table. I took one of his hands in mine. "Did you hear me?"

"Yeah," he finally said.

"Well?"

"Deep subject." He turned my hand over and rubbed my palm with his finger, not like he was trying to excite me, but like he didn't know what else to do.

"Dick, say something, please."

"Baby, I got to get used to this. It's not every day a man's told his gal's in a family way."

The waitress interrupted us with cheeseburger, fried potatoes, slaw. When I smelled it I wanted to crawl away like a dog finding grass and throw up—alone.

"Wanna potato?" Dick splorched catsup on the pile.

"I'm not hungry."

"You sure it's mine?"

I didn't know whether to cry, hit him, or both. "What kind of question is that?"

He pointed a dripping French fry at me. "Legit. If I'm going to own him, I got to know if anybody else's been messing around you."

"How can you say that? You know you're the only one."

He dropped a gob of ketchup in his lap. "Well, shit. If that ain't a fine how-do-you-do." He ate the fry, then wiped himself with three or four napkins. "I just got this damn suit cleaned, and now look. Say, how about your boy, what's his name, Pete?"

"I haven't seen Pat since March. Besides, we never—did what you and me did."

I stubbed up in the booth and looked around while he ate in silence, like a dog, steady and fast. Patrons were beginning to leave the Plaza and come in for supper, but no one paid us any mind. The milkshake would not go down. "Penny for your thoughts," I said. It sounded dumb, but I didn't know what else to say.

"I just need some time, that's all. Got to get used to this idea."

"I haven't heard you offer to marry me."

"Priscilla, you ain't heard me throw you away, neither." He wiped his mouth and lit a cigarette. "I just got to think about this a while."

"When can I see you again?"

He waved his cigarette in the air. "Next weekend?"

"Sure. We have to talk about this soon. Figure out what to do."

"Whatever. We'll talk Saturday night. Want me to take you home?"

"I'll get the bus."

He stood, examined his pants, and kissed the top of my head. "See ya." I couldn't read anything into the rhythm of his walk. Outside, he threw his cigarette into the street, lit another, and walked into the night.

December fourth I waited like a sap until seven-thirty, when, crying, I took the bus home. I wanted to throw my arms around Wanda and tell her everything but she wore a thunderstormy face so I went to my room and cried myself to sleep.

I never saw Dick Snipes, if that was even his real name, again.

Christmas Day we had the usual turkey and dressing, or rather my folks and sister ate while I puked in the bathroom.

After dinner Walker settled downstairs by the radio, and Wanda came into my room and shut the door. I was lying on the bed, my back to her, staring at my teddy bears as if they might take my hand and lead me to a place and time where I had never heard of Dick Snipes.

My bedsprings griped when Wanda sat on them. "Priscilla Ruth Lance," she said, and from the tone I knew her lips thinned like somebody had zipped her mouth from the inside. "Look at me."

I slowly turned onto my back and tried not to cry.

"You're in trouble, aren't you?"

I nodded.

"What do you know about the father? Anything?"

I sobbed and shook my head.

"Does that mean you won't tell or you don't know?"

I raised on my elbows, still crying. Instead of sympathy I got a handkerchief scented with fake Shalimar, which nearly sent me back to hug the commode.

"Honestly, girl, anymore I don't know if you're lying or not. Does he go to your school?"

I shook my head and blew my nose. A patch of sunshine slowly crossed the hooked rug at the foot of my bed where Puddy Tat lay, despite the interruption, spread out like a hot breakfast.

"Let's have it, Priscilla Ruth. I'm not leaving until I know."

I sat up, hanky in my lap. "He's in college. He said his name was Dick Snipes."

"I bet he also said he loved you."

I shook my head, and that was the truth. He never said such a thing nor did I to him.

"All the worse. Where's he in school?"

I told her.

"Does he live on campus?"

I shrugged.

"Where's he from?"

"Somewhere toward the coast."

"He might as well be a moth-eaten tomcat for all you've told me. Do you expect to see him again?"

I shook my head.

"Lord have mercy, child, did you even know this boy a month before you got pregnant? I raised you better than that."

"Mama, I'm sorry."

"You ought to be. I don't know how I'll keep going to church. And whatever will you tell that nice Pete Allen?"

"Maybe he'll understand."

"Yeah, and maybe the sun will stand still like at Jericho. Priscilla

Ruth, you're damaged goods. If you ever get married it'll be to a lowdown drunken sot." She made an abacus of her fingers. "Middle of July, then. First babies are most always late so it might be up into August."

"What are we going to do?" I asked.

"'We?' Daughter, I didn't spread my legs for some sweet-talking Romeo."

I began to cry again.

She stood and looked out the window, blocking sunshine like some spiteful eclipse. She turned and grabbed the footboard like it was a lectern. "Okay, girl. Listen. We got to figure this out. I know one thing. I'll not be party to getting rid of it, whether douche or granny woman or doctor. That is nothing but murder.

"And you can't have it here. A pregnant girl in Crawford would stick out like a polka-dotted rhino. What would people say? I have to be able to hold my head up around here. Even Asheville's home for unwed mothers is too close." She picked at a bit of fuzz on her sweater. "Child, if your daddy gets any idea you're in a family way the first thing he'll do is try to kill that boy, know what I mean? If he can find him, that is. You told the boy, I reckon?"

I nodded.

"And I bet he vanished, pardon my French, like a fart in a whirlwind, gone to wherever he thinks nobody can find him. Hmp. Unwed fathers. In my day they ran to California. Anymore they might not get past New Orleans. You'll never hear of him again in any case."

"Mama?"

"What?"

"What if I try to raise the baby myself?"

She snorted. "You? How in the world would you do that?"

"I could…"

"Nonsense. You'll give it up and start your life again."

"But…"

"I'll hear no more of that. Now, I'm going to leave you to ponder your sins. But hear me—you have to stop throwing up. Even Walker will put two and two together eventually. We have to keep this under our hats."

"What about Grace?"

"I'll put the fear of God in her. She'll have to help, whatever we decide."

She left without a kiss or go-to-blazes. At least she didn't slam the door, likely because by then Walker was asleep. I guess she had a heart-to-heart with my little sis that afternoon. I didn't come out except to brush my teeth and get ready for bed.

*   *   *

I remembered, like a punch in the belly, a G.A. field trip when I was ten or eleven. One Wednesday night our leaders were kind of secretive, so we figured it was some home missions outing, no foray for ice cream. It was cold, October, dry leaves rattling everywhere. Three cars, four girls in each backseat, two adults up front—were they worried we might hijack them?

Maxine's father, fedora perched back on his head, drove the car I rode in. He kept looking in the rearview, saying in an ominous tone we sure would remember this field trip. Except for his patter we went all the way from Crawford through West Asheville and over the river in silence.

We wound into Montford, a section of stately homes with alleyways and carriage houses out back. Large porches, turrets, slate roofs. Houses of people who mattered—doctors, lawyers, businessmen.

We parked before a beetle-browed house sitting on a rise like a judge in court. A high fence guarded the back lot—low rock walls covered in moss and lichens surrounded the rest.

"Well, girls, here we are," said Maxine's dad as he ratcheted the emergency brake.

"This place is creepy," Maxine said. "Why are we here?"

"You'll see."

Maxine's mother herded us to the porch, where a dim bulb, trying to light a great darkness, failed. "Young ladies," she said, "be on your best behavior inside. This is a Home for Unwed Mothers. These girls are in trouble, and you mustn't cause them distress."

We shuffled into an entry hall which could comfortably contain an entire Crawford house. A staircase wide enough to allow four abreast rose to a dark landing. A glass chandelier hung overhead, two electric bulbs making cut glass pendants sparkle. Beside the front door sat an entry table, where visitors used to leave calling cards. Now it held a dog-eared Gideon Bible.

The odor of fried pork and steamed cabbage trumped pine disinfectant and the mothball smell of old ladies. A parlor to the right with a line of straight chairs, their backs to us, was barely lit with what I called funeral home lights—wall sconces and a couple of tall torchieres. A wan fire hissed and spat in the north fireplace. "This way, girls," said a hefty woman with eyeglasses like goggles over eyes too close together. "I think we have enough chairs." Her white uniform crackled with starch.

Sitting, we stared at a three-panel screen decorated with fabric prints of long-necked feathery birds. Behind it sat three girls, their feet all we could see. The middle one's ankles were swollen like tennis balls.

"Crawford Baptists," said the matron, "your visit is to make sure I never see you in here after tonight. Three of our clients will tell you what it's like here. Polly, please begin."

By her accent, Polly was a mountain girl—I started to inventory Crawfordites to see if one was missing.

"I got in trouble in August so they decided I needed to stay until… well, until it's over. We have roommates and we live upstairs and we have to help in the kitchen and laundry room and sweep and mop. It's okay here… but I sure miss home."

I thought "in trouble" must be pretty bad if they took you from your family.

The second girl sounded like a Yankee. "You have to work here," she said, crossing and uncrossing her puffy ankles. "But they let you listen to the radio Saturday night, and breakfast is good, except for grits."

"Edna, is that all you have to say?" asked the matron.

"Yes, Ma'am."

"Hmp. We will talk later. Arlene, what can you tell our young guests?"

This girl was definitely from off. Her "outs" were "oots" and her "house" was "hoos." Midway she broke down. While Edna and Polly led her away she kept sobbing, saying, "I'm sorry, I'll never do it again." Enough to give me the fantods.

"You girls have questions?" said the matron, tapping an open palm with a yellow pencil.

I wasn't about to ask how you get "in trouble." Nor was anyone else. We just wanted out.

"Girls," she said, "after these young women have their babies—then they can go back home. Or to wherever they are welcome."

I'd been fiddling with a loose coat button. So what was the connection between "in trouble" and having babies? In my experience, before you became a mother your belly got bigger, then you either had a baby at home or hospital. Everybody was happy.

Maxine raised her hand. "So why must they be here?"

The matron smiled like Maxine might have been a feeble-minded, three-legged dog. "Because they are not married." The same tone she would have used to say they had leprosy. "They chose not to embarrass their families. A kind of common courtesy."

"Common" sealed it for me. I wanted no part of it.

Maybe we should have asked more questions. I was among the oldest in this group of G.A.s, but had no idea how babies were made, except I didn't believe Walker, who said pregnant women had swallowed watermelon seeds. We knew you had to be married to have babies—at least until that night—but had no idea why. And, coming home, we didn't even get ice cream.

The memory of that trip flooded my mind after Wanda went downstairs. How in the world, after that, did I wind up in this shape? Why had I thought myself immune to the wages of sin? Why, for that matter, had I not thought, period? Was there no help for me?

When I tried to pray, words bounced off the ceiling like cracked ping pong balls. Lonesome, worthless, sick to my stomach, I had never felt so lowdown mean. If the Lord had given us pistols instead of hands I would have used them on myself.

Except, God, there was that baby. Which Wanda was determined I would have, then abandon. So I decided it better be a boy. I'd not want to cause another girl to go through what I was about to.

Except for my dancing streak I was what you might call quiet. Not really shy but not the life of the party either. I had friends but we weren't like some girls that you couldn't pry apart with a crowbar. When I turned up pregnant I seemed to fold into myself. I wanted to be alone. And, really, who could I tell?

Certainly no one at church. Our preacher seldom smiled and my Sunday School teacher wore gloves Sunday mornings. During worship I was certain I was no longer welcome at the communion rail. Through the window I had a view of the distant ridges, where I lifted my eyes but found no help.

School? Our school nurse looked like she had been midwife to Teddy Roosevelt's grandmother and I was not close to any teachers. Our cheerleader sponsor was so goody-two-shoes I wouldn't have told her I had a hangnail. Principals and such, forget it.

I had to tell Pat. Oh, he wasn't due back until fall and I suppose I could have kept writing like nothing was wrong and he'd never know any better. But every time I thought about that, something gnawed at my tummy like a squirrel after a walnut. I had to tell him.

I must have started a letter a thousand times only to wad it up and burn it in the backyard. But one afternoon it wrenched its way out of my gut.

*   *   *

December 22, 1948

Dearest Pat,

There's not a cloud in the sky. I'm home in the Wednesday afternoon sun. It's warm for December, feels like an Indian summer day you wish would never end.

I hope you are well and don't hate me for not writing last week. It was a busy week but I thought of you every day and want so much to be with you that I don't know what to do. I have a thing to tell you that should be told face to face but can't wait.

Promise you won't kill me if you ever see me again. I admit I deserve killing. I have not been a good girl. In fact, I have been about as bad as could be. Bear with me, Pat. I need to tell you but could almost die for the telling of it.

I met this boy. Now, before you tear this up and heave it over the side of your boat let me say I'll never see him again so you don't have to worry about killing him or anything. He meant nothing to me. Not anything like what you do.

About all I can say on my behalf is that I was lonesome. I missed you so bad and he flirted with me. I really tried not to go out with him. I used every excuse in the book—I even said we were engaged but that didn't faze him. He kept popping up like a jack-in-the-box. I finally thought if I went dancing with him he might quit chasing me.

I went out with him four times. I swear, that was all. Four times, and—I don't know how to tell you this, but here goes—I'm going to have a baby. There. I've told you.

I don't know how it happened. Oh, what I mean is I don't know how I let it happen. It just seemed natural and how likely was it that the first time I ever did anything like that I would get pregnant? Just my luck, I suppose.

If you're still reading this, please know I am SO sorry. Every day Mama is a one-woman judge, jury, and hangman. So don't think I need reminding how bad I've been.

I will give the baby up. It will be adopted out. I hope to a good home. Sounds like a puppy or kitten, doesn't it? "Free to good home."

Best anyone can tell I will have it in July or August. Will you be home by then? And if so will you even want to see me?

I wouldn't blame you if you didn't. In fact, I wouldn't be surprised if you haven't already torn this up and thrown it away. You're too nice a boy to get tied down with a wretch like me. I mean, with all the girls in the world why would you want to stay with one who has cheated on you and had somebody else's baby?

I just answered my own question. Of course you wouldn't. You deserve better than me. All I can hope is that you might forgive me, nothing more.

I wish you a fine life, Pat, with success and love and children and everything we talked about. I hope you find a nice girl to settle down with. And I hope you will remember me as one who loved you except I slipped and fell. It would be a comfort to know you thought of me every now and then in a kind way instead of hating me forever. Which I richly deserve. Goodbye, Pat.

With much love,

Priscilla

P.S. Please don't tell anyone who knows anybody here about this. It just HAS to be kept secret.

Between tears and runny ink I pretty much ruined a Blue Horse tablet but that night I copied the letter out so he could read it. When I dropped it in the mailbox my heart raced like I had set something totally unknown in motion.

I was a mess that Christmas. For one thing, they asked me to be Mary in the nativity scene and I couldn't think of an excuse. So there I was, three evenings out in the cold, wearing a blue scarf and looking at a sixty-watt lightbulb in a manger and thinking what kind of pregnant hypocrite pretends to be the virgin mother of Jesus. Whatever was in my belly certainly wasn't the savior of the world and I began to think that the real Jesus wouldn't even save me anymore because he'd be so sad over my sin.

Our preacher talked about Mary one Sunday, how she wasn't the Queen of Heaven like Catholics say, she was just the earthly mother of Jesus. Like a glass dish they grow mold in.

I was mad, because I was beginning to see that being a mother even of a normal baby is no simple matter of planting a seed, sitting around, and letting it grow. And being the mother of God is, I'm sorry, a big deal. A really big deal, something a man shouldn't belittle.

Then I felt guilty—you don't question a man in the pulpit.

So I tried to get through the holiday with pure thoughts, although it was difficult. Especially since I had no word from Pat. I sent him a jar of honey. The best gift from him would have been a nice letter. But I wasn't even sure if I'd ever see him again.

For a while I got the usual chatty letters, every other day some goofy detail about his routine, until one day, nothing. Nor the next. Nor the next. So he had gotten my letter. Or something bad had happened. Or both.

The new year brought a reply.

January 19, 1949
> *Priscilla,*
> *Your letter hit me like a ton of bricks. It was days before I could think straight. I mean, I was in a fog, only making it through the day because I know the routine and salute automatically. Nothing has ever hurt so bad.*
> *I've been around guys who have gotten "Dear John" letters. One threatened to jump overboard. Another plans, like you say, to kill his girl's new fellow—and her, too, for that matter—the minute he gets home. I mean, he's got it all figured—the weapon, the place, the time. Another guy shrugged it off and said there's more fish in the sea and went on about his business.*
> *I guess I was somewhere in between all that. I mean, you say he's out of the picture and I gather all you're focused on is having the baby and getting on with your life. So I don't need to plot revenge like some Shakespeare character who's dead in Act Five along with half the cast.*
> *I still don't know what to say. Except I'll write again when I've had more time to think.*
> *Love (for your news doesn't change that),*
> *Pat*
> *P.S. It's a ship. Boats are smaller than most anything this man's navy puts on the water.*

I wrote him a thank-you letter but didn't know whether to keep writing like usual or not. Meanwhile I felt myself changing, getting softer, wanting odd things at odd times of the day, getting ready. From then until February took about three years. Finally, this:

February 1, 1949

Dear Priscilla,

Sorry I have taken so long to write. I kept thinking what to do, what to do, almost went AWOL, which is hard in the middle of the ocean.

I took your letter to the chaplain. I'm sorry if you get mad because I've broken secrecy, but we can trust the chaplain. He's a Presbyterian but I don't think that makes much difference. He isn't too far out with his ideas or anything.

He read it over once, shaking his head a lot and almost smiling in places. Then he read it again and gave it back to me like he was handing me something really valuable. "Tell me about this girl," he said, reared back, and lit his pipe.

So I told him how I'd had my eye on you forever. How your hair curled up in back and how you had the whitest neck and how you loved chocolate and little kittens. How I always tried to sit close to you in church and how good you looked Sunday mornings. How we had fallen in love and how we had promised to be faithful to each other while I was away.

And then I broke down and wept.

"Son, tell me why you're crying."

"She broke her promise."

"And that hurts only you?"

"Well, I expect it hurts her, too."

"Sure it does. She says so. Besides, she's the one having the baby, not you."

Then he read from John, the chapter where they bring Jesus a woman "taken in adultery." Where Jesus ends up saying "Go, and sin no more."

"Can you do that with Priscilla?" he asked.

"I don't know."

"Think about it, son."

That's all I have thought about for three days.

When I get home, if you will still have me I'd like to take up where we left off and see if we can make it work. That'll be in October. The baby will be gone. You'll be shaky and tender and I'll be walking on eggs, but we can try. I expect we will have difficult times—I know how bad you beat up on yourself when you mess up on a test, so you must be in pure agony over this—and we may not be able to put this behind us. But I'm willing to try. Here's hoping we have a happy new year in 1950.

Your picture still graces my berth. You are the same pretty girl I *left behind, no matter what your mother says. Try not to listen to her overmuch. You have made a mistake, sure, but we all do. She might not be able to forgive you but I can try. Only you can forgive yourself.*

I'm off to watch some Gary Cooper movie, just to take my mind off things. I would wish you could see it with me. Maybe in October.

I love you despite everything. Please believe that.

All my love,

Pat

I cried for the better part of a day, torn between belief and unbelief. That I was so lucky to have Pat—or that I was so undeserving of him that he was only building me up to come back and dump me like some worn-out mop. I finally pulled myself together to write this letter:

March 1, 1949

Dearest Pat,

Can I really be lucky enough to hope you and I might still be engaged? That after my ordeal is over you might really marry me? It's almost too good to be true. Hope will get me through the next seven months.

Your chaplain sounds like a wise man. I wish I had someone like that to talk to but there's nobody. I'll just use the US Mail to talk to you.

You mentioned the woman in Jesus' story. It's funny—maybe there's a better word—but I always thought I was better than her. But here I am, having done the very same thing (I broke the seventh commandment same as if we were married) and gotten pregnant to boot.

And here you are telling me (I hope) like Jesus told her, "go and sin no more." Well, that's my plan. I've learned my lesson and hope to show you how grateful I am. I'll be the best wife ever. I promise.

I read your wonderful letter at least twice a day—when I get up and when I go to bed. It keeps me going.

All my love, (Really!)

Priscilla

I was nervous as a chihuahua at the vet's office until I heard from him. His words were kind and sweet. He wrote almost weekly while I was expecting, and never gave me reason to fret, but I'm a worry wart, so never let myself believe a hundred percent.

So this "Who am I?" became tangled—more like "who are we?" See, I had become plural. From a blonde-headed high school senior without a care, to an unwed mother-to-be, scared of a shadow.

A girl "in trouble," in other words, a slut, tramp, whore. Damaged goods, as Wanda was fond of saying. (She never called me "April Fool" again.) Not worthy, certainly, to be a parent.

At least Walker left, not to return until October. He'd been hired as lead carpenter by some firm building tract housing in New York state. Hugging him goodbye was really the only relief I had that winter until they decided where I would go.

Wanda certainly offered no quarter. No day passed without at least a disgusted look from her, and most days contained at least one cutting comment.

I came home one Thursday almost in tears—which was, now that I think about it, mostly normal. I had made a B- on a math test. Wanda asked what was wrong, and, I don't know, I kind of lost it. She listened for a little while, then slammed the dishtowel on the kitchen counter. "I don't want to hear any more of this," she said. "It's your own fault. You didn't study."

"Mama, I did too. I studied hard."

"Well, I've read that girls that get in trouble are often feeble-minded."

Never mind flies—my mouth hung open wide enough to catch passing sparrows.

"I just hope your baby doesn't inherit that. Nobody wants a half-witted baby."

I spent that afternoon in my room and wouldn't come down for supper. Grace sneaked me a plate, bless her, or I'd have starved.

About a week later Wanda knocked on my bedroom door. "Priscilla, can I come in?"

"It isn't locked."

She stood in the doorway and looked at her fingernails. "I've checked on that home for unwed mothers in Charlotte. They want a substantial fee—a "contribution"—to cover room and board and agency fees. There's no way to hide that from your father."

"So what am I going to do?"

Wanda had sighs for various occasions—irritation, boredom, sleepiness—but this one, coming from some depth of soul, I had never heard. "Maybe you could stay with your aunt Pearl until you give up the kid."

"You haven't seen her in years."

"You give me no choice. Meantime, a Miss Maxwell with the welfare department is coming tomorrow. She wants to talk about—the situation. You best tidy the front room."

We didn't use that room much—only when visited by the preacher, some long-lost cousin, or the Fuller Brush man. That afternoon—a Tuesday early in March—I put away the bedsheets that normally swaddled the upholstery, swept and mopped, dusted flat surfaces, cleared the corners of cobwebs, fluffed pillows. I even cleaned the insides of the windows and wiped down the Venetian blinds. After supper Puddy Tat and I came upstairs, where I hoped for a good night's sleep, then a long bath before Miss Maxwell's advent.

Next morning, Wanda and I were both nervous. She paced from kitchen to front room, peeking through the blind on each lap and letting a shaft of sunlight full of dancing dust light up the room.

"I thought you cleaned in here," she said.

"I did."

"You'd never know it. Honestly, Priscilla Ruth, I don't know about you anymore."

The smell of freshly perked coffee began to blend with our morning bacon, and the clock was nearly as loud as our rooster. Our guest, mercifully, drove up as the clock chimed ten. "Well," Wanda said, "there she is. Finally. Now remember, if anyone asks, she's your cousin stopped for a flying visit. I told her not to bring a briefcase or anything to give her away."

Miss Maxwell neither wore a sign on her back that said "Welfare" nor a false mustache and glasses. A willowy brunette, she wore a tailored tweed jacket and skirt and a cream-colored silk blouse. A silver dogwood blossom decorated her lapel. She carried a patent leather purse big enough to hold a fair-sized cat.

Wanda welcomed her warmly enough, offering coffee and pound cake. I said just coffee, please, and so did Miss Maxwell, who probably avoided anything fattening. She sat in one wing chair, kind of on the edge of the seat, while I sat on the sofa, fiddling with my necklace (Pat's ring was back).

"Miss Lance, I am pleased to meet you. I hope you are well this morning," she said.

"You can call me Priscilla, Miss Maxwell. And, yes, I'm fine."

"Then I'm Elaine. We'll get along well."

She was twenty-five, maybe, with no wrinkles to indicate husband, children, or worries. Probably a college grad. From her handbag she pulled a folder crammed with papers. "I need to ask some questions, just to introduce you into the system, so to speak. And, of course, to get to know you so we'll do what's best."

Wanda reappeared with a wooden tray holding three cups of black coffee, a white cream pitcher, matching sugar bowl—and three slices of pound cake. "We may get hungry," she said.

"I'll doctor my coffee," said Elaine. "Then we'll proceed." She dropped two spoonfuls of sugar in her cup and stirred. "Mrs. Lance, did you make that cake? It looks scrumptious."

Wanda had settled in the other wing chair. "I bake one a week when my husband's home. He's a builder, you know, right now he's in New York. You never can tell where he'll be next."

"That must be interesting," said Elaine. "To change scenery often."

"I wouldn't know," said Wanda. "I've lived here forever—never much wanted to go anywhere else. Until..." She locked eyes with me.

"Yes, well..." said Elaine. "Let's begin. Priscilla, please fill out this form." She handed me a paper asking for birth date, height, weight, that kind of thing.

"Who sees this?" I asked.

"Just me and my supervisor. When your baby is adopted, the new parents will have the right to non-identifying information—your height, hair color, years of education, but never name, address, or anything like that. They can choose to tell the child—or not."

"So... I have to give up the baby?" I really didn't know where that came from. I hadn't much felt like a mother but maybe...

Elaine and Wanda eyed each other as three cups rattled into saucers. "Of course you do," said Wanda. "Don't be stupid."

I glanced from one to the other. Wanda was in full-blown business mode and Elaine looked to need fortification.

"Do I?" I asked her. "Really?"

She took a deep breath. "No, of course you can choose to raise it yourself. But your mother says you'll stay single. You haven't graduated from high school, and therefore are in no position to give a child what it needs in terms of finances and housing and, especially, opportunity.

Under such circumstances, keeping a child simply means trouble—a struggle to get by. Also, studies prove poverty leads to crime, with negative consequences for everyone, including society itself."

Wanda seemed about to cloud up and rain all over me. "Priscilla Ruth Lance, how in the world could you, in your condition, keep a child? It's preposterous."

A word she likely learned in *Reader's Digest*. "So, Mama, you wouldn't help me?"

She snorted. "And why would I do that?"

I rubbed my belly. "It *is* your grandchild."

"Whatever it is has nothing to do with me, young lady. I'm certainly not going to own a bastard grandchild."

Her words cut me to the blood. When I started crying, Elaine sat beside me, handkerchief in hand. "Here," she said, and put an arm around my shoulders. "I'm sure Mrs. Lance didn't mean that."

"Yes I did," snapped Wanda. "Maybe I shouldn't have used that word, but nothing will ever change what that child is. It's a… woods colt, a mongrel, a misbegotten—let's not mince words. It's a bastard. And tell me this, young lady—suppose your sin—which you likely now have a taste for—gets the better of you, and you run off with some sex maniac? Blamed if I'm going to raise such a child."

"Whoa," said Elaine, who returned to her chair and smiled thinly at us. "Please excuse me, but I simply *must* have some of this scrumptious cake." We watched her eat the whole piece quickly, like she enjoyed every bit. Maybe she needed the sugar. Or simply needed a break to decide whose side she was on—mother's, grandmother's, child's.

Brushing crumbs from her lap and patting her lips with a paper napkin, she turned to my mother. "Mrs. Lance, that was delicious." Then she cleared her throat. "Priscilla, I see women like you all the time. You are scared and need a place to turn to. Public Welfare provides that place. We promise to ease your baby into a family that will love him or her like their own. Our pool of parents-to-be generally have been trying so long to have a baby that they're older, so have stability—savings, house, car. They can give the baby what it needs. Good food, clothes, a college education. Do you think you could provide that for this baby?"

"I… I don't know."

Elaine raised her hand in a "not yet" to my mother.

"It's not terribly likely. Mrs. Lance says the father abandoned ship, so to speak. So you're going to be by yourself, right?"

"But Pat says…"

"Wait. Who is Pat?"

"We're engaged. He's in the navy. Lord knows, I am sorry as I can be for what I did. I was… lonesome."

"Oh. Mrs. Lance didn't tell me that." Eyebrows arched, she looked at my mother. "Does this Pat know your… situation?"

I nodded and blew my nose in her expensive hanky.

"Do you really think he'll marry you?"

"I… think so. But… oh, Elaine… I don't… I can't… know for sure."

"That's Miss Maxwell to you," barked my mother. "And he'll not take another look at you. Mark my words."

Elaine sipped her coffee. "Priscilla," she said, "in my experience, Mrs. Lance is right. Maybe one in a million, no matter what they say, will follow through on such a promise." She sat the cup on the tray. "Have you given any thought about where you would live?"

"Not here," my mother said. "She needn't think that."

"I guess I'd get a job somewhere. Find a room."

"Okay, Priscilla, let's get clear-eyed here," said Elaine. "Say you've found that room. You're there with your baby, sick with fever, he or she won't stop crying. You need help—where's it coming from? Or, say, he's well, but you need to work. Who will you leave him with? That will cost money, of course. Now, he's seven, you're scraping to put food on the table, and he needs school shoes. Or, later, he wants to play trombone in the high school band. Musical instruments cost serious money."

She crossed her legs and smoothed her skirt. "I have prospective parents for whom money is not a problem. They can provide that and much more. Travel. Enrichment. Advantages. You must think about the big picture—that you are doing your baby an immense favor. Priscilla, trust me. It's the right thing to do."

After that, what *could* I say? That I wanted to condemn my baby to a life of poverty? That I wanted to keep it and hope for the best? That my mother would ever love it? That I had anything but pie-in-the-sky hopes Pat and I would ever see each other again?

I sniffled and filled out the form while she and my mother made small talk. They sounded relieved. Elaine said I'd see a doctor when admitted to the hospital. That it was best I didn't return to school.

"I know you've ruled out the Compton Home for Unwed Mothers," Elaine said. "Have you all worked that part of the problem out?"

My mother's voice sounded hollow, I hoped from remorse. "I haven't decided," she said. "I might ask my sister if we can make some kind of arrangement."

"Where does she live?"

"Just south of Asheville, by herself, in a big old rambling dump. Priscilla Ruth, we haven't talked about it, but do you think you could put up with that?"

It was the best idea I'd heard in a while but I only managed "Guess so." I wasn't about to give her reason to be happy. Calling my baby a bastard had pretty well undone nearly nineteen years of mothering.

I sat in stony silence while my mother walked Elaine to the door, saying she shouldn't need to see us here again and to be in touch by mail, because we shared a party line with nosy neighbors. Elaine called a cheery "Good-bye, Priscilla," but all I managed was a shallow wave of my hand. Which still gripped her handkerchief like an owl's talons a mouse.

My mother and her sister had a falling out years before I was born. I never really knew why, and figured it had been so long neither of them remembered, either. But it was strong as a bobcat. While their mother was living they saw each other only at Christmas and Easter—after she died, almost never. But my predicament drove Wanda back to the family bosom.

She and Aunt Pearl were as opposite as siblings could be. My mother dressed better than we could afford and never let anyone see her without makeup. My aunt never wore a belted dress and I doubt she owned two pairs of stockings. My mother would not smoke and swore lips that touched alcohol would never touch hers. (When I realized Walker made regular trips to a brown bag in his truck, I buried that, like many other things.) Despite warnings about everything from hell fire to health, my aunt smoked cigarettes, drank apple brandy, and read novels bought from wire racks in the drug store. I never knew her to go to church, either. I loved her.

She had married Uncle Mark right out of high school. His was a dead-end branch of a family tree whose roots went deep but had lately produced meager fruit. When a stroke laid him down in a trout stream, she inherited a little money and his old Miss Havisham frame house in a patch of woods south of Asheville.

My mother might think it a shack, but I loved it. Easily four times the size of ours, it had a front room, kitchen, and dining room downstairs, four bedrooms upstairs. Two rear sleeping porches were stacked like rabbit hutches. Wiring was stapled to the doorframes, light switches were dials. Aunt Pearl kept electrical tape in her pocket to remedy spots where copper peeked through cloth insulation.

She was what my mother called a pack rat. She wasn't as bad as those New York Collyer brothers they found dead the spring before I got pregnant but still, she couldn't hardly throw a thing away. Balls of string, tied-up newspapers, paper bags, Mason jars, you name it. She seemed to have at least one of everything. There was even a canoe on the front porch, although Aunt Pearl would have capsized it even without that hole in its side.

She liked to be considered odd—it kept people away, which gave her time for her real love, art. Oh, I don't mean fine paintings or fancy sculpture, but in her upstairs studio she made—Lord, I don't know, objects. Brightly colored ceramic hearts, fish with goofy faces, snails, all about the size of a golf ball, which she arranged into shapes to hang on the wall. It took maybe a hundred, for example, to make a multicolored life-sized guitar. She made unnaturally pretty flowers, too, that became pins and earrings, which she wholesaled to a tourist trap on the Spartanburg highway.

When I was a girl my mother sometimes let me spend Friday night and Saturday there, if Walker was home to carry me back and forth. I helped with Aunt Pearl's projects. When the light wasn't right or she was tired we'd play cards or board games. She had a new Monopoly set I was fair at but I always misplayed the Checkered Game of Life, a game so old she swore Noah and Mrs. Noah used it on the Ark.

I moved in with Aunt Pearl the week after Elaine's visit. My mother's story: Pearl had broken a hip and there was no one else to care for her. I would drop out of school to cook and clean and whatever else until she was back on her feet. Her place, my mother thought, was far enough from Crawford that I wouldn't be seen by every church lady in the county. The school let me keep up with studies by long distance, so to speak, so I kept my picture in the annual and all that. Camouflage.

My mother let me out in the driveway and drove away after a pretty stiff "Goodbye, Priscilla Ruth." I didn't say a thing. I had a cheap suitcase, a paper grocery bag full of canned cat food, and a cardboard box in which Puddy Tat suffered. Aunt Pearl came to the porch, wiping her hands on her apron. "Lord, child, what all have you brought? Is that a cat?"

"Mama said when I left she'd get rid of him."

"Her usual compassionate self, eh? You take the cat. Give me your bags."

I sat the box down on a bare spot in the hall. As I began to open it,

Puddy Tat shoved himself out and zinged down the hall, for a bout of hissing and growling with Aunt Pearl's cat.

"That's Van Gogh. They'll get used to each other," Aunt Pearl said, as we hugged.

She was kind of everything I wasn't—overweight, dark-haired but turning to gray, nearsighted, unhealthy. Her eyeglasses fit her face like a question mark. She kept her hair in a tight bun and wore a homemade house dress with full pockets, in which keys, bottle caps, and Lord knows what else jangled. "I'm grateful you let me come," I said.

"Glad to do it. So Miss Priss is in trouble?"

"Wow, you haven't called me that in years. And yes, she is."

"I bet Wanda shit a pickle." Aunt Pearl lit a cigarette and held the pack out. "Here. Or has this fallen woman taken them up?"

"Actually, I haven't. Boy, you're right, she *was* upset."

"Hell, she gets upset over a hangnail. There's got to be a better word for when she found she had a daughter gone bad."

"Maybe 'mad as hops'?"

She grinned like the chessy cat. "Your granny used to say that. Never knew exactly what it meant, but yes. Let's talk in the kitchen."

"So you don't mind me staying here?"

"No, kid. I always liked you." We shuffled down the hall past pet toys, slut wool, stacks of magazines, the odd stick of firewood. She sat at the table and motioned me to a chair.

The room hadn't changed much, except to add an electric range next to the old, wood-burning Home Comfort. I don't know who had talked her into the sleek, white-enameled stove, but it was apparent Aunt Pearl preferred the old, ornate wood range, a feast of cast iron and steel, eyes warped with heat, firebox nearly always in play. Aunt Pearl claimed no electric range would ever bake a decent biscuit or simmer a respectable pot of soup beans.

An ancient waffle iron sat next to a food mill bolted to the edge of the right-hand counter. To the left of the sink was a half-full dish drainer and a bread box with a stenciled sunflower. A calendar with a picture of Jesus suffering the little children said I'd be there a while.

Aunt Pearl shoved a stick of wood into the firebox. "Let's see if I understand the plan," Aunt Pearl said. "You're at the hideout until you're off to the hospital?"

I nodded.

"Then what?"

"I guess I go home, if Mama will have me. If not, then I don't know."

"What about the kid?"

"It'll be adopted."

She flicked a long ash into a brimming glass tray shaped like the state of Tennessee. "Just like that. It'll be adopted and you'll go home and life will be like nothing ever happened."

"Well…"

She shook her head, her hair tickling her cheeks. "Let me tell you something, little girl. This ain't going to be like giving away a puppy."

I stared at my hands lying in my lap.

"Look at me, darling. I'm serious. Having this child is going to hurt. If you think you're easily going to give up something you worked so hard for, you got another think coming. 'Give up.' That's one word. I might have said 'abandon,' 'renounce,' 'discard,' 'throw to the wolves.'"

She stood and looked out the window. I was about to cry. "Ever consider keeping it?"

I shook my head slowly. "Mama wouldn't hear of it."

"Wanda ain't having this young'un."

"Aunt Pearl, there's no way she'd let me back home with a baby."

For the first time I noticed one of her art things on the wall, a fish the size of a sturgeon, belly about to burst with multicolored hearts. Me, soon enough.

"Bring him here. Hell, I'll help you raise him. Her. Whatever. I'm not as helpless or sinful as big sis thinks."

"I'd never be able to provide for it."

Aunt Pearl put out her cigarette and walked over to me. "Lord, listen. You sound like a welfare worker. You been talking to them?"

"Her name is Miss Maxwell, Elaine Maxwell. She's nice."

"*Miss*, eh? Means she don't know a blooming thing about babies. I bet 'Miss Maxwell' wears good suits and ain't ever done any babysitting. She's fed you a line. I bet she said his new parents will send him to college and Europe and everywhere else."

"As a matter of fact…"

"And I bet she also says to give her up is the Right Thing To Do."

With that the faucet opened and I fished for a handkerchief.

"Listen, girl. There's always more than one point of view. Hear this—it's your kid. No law says you got to give him away. Anybody ever say that?"

By that time I was bawling like a calf beside its dead mother.

Aunt Pearl put her hand on my shoulder. "Well, think about this. Just because my sister has her ass on her shoulder is no reason to abandon a perfectly good kid. She'll get over it. Hell, it's her grandchild."

"Aunt Pearl, she's already called it a bastard."

"Wow. Really?"

"Yes, and I don't believe anything else has hurt me so."

"I bet. Want some coffee?"

"Please."

"I'll make a pot. And I'll give you all the help Wanda will allow—including free advice." She poured stale coffee down the sink, threw the grounds out the back door, rinsed the strainer, and filled the pot with water.

"Aunt Pearl, I'm so scared."

"Of your baby coming? Or your mother?" She filled the basket from a red bag of Eight O'Clock coffee.

"Both, I suppose."

She chunked a stick of rich pine in the firebox, set the pot on a warm eye, and looked at me like I was the only other person in the world. "Don't be scared of having your kid. You ain't a bit better or worse than thousands the world over, hatching them this very second. What you got to figure out is how scared you are of Wanda Lance. Then you can decide whether to keep your baby. I'm with you, whatever you choose. Now. Don't I remember something about you being engaged? Some boy in the service?"

"That's right."

"Does he know about this mess?"

"Yes. And he says when he comes home in October he'll—we'll—see if we can make things work."

"That include the kid?"

I did a quick mental inventory of his letters. "No, he assumes it's just me and him."

"Then maybe that's an argument for adoption. Tell me about him."

"He's quiet, strong, a pretty good basketball player, likes to fish. Daddy likes him."

"Fisherman, huh? Never did my Mark any good. Have y'all talked about children?"

"Not really. Just in general. I mean, we've talked about me going to school before we start a family."

"You still want to do that?"

I nodded.

"Here, but be careful. Woodstove coffee's hot enough to set your mouth afire." I blew across the cup, then inhaled its aroma. Aunt Pearl sat and patted my arm. "Maybe I'm jumping the gun here. Say he comes back and y'all decide to try to make it together. That'll mean he's got to trust you enough to let you out of the house every now and then without you getting pregnant. Don't laugh, men are jealous Joes. That'll be hard for him. Maybe too blasted hard if you keep the baby. After all, it's a reminder of what happened while he was gone. Sadly, he might never see anything besides that, so maybe that's best—adopt it and start over. If you think your Pat is worth the trouble."

"I love him, Aunt Pearl. I really do."

"Then I hope you work this out. But we don't have to decide today. Okay?"

I didn't sleep worth beans when I was expecting. Too much to think about. How bad will it hurt? When will I be back to normal? What if Daddy finds out? Will Pat change his mind? Will we still love each other a year from now?

I probably should have fretted over whether I would have a boy or girl, or whether it would be healthy and have a good life. But after the slapdown with my mother and Miss Maxwell, I tried to suppress motherly feelings. They say God takes care of fools and little children. Well, on a good day I figured I was one and the baby the other and, somehow, we would be fine.

Aunt Pearl seemed more interested in the baby than I was. She made me eat greens and stuff, things she said would make the baby grow fingernails, or whatever. I held the line at calf liver but managed broccoli and Brussels sprouts. Every day she fed me some kind of fruit. When I had heartburn, she said the baby was growing hair. If so, this kid would have hair to rival a mountain goat. Once she fed me cinnamon toast laced with cayenne so the baby would have some spirit about her. (I say "her" because Aunt Pearl said I was "carrying high.")

At first I didn't feel too motherly. Once I got past the throw-ups I figured I was just in for an eight-month ride with odd cravings. I never felt "butterfly wings" or any of that fluffy stuff in women's magazines, or if I did, I figured it was indigestion. But in late March something changed—I called it "flitters," a feeling that something really was alive in my belly. Light turns, flips maybe, not full-on kicking, but, girl or boy, it responded to my voice, and to my fingers when I rubbed my tummy.

Aunt Pearl and I ate like thrashers. One morning as Aunt Pearl and I were fixing breakfast—frying bacon, cooking grits, baking biscuits—I felt the baby, and sort of grunted.

"What's the matter?" asked Pearl.

"Nothing. The baby just moved."

She grinned and turned another slice of bacon. "That's pretty neat. How long has this been happening?"

"Hard to tell. Maybe a week or two?"

"There's a name for it, you know. 'The quickening.'"

"What a pretty way to put it."

"Yeah, it really is. Might make a good movie. *The Quickening*: starring Gregory Peck and Rita Hayworth."

She checked the woodstove while I stirred grits on the electric range. "Should I tell Pat?"

"About bouncing baby girl? Sure, why not?"

"Well, he hasn't been a bit curious about any of this."

"Tell him. Might be your best way to see if keeping the kid is an option."

I spooned grits into a bowl as she forked up bacon. "You mean..."

"Look, if you want to keep her, you gotta know he is all right with that. If he ain't, then you gotta decide between him or the baby. Either way, you need to know."

We wolfed down scrambled eggs, bacon, grits, milk gravy, and biscuits, washed down with strong coffee. I don't know why that breakfast lingers in my mind, but I still remember flecks of pepper and bits of bacon in the gravy. We finished with a butter biscuit slap full of blackberry preserves. I spit seeds all morning.

After we cleaned the kitchen I went upstairs, figuring to write to Pat in the interval between breakfast and dinner. After finding my stationery and fountain pen, the letter kind of flowed, like I finally had permission to ask.

March 29, 1949

Dearest Pat,

I hope this finds you well. I can't begin to imagine what you're doing today, but I hope it involves sunlight and ocean breezes.

Aunt Pearl and I get along real well. She's good for me—doesn't criticize, always supports. I don't know if Wanda and I will ever be close again. Aunt Pearl and she are polar opposites, that's for sure.

I don't quite know how to put this, so I might as well haul off and ask. Do you want to know anything about—my progress? I haven't had much to report, until about a week ago, when I began to feel something besides heartburn. Like she is jumping a little. I call it "flitters." Aunt Pearl says it's "the quickening," a lovely way to put it, don't you think?

So I guess my big question is, do you want to hear about this? Be honest, please.

Not much else to tell. It's a bit warm for this time of year. Crocuses are over, daffodils are past their peak, but Aunt Pearl has flowers galore, so something new will be blooming all spring and summer. I have that to look forward to. Not to mention having you home!

All my love,
Priscilla

A couple of weeks later, on an unseasonably cold day, our grouch of a mailman brought Pat's reply, along with an electricity bill (which would grump Aunt Pearl) and a furniture store circular. I opened Pat's letter at my desk and settled into a small puddle of sunshine as Puddy Tat rubbed himself on the backs of my legs. (He and Van Gogh kept an uneasy peace.)

April 17, 1949
Dear Priscilla,

Today's been sunny. My usual ocean life is in the radar room, green lines on glass screens, so when, like today, I loafed a little above decks, it's kind of overwhelming.

The sun at home is never as bright as here. I guess the mountains sort of absorb it. Out here it ricochets off the water and hits you in the face. Maybe regular swabbies get used to it, but to me it's kind of overpowering.

You asked about news of your "progress." I'll be honest. I hope not to hurt you, but I really don't want any details. It's not that I don't care or anything. It's just, well, like my picture of you got parked when I left, and I'm bent on coming back into that picture beside you—and what happened while I was gone can't really matter. Oh, I know it matters immensely to you—but I can't let it mean much to me or I'll think about you having a baby instead of you, and that would sour the milk.

You know, if you hadn't told me I probably would never have been the wiser. Mom thinks you've dropped out of school to care for your aunt, and I would have had no reason to question that. (Don't worry, I haven't told Mom a thing.)

But I'm glad I know. I'm beginning to get used to the idea, and to think, yes, we can make this work. What used to be an awful hurt is now some better. The chaplain, who I see every so often, says I need to reach inward for faith, which will help restore you and me.

I'll be home in six months. Everything will be behind you then, so we can try to make a go of it. I hope and pray we will. I love you very much.

That's about it from here. Tonight we get an oater starring Roy Rogers. It's strange enough to see a Western stateside, but out here it is really weird. It makes you realize how unreal those stories are—nobody ever was that good a shot (or bad—cowboys never miss, Indians never hit), nobody ever got shot without bleeding. Real cowboy life had to have been rough. You didn't ride all day, then take down your guitar and sing.

I hope you understand. Remember, you asked me to be honest. I love you very much.

Pat

Wasn't exactly what I had expected. I started crying halfway through, and after reading it twice I realized I hadn't felt the baby since I sat down. In between sobs I rubbed my tummy, straining to feel its presence. "It's all right," I whispered. "He just doesn't know you." I felt my belly move as if the baby backed up to my hand like a cat. (Puddy Tat, from the window seat, looked at me like I had lost my mind. Which, I suppose, I had.)

So, I thought. He wants no details. Well, he'll not get any. He can keep that picture he's so proud of—where I don't change and "what happened while I was gone doesn't really matter." Did he really write that? Yes, he did. And I'm "parked" like some big blue Buick where I did something I shouldn't have—but that really, really does matter. Does he think the most important thing that ever happened to me can not matter, even after I give this baby up?

He thinks cowboys have a rough life. What about a pregnant girl?

59

Does he expect me to go through my day—or for that matter, the rest of my life—playing and singing as if nothing ever burdened my soul?

I raced downstairs to find Aunt Pearl in what we called the "warm room." We stayed in it during cold weather, because its picture window faced south and on the north wall was a big fireplace, beside which she kept a squatty ladderback chair painted dark blue. Aunt Pearl's hips spilled over both sides of it as she jabbed a locust log with a brass-handled poker.

"*Yet man is born unto trouble, as the sparks fly upward,*" she intoned absently, gazing into the fire. It seemed five minutes before she noticed me. "What in creation's got into you?"

I simply held out the letter. She adjusted her glasses, glanced at it, and laid it on the mantel. "Hell, Priss, I can't read something like this stone cold sober. You want some, too?"

"At this time of day?"

"I expect it's dark in the basement," she said, shuffling toward the kitchen. She returned with two jelly glasses half full of fairly clear liquid smelling like gasoline and apples. "Brandy," she said. "Down the hatch."

She finished hers in one gulp but I just sipped mine. I was afraid of upsetting my already flip-flopping stomach.

She lit a Camel and read the letter. Twice, shaking her head, smoking. "Well, gal, you got your answer. This one ain't ever gonna fall for a baby that ain't his, even if it's cute as a speckled pup, holds out its arms, and says Da-Da in Latin. So this much is clear: keep the kid and lose Pat, or keep Pat and lose the kid."

"Until the last couple of weeks that would have been easy." I patted my tummy. "Now, I don't know."

"Your decision, girl." She walked over and patted my head. "You want a speech from your old Auntie?"

I nodded.

"Was it up to me, I'd tell him to stay on that boat of his, keep my kid, and take my chances. To hell with his sour milk. But you love this boy, so listen up. He's short-sighted, like all men. Their brains ain't in their heads, if you follow me. Even though he says he loves *you*, he loves his memory, which isn't you anymore. You need to make him deal honestly with that."

She took my drink from my trembly hand and set it on the mantel. When she sat to worry the fire, I didn't know which popped louder, her knees or the locust.

"Priss, you're probably lucky that Big Dick cut out on you. You're also lucky you got a man, if you want one. But old Pat ain't on the hook yet. He's been burned too, and you'll have to give him time, re-introduce yourself to him, so to speak. Make him realize you're not the empty-headed girl in his stupid picture. And he don't know it, but he's changed, too. He'll have to deal with that, if he ever realizes it."

She stood and looked at my glass. "You ain't no common tramp, either, despite you had a kid and all. So don't let him in your knickers right off."

Whatever raced across my face made her laugh. "Don't look so danged shocked. You know he wants to screw the britches off that girl he remembers. You got to re-establish that you're a proper young woman, despite all, and he's going to have to earn you. To *deserve* you. Because you're worth having. Hear me?"

I nodded. To tell the truth, I was getting a little swimmy-headed, whether from the brandy or simply knowing Aunt Pearl was right—I had more work to do than having the baby.

"Well, think about what I've said. It's going to be a brand-new dance. You both will have to learn the tune. I ain't saying you can't do it, just that it will be harder than he thinks. You know it already, but he don't."

She drained my glass. "You don't like these apples?"

"It's a little rough."

"That's okay—now that I think about it, it might not be good for junior in there. I'll find you some lemonade."

After the baby became active, I realized there was no simple answer (if there ever was) to "Who am I?" Because I was plural—or dual—or at least more than I was before I met Dick Snipes. The question was "Who are we?" No longer a carefree twit, I was actually two people. Or one person carrying another inside her. Which meant responsibility. Obligation. Guilt. Gloom.

Oh, sometimes I'd feel her—kick isn't the right word, but when Aunt Pearl's radio played Dinah Shore, I'd almost feel she was dancing. The nicest feeling, one that made me smile until I knew this wouldn't last—and that if I allowed myself to love this baby I'd never give her up.

I'd be rich if I had a nickel for every night I lay in bed, hands on my belly, feeling her piddling around in there, crying myself to sleep because I didn't want to face the difference between what I felt she needed me to do and what I felt I had to do. Then wake in the middle of the night and wonder why she wasn't moving. Asleep? Is she okay? Then to feel her again and go back through all that indecision. I was going to be a mental case if this went on much longer. Did they deliver babies at Broughton Hospital?

Aunt Pearl seemed to sense I was fighting this battle inside my head and needed to do it mostly by myself. We cooked and ate three times a day but sometimes we wouldn't say a word in between. Until I got too big, I'd weed flower beds or help put up snap peas, but there were days when sunshine and bird calls and a dancing baby would make me want to spend the rest of the day in bed, shades rolled down, eyes shut tight, trying not to let myself enjoy life one bit. Feeling like I didn't deserve sunshine. Or my baby.

When that happened, Aunt Pearl, kind and wise, insisted we walk in the woods instead of staying in the house or puttering in the garden. She'd show me brown or yellow mushrooms, the strange green of turkey track, red moss, woodpecker holes, deer tracks, whatever crossed our path. Evidence of God's grace, she said. She said she loved to worship at Rabbit's Church of Nature, a place that kept me from going totally insane.

I'd be okay for a few days, then down again. I'd never had ups and downs like that before, and was getting pretty tired of it.

From "the quickening" to a steadily growing baby is a mighty long haul. I was, simply, tired. Physically—and emotionally—exhausted from wrestling with right and wrong.

Summer's heat tipped the scales toward adoption. Weariness, aching shoulders, swollen ankles, and sweat—plus the growing certainty I wasn't ready to commit twenty-whatever years to raising a child by myself—made my mind up. So when Miss Maxwell came in July to make arrangements for the hospital, and for me to sign papers, I was ready.

She wore a yellow suit that perfectly offset her brown hair and eyes—which, I could tell, were distracted by piles of stuff in the house.

"Priscilla, it's good to see you. You look great."

I laughed. "I don't *feel* great."

"Well, I mean it. You're the picture of health."

"I've made her eat good," said my aunt. "And I've tried to keep her mind off things. We've played a lot of cards. She's good at it, for a Baptist."

"Thanks for that. We like to know our clients are being well taken care of."

First time I had thought of myself as a "client."

After some small talk she found the permission papers. "You're absolutely sure you want to go through with this? Once this is in motion you can't back out."

"I want to," I said, running my hands over my bulging belly. "I just want this over with." I signed quickly.

She nodded. "Just so you are clear. This is a legal document. If I tear it up, you can keep the baby. Once I file this paper, that's impossible."

"I know," I said. "This is best."

"Glad you see it that way." She stood and shook my hand. "Be brave."

When my water broke, Aunt Pearl called the number Miss Maxwell gave us, which summoned a yellow cab. I got in the backseat and rolled the window down. Aunt Pearl lit a cigarette and leaned in the window. She reminded me to keep up with my bag and said she'd take good care of old Puddy Tat.

"I'll see you tomorrow. Then you'll go back home, like Wanda wants. You let me know if I can do anything."

"I will. Thanks, Aunt Pearl. You've been a lifesaver."

"I don't know about that, but I love you, kid."

"Love you, too." I rolled up the window.

The cab smelled like dead cigars and something akin to the smell of fear in the school hallway. The cabbie took a look at my belly and turned the radio up, like he didn't want me talking to him. I'll never forget Perry Como singing "Some Enchanted Evening." Hmp. Don't tell me God doesn't remind you of your sin.

He drove to the hospital's back entrance, where a green-eyed orderly gave me a rough ride in a wheelchair into a dark elevator. On the maternity floor a nurse barked "Take her to number three," a small room bare of much of anything except green paint, fluorescent light, and an examination table that looked like some torture machine. A nurse helped me into a shortie smock and arranged me for the doctor.

Between contractions I trembled from cold and nerves and whatever else. I had goose bumps the size of, well, geese. I waited alone for an eternity. Finally the nurse reappeared with a gray-headed doctor smelling of tobacco. I might as well have been a piece of meat he was inspecting. "Prep number three," he told the nurse. "It won't be long."

First time I had thought of myself as a number.

A woman came in carrying a tray with a straight razor and mug. "What's that for?"

"Honey," she said, in as country a drawl as I'd ever heard, "you gonna get shaved. Can't have scootchie hairs in baby's eyes, can we?"

Beside her was a stainless steel stand with a red rubber bag and long tube with an evil-looking thing on its end. "What's that?" I asked, as she lathered up a storm.

"Honey, you're getting an enema."

"What's that?"

She looked at me like she wondered where I'd been all my life. "We got to clean you out so's you won't shit all over the doctor."

I started sniffling. "I... I... didn't know this would happen."

"Honey, this ain't no playground. It's the curse of Eve, you know. You planning to see this young'un?"

I bit my lip and shook my head.

"That's likely best."

In the delivery room they gave me a shot, then strapped my hands to the bed. By that time I was too woozy to resist. I don't remember a thing about the delivery. And I never saw the baby. Boy, girl, I didn't know. Who was I? Empty. That was all.

DATE: August 6, 1949
NAME: Baby Lance
SEX: Male
Weight: 5 pounds, 2 ounces
Time of birth: 3:37 A.M.
Delivered by: Frank A. Thomas, M.D.
Silver Nitrate: ✔ yes no
Name of Mother: Priscilla Ruth Lance
Name of Father: NONE NAMED

II.

A Slot in Time

Martha Atkins Blaine

My doctor gave me this blank journal and said to write down things that happen. Or things that used to happen. So I can figure out why. That might be too hard. I've heard God never gives you more than you can bear, but I'm living proof of the untruth of that.

I wonder where that redbird's going, flitting in pine leaves like a feathered drop of paint. He's free. Free. Means you can have it for nothing. Also means you *don't* have something. As in "free from suffering." I'm free from my son but I'd rather have Willie Lee than silver or gold.

The Bible says to everything a season. A time to be born, a time to die. A time to adopt, a time to cry.

My doctor's name is Jackson. Nice man. Round glasses, a little mustache. He wants but I can't. The story. How years ago the welfare people gave Willie Lee to me... Not today. I'll just say the Lord's Prayer. I start and end my days with it. Makes me feel safer. Usually.

Dr. Jackson said to maybe start with my parents. Tom and Ella. Thomas Jacob Atkins his full name. About the turn of the century he pulled up roots near Spartanburg, South Carolina. Came to Buncombe with a little money and a wife named Ella Rose and, as he told it, a hankering to sleep under a blanket of a summer's night.

In his prime Tom was six foot two, two hundred forty. Wore muttonchops and a bushy mustache and his dark hair was kind of curly so he looked fearsome to a little girl but he was a pussycat really. Even when drinking.

He said Asheville would grow west, so bought land in the Sand Hill section, on a hill with a view of Mount Pisgah "from the shoulders up." On this lot he built a two-story structure, food store downstairs—he called it Tom's General Store—him and Ella lived upstairs. He sold milk and bread, cheese and crackers, mostly on credit, at prices you could beat in town—and also stocked horse feed, axe handles, nails, nuts and bolts. You could buy fresh eggs and butter—but talk, Lord, talk was free and evenings Tom sold bottled comfort to men, at first for cash money, later on credit.

Ella Rose was kind of mousy, not skinny but not fat either, kept her brown hair in a tight bun, wore most anything handy. She'd put on Tom's big old shirts like some artist's smock. Or might wear the same apron a week. She didn't care, really, except Sundays, when they dressed up and went to the Presbyterian church, a square brick chapel across the road from the store. It was handy, so it suited them. If it'd been Catlick or Jewish they'd have gone there just the same.

If they weren't happy back then…

Yesterday they got me for therapy so I lost my thread of thought. I was telling about parents, how Papa was a drinking man. Me, I'm a teetotaler, afraid to touch it. Ella Rose was a Dodd, with all that clan's quirks. Her ears were big and she had kind of a crackly voice and a heart condition, as far as I know she never worked hard. A little embroidery, some knitting. She took a drink of a night if she specially needed sleep, otherwise didn't mess with it.

But love of liquor ran like a waterfall down the Atkins branch. Mama had to forgive her future father-in-law for being so cockeyed he passed out, just fell into the aisle, at her wedding. Over the years she did a lot of forgiving, mostly of her husband. When they were first married, one or two days a month Tom got tanked but that changed, not all of a sudden, but like when a kid grows up and you think, how'd she get to be that old?

In time, Tom drank every day except Sunday, he was right strict about that. I reckon the only way Mama put up with it was he wasn't mean. If a customer caught him right he'd give her a sack of flour or a tin of coffee, on the house. And he never hit Mama. She'd have left him, sure.

Toward the end he'd light in at dawn, so midday patrons might find him in black shirt and trousers, covered by a stained butcher's apron, a-snore in a leather chair in the corner. Snuff-drooled chin. They stepped quietly, wrote their buyings in the ledger, settled up at month's end.

Ella Rose's mind and Tom's liver began to fail when I was in seventh grade. At thirteen I quit school to be full-time nurse, cook, laundress, house cleaner, shopkeeper all rolled into one.

Their first child Frank Eugene Atkins was born in 1906. The next year Asheville went dry. Mama said Papa felt the world was about to end, but she was already with child again, bearing Jacob Hugh in early 1908. Jacob favored his father, large, loud, loved to tell tall tales. He also liked to fight, and, in time, followed father's footsteps on the path of strong drink.

I was born May 3, 1913. Saturday, a guarantee I'd work for a living. Mama said Papa said he'd hoped for another boy, so this puny girl might be the last. Don't know why she told me that.

Frank was quiet, serious, eager to please. He favored our mother, did well in school, but died of the Spanish flu when I was three. Tom, I am told, grieved like David for Absalom.

"Ella Rose, it's awful hard to lose a son. I'd rather it'd been me. We'll have no more if I have anything to do with it."

And, you know, I guess he did, because they didn't. So by myself I cared for a straying brother, a father sneaking toward his final bleed, a mother waxing loopy as an addle-pate ferret.

Dr. Jackson says tell about being a little girl. I honestly don't remember much. I liked church. A rag doll named June slept beside me in a pine box with a little bitty quilt in it. Until… I can't remember.

Mama said I couldn't say r's plain but grew out of that. One time grape juice gave me hives. Had the earache a lot. Measles. Mumps. Didn't like school until I got a pair of glasses, then did fine. But one day I turned in library books and the next day was home caring for broken people. That's about all.

Yesterday's shallow ending got filled in after dinner. When it's quiet, after all the people settle down, I can remember.

My mother's sister had a baby to die. They took me to the burying but I was maybe four or five and had no business there. They made me look in its little casket. He lay on his back in a white dress and booties and seemed kind of asleep, but not quite, and his color was off. The box was lined with white silk with a ruffly band and I screamed, they chased me over half the cemetery before I calmed down.

Next day I laid my doll June in her box, covered her with the quilt, took her to the backyard. Me and Jacob were burying her when Ella Rose stopped us. I never played with that doll again. Or, for that matter, any others. They got me one that her eyes opened and shut, she wore a frilly dress but I never messed with her. You might say from that time dolls were dead to me.

*   *   *

Dream—I'm inside a cold room, door locked, nobody knows or cares where I am. I shout and scream and cry but nothing doing. I'm so cold I'm like that dead infant. I wake in a sweat and for a minute don't know where I am.

Dr. Jackson says it's good to write down dreams, they always mean something. At least I know this one's begats. Behind our store's back wall was—well—storage. The left half, where we kept paper goods and canned stuff, was open. The right half had thick walls and a big door with a latch. Before refrigeration, blocks of river ice kept it cold.

When I was about four I wandered in there, and as I saw meat on hooks the door closed, the latch clicked—the room went dark as a coal pile. Talk about screaming bloody murder! There wasn't a sign of a door handle and I kicked and hit it and my heart was about to leap from my mouth when Jacob opened it, big grin on his face.

"Saved you!"

"I'm telling Mama."

Best I remember he got his tail beat and I had ice cream. Years later, going there still gave me the fantods.

Like I said, we were Presbyterians. The religion had preacher words, like predestination, I didn't know how to spell, but I sure understood. I'd think, oh, yes, God from the beginning knew everything, even that I would take care of my parents. His Plan proved He was in control. And if I strayed He would gently push me back, like Jesus used to lead His disciples around the Holy Land. Where I'd love to go if I was younger.

I also knew Jacob as a little shaver was predestinated to steal liquor. When I quit school, Jacob was a high school senior, some days. Others he stayed home to tend the family shop, sample joy juice, filch a dollar or three.

He sometimes hitchhiked seven miles to the Crawford Springs, where he might wake up on the porch, five in the morning, pockets out-turned, money gone. When he dragged in I fed him hot soup and put him to bed. Didn't give him down the road, either. Maybe I should have. That summer—let's see, I was thirteen so that was 1926—he went down east, like storybook people that go to seek their fortune. Except instead of a hobo's bindle he carried a cardboard suitcase.

Dr. Jackson says dig deeper. I've said I've remembered all I want to, but he shakes his head and smiles behind that mustache. So here's something I thought of this morning while we were all sewing.

Sand Hill was a goodly neighborhood, stretched maybe a half mile in any direction from our store. We were at the top of the hill where the Asheville road and Oak Street crossed. I say street, they weren't paved until the 1950s, they were just dirt and gravel back then. Oak ran north-south, Sand Hill School at the north end, Mr. Crowder's dairy at the south. The Asheville road ran from West Asheville straight through our neighborhood to the textile plant and beyond. Crawford, Canton, Clyde, Murphy.

Most houses sat fairly close to these roads, and had a patch of woods behind. Woods trails linked us all together.

The oldest families descended from Colonel Moore, a long-ago Indian killer. Their names, the families I mean, were Whisnant and Elder and most of them, the men anyhow, drank.

The biggest house on Oak belonged to Miss Elder, a tall, big-boned woman, secretary to some high-up at the plant. The house was red brick with white shutters, dormers across the front roof like exclamation points. Miss Elder, a temperance crusader, had a hard-drinking brother who lived in Gastonia but worked a sales route west. He stayed with her a right smart.

A back porch faced woods that joined Mr. Whisnant on the north-west. Whisnant and Miss Elder were cousins. Mrs. Whisnant, nee Fox, had "married up." In cahoots with Miss Elder, she carried on a constant campaign to save people from liquor, while Mr. Whisnant and Miss Elder's brother met in the woods to drink and, I suppose, carp about women who didn't.

One day—I was maybe seven—it was summer, I wasn't in school—Ella Rose shooed me out for some fresh air. So I crossed the road and walked down Oak, past Mr. Norvell's place. He wasn't kin to the old families—he'd moved from West Virginia with his brother, who had stuck an e on his last name, to make it look French or something. Mr. Norvell accented his name on the first syllable, Mr. Norvelle on the last.

Anyhow, (see how good my memory is?) across the road from Mr.

Norvell's I cut down toward Mr. Crowder's and ended up in the bottom land along Hominy Creek. There were usually red-winged blackbirds there but that day I seen a bright red bird with black wings. A tanager, somebody said later. I kicked up sandy soil but no arrowheads surfaced. My brothers had found hundreds so I figured I was just unlucky.

Heading back up the hill it was hot on the big road so I cut into woods behind Mr. Whisnant's, where my brothers had dammed a little bitty creek, to catch crawdads and stuff. I thought to put my toes in the water.

When somebody laughed I kind of froze because I hadn't seen a soul. The laugh turned into two, then three and I knew at least one of them. Then there was music.

They weren't in the wading hole, but closer to Miss Elder's house up a path I'd never noticed. When I finally seen them my mouth opened like a big woodpecker hole. There were empty Schlitz cans and wine and liquor bottles in a heap, I swear, the size of a T-Model-Truck. Mr. Whisnant and Miss Elder's brother sat beside it on a log. Mr. Whisnant played "Turkey in the Straw" on a mouth harp and his cousin played the spoons. My brother Jacob?

Nearly falling-down drunk, shirt tied around his waist, pants belted around his head like a court jester's hat. He brandished a bottle in each hand as Miss Elder's brother hooted and egged him on. I almost thought Jacob had hooves he was prancing around so. It'd have been funny if it wasn't so pitiful. Or maybe the other way around.

I wasn't about to embarrass those men by making my brother come home, and he probably wouldn't have anyhow. Besides, who wants to walk up the road with a stumbling upside-down-dressed goat-boy, stinking of whiskey and beer?

I snuck out of the woods and came home.

Papa always closed the store at six, or at least shut the door long enough to eat supper before returning to let drinkers in. About five-thirty I was cooking when I heard something clamber around out back. Mr. Whisnant and Miss Elder's brother held up Jacob, pants and shirt back on, limp as a rag doll.

"Here, little girl, help us get him hid afore old Tom finds him."

We somehow snuck Jacob by Ella Rose and tucked him in. Maybe the men skittered out the window, I don't know. I told Papa Jacob was gone to Crawford and he just shook his head.

After supper I woke Jacob and fed him soup. He had no idea how he'd gotten home and I didn't tell him what I'd seen. Wouldn't have done either of us a bit of good.

Dr. Jackson wanted to know if I hadn't made part of that story up.

I told him I wasn't telling a story. It really did happen.

Then that look jumped on his face.

"You were around a lot of alcoholic men when you were little. Did any of them ever hurt you, Mrs. Blaine?"

"One time Papa nearly broke my foot stepping on it as I was trying to get him into bed."

"No, I mean not by accident."

"Papa wouldn't hurt a flea. And even the old drinkers, they'd fix fence for people whose cattle got out, in the spring they'd plow and plant for a man who was down sick. Good-hearted people, stood up for their neighbors."

I hope Dr. Jackson believes me.

Dr. Jackson asked if I never played when I was a little girl. Of course I did, but mostly by myself because my brothers usually wanted nothing to do with a kid sister. With them it was baseball, fishing, or nothing. Oh, every now and then we'd play rummy or checkers, but they always cheated and we'd end up fighting.

I never had a birthday party.

That shouldn't sound like poor pitiful me, because nobody at our house noticed birthdays except to give the lucky one extra dessert. We didn't do cakes, candles, presents, nothing kids have these days. Never had a sleepover, I think they call them. How many girls' parents let them spend the night at a booze hound's house?

Anyhow, I guess I never played much. I've told about trouble with baby dolls. Ella Rose let me do paper dolls so later I could cut out dress patterns without hacking my fingers off. Play that taught Something Useful.

We hardly ever went anywhere, either. Papa said when he put down Sand Hill roots, that was the last moving he'd do, and, you know, it was. And he never owned horse, car, or truck. Said if he had to travel he had two good feet but if they weren't fast enough he'd stay home.

His brothers and sisters were scattered over South Carolina and Georgia, but never visited us, and if they had reunions, didn't tell Papa.

Mama's family? I can't think of a sociable Dodd—and can't remember her telling family stories except how her mother died of the sugar, with all that horrible numbness in her feet, them turning black and toes falling off. Mama was not a cabinet of pleasant memories.

I wouldn't call my childhood happy. Oh, nobody beat me, I didn't beg for gruel or eat hog slop. But I had no long happy afternoons playing with girlfriends. Our household was three males, none any good at cooking or washing, plus two females, one that was delicate, which left me to do most everything.

I liked to read, at least after I got glasses and had time. Wasn't much to read at the house except the Bible, a catechism, a couple of cookbooks. County didn't start the bookmobile until I was sixteen, so until I dropped out I used the school library. I read about Clara Barton and Joan of Arc over and over. *Black Beauty. Little Women.* I memorized "The Bells" by Edgar Allan Poe. Can still recite it, too.

But Bible stories I loved most. David and Goliath, Moses and Pharaoh, Jesus and Lazarus, anything, really, about Jesus, except that fig tree business. I liked Rachel at the well but until I was an adult didn't figure out why Sarah ran Hagar off. And that creepy story about Abraham and Isaac? I never read that story to children.

I sure didn't understand adults, and sometimes church people were hardest to ken. How could they sing about heavenly sunlight on Sunday, shake hands and hug everybody, then Monday backbite like barracudas? Even what I called paid Christians, preachers, missionaries, and such, sometimes presented themselves a living but unacceptable sacrifice.

When I was real little we had a preacher, Mama told me, I don't really remember him, that used to thunder about sin all the time. A good-looking cuss with a meek little wife and two kids, a boy and a girl, who nobody much liked. Mama called them Sin and Sorrow, but not to their faces.

One Sunday he didn't show up.

The elders who kept emergency sermons in their inside pockets drew straws to see who would preach, which I guess is like casting lots in the Bible. The chosen one looked for the choir director to see what she'd practiced Thursday night. She wasn't there, either.

Mama said she was a pretty good soprano, with short black hair, and, I can hear Mama saying it now, "her butt stuck out," as if that explained everything.

Anyhow, she and the preacher'd snuck off Friday to Knoxville for a weekend on Gay Street before heading west to start a new life.

The choir director's husband wasn't at church, either. He'd smelled a rat, or anyhow extra perfume, and tracked them to their room, where they, well, you know. Shot and killed her, bullet through the heart. Wounded the preacher in the face and groin. Then a bullet through his own head. That hotel room must have been an ungodly mess.

The preacher's wife took Sin and Sorrow home to Ohio, no forwarding address. The preacher lived a couple of months before blood poisoning took him home. I hope he was able, at least in his mind, to ask God to forgive him.

One hot Sunday when I was seven or eight, we had a new preacher we didn't yet know well. It was already heading toward ninety degrees, and in our pew we tried to flap up a breeze with those funeral home fans. Through open windows, birds sounded sweltery.

The preacher—Reverend J. C. Dixon—droned about loaves and fishes when this grey striped cat jumped onto the windowsill behind him. People elbowed each other, grinned, The cat scanned us like he wondered did anybody have two fish. Silently it jumped into the choir loft, walked up to Reverend Dixon, and jumped onto the pulpit rail.

You should have seen the preacher's face. Like well, you've gone and ruined my sermon. Then he smiled, reached out, rubbed the cat's head.

"Friends, we'll take a short break—for catechism."

We laughed our heads off, because we had not known him to have a sense of humor.

Come to think of it, a dry baptism might have soured him.

See, our church's baptism font was a hollowed-out Jordan River rock a little bigger than a catcher's mitt. A glass ashtray in it held water. Well, it was the preacher's job to make sure it was full for a baptism. But Reverend Dixon—he being brand-new—took for granite the elders did.

His first baptism was little Teddy Brown. Everything was fine, the sun shone, we wondered if the baby would wake up and fuss. The preacher, reading from *The Book of Church Order*, right before "I baptize thee in the name of the Father" dipped fingers into an ashtray as dry as the Wilderness of Sin.

Didn't miss a beat, baptized that baby with air. Which, best I remember, is not biblical.

Elder Norvell, four rows back, afterward cornered the preacher.

"You don't baptize with water, it won't take."

"What do you suggest I do?"

"Do it right. We can't have a chap going to hell if he dies."

So they brought Teddy and his folks back, this time with water. When Teddy cried, Mr. Norvell smiled like the heavens had opened.

Afterward Reverend Dixon noticed Mr. Norvell whispering to a circle of elders, jackets folded over their arms, under a pine tree. When they seen him they got quiet as fish. Enough to make him nervous, I would think. Or at least curb his sense of humor.

By the way, that second baptism took. Teddy Brown made a missionary to Japan.

Along about then they took me to a show put on by athletic supporters at the plant. Their industrial league teams, bowling, basketball, baseball, what-have-you, needed uniforms. Papa hollered about the thirty-five-cent admission, but Mama said it was a good cause—the plant workers put bread on our table, and besides, I got in for a nickel.

In the Sand Hill School auditorium two aisles and three courses of seats sloped down to a wide stage. High narrow windows on the sides, thick maroon velvet curtains. Every seat came with at least one rock-hard gum wad.

With the stage curtains closed, folks played music that started slow but ended up gay and fast. Something you could dance to. A piano woman, men with banjos and fiddles, one guy with a saxophone as tall as he was. They wore black suits, white shirts, black bow ties, and played well together.

When the curtain rose I was startled. About half of the stage people looked right but the rest wore suits with huge lapels, loud patterns, clashy colors, unmatching neckties. Nothing really fit, either too large or too little. A man decked out in a bright red wig wore a dress over houndstooth leggings. And their faces? They were black.

Not healthy-looking black, but like somebody had rubbed burnt bark everywhere except around mouths and eyes. Made their lips look two inches wide. About as natural as a purple goldfinch.

At first they sang stuff I'd learned in school, "Camptown Races," "Swannee River." But I couldn't figure why the black faces. When I asked Tom or Ella Rose they shushed me.

"Listen to the music, child."

After an intermiddle the people in strange costumes lined up at center stage. The one on the end started asking questions. One by one the others fired back and after each answer a man banged a drum, the crowd roared and slapped their legs. Stuff about watermelon and coons. Preachers and fried chicken. The actors, Tambo, Rastus, Bones, talked in outlandish accents, like nobody on earth ever talked.

No colored people lived in Sand Hill. One, Mister Jerry, worked on the truck that delivered canned goods at the store. The driver, his boss, was a grumpy white man who, when he had to unload by himself, threw stuff around like he was mad at it. Mister Jerry always unloaded with care. His face was a pretty brown, like rich people's furniture. He wore a proper suit and tie, and had a smile and good word for "little Miss Martha."

I asked Papa where Mister Jerry was.

"He wouldn't care for this show. Besides, there ain't a balcony."

"What's a balcony?"

"You know that upper tier in the back like in the Paramount downtown? Well, that's the balcony. Negroes sit there."

"Why?"

"Honey, it's just the way it is."

"Do they like it?"

"Sure they do. Quit asking all these blooming questions."

That night in bed I remembered the man and his wife behind us, whistling and clapping, laughing like funnybone monkeys.

"Whoever put this together sure pegged them n****** right."

"They sure as creation did."

A word I'd heard on playgrounds. When I was little and brought home "Eenie meenie minie moe, catch a n***** by the toe," Mama threatened to wash my mouth out with lye soap.

I decided I'd never figure adults out.

There was one thing. When I was fourteen, maybe fifteen. And I couldn't say if it really happened or was a dream, cause there's no shred of proof left.

See, this couple moved into the neighborhood and nearly made criminals of the lot of us.

They were Yankees. Not that I'm prejudged, it's just that some people are lazy, or shiftless, or bona fide—others, just Yankees. (Some say damnyankees like it was one word.)

They bought land from Mr. Crowder—we were amazed he sold to people from New York, New York—and had this man from Crawford, Walker Lance, build a house on it. Sometimes of an evening he joined the old drinkers.

We were curious about the first new house in Sand Hill in forever. Mr. Whisnant and Miss Elder's brother and lots more wore a path through the woods to the back of the building site to get a good look. Of course, pretty soon Mr. Lanzio, that was his name, noticed. He had squared-off shoulders and pomaded black hair parted in the middle.

"You jerks rubbernecking, or do you need a job?"

"Just making sure your carpenter knows what he's doing."

"That's what I'm paying him for. Now scram before I get my baseball bat."

"You play? We could get a game up."

Mr. Lanzio stomped to a black Reo Flying Cloud, a car with a hood long enough to hide a Model-T in, roof that stuck out beetle-browed over the windshield. He came back with, Mr. Whisnant told Papa, a black bat that looked like it had been through the world war.

"Let's get out of here, boys."

Mr. Lanzio had Mr. Lance fence the rear of the place, so our old men were flustrated and had to stay out front and peek through the woods with the rest of us while Mr. Lance framed and finished a two-story house bigger than Miss Elder's, with four kinds of wood in the floors. So much room, we clucked, for two people. No matter that Miss Elder was only one lady in a bigger house—she was one of us.

Mrs. Lanzio didn't use our store. I reckon Sand Hill goods weren't good enough. She didn't shop in West Asheville, either, we seen them coming home in their big fine car, its back full of packages from Carpenter-Matthew and Bon Marché, Ivey's and Enman's. Never from anywhere as common as Eifird's or, Lord forbid, Fain's. Groceries delivered in, too. They didn't go to the Presbyterian church, either. Sunday mornings they went over town, somebody said, to the Catlick church with all the statues.

When somebody shuts themselves off like that the neighborhood gets mighty curious. Our old men couldn't stand not knowing, so they made stuff up. He was a stockbroker. A mobster. Maybe a retired baseball player except not old enough to be a retired anything.

She was an opera singer. Fashion model. Clothing designer. Maybe recovering from TB. Maybe widowed early and Mr. Lanzio was her "rescue husband."

There likely wasn't a lick of truth to any of that. But it made us feel better. You don't want anything in your midst you don't know beans about. You need to know where they came from—their story—true or not. You adopt them, kinda.

Anyhow, what happened to me was so icky it might have been as made-up as the Sand Hill version of the Lanzio family history. Or maybe I dreamed it. But it feels real.

I was by myself in the store. Papa had gone to pick up something, I guess. I was wiping the counter when Mr. Lanzio came in, looked around.

I knew right off who he was. Dangling cigarette, long coat, hands in pockets like he might be fingering a pistol.

"Hello, Mr. Lanzio. What can I do for you?"

He looked everywhere but at me.

"I'm right over here. What can I help you find?"

When I came out from behind the counter he smoked me over. Slow. Like he was enjoying himself.

"Got any Royal Crown pomade?"

"It's in the red can over there."

"Show me."

Like Zacchaeus I was little of stature. Papa always said I was "picked too green" to be much tall. Mr. Lanzio followed me to the shelf and when I reached on tippy toe for the hair goo he grabbed me, well, *there*.

About the time I screamed Papa opened the door.

"What do you think you're doing, Bub?"

I ran behind the counter. Papa lifted him right off the floor by his necktie and slung him against the wall.

"I'm a good mind to kill you, you horny-toad Yankee bastard."

"I didn't mean anything."

"The hell you didn't. Get out of here before I tear the smart-ass off your puss and feed it to you."

Mr. Lanzio took off quick as a banty hen in a hailstorm. Papa calmed down once he realized me or the store wasn't harmed but that evening grumbled a bunch to the old drinkers.

Late that night Mr. Lanzio's house scorched up in flames, along with Mr. and Mrs. Lanzio for all we ever knew. Wasn't hardly a thing left but a two-story chimney with hearths stuck on like false teeth. Burned down that rear-end fence, too.

There was talk that the firemen could have saved it, except they took their time arriving and mostly wet down the woods.

We also heard that the sheriff never did much besides ask his men to rake the ashes for "evidence." No bodies, but there was melted silver and four or five lead slugs some said had seen duty in blackjacks. The bat in Mr. Lanzio's car was leaded, too. The Colt pistol and box of ammunition in the glove box led to more stories.

The county sold the car and the gun, and after a while nobody spoke of Mr. and Mrs. Lanzio. I still don't know if they were in that house. Shoot, sometimes I wonder if I made all that up. There's no trace of the Lanzios in Sand Hill. The chimney was torn down, the fancy car went to Georgia, no bodies were buried. Papa and the old men who watched over our community are now gone, and besides, none of them ever told what really happened.

I can still feel that dirty old man's hand, though. Or can I? It's real hard to tell. I used to dream about that sometimes. Am I remembering a dream? Enough to make your head hurt.

Dr. Jackson says that's called dis-... I forget what but there's a reason for it—the mind shuts out painful stuff. But in my case it's good to remember it, I forget why. He also says I need to sort out how I feel about, you know, relations, but why a woman my age needs to do that is beyond me. Maybe sometime but for now I'll gee this mule of a journal into happier territory.

One spring—I was nearly seventeen—a boy about my age showed up at church. Sharp blue eyes, thin brown hair, wrinkled suit, collar buttoned, tieless.

He'd smile and I'd look away because, I don't know, smiling back seemed bold—and scary. It might make him ask me out or something. Oh, half of me wanted that. But another half wanted nothing to do with men. Another half was curious. I was what you call confused.

He started coming in the store every day after his shift, did what Papa called "turning things over," looking at everything, even though it was plain as the ears on your face why he was there. Then he'd sidle shyly up to the counter and lay down a penny for a jawbreaker or blow gum. He'd smile, say thanks, and leave. I wondered when he'd try his hand at talking.

Must have been a month before he cleared his throat, scratched his head.

"Want to go fishing?"

I didn't know much about that. Papa was no outdoor man, and Jacob had taken me to Crowder's pond once, then gave up—I wouldn't bait my own hook because I didn't want to hurt the worms. But here we were.

"Where?"

"Don't matter."

"Really?"

"Fish don't live in ugly places. Anywhere they are, I'm happy."

My ears perked up.

"I guess. When?"

"Now?"

"No, Papa's sick, you see, and Mama's mind ain't the best, so it's got to be a day we're closed, and a good day for her too, so I can leave for a little while."

"Would they mind you fishing on Sunday? Or does it have to be July Fourth or something?"

I shook my head. Except for Christmas and Easter, Tom and Ella Rose weren't strict about holidays.

"Then let's see about Sunday after church."

"Okay."

Henry Blaine, no middle name, left Haywood County to avoid farm work. But he wasn't running from fish. He'd already found Mr. Crowder's pond, where we went the next Sunday.

So here came me and Henry through the woods, not saying a word, him with two fish poles and tackle box, me with picnic basket full of crackers and cheese, bread and jelly, a jug of lemonade. A calm day, not too hot. We'd already had dogwood winter and blackberries were getting ready to bloom, which meant another cool snap soon. Pee-wees wagged their tails on overhead limbs, crows jabbered. In sunny spots honeysuckle and fire pinks flowered and down close to Crowder Branch orange jewelweed looked soon to bloom. You could smell summer around the corner.

At the pond he put finger to lips as if we'd been a pair of chattering magpies. He set down his gear, motioned me to sit beside it, then sat next to me.

"Ain't you going to fish?"

"Yep. I just need to study about where they are."

He showed me little pocks made by water spiders, the blips bream make when they feed, how dragonflies—he called them snake feeders, which I thought funny—hover and dart like they didn't abide by the same laws as us. He showed how to look for what he called structure, tree limbs under water, or maybe something Mr. Crowder had sunk for bass to hang around. A kingfisher dipped and yelled like a blue maniac.

"Look yonder."

He pointed to cattail reeds.

"What am I looking for?"

"Watch. He'll turn in a minute so you can see him. It's a blue heron."

I finally seen it fishing slow in the shallows.

"I never seen one before."

"This'n's used to people. They're usually spooked by anybody."

"It's grey. Why do they call them blue?"

"He's silver in some lights, blue in others, white sometimes they say. Can even hide on a naked branch."

It felt like an hour before Henry rigged up the poles, but I didn't mind. Fishing takes patience I don't naturally have, but Henry seemed to know this spot. Worms, tadpoles, tree frogs, cardinals, sparrows, red-wings, even what kinds of ants there were. Snakes, too.

When he was ready he baited my hook with a fat nightcrawler.

"See the end of that tree's shadow? There's a fish waiting for you."

Of course I fouled up the cast.

"Here, let me show you."

He laid that worm right at the shadow's edge and darned if line didn't start running off that reel.

"Bring him in, gal."

"No, Henry, you do it."

Six or seven head of cattle came to drink and stayed to watch us. After about three hours we came home with three nice bass. Good time—I didn't want to leave but also didn't want Mama to be with Papa any longer than she had to. Henry and I ate our snack and drank lemonade and had some laughs. He didn't try to hold my hand on the way back but I thought he wanted to.

He offered to cook supper—fried fish, potatoes, slaw—but I couldn't eat another bite. So Monday after work we fixed supper at my house together. I enjoyed that, and thought this might be predestinated. Mama liked him—of course she liked anybody, and probably wouldn't remember him tomorrow. But I felt this wasn't just settling. So I offered to fix the sleeve on his suit coat. He grinned.

"Sure, gal."

That's how we started courting.

Christmas 1930 I had fixed up the store, put up a tree with colored lights, tinsel, popcorn strings. I wrote Merry Christmas on the windows, even found a radio station playing Christmas music every other song. The store looked pretty, and our customers enjoyed it.

December 16, a windy Tuesday, didn't get much above freezing. I was fixing to pay bills when Mama hurried downstairs, the strangest look on her face. She pointed toward the ceiling.

"Something's wrong."

I ran upstairs and, Lord, I had no idea a body held that much blood. I called the doctor but didn't need to because Daddy was dead as a door-catch, wouldn't anything put all that blood back. Took forever to clean it up, I had to burn no telling how many towels and sheets.

I didn't see much sense in taking down the Christmas, so the funeral people laid him out beside the tree, and the line of mourners snaked among shelves of snuff and light bread.

Mama hadn't worn her black dress in a coon's moon. She'd put on some weight, so I had to let it out—it fell on her like a maternity dress. When she came downstairs wearing a white and blue afghan around her shoulders I didn't have the heart to say anything. People would just have to understand.

Henry was in the rear of the receiving line, took forever for him to get to us.

"Mama, you remember Henry?"

"He's your beau?" asked Ella Rose.

"Oh, you remember, he sits with us at church."

She wouldn't let Henry's hand go, smiling and nodding at me.

"I'd *hoped* you'd marry in church."

Henry looked from Mama to me and back and grinned despite the mournful time. And I admit I grinned back. Mama was happy, too. Daddy, well, he'd gone beyond, too far to come back, off somewhere with Jesus and Frank.

*　　*　　*

Papa left a pure-T mess. I don't mean when he bled to death, although that was gruesome. I mean the store. I found folders of unpaid bills, cash stashed in odd places, closets full of empty bottles, unbalanced ledgers—and the Bad Book, full of uncollectable debts.

After I fixed all the credit accounts I had some *former* customers, for Papa was a softie about collecting. Luckily there weren't many. I got rid of the liquor, too, so those thirsty grizzles who hung around the Warm Morning heater went elsewhere—especially after I made them pay their tabs. So by summer I was actually making a little money.

Henry moved in with me and Mama after we got married. Saturday, Flag Day, 1931. We didn't have a honeymoon—no spare money or car. He went to the plant Monday morning and I went downstairs to tend shop. Just a normal day.

Here's where Dr. Jackson thinks I need to write about, you know, what we did on our wedding night. Or not so much *what* we did as *how I felt* about it.

Ella Rose's mind had started downhill before I needed to know about the birds and bees and I quit school before girls much started talking about that, so I didn't have any real picture in my mind. Oh, Henry had kissed me plenty of times and that led to feelings, you know, but I didn't know whether he was supposed to grab me like Mr. Lanzio or what.

I also knew the Bible stuff about Ruth uncovering Boaz's feet and men going in unto women but I didn't link that with pleasuring. You might say I was ignorant as a pewter spoon.

So that night in the bathroom I put on my nightgown, brushed my hair and teeth, threw my robe on, came to the bedroom. Henry had the ceiling light on and was in the bed with a kind of worried grin on his face.

"It's too bright in here."

"I want to look at you."

"You can look in the dark."

I turned off the light, took off my robe, got under the covers.

"Okay, God made women in Braille. Come over here."

He was gentle, and that was good because those darn bedsprings were noisy enough to wake the dead. Mama was more than half deaf, but I worried that neighbors might call the law.

Next day he bought a new set of bedding at Crawford Furniture.

To tell the truth, I was glad, because I came to enjoy what he called playing in bed. I'd been scared. But I got to where I couldn't wait for bedtime. And when I knew what you did to make a baby felt good, too, that was fine. I figured children would come soon, and me and Henry would build us a big happy family.

There. I've written about relations, which I hope makes Dr. Jackson happy. I suppose that's a normal part of life—and it was important for a fair time—but it still embarrasses me to write about it. At least only Dr. Jackson and I see this book. I keep it well-hid.

After Papa died, Henry said we should change the name of the store. We agreed to call it The Top of the Hill Grocery. Which meant we sold all the farm inventory in favor of food and candy and such. We became a convenience store before that was all the rage.

And Henry could fix anything. He decided to put a two-bay garage on the west side of the shop. He scrounged lumber, built it himself, dug out and poured pits for oil change and all that, arranged for a buried gasoline tank, and before you knew it we became The Top of the Hill Grocery and Garage, the only repair shop between West Asheville and Crawford. He spent weekends working on cars until we hired a real mechanic. We soon made more off the garage than the store.

Ella Rose seemed content to rock and embroider pillowcases and knit baby booties I sold as a sideline. Hardware salesmen began to call on us, so we started selling pot holders, throw rugs, metal trivets, craft supplies, what have you, along with bread and snacks. We did pretty well despite the Depression. At least we kept the lights on and the government happy.

The mill had started Henry as a sweeper, just to make sure he wouldn't harm anything important, then let him cart bobbins from one station to another. When they tried him as a doffer in the reeling section he asked to transfer to groundskeeping, because he was tired of sick headaches and clearing his throat all the time. By 1935 he was assistant foreman of the yard crew, making ten dollars a week. I expect we matched that money with the shop.

But a big hole could only be filled by a child.

It wasn't from lack of trying. Sometimes twice a day. For five whole years.

Was I barren for some reason important to God's plan? Was I like Hannah, mumbling the Lord's Prayer every day, waiting for God to hear? Was it punishment for some forgotten sin?

Or had Henry done something unspeakable he hadn't let on about?

Or… what kind of God wants us to have no children? God is stern and judgmental but He isn't cruel or mean. Is He?

That dream again. I've had it for years. It might start different but always ends the same. Somebody gives me a baby to keep while they go somewhere—or I've adopted one—or I'm tending the church nursery. Anyhow there's a baby and I lose it.

I can't remember whether I laid it in a dresser drawer or threw it out with table scraps or some animal got it, but it's gone and its parents are coming back or the agency wants it or church is about to let out and I'm screaming and nobody will help me and I can't find it. I never do.

Lord, I pray to get better!

At first Reverend Dixon wasn't much help. He muttered about God working in mysterious ways, said His plan is sometimes, what was the word, inscrutable, which didn't do me one bit of good.

"Why don't you adopt?"

Truth to tell, it hadn't crossed my mind, at least not seriously. Henry and I were still trying.

"Look at it this way. God has a plan. Part of that plan is to fulfill women like you, who crave a child. Somewhere a girl in trouble can't keep hers. So she gives it to you. All things work together for good to them that love God, right?"

Well, I smoked that idea over, took it to Henry. He was jumpy as a cat having kittens with barb wire tails.

"Are you sure you want to adopt a kid?"

"Henry, I want a baby so bad I could scream."

"Martha, I'm not ready."

"Sit down, tell me your fears."

He looked out the window, then turned toward me.

"You don't know what you're getting."

"What in the world do you mean by that?"

"Well, it's like buying a car. A new car, you know all about it. You know where it comes from. But a used car, you don't know where it's been, how it's been kept up. Kind of a pig in a poke. Adopting's like that. You really don't know what you're getting until you get it—then what if something's bad wrong? You sure can't take it back."

I probably looked ready to kill him.

"What? Did I say something wrong?"

"Henry Blaine, sometimes you have sawdust for brains."

"Well, don't I have a point?"

"Your head's pointy, that's all. Listen. We're going to have a baby one way or another, if I have to steal one. So think about it. We aren't getting any younger."

"So you think it's worth the risk?"

"Absolutely. Let me know when you're ready, because this takes two, darn it. If it was up to just me we'd already have one."

Reading this journal, it's the funniest thing. There's times I feel like I'm reading about somebody else, a character in some book. I mean, on one hand I know this happened to me—but on another it seems so far away, so strange, like it's Martha Blaine—a woman in some dreary soap opera. I'd not believe a lot of it had I not lived through at least some of it.

Henry's father died from a stroke in 1938, which left Henry's mother alone. Which, as far as I was concerned, she could have stayed, for I never much liked her. In fact, I figured her husband's body shut down so he'd not have to keep listening to her gripe.

Did anybody ask me if Mama Blaine could move in with me and Mama and Henry? No. But I told Henry I could put up with anything once we had a baby. Might even gentle the old woman some, who knows?

It was all right for a while, because she complained to Ella Rose, who felt sorry for whoever this was who had flitted in the window like some cranky, oversized bird. And that was okay, for Mama Blaine had an audience, Ella Rose had company, they spent days embroidering, knitting, in what Henry called dueling rockers.

Then that blankety-blank war broke out.

Henry wanted to go, and who could blame him? The war was needful and he'd have a better chance of not being cannon fodder if he enlisted. Besides, at work he was foreman of the yard gang, with fifty-nine men to keep busy and happy, and a ton of paperwork. At home he had three women, one dotty, one mean, one just plain aching.

January 11, 1942, me and Henry and Mama Blaine boarded the rickety old P&L bus in front of the store. It was a pretty morning, crisp, frost persisting in the shade at ten o'clock. We rode through West Asheville with tears popping down our coat fronts, and when we passed the Isis Henry said we'd see a movie there next year. Made me cry—and Mama Blaine snuffled like some goat with a head cold. People turned to gawk at the us. I didn't blame them.

At the big bus station we hugged and cried and when he waved to me from the Trailways window I waved back and after the bus pulled out I looked at a mournful Mama Blaine and wondered how long I could stand it.

Maybe the trouble with Willie Lee happened because I couldn't love Henry's mother. If that's true I reckon I'll just have to split Hell wide open. God will have tons to forgive with both of us. And maybe with Henry too, for never asking if she could move in.

Mama Blaine had seven children. Oh, I didn't envy her for that—yes I did, who am I fooling? But you don't detest somebody for that. What I hated was, she didn't think any more of them than to keep them stirred up like October yellow jackets.

Her favorite sport was to write or call one and tell how another had treated her bad. A pack of bald-faced lies, at least what she told about Henry. One time she said he'd not gotten her laxative at the drug store, so she was plugged up like a horse took a founder. Truth was, Henry bought it every week, she ate Ex-Lax like it was Whitman's Sampler. No, she enjoyed telling a lie about somebody to see what would happen.

When Henry left I had to take care of the old battle axe, although two of her children lived nearby. I guess they knew better than to offer to help. I'd have driven her to them with a coachwhip.

In 1943 the government took all the copper to make wire and ammunition and started making pennies out of zinc. No, that's not right. The coins were zinc-coated steel. Some weeks in the store that's all I got, those weird pennies. They didn't feel right, and counting them turned fingers stinky. But the bank took them, so we kept food on the table.

Such as it was. You couldn't hardly find sugar, and they rationed meat, canned food, I don't remember what else. Coffee. Gasoline, except we had sold our car so that was okay. I went the whole war with two pair of nylons. What we gave up to give our soldiers what they needed! I don't think for a minute we'd do that again. People nowadays, with the Vietnam mess, wouldn't stand for it.

But back then we had paper and scrap metal drives, planted victory gardens, and generally got by. People grumbled in the store—I couldn't sell meat, for instance, without ration stamps. You were allowed something like two-and-a-half pounds of beef a week. People mostly put up with the rules, but I complained, too, because paperwork was a headache. The real griping, though, happened upstairs.

When Mama Blaine heard the enemy had taken the Philippines—a big source of sugar—all she heard was "sugar," which made her want pecan pie. Or she whined to take a Sunday drive when she knew good and well even if we had a car we couldn't just joyride, and besides, none of us knew how to drive.

I bit my tongue so often it's a wonder I can still say a word. And if Jesus was right about looking at a woman being the same as sinning with her, I'll burn in hell, for I murdered Mama Blaine in my heart two dozen times a week. I dread the judgment.

I never would have gotten through the war without my friend Boots. She literally kept me from murder, suicide, nervous breakdown, or all three. We were close because our husbands worked at the rayon mill and we all were Presbyterians.

Her name was Ethel and she was a nurse, but aside from hospital people nobody called her anything but Boots. See, when she was little she had this black kitten with white feet, named Boots. When her daddy backed over it and killed it, Ethel cried for weeks, so its name attached to her like a cockleburr.

Her husband, Howard Franklin, worked with Henry's crew at the plant for a while, then decided he'd rather work production. They assigned him to the acid bath, where if you didn't pay attention you'd lose an eyeball or worse. But it seemed to suit him fine.

His buddies called him "Puss," which made me smile every time I saw Puss 'n Boots cat food. I never asked why he got that nickname.

Boots had worked summers in Dr. West's office in Crawford, stocking cabinets with bandages, emptying wastebaskets, holding nervous hands. He encouraged her to apply for nursing school at the Asheville hospital. She graduated in 1936 and immediately got a job there—they hired only their brightest grads—and then she married Howard. Between his job and hers, they did well, Depression or not.

Boots was three years younger than me but already had a good start on a family. Her Tommy was a doll, just turned three when the war broke out, big old brown eyes and a cowlick and freckles, a combination I don't think I've seen before or since.

Every now and then Boots and I talked Mary Anne, the girl that helped in the store, into babysitting so Boots and I could take in a movie or have a burger at the drug store. Anything to get out of the house, away from my old women. Who loved little Tommy. Mary Anne said they'd sit there and watch him play, like they'd never seen a child before.

One time Boots and I went to see *Casablanca*—the spring of '43, I remember because lilacs were in bloom and I figured Ingrid Bergman wore lilac perfume, what was her character, Elsie or something, anyhow, it was on at the Imperial Theater in the middle of downtown, the matinee so we could get back before dark. When we got home all kinds of racket streamed from upstairs, like somebody was torturing cats with a jackhammer.

We jerked the door open to find little Tommy in the middle of the living room beating every upside-down pot and pan with wooden spoons. Giggling hard enough to cry. My mother and Mama Blaine were singing different songs together (neither one could carry a tune in a bucket) and Mary Anne stood in the corner like some crazy choir director, like this was the most normal thing in the world.

Two broken spoons became kindling, and one thin pot that never sat level on the stove again went in the next scrap drive. But it was worth it to see the joy on all those faces.

Mama Blaine and Ella Rose never sang again that I remember but they got along okay, unless Mama forgot and sat in Mama Blaine's chair. And little Tommy adored those old women, because they let him do anything he wanted. Boots never seemed to worry that they'd spoil him to death, either. He turned out okay, too. Made a lawyer.

*   *   *

Dr. Jackson says I'm doing well—I might get to go home soon. He wants me to keep up the journal, says one day it'll help me break through my condition. So here I'll tell about where we lived over the store.

You came up the stairs into a long room—the left half the kitchen, the right half our sitting room. On the back wall four doors led into three bedrooms and a bath. Mine and Henry's room was off the kitchen. Ella Rose had the next one, then the bathroom. Mama Blaine's back room I called the lion's den.

The kitchen's wood range sat next to a sink on the outside wall. We ate at a veneered-top round table with four mismatched chairs. A radio over the icebox spit out war news, music, soap operas. Two pictures flanked a funeral home calendar—sweet young Jesus in the temple, FDR in profile, chin stuck up like he dared Hitler or Tojo to hit it.

In the sitting room three upholstered armchairs circled a low table holding my Bible, Mama Blaine's snuff, everyone's sewing and knitting possibles.

Sitting there we looked at a cold fireplace, which, until a scrap drive, had been covered with sheet steel. I'd stuffed a ratty quilt up in it to keep the drafts out. We watched what I thought of as ghost fires, laid on vanished fire dogs, all this metal now part of Henry's tank. A coal heater's stovepipe elbowed into a flue above the mantel.

On the mantel sat a picture of Henry in uniform, grinning like he was proud as a possum to serve his country and no bullets in creation sported his name. Before Mama Blaine moved in I had three or four pictures of Ella Rose and Tom. Mama Blaine replaced some of them with a big straight-on picture of her with some speech about fairness and balance. I doubt she ever noticed I dusted everybody but her.

Before the war I didn't dream often, at least not to remember, except for the one about the lost baby. I guess before Henry went to war I felt pretty safe, but that ended when he left me with Ella Rose and Mama Blaine.

One dream I kept having—Henry was sick or in trouble and I had to get to him pronto. So I headed out in the car. I hadn't driven three feet in my life but I reckon my brain didn't know that. I'd run it up on a sidewalk or into a building or through a crowd, but I'd never get to Henry.

But always, somewhere in the crowd, Mama Blaine stared at me like I was plain dirt. I never run over her, just other people. Or maybe the car would mire in quicksand. But I never got to Henry and never killed

Mama Blaine. I'd generally wake up when I heard sirens and I'd not only not know where I was for a while, I'd not know *who* I was either.

At first Henry wrote every week, sometimes twice. Chatty letters about tank mechanic school or a movie or how hot Mississippi was. Sometimes his first and last sentence was that he didn't have much to say, but I didn't care, I figured that right then he had been all right.

In 1943 I went six weeks with no letter. I *knew* something bad had happened. He had said he was shipping overseas but couldn't say where. Later I found out he was bound for North Africa on a Liberty ship, the *S.S. Florence Crittenton*. But until I heard, I was afraid Ella Rose and Mama Blaine would have me and him both to bury, a thought about as welcome as goats in a strawberry patch.

Ella Rose forgot how to cook, or she'd have burned us out for sure. Mama Blaine? As long as there were able bodies she'd starve before she'd cook. So I made breakfast, then went downstairs until mail time. Ella Rose washed and dried and put up dishes while I was gone, then swept the place while Mama Blaine embroidered or read the paper.

I'd come back to fix lunch, which usually meant a can or two of soup if we had them or sandwiches if there was bread, or leftovers. Then back to the store until six. Supper sometimes was breakfast again, for it was easy.

One evening Ella Rose wasn't interested in eating, so Mama Blaine snatched her plate.

"Here, I'll take care of this. Martha, I never did see what Henry saw in you. A woman ought to have a little meat on her bones is my way of thinking."

She had plenty on hers, all right. But in spite of bulk she was always cold. After supper she shoved snuff in her cheek followed by a "tooth-brush"—a frayed birch twig—and puffed up like a penguin.

"You'd think my Henry would have married somebody who cared about his mother. Here I am freezing to death and you won't do nothing about it."

"Mama Blaine, we barely have coal to last the month. Just be glad we didn't give the heater to the scrap drive."

Ella Rose was knitting a surprise for Mama Blaine—a green-and-white afghan big enough to cover her *and* her chair. Finished, it made the old bag look like a festive turtle, chin and toothbrush peeking from its shell. But she complained less about the cold.

After supper we might listen to the radio. We liked *Fibber and Molly* and *Sherlock Holmes*, but news irritated Mama Blaine and I didn't care for wartime drama, for it reminded me my man was liable to be run over by a tank, shot, captured. Other nights I read the newspaper or the Bible aloud before lights out. Sometimes we all said the Lord's Prayer. It seemed to help.

Next day, again. Over and over. I thought that war would go on forever and some nights I could have killed Henry for leaving.

February 21, 1944. Mama Blaine's birthday. A Monday. I got up early, put on my robe, said my prayers. Then I wrapped the gloves I had gotten Mama Blaine for her birthday.

My family says giving gloves is bad luck for whoever gets them. To my mind there's no such thing as luck, but it didn't hurt to try. Sinful, but I didn't care.

I hadn't heard Ella Rose stir—she was usually first one up. So I laid the present on Mama Blaine's chair and tapped on Mama's door.

"Mama, you okay?"

I found her in bed on her back, mouth and eyes gaped like the last thing she seen had turned her to stone.

I shut the door and sat with her a while. I cried, sure, she was my mother, and maybe bad luck had slapped back at me, but there was relief too, because her journey was over, she was with Tom and Frank and Jesus, wasn't confused anymore.

"Ain't nobody going to make my breakfast?"

I patted Ella Rose's cold hand. "At least you don't have to hear that horse manure anymore."

In the sitting room I told Mama Blaine my mother was dead.

She slumped in her chair, fingered the package, began to sob. I put my hand on her shoulder.

"There, there."

A startling moment of sympathy.

"Why'd she have to go and ruin my birthday?"

I wondered if the funeral home might give a two-for-one special.

*   *   *

Before I called them I rang Boots, who was working off graveyard and had just gotten home. Wasn't ten minutes until she came up the stairs.

"Anybody want breakfast?"

Mama Blaine stopped crying and blew her nose on a handkerchief.

"Lord, yes. I was wondering when an old woman might get fed."

Boots walked over to me and winked.

"Honey, you take it easy. I'll fix breakfast. Have you called the funeral people?"

"No, but I will."

"No, I will. Also the church. You rest. I'm in charge."

Bless her, she knew how to make things right. Plus biscuits.

A fair number showed up for her service. The army had taken Reverend Dixon as a chaplain, so his fill-in, some retired fossil from Montreat, old-fashioned enough to wear a four-in-hand tie, led the service.

Not knowing Ella Rose in her right mind, he read a ton of scripture, droned through the thirty-ninth Psalm (*Thou has made my days as an handbreadth*), the ninetieth (*we spend our years as a tale that is told*), and an odd piece from Ecclesiastes (*man goeth to his long home, and the mourners go about the streets*). Several shifted in the pew, coughed, and dabbed eyes with handkerchiefs. Mama Blaine carried on like she was blood kin cheated out of a huge inheritance by some conniving in-law.

At the graveside—it was warm for February, nearly sixty—a mockingbird sang its head off from an unbudded dogwood. While I sat listening to that bird a gray kitten walked from behind the dirt mound and went right up to the edge. Looked in that grave like he was seeing if Ella Rose might find rest there.

Was this the great-great-grandchild of the cat in church when I was a girl? They breed fast, you know.

It hightailed away like it was happy. I couldn't help but smile.

The preacher said Ella Rose's life was now eternal.

That was a pretty thought, but I was afraid that, without mother and husband, mine would *seem* everlasting with no heavenly benefit. And then I'd die and face the judgment.

He closed with Revelations: *Blessed are the dead which die in the Lord from henceforth: Yea, saith the Spirit, that they may rest from their labours; and their works do follow them.*

93

Proper send-off words for Ella Rose. I wondered what they would mean when said over me. What followed me?

So far, barrenness, a world war, a mother-in-law from Satan's britches. And guilt. I never should have given Mama Blaine those blooming gloves.

That night in my room I couldn't think of any scripture that promised life would be fair so I closed my eyes and said, over and over, deliver me from evil. After a while I felt something like a hand on my shoulder and in my heart a gentle voice said *this too shall pass*. I'm pretty sure that was Jesus' hand and if those words weren't scripture they ought to be.

Have had a cold, haven't felt like writing. It's funny. I hadn't ever written much more than a friendly letter. When Dr. Jackson gave me this book I thought, shoot, I'll never think up enough stuff to fill five pages. But here I am halfway done with it and, I don't know, it's like I *need* to write. I feel guilty if I don't open it every day.

August 15, 1945, I had the radio on all day. They reported the Japs (oh, I know you aren't supposed to say that now, people stand in line to buy Hondas and such, but I can't forget those awful people built airplanes to kill our boys with) had surrendered in the night but nothing official yet. They kept saying they'd announce something soon, and, I don't know, they said wait for the President to tell it—then somebody laid down on their car horn.

I went out front. As the screen door banged, another car came, horn blaring, driver's head out the window yelling "It's over!" Our mechanic came out cleaning his hands with a rag, grinning like a mule eating briers. He yanked our American flag from its holder and paraded around the top of the hill all afternoon.

I gave away apple juice and crackers—I didn't have anything stronger, but here came old Mister Whisnant, grinning like a totem pole, with two bottles of whiskey. It was a wonderful afternoon. And a little after dark, when they announced an unconditional surrender, there wasn't a happier person than me.

Henry had gone from Tunisia to that horrible fighting in Anzio, then transferred to General Patton's army in France. Now I hoped he'd be home for Christmas.

He wasn't. But nearly.

*   *   *

January 15, 1946, a Tuesday, I don't think there was a nervouser person in North Carolina. It was cold but I was sweating like a harlot at a revival. I hadn't seen Henry in four years and three days and I didn't know if he'd be different or we would easily pick up where we left off. It both scared and thrilled me to know he'd soon be in my arms.

I took the 9:45 P&L to town and paced until I seen a red and silver Trailway with Knoxville on its sign. It stopped—so did my heart, hearing air brakes and seeing people getting off who weren't Henry and still weren't Henry and then this man who might be Henry but... I kept biting the back of my hand and almost tore my handkerchief when a man who *was* Henry climbed down, grinning like a possum in a dishpan of kitchen scraps.

He'd lost weight and hair but his eyes were still cornflower blue and when he grabbed me I thought—hoped—he'd never let me go. We kissed on the mouth right there in front of God and everybody. The feel of him in my arms about set me on fire. The war had flinted him up, and I could tell he wanted me as bad as I wanted him.

We caught the 2:30 back to Sand Hill, me and Henry and his duffle bag squinched up in that seat like we'd never come apart. I was the happiest person in the world.

That afternoon and evening proceeded to last forever. I had to fix Henry a bait of cornbread and beans, and catch him up on Mama's death and all, and of course Mama Blaine asked about everything in the cotton-picking world. Could you get regular hen eggs in France? Did they have Irish potatoes in Italy? Did he find any French harps? I thought I'd have to strangle her to make her shut up.

She finally waddled off to the lion's den, and I just sat in his lap and closed my eyes, glad for the familiar smell of him (except he'd took up cigarettes, courtesy of Uncle Sam sticking Lucky Strikes in his ration kits) and the touch of his hands on my arm. When we heard her sawing wood we tiptoed to the bathroom and brushed our teeth. She still snored when we cut off the light and closed our bedroom door.

Even making up for four years' absence didn't make me pregnant.

Maybe I didn't catch, but I did have one quick joy. Henry seen that living *close* to his mother and *with* her were as different as cats and armadillos.

He said he deserved killing for saddling me with her, then told his family he'd throttle the old woman if one of them didn't take her in. Nobody volunteered, but they got together and rented a little house for her. When they moved her out I came upstairs for lunch and had the place to myself—Henry was back at the mill—and that was almost divine.

Almost. I ached for the noise of a child.

One evening Henry lit a cigarette and built a fire in our new heater against a late cold snap. He sidled up to the expanding metal and smoked. I looked at him over the evening paper, listened to coal settle on the grates, smelled the heating metal.

"It wouldn't be so quiet in here with the patter of little feet."

He slid the front vent open and dropped in his cigarette butt.

"You mean… you're…?"

"No, Henry, I'm not. But we could adopt."

"Are you sure?"

"Henry, I want a baby so bad I could turn inside-out."

He pretended to be interested in the sports section, then looked at me.

"Martha, war changes a man. I seen things I don't care to remember. What if I couldn't stand to hear it squalling? What if that shoved me over some edge I don't even know is there?"

"Honey, I know it was hard. It was here, too. But think of the love a little baby would put in our lives. It would smooth over all that pain and suffering you seen."

"Maybe. I guess I'm scared."

"And I'm desperate. I'll be thirty-three come May. I can't wait forever. Think hard about it, Henry."

He lit another cigarette and smiled.

"I will, baby. I promise."

To tell the truth I was scared, too, because he had nightmares where he'd be sweaty and wild-eyed and still asleep. One night he shook me like a rag doll—I screamed to wake him up.

The scariest thing, though, was one night, I heard racket downstairs.

"Henry, wake up."

When I poked his arm he grabbed me by the throat with one hand and hit me in the face with the other.

"I'll kill you, you blankety-blank Kraut so-and-so."

I hollered till he woke enough to know what he was doing. Then he started crying, got out of bed, knelt, prayed for me to forgive him. By the time we'd hugged each other and calmed down, downstairs was quiet. I didn't sleep another wink. Had a shiner the next day. Said I ran into a door. What was I going to say? I know I never woke him all of a sudden again.

Here's one thing I worried about in the middle of the night: what if a slot in time opened for a moment, then closed and you hadn't even known it was there? Like somewhere the baby God wanted me to have was out there but I didn't know where, and I missed my one chance. All because of that stupid war. That dirty stinking stupid filthy war.

My ache worsened in 1947 because all these women got pregnant after their men came home. You couldn't go ten feet downtown without seeing a bulging belly or a baby carriage. In church, too, sitting there all glowing, pleased as prunes, me staring like a starved stray dog. When Reverend Dixon sprinkled babies, more water streamed down my face than on their little heads. I almost quit going.

Boots, too, got a belly pretty quick after Puss got home. Her daughter, Amelia Lee, was a joy to watch—depending on your viewpoint. She just made me think more about adopting.

Henry got better, thank Jesus. He looked at how many cars were being sold since the automakers quit building tanks and such, and offered to quit the plant and become The Top of the Hill's chief mechanic.

"Are you sure?"

"Not a car goes off a lot that won't need fixing. We're the only repair shop between Crawford and Asheville. Baby, I'm sure."

And he was right, and happier than I'd ever seen him.

One day he actually mentioned adoption on his own. It must have been the spring of 1948. We'd gotten a dark green 1936 Chevrolet coupe, grey mohair seat covers, ran like a top. (This was before Henry bought our Plymouth, the 1949 that he loved so much.) One Saturday he said let's have a picnic. I could have fallen over, because Saturdays he always rooted around in the engine of some car, his stubby fingerprints lined in grease.

It didn't take ten minutes to pack a basket. I left Mary Anne in charge and we headed west. When the Crawford road veered south we chugged over the twin bridges and up South Hominy toward Mount Pisgah.

I thought we'd go to Camp Laurel at Pisgah's foot, to wade the creek or build a fire and roast marchmellers and hot dogs or just spread out beneath sheltering hemlocks and nap in the shade. It smelled comfortable, like your grandmother's kitchen. But we sped by it like it was standing still, which I guess it was.

Henry stuck that Chevy in second gear and headed up the mountain, throwing gravel through switchback turns like Barney Oldfield. I yelled slow down but he grinned and goosed it. Never mind that my heart raced and my hands white-knuckled the dashboard.

We stopped at a picnic area down from the old Buck Spring Lodge, which in those days was still used, by the Vanderbilt descendants, I suppose. Nobody was around that day, not even a caretaker. This was before the television tower, before the Parkway come through, so not much traffic. I forget how high you are—nearly six thousand feet, which meant a good ten degrees cooler than at the store. Smelled like cold, dark green moss. But you could see forever, and look down on hawks and crows going about their business, in light somehow brighter than Sand Hill's.

Wasn't long until we seen a biplane off to the east, about level with us, headed toward Asheville, maybe to the Emma airstrip. We heard its motor drone a few seconds later.

"I'd like to do that sometime."

I smiled at Henry.

"What, fly a plane?"

"Ride in one. Free as a bird. One of these days we'll get somebody to take us both up."

"Henry Blaine, I'll keep my feet on solid ground, thank you."

We washed down baloney sandwiches and sweet pickles with orange Nehis. We joked and laughed like a couple of goofy teenagers, not old married fogies.

After a while he got quiet, put his hands together like some prayerful monk. I shut up and waited. He stared at the mountains for a good while, then at me.

"Look yonder, Martha. See all that? Wouldn't want to live anywhere else."

I squeezed his hand, for it wasn't like him to get broody.

"Makes a fellow think. About where he's at, how that's worth fighting for. And how where he's at is part of him, you know, what he's made of, and that's worth passing on to a kid."

"Henry, you mean...?"

"It's been on my mind. Up here I see there's something a lot bigger'n me I need to think about. Like this big old world, and your feelings, and, I don't know, I'm a lot better. Maybe we can talk about that adoption stuff."

"Oh, Henry, you make me so happy!"

I leaned over and kissed him and he kissed me back and would have pulled up my dress if I hadn't squealed.

"Henry Blaine, not in public!"

"Shoot, girl, you can't blame a man for trying."

Mama Blaine grudgingly had started cooking, although she said she didn't. Mostly fried pork, boiled potatoes and steamed cabbage, and every Monday she baked a cake that was gone by Friday. Sundays, her Asheville children took turns hosting her for dinner. Where you'd have thought she hadn't eaten a bite all week.

Honestly, a chicken dinner meant I had a leg and gizzard, Henry grabbed a back and heart, she inhaled the rest. One time Henry reached for the pulley bone and she about speared his hand. If we got white meat it wasn't on a Mama Blaine Sunday. Which I came to call Dark Sunday. Even Henry laughed about that.

"Mama, how'd you like to be a grandmother?"

This was one Sunday in the fall of '48.

She shoveled out another helping of mashed potatoes.

"I thought I was."

"I mean from me and Martha."

"Son, I give up on that long ago."

"Mama, we might adopt a kid."

She shot him a look to do a snake proud.

"What do you want to raise somebody else's mongrel for?"

"Mama, it ain't a dog."

"Only thing different, one's got a tail."

"That ain't fair."

"Why not? It'd be the fruit of somebody's sin, out there doing what they ain't supposed to be, probably drunk to boot, no telling how many problems you'd bring into your home."

I really did bite the blood out of my tongue at that.

"Henry, it ain't your fault you can't have children. I told you when you first brought her around she wasn't no prize. And I ain't seed no reason to take that opinion back."

I broke a plate on the table and spent the rest of that day locked in bedroom or bathroom.

I came out way after dark. Henry had taken the old biddy home, cleaned up the kitchen best he knew how, sat smoking on the back stoop. I looked the kitchen over—I'd have to rearrange every fork and pot and dish—and came out and sat beside him. North of us the train rumbled toward Asheville. When he put his arm around me I laid my head on his shoulder and tried to look at the stars.

"Martha, I'm sorry."

"It isn't your fault."

"But she's *my* mother, dang it. If I could keep her from saying hurting things I would. But she's done it all her life."

"I know. Don't worry about it."

"She ain't coming back here for dinner."

"Henry, you can't do that to her. She's your mother."

"I ain't putting up with her being hateful to you no more."

"Henry, I'll manage. Now don't talk about it again."

The crickets were getting quieter, maybe looking toward first frost.

"What about… you know?"

"Adoption?"

"Yeah."

"Now even *I* got to think about it some more, Henry Blaine. I'll let you know."

We met a caseworker in the spring of '49. Her waiting room's wall clock was shaped like a black cat, clockface in its belly, eyes and tail moving back and forth to mark seconds. In one dirty window sat an unblooming begonia and beside the other hung a poster urging you to have your kids vaccinated.

I wore a nice frock and was well-armed, a handkerchief for each hand, and my black patent pocketbook held several more. Henry looked a little starched. He'd bought a blue necktie with a bird dog on it, the knot was loose in his collar until I tightened it.

The caseworker ushered us into her office. Tall, trim, late twenties, silver dogwood bloom pinned to her lapel. Brown hair in a permanent that flipped up on her neck in back.

Quite a contrast to her office. Every flat surface except for three chair seats was piled with papers. Two file cabinets overflowed to boxes on the floor and a work table groaned with paper that spilled to a typing table that fed another stack on the floor.

"I'm Elaine Maxwell."

"Pleased to meet you."

"Please have a seat."

"I need the closter chair cause I don't hear that good."

"Please take it, Mr. Blaine. May I offer you all some coffee?"

"We're fine."

She sat behind her desk, opened a deep drawer, fished out a manila folder, cleaned off a desk corner, arranged a bunch of papers.

"Please fill these out. We need to know medical history, finances, employment. I can't stress enough how important these are. Be honest— if you lie about anything—not, Mrs. Blaine, that *you* would, but some do—you will be denied. And possibly charged with a crime."

"Holy moly, weren't this much paperwork in the army."

"Mr. Blaine, I'm afraid it's necessary. Please write legibly—I type this up myself."

"I'll say one thing. When I die, if somebody gives me a form to fill out I'll sure know where I'll spend eternity."

Miss Maxwell smiled and began to slide the papers into an envelope.

"Do either of you have questions?"

"When will we..."

"Be accepted or denied? Within a month. If accepted, when you get a child depends on who is in the chute. Sometimes we're awash with potential adoptees, sometimes not. Right now, we have plenty."

I sat straight in my chair.

"Do we have any say in how old the child is? Or whether it's a boy or girl?"

"Normally, we place infants with younger couples. Do you particularly want an infant?"

"That is my prayer. I want a baby to be *all* mine. Ours. A teeny baby will grow up to remember *one* set of parents. Us. That's important."

"I'll see if it can be arranged. But which sex is almost entirely a matter of who is available, you understand."

"It'll be white, won't it?"

"Henry, shame on you."

"No, I'm serious. There'd be problems..."

"Henry Blaine, I'd love it regardless."

I figured I wasn't going to cry so put one handkerchief in my bag.

"Our policy pairs parents and children racially. And we certainly wouldn't place a child where one parent objected."

"Pay no attention to him, Miss Maxwell. I have a bigger question. Will he—or she—ever know about its... other parents?"

"No. In this state such records are sealed. The child's legal birth certificate—the only one he or she will ever see—will name you. Should you be accepted, pardon me, I have to keep saying that."

"Will we ever know about them?"

"Not really. Certainly nothing to allow them to be identified."

"Fair enough."

"Is there a fee?"

"No, Mr. Blaine, this is your taxes at work."

"It'd be the first time. You really know where ever thing in here is at?"

"I do, Mr. Blaine. I guess if I died they'd have to bring me back to make sense of it all."

That night we started to make the center bedroom into a nursery. I had no idea why Henry first thought it should be the farthest room.

"It has to be next to ours. In the first place, you can't hear it thunder. And, no offense, that was the lion's den, and I will not cloud my child's future with your mother's vapors."

We swept, wet-mopped, dusted. I thought the dresser and mirror would make a fine changing table and had found a diaper bucket. When we knew pink or blue we could paint and pick out nice pictures. What kind of stencil might go on a toy box. Important decisions.

"Look at this, Henry. A promotion from one of our suppliers." I unwrapped a package I'd been saving—in it lay a soft brown teddy bear.

"You're going to love living here with our new baby."

I said that in a squeaky baby-talk voice.

"Now Martha, we might get a ten-year-old."

"Miss Maxwell wouldn't do that. I just *know* she wouldn't."

"Well, I'm not buying a crib yet. Those things are expensive."

"Nothing's too good for your kid. Oh, listen. Hear the radio?"

"Can't say I do."

"Come out here. They're playing our song. Perry Como."

Some enchanted evening, we would meet a stranger, a new baby of our very own. Henry and I danced, tender, quiet, expectant. I dared hope sooner rather than later.

*   *   *

August 22, a Monday, I received a carton from Zenith, two clock radios and three regular ones, all encased in hard brown plastic. On that humid morning my bangs stuck to my forehead. I tagged the radios with retail price and cost codes and as I arranged them near the front counter I heard a car door shut and a woman's high heels focus on the front door.

Miss Maxwell, huge smile, extended hand. Her dress was between the yellow of March flowers and crookneck squash.

"Mrs. Blaine, I wanted to tell you in person. I bring glad tidings."

I balled my fist, touched my lips, couldn't say a word. I reckon she worried I might explode. About that time Henry, wiping his hands with a red rag and looking hopeful, came into the store.

"Oh goody, I can tell both of you that we have a baby for you."

"Is it… when… can I… we…"

Miss Maxwell hugged me.

"One thing at a time, Mrs. Blaine. He's a boy, born two weeks ago Saturday. He's been in the hospital because he was jaundiced. He's fine now. You and Mr. Blaine can pick him up anytime after two. Just tell me when so I can be there with the final paperwork."

"Oh, thank God."

"We can't wait, Miss Maxwell. How can we ever thank you?"

"Just love him. Raise him right. That's thanks a plenty. Two o'clock?"

"If we can stand to wait that long. Yes, two."

As I waved goodbye I realized Ella Rose had trimmed my handkerchief in lace, and wondered if she was looking down on me. I sure hoped so.

"Dang it, Martha, I've got to buy a crib. He needs better than a dresser drawer."

He threw down that red rag and ran off down the hill at full speed, thumb up in the air. I yelled at him to take our car, but a man in a pickup truck pulled over and said get in.

"How far you going?"

"Crawford Furniture. Got to buy me a baby crib."

The man looked nervous.

"Kinda in a hurry, ain't you, Mister?"

"You just don't know, brother. Step on it."

The store's center aisle was covered in black-and-white checkered linoleum, on either side of which sat rocking chairs and coffee tables, dinette suites and sofas. Henry said he hit the door running, waving a twenty.

"J.T., it's a boy!"

He took the stairs two at a time, stair treads creaking with what I bet Mister Chappell thought was fright.

Wearing sleeve garters and a green eyeshade, he grinned and followed Henry, who had found the white crib bathed in sunshine. It let down on both sides and came with an innerspring mattress and bolster cushions. Bright-colored butterflies bounced from the mobile. The crib sported two ribbons, one pink, one blue, J.T. laid the pink one into the adjacent baby bed and made sure the sides slid properly.

"There's cheaper, you know."

"Nothing but the best for my boy. I need it at the house—it's unlocked."

"Consider it done. Congratulations."

J.T. tucked the twenty in his shirt pocket and shook Henry's hand.

"Now I got to get back. We get him at two."

"What's his name?"

He looked at J.T. in some wonder.

"Lord, we got to see him first."

And with that, Henry jumped back downstairs like an insane jackrabbit. It's a wonder he didn't get run over thumbing back to work. I never seen him so happy. And so was I. Lord, the happiest people in the whole wide world. That slot in time had opened, and I felt saved at last.

This winds up the hospital blank book. I'd thought never to come close to filling it, but Dr. Jackson was right—writing about things helps. After I came home I kept at it. Now, if I go two or three days without writing, I get crabby. Better than pills to keep me on the level.

I was in pretty rough shape when I started. I'm a lot better now, home after those treatments. And understanding how I became so wrapped up in my son. I mean, it's on practically every page, how from birth I let other people define me—parents, brothers, husband, child—and when they all left except my adopted son, I clung to that boy like I was poison oak and he a tree, which I couldn't see was horrible for both of us. Then he about broke my heart.

III.

Missing Pat

Priscilla Lance Allen

Priscilla Ruth Lance, teenaged mother, child relinquisher. A woman abandoned by the baby's father and orphaned by, or at least estranged from, her mother. Engaged, however precariously, to a man not the father. Lying adrift in a Catholic hospital. How in the world to lead even a halfway normal life after I'm sprung from here?

A maternity ward stuffed with orchids, chocolates, and Hallmark cards was not meant for me. They stuck me at the tail end of a hall, hidden by a roll-around screen, so I wouldn't louse up all the Virgin Marys feeding no-crying-he-makes kids. I didn't care for company anyway. I just wanted to go back to Aunt Pearl's to hope against hope for my sailor's return.

My "room"? Metal bed, bedside table. No visitor's chair, closet, or window. Plaster walls painted a kind of yellowed ivory. Over the footboard a small-scale Jesus suffered big-time on his cross. A metal pitcher, a box of tissues. A wall mirror to the right of the bed.

Every so often a prolonged swish of cloth announced a starched sister coming down the hall like an overstuffed toy penguin. None paid me any attention, even when bringing fresh water. Actually, that was fine. I was afraid they might try to make me feel even guiltier.

I wasn't supposed to get up, but *had* to look at myself. I sat up and glanced at Jesus like he might say *Aren't you sorry now? Bet you won't do that again.*

I was a bloated husk with sore breasts. For that matter, everything hurt, from conscience to tailbone. I pulled my robe tight, shuffled toward Jesus, and covered him with a tissue. In the mirror I saw some stringy-haired slut, bruises under bloodshot eyes, in dire need of lipstick. I was trying to rub some color into my cheeks when I heard leather heels heading my way.

Wanda, big as life, arms crossed, handbag dangling across her middle, hat and belt to match, every hair in place, scowling like she'd spotted a rat in her pantry.

Wasn't she my *estranged* mother, someone never to play bereaved grandmother to a relinquished child?

I wanted her to go away, to stay out of my life. I wanted her to say something simple, like "I love you." I wanted her to hug me.

What came out was "Mama."

"Priscilla Ruth, get back in bed and don't start crying. You'll come home with me soon."

"But…"

"Don't talk back. That's what started this... mess in the first place."

She rattled through a paper grocery bag for my brush and comb. Compact. Lipstick.

"Here. You look a fright. Now, listen. Everybody thinks you've been tending to Pearl, so we'll have to have our stories straight at home."

Home. I didn't know whether to laugh or cry. Of course, I cried.

She uncovered Jesus and fidgeted with the tissue until it disintegrated. "You'll have emotions until the baby stuff flushes out of your system. Then you'll be fine. When you've had a good cry, fix your face. You'll feel better."

"Why are you here?"

Our drama teacher would have made her tone down the sigh and eye roll. "I've been thinking a lot here lately. It's my Christian duty to see this story through. I'll not stand by and let you ruin your life any further. Now, be sure and eat your lunch when they bring it."

She leaned down and kissed my forehead.

"Priscilla Ruth, despite everything... Well,... Child, I'll see you to-morrow." I swear, she almost teared up before she took off up the hall, heels clicking like rifle fire. Maybe one day she might forgive me?

I freshened up, then covered Jesus again. I couldn't stand to see him all sorrowful like I'd nailed him there instead of Roman soldiers. I sat up in bed the rest of the morning, staring at foot-lumps under stiff covers. Did they even starch blankets? I tried to doze but hospitals are noisy—phones ringing, nurses yapping, carts wheeling here and there—and underneath all a murmur, a kind of electric buzz, a burden both heard and felt, either from lights or the unceasing war between life and death.

The lunch cart sounded like it rode on roller skates with flat-spotted wheels, pushed by an older lady about as big around as a broom. She wore civilian clothes, thick black-rimmed glasses, gray hair in a bun, and she carried on a constant wheezing conversation with herself—or someone.

On the table she laid a metal tray with some kind of chicken dish—or was it fish? turkey?—anyway something dried-out white. On the side a wilted salad, hard roll, dessert. She spotted my covered-up Jesus, crossed herself, and backed up the hall, muttering. I wondered if they kept her in the basement.

I managed to choke down a cube of green Jell-O. I brushed my hair again but when I sat on the side of the bed I felt trembly and weak. As Walker would say, I couldn't have pulled a greasy string out of a cat's behind.

When I realized how much I missed him—and what he'd do if he knew where I was and why—I wept again. And after I thought how much I wished Pat was there—Lord, I was dizzy-headed over the men I had betrayed—I cried a bucketful.

Later, a rumpled Aunt Pearl showed up, fished a handkerchief from her purse, and tossed it in my lap. "Hey, Miss Priss. You look like warmed-over dog poo."

I tried to smile. "I don't feel so good."

"No, I expect not. Dear sister says you won't be returning to the manor."

I shook my head and focused on black-and-white hexagonal tiles streaked with wheel marks random as shooting stars. "I don't want to go home."

"Don't blame you. But, hey, you've hatched a baby, you can do anything, including putting up with Wanda until you fly the coop. You always have a home with me."

She uncovered Jesus and straightened the cross. "Tell you a secret, Priss. Under wraps, he'll not help you. I may not go to church but I know the power of the story. Good Friday's pitch black—but Easter is bright green."

She rummaged in her handbag. "Care for a Life Saver?"

"No, thanks."

"Fingernail file?"

I shook my head.

"Church key?"

I almost laughed—her bag was big enough to feed this routine all afternoon.

"Well, here. It came yesterday."

Through tears I made out Pat's spidery hand across a penny postcard.

"What does he say?"

"Honey, I don't read other people's mail."

I took it with fear and trembling, like it might bite or, maybe worse, vanish.

Hope you're okay. See you soon. I love you. Pat

Started me crying again.

"Lord, child, has he abandoned you?"

I handed her the card.

"Priss, you need to get down on your knees and thank God for this boy. He's dumb or wonderful or maybe both. When will he be home?"

"The middle of October."

108

"You'll be off the roller coaster by then. I wish you two a long and happy life."

"I don't know why he'd want me."

"There's God's plenty of tramps out there. You're not one of them. Here's a big hug. Need anything, you know where I am."

Soft and warm, she smelled faintly of honeysuckle. "I love you, Aunt Pearl."

When I looked to Jesus for some kind of word I saw, hanging from the right arm of the cross, something bright green, either left by a miracle or my aunt. I almost didn't touch it for fear of being burned. Maybe a grape or flower in Aunt Pearl's favorite green, the color, she insisted, of hope, not envy. I dried my eyes, picked it up, and laid it on the table. A ceramic fish.

Jesus was a fisherman. Or at least called disciples who were. I took it as a hopeful sign. I longed for sunshine to make the ornament gleam. I spent the rest of the day holding it while prowling in Gideon's Bible.

Those barren women—Sarah, Rebecca, Rachel, Hannah—all eventually bore fruit. Hannah gave hers to God. Where was mine? Who would he or she become? God, what had I done? I didn't even know if my baby was a boy or a girl.

Reading Luke it hit me that Mary might have told Gabriel to get lost. Because she didn't, we have Jesus. When I had a choice, to raise my baby or give it away, I took the coward's way out. And they talk about comfort in scripture.

Cried myself to sleep. Woke every thirty minutes to read Pat's note and make sure my fish hadn't disappeared. By morning (heralded by shift change, not sunshine) I decided Aunt Pearl was right. I could stand anything until I saw Pat. And maybe—please, Jesus—I could hope to become Mrs. Pat Allen. That is to say, somebody. Somebody with half a chance of happiness.

Still the question waited to pounce: *Will I ever stop thinking about all this?*

So a scared, pregnant girl became a mother, immediately lost her child. A girl can become childless two ways. One, her kid dies. They are apart until eternity, when they will meet again. Two, she gives it away. This may also be until eternity—except he or she might show back up. You don't know. The relinquished child might be dead—or living in Timbuktu—or three doors down the street. You just don't know.

Certainly nothing anyone, including me, wanted to talk about.

The afternoon I came home Wanda sat me and Grace down in the front room, in which nothing had changed since I met Miss Maxwell that morning that seemed years ago.

Grace and I faced each other in the wing chairs. I hadn't really looked at my sister in a while. She was a cute fifteen with no more figure than a boy. Maybe her salvation. I favored Wanda's side of the family—light-skinned, blonde, well-rounded. Grace favored Walker's mother, skinny, high cheekbones, fine brown hair. On a humid day Grace's bangs looked like question marks hung upside down on a clothesline.

Worrying a handkerchief, Wanda sat forward on the sofa to reach both of us. "Now, girls, nobody must say a thing about what really happened. Nothing, you hear?"

Grace and I nodded at each other.

"Promise."

"We promise." Said in as much unison as Grace and I ever managed.

"Put your left hands on the Bible, raise your right hands, and swear."

"Mama, this isn't a courtroom," I said.

"I don't care. Your father must never get wind of what happened. I *have* to have your solemn oath."

"But Mama," said Grace. "If we swear on the Bible that Priscilla went to help Aunt Pearl with her broken leg, isn't that a sin? I don't want to go to hell."

"You're not swearing that story is true, honey. You're swearing never to tell the real story. It's very different."

"I'm really confused."

"Look, we're in this together. Here's my hand on the Book with you. Swear to say nothing about hospitals, babies, adoption. Just like it never happened."

We swore. Sorry, Jesus, we didn't have much choice.

I didn't cut Grace any slack either. That evening I washed dishes while she rinsed and dried.

"What was it like?" she whispered, glancing after Wanda, who was on the porch reading the paper.

"What was what like?"

"You know. Did it hurt?"

"Little sister, it hurt like hell in a petticoat. And if you don't keep your legs together until you get married I'll kill you. Understand?"

"So where's your baby at?"

"One more question and I'll break this bowl over your head."

"So, like Mama says, just like it never happened."

"That's right. Shut up and dry."

It wasn't too bad, really, to be home. Wanda seemed happy enough to have me around, especially with apples to put up, kraut to make. Kept us occupied. But it was hard to keep stories straight. At "How's your aunt?" I'd be evasive, not wanting to lie outright, especially at church. "Oh, she's fine."

"Is she still on crutches? Haven't seen Pearl in years, but if she's still a bit stout, she must have had trouble." How should I know? I'd never been around anybody with a broken leg.

Wanda enjoyed the attention. "Oh, I bet you missed your little girl something awful," they'd say, and she'd nod and pat my shoulder. "Don't know how I managed without her." I didn't know whether to cry or throw up. I mean, she never called while I stayed with Aunt Pearl. Where was the truth? Likely somewhere between my version, in which Wanda, happy to be rid of me, read magazines and ate chocolates, and hers, in which she pined for her darling Florence Nightingale daughter.

At least Aunt Pearl had brought Puddy Tat back. Away from Van Gogh, the little black furball rubbed against my legs and purred like she harbored a ten-horsepower motor. Wanda hadn't messed with my room, either. I had feared she might give away my stuff, thinking a girl old enough to birth a baby didn't need teddy bears and dolls and their big house.

It was good up there, even with bars on the window. It smelled of warmth, clean clothes, perfume, cat hair and, once I had opened the window for the first time in months, fresh air. It felt safe—until I had time to dread Walker's homecoming.

It was a Friday—I think the sixteenth of September, a day anyway hot enough to wilt sunflowers. I had been antsy all day. All day? All month, more like it. A combination of heat, guilt, and nerves whopped me going and coming. Every time the phone rang I jumped a mile.

As Walker got out and stretched—he'd been driving all day—his little women, as he called us, ran to him. "Sweetheart, how are you?" he asked as he enveloped me. He smelled, as usual, of sweat, sawdust, and what he called hair tonic.

"I'm fine, Daddy."

"You look great. Hey, there's a graduation present in the truck bed."

"You shouldn't have."

"What? You only do that once, Sweetheart. Unless you're like your dumb old daddy, who never did. Just wish I had been there."

Wanda waved a gold tassel she had somehow come by. "Yes, we're so proud of her." I smiled through gritted teeth. I mean, instead of an honors tassel I got a baby—then gave it away.

"I want to see that diploma, too," he said.

Thank Jesus they let me keep up with my work at Aunt Pearl's. Just a couple of weeks ago I finished my tests and had gotten a diploma in the mail.

He gave me a cedar chest small enough for the dresser top. "They call it a hope chest. When you and Patrick get hitched you can put girl stuff in it," he said. "That, too," handing me the tassel.

"Sure," I said, wondering exactly whose memento he held in his stubby fingers.

As usual, after finishing a long job he took a few weeks off, repairing stuff at the house (my window bars came down his second day home) and "loafering," as he said, at the barber shop. Telling tall tales, I suppose. Evenings he made two trips to his truck—once before supper and once before bedtime. Hair tonic seemed to make him happier. After a few days I relaxed—he would not learn anything from his little women. We'd sworn.

Then we got ready for Pat's shore leave, and he *knew*. "Wervous nerk" time again.

October eighteenth—a Tuesday—his bus was due in Asheville at two. Wanda tried to talk me out of meeting him, said I'd look too eager. I didn't care—I was going and that was that. Besides, his mother worked days and a man shouldn't come home from service with no one to greet him.

I'd thought I was anxious when my water broke, but this day's fretting was enough to send me to the loony bin. I took a bath first thing, but by eleven needed another, so barely had time to dress, itself a worriment. I mean, what do you wear to meet a man who knows you've cheated on him? I had a nice red dress Pat liked but the Scarlet A color wouldn't do. I'd not have felt right to wear white, either. I finally settled on a soft yellow dress—a nice spring color for good luck.

I ran for the bus stop, hoping not to trip, skin my knees, and ruin my nylons. I'd gone hatless but as I caught the town bus I wondered if that made me look too flighty. I couldn't win. I even dropped coins in the floor beside the fare box.

So there I sat, worried sick, can't-wait excited. Lunch? No way. I'd have thrown up for sure.

The ratty old P&L station was a block west of the new Trailways station. Red and chrome, it had a lunch counter and a self-service booth that made little square black-and-white pictures for a quarter. It smelled of fried food, diesel exhaust, and something I'll call anticipation—whether good or bad depending on who was coming or going.

It had dark corners where seedy-looking men eyed you, benches where down-and-out men snored. A space full of sudden hellos and good-byes—would these people ever see each other again? For that matter, would Pat and I... oh, if he didn't show up soon I might explode.

Ten minutes late, the bus stopped in a flurry of hissing brakes and flashing lights. A uniformed man opened the cargo compartment filled with military duffle bags. And a big box with "Fragile" stamped on the side.

I wish I could say when he came out a light flashed, a bell rang, or Jesus whispered in my ear but all I remember is being held. His arms folded around me, my head on his shoulder, heart in my mouth, his uniform so white, his hands on my waist, not moving much or saying a word. Just holding each other. I quietly leaked tears on his shirt front and he on my shoulder. Hearts going ninety miles a second.

"You smell even better than I remembered," he finally whispered. I tried to pull back to look at him, but he resisted. "Just hold me, Priss. Just hold me."

So I did, until the baggage man poked his arm. "This your bag, sir? It's the last one."

The local bus left us at the Crawford P.O. We hardly touched ground before people said, "Well, look who's home" and "How's it going, sailor?" A few asked "How's your aunt?" and said "Good to see you two together again," in a tone I searched for sarcasm. Finding none, I said "Thanks."

His mother had hung a circle of bittersweet and turkey track on their front door. A white paper banner across read "Welcome Home Patrick."

"Marie's still at it," he said.

"She's the best wreathmaker I know."

"Heck, she's the only one I know. But yeah, she's tops."

"Pat…"

A brief "Here it comes" look flitted across his face like a bat at dusk. "Pat, I'm sorry."

His hands engulfed mine. "Me too. But it's water under the bridge. It's gone." He kissed the tip of my nose. "I believe you, and I trust you, so do me a favor."

"What?"

"Don't say you're sorry again. It's behind us, let's keep it that way."

"Oh, Pat, I love you more than anything."

"And I love you, Priss." He fingered my necklace. "So you're still wearing my ring?"

"I didn't for a while—I was ashamed to. It was like I threw dirt on it."

"I said 'No more.' Let's look to the future. Ours."

"So… we're… still engaged?"

He dropped to one knee. "I have thirty day's leave. Is that time enough to get married?"

"Oh, Pat, do you mean it?"

"I do. Will you marry me ASAP?"

"I don't know what that means, but I will if you'll have me."

I remember that kiss—soft, thoughtful, sweet. I think I might have floated a few inches off the floor. It stirred me, too, which was reassuring—I had wondered if that might never happen again. But I didn't lean into him just yet. After all, Aunt Pearl said I wasn't a tramp.

The 3:40 mill bus let off a dozen passengers, women all wearing work uniforms, men mostly in overalls. Marie, waving like her hand might fly into orbit, trotted up the road.

"Okay if I tell her?" he asked.

"Sure."

He bear-hugged her and whirled her around. I stayed on the porch wiping my eyes, tears anymore my reaction to good news or bad.

They stopped with his back to me. Pat was a good head taller than his mother, so for a minute I didn't see her. Then an "Oh my Lord!" exploded, her head peeked out, and she shot around him, heading for the porch.

She grinned like the Grand Canyon, jumped on the porch, and hugged me. "Congratulations, Priscilla. I've hoped and prayed for this."

I hugged his mother. "I love him. I'll treat him right."

"I know you will, honey. We still going to your house for supper?"

"Yes, Mama's been cooking for days."

"Well, I made pumpkin pie and banana bread. And I got to get out of this stinky uniform and freshen up. Patrick, you have to stow your gear—is that how they say it in the service?—Priscilla, we'll be over about six."

We had no dining room but our kitchen was efficient. Sink and cabinets on the north wall, range and refrigerator on the east. A six-foot food bar jutted into the room from the west, separating a dining table on the south wall from the kitchen. The whole family—me and my father and sister and—goodness—my soon-to-be husband and mother-in-law—pretty much filled the table. Wanda had gone all out—preacher dishes said we were important, paper napkins said we were modern.

Wanda would no more sit down to such a meal than show up in underwear. She was the servant hostess, nibbling at a chicken wing and mashed potatoes from a plate at the food bar while making trip after trip from stove to bar, lugging platters of baked ham and roasted chicken, bowls of vegetables, baskets of bread. She passed mashed potatoes, green beans, creamed corn, lima beans, two kinds of gravy, biscuits, dinner rolls. On the table sat apple butter, sweet pickles, two kinds of jelly. Not to mention butter, cranberry sauce, a Jell-O and fruit cocktail mold, and a marinated cucumber and tomato salad. Then chocolate cake, apple pie—and Marie's pumpkin pie and banana bread—washed down with milk or iced tea.

One of the happiest gatherings I can remember. Pat and I were toasted many times, and Walker—who usually hated such occasions—went to his truck twice before supper and seemed well-pleased.

Between supper and dessert he started to tell a story I'd never heard. And, for that matter, shouldn't have.

"Me and Wanda ran off to South Carolina—I was eighteen, she was sixteen. We found a justice of the peace, said our vows, then left his house. She asked 'Now what?'

"'Got a surprise,' I said, and we started down the street. Saturday night, folks strolling around, having a good time. I turned us into the swankiest place in Greenville, the Poinsett Hotel, the kind of place where you leave your shoes in the hall and they shine them for you. I mean, in the lobby an orchestra I guess you'd call it, all dressed up, played high-fa-lutin' music in amongst the potted palm trees.

"They were fussy, too. Wanda looked so young I had to show them our marriage certificate. But we got that straightened out, and went upstairs…"

"Don't you dare say another word," Wanda said. My mother hadn't turned that red since she found out I was pregnant.

"But, dear…"

"'But, dear,' my foot. Walker Lance, if you embarrass me in front of our future son-in-law and his sweet mother, I'll fill your lap with scalding coffee."

She meant it.

"Hell, Wanda, can't a man have a little fun?"

"Not that kind. Anybody else want coffee?"

Only my parents drank it that time of night. He took a sip, lit a Chesterfield, and rubbed his belly. "Patrick, I'd give you a cigar but I'm fresh out."

"That's all right, Mr. Lance, I don't smoke them."

"Son, we're going to be family. I'm Walker. Got that?"

"Yes, sir."

"When you two hatch a baby, be sure and pass out nice cigars. No cheap stuff."

Four females blushed.

"I guess you all aim to hitch up at church?"

Guarded glances all around. "Tell you what," he said, producing a wallet. "I'll pay you lovebirds to run off. Cost me a sight less than a church wedding."

Everyone's eyes darted toward me. I raised an eyebrow and nodded discreetly at Pat.

"You're on, Walker," he said, to an insuck of feminine breath.

Walker pushed five twenties toward Pat. "A hundred bucks. If you elope." Wanda, slowly sliding an ashtray toward her husband, glanced from me to Pat.

I looked around the table before settling eyes on him, and smiled. "Maybe that's best."

"We can leave for South Carolina in the morning," Pat said, picking up the money like he'd won with a royal flush. "Maybe we'll get a room and come back Sunday."

"Son, I'll pay for that, too." Walker slipped him another twenty. "Get a fancy place. And if you don't stay forever, take my car." Wanda's face radiated pure wonder. Her silence was breathtaking, like she didn't quite believe, but didn't dare jinx it.

"Well, now," said Pat. He raised a glass of tea. "Here's to my bride. May we live happily ever after." Glasses clinked all around. "And here's to my soon-to-be mother-in-law. Mrs. Lance, I never had a finer meal."

"Call me Wanda. And thank you, Pete."

"It's Pat, Wanda," he said.

"More pie?" she asked.

We were full as ticks—even I had lost my butterflies enough to shovel it in. That night we acted like family—telling stories you could finish without being threatened, laughing at each other's jokes, even looking toward a future. After not another morsel could be stuffed into anybody, Walker and Pat went to the porch while we women, thankful things had gone well, tidied the kitchen.

After Marie left and the family went to their bedrooms, Pat and I sat on the porch and talked long into the night. About how excited we were. About what he might do after the navy. About me going to business college. About the future, something I had not allowed myself to think about for a long time. I dared think things would—maybe—work out. That all would—finally—be well.

Our first day of wedded bliss didn't start so great. We headed out in Walker's new car, new to him, anyway, a 1939 Plymouth a man gave toward a down payment on a job. It ran fine through Asheville but gave us a flat north of Hendersonville. After Pat changed it we drove through Flat Rock where the rich people lived. Down by Tuxedo and Camp Mondamin, I swear, the leaves looked like red and yellow coins glistening in the trees. Between there and the state line we were treated to a series of Burma-Shave slogans, each cornier than the last.

Pat pointed to the sign at the South Carolina line and grinned like a carnival barker at a girlie show. I tried to look innocent but I'm not sure I succeeded.

He soon slowed and pulled into a gravel parking lot in front of a wooden building that seemed all front porch. Between its balusters spiders had built webs that glistened in the sun. A red-letter sign on the roof spelled out FIREWORKS across half the building.

"Why are we stopping?"

"It's South Carolina. You gotta buy firecrackers or something."

"Why?"

"Just because."

I put my arm around him.

"Pat. Let's head down the mountain. We don't need a thing here."

"Maybe you're right. Fireworks tonight, right?"

I simply looked at the gravel and almost nodded. He took that for a good sign.

Winding down the mountain toward Marietta, kudzu hung from rocks like it wanted to pounce. We stopped for a picnic—last night's leftovers—outside Travelers Rest. Blue jays shrieked when they saw cooler and basket on the concrete slab table—I guess they thought that meant leavings.

Ha! Not a crumb. I'd gone to bed convinced I couldn't eat another bite but ham biscuits tasted really good.

"Well," said Pat, gnawing on a chicken leg, "tonight we'll be man and wife."

I tried to blush.

"Wanna hear the rest of Walker's wedding night story?"

"Did he tell it while we were cleaning up the kitchen?"

"Sure. Remember how it went?"

"Mama cut him off just as they'd gone upstairs."

Pat laughed. "Well, she didn't cut him off that night. He said they came inside and pretty quick—did the honeymoon thing."

"Pat, did he really say that?"

"I cleaned it up for your tender ears. Afterward your mother wanted a cup of ice and a cola dope, so your father went out and found some, laid back down, propped himself against the headboard, and started to read the paper.

"All of a sudden Wanda gets a piece of ice hung in her throat. I mean, she can't speak or breathe and he's fixed on the baseball scores so she knocks the paper away and sprawls across his lap, gasping and clawing.

"'Damn, Wanda,' he says, 'you want it again *already*?'"

I hit his arm. "Patrick Allen, how dare you?" I laughed so I'm sure he didn't think I meant it. The notion of my parents' wedding night was creepy enough, but to think of my mother…

"I hope I didn't jinx, you know…"

He hadn't.

In Greenville a half-deaf justice of the peace took our money and pronounced us—or anyway people named Pete and Drusilla—man and wife. Our witnesses were his wife, a woman they invented "dowdy" for, their thousand-year-old neighbor lady, and a bored one-eyed hound named Fritz.

Pat could be stingy. "I bet the Poinsett'd cost that whole twenty," he said. "Let's find something cheaper."

"Sure." But something in my head said "Please, not *too* cheap."

We stopped at a run-down north Greenville tourist court. The chill of car wheels on gravel, the buzz of old neon in the parking lot. Pat came out of the office grinning, with a key. I took a deep breath. Who was I tonight? The virgin he thought at one time to marry? A "hot mama"? Or just a scared girl with a scared boy?

He carried me across the threshold—after it took five minutes to get the door unlocked—and sat me on the bed. Which creaked like a swinging bridge. He started to kiss me but I wrinkled my nose. "This place doesn't smell good. And what's that noise?"

The commode was running through. The windowsills harbored piles of dead bugs, and the ancient Admiral radio picked up only a scratchy gospel station.

"I'll take care of this," said Pat. "Back in a minute."

It was more like ten before he threw his hat on the bed in disgust.

"Old rascal says 'no more room in the inn.' That's exactly how he put it, like he wanted me to think how darn clever he is. And he won't give our five bucks back."

"Pat, honey, that's bad luck."

"What?"

I picked up his hat and re-creased the brim. "Putting a hat on a bed. Didn't you know that? Now, what will we do?"

"Well, the Plymouth has a big backseat."

Like I was going to spend my wedding night being reminded of what started the worst time of my life. I hit him with his hat.

"Hey, Priss, I'm sorry. We'll find somewhere else."

After a while we saw in Travelers Rest a place run by a nice family named Edwards. Flowers around each cabin, grass nicely trimmed. Mrs. Edwards gave us a box of chocolate-covered cherries. Quiet, clean room, away from the main road, a firm bed—and I didn't need a cup of ice as an excuse to turn a second time to my husband—my really, as he said, first-timer husband. About the best ten dollars we ever spent.

I thought that might be our last lovemaking until we moved to Virginia. Upstairs in my bedroom, Pat said the thought of Walker's ears, sensitive as the radar he was used to tending, below us unmanned him—his word, not mine—and I understood. You never went anywhere in that house without Walker knowing it. Wanda? She could sleep through Armageddon.

But Walter soon left for a job in Alabama. After that I wasn't worried about waking Mama, and figured Grace had to learn about things sometime. In fact, one afternoon I told her about the birds and bees, because Wanda never would—or, worse, might give her that same awful book. I'm proud my little sis never got knocked up.

One Wednesday Wanda packed a bushel of food and put us on a bus to tidewater Virginia. It said "Express" but stopped at every pig trail between Asheville and Norfolk. Down the mountain to Old Fort, across the piedmont to Durham, where we switched busses. Ran most of the night beside Virginia peanut, cotton, and soybean fields. Finally, at dawn, we saw big water, the James, the Chesapeake, the ocean. My first view of it.

Didn't excite me a bit. Maybe I was tired, and maybe I knew on some level water was about to rob me of my darling for the next six or eight months. I couldn't say I loved the country, either, flat as a dinner table. Out the dirty window I saw Norfolk streets lined with pawn shops, gun dealers, peep shows, tattoo parlors, bars. I figured to stay home a lot.

That evening's temporary quarters had a filling station restroom's privacy. It took most of a day to transfer Pat from bachelor quarters to married housing, so Friday evening was our first night really alone.

Our duplex half was a combination living room and kitchen, small bedroom, and a bathroom barely big enough to turn around in. The view from the kitchen window was across a teeny courtyard to another brick building, partially hidden by sheets and shirts on a rotating clothesline. The apartment smelled of linseed oil and government green paint but it was clean and spider-free.

Outside, the smell of salt air and low-tide mud had somehow stirred us up. He hugged me and slipped a hand to my breast and I cuffed him. "Not out here, silly." Inside, we explored the living area, he seeing if windows opened properly, me eyeing flowered slipcovers, both inching toward the bedroom. He began to whistle through his teeth, a habit I thought cute. He entered—I followed. He looked outside, drew the curtain. I sat on the bed, bounced once—no screaky springs. When I patted the mattress and whispered "Honey?" he smiled and reached for my shoulder as my hand brought his face to mine and we tilted bedward like a pair of trees in a windstorm.

A mid-kiss knock at the back door made me growl like a bulldog. I jumped to answer while Pat swore and adjusted his trousers.

I opened the door to a woman about my age, maybe five feet tall in heels. Red hair tied by a blue scarf, lipstick several degrees brighter than anything in my palette. She offered a clay-potted yellow chrysanthemum. "I'm Kat. Your next-door neighbor. Welcome to the dog pound."

"It's beautiful, Kat. Thanks. I'm Priscilla. Please come in." As she set the flower on the counter Pat emerged from the bedroom.

"You must be Mister Priscilla," Kat said, snapping chewing gum. "Either that or Priscilla here's got herself a personal bedroom inspector."

He laughed. "I'm Pat Allen. Nice to meet you, Kat..."

"Szabo. I'm a Kentucky Cope married to a Pennsylvania Hunkie on submarine duty, due back in December."

"I'd be worried sick if Pat was on a sub," I said.

"Oh, you know about a submarine—it's long and hard and full of seamen," said Kat, laughing. "When do you ship out, Pat?"

"I'll get orders tomorrow."

"Well, while you're gone me and Priscilla will take care of each other, hey, honey?"

I beamed. "Sure thing."

"How long you lovebirds been married?"

"A couple of weeks," I said.

Kat eyeballed me. "You're shipshape for a newlywed. My first month I couldn't hardly walk for floor burns fore and aft. Well, gotta run. Just wanted to welcome you aboard."

She hugged me and whispered, "Tell him to quit wearing your lipstick if he wants a promotion," and left with a wave.

"Our neighbor's a character," said Pat.

"And I'm going to lock the door," I said, a gleam in my eye.

Tidewater Virginia and mountain North Carolina were about as alike as jellyfish and possums. The rank odor of low-tide saltmarsh, when I had been used to crisp air, mown grass, apples. And they sounded different. Port, naval base, and air station constantly clanked, whooshed, growled. Sirens and car and ship horns kept you up at night—I used to sleep beside an open window admitting no more racket than a distant barking dog, hoot owl, or train whistle. And they sure looked different. It wasn't natural to call ground six feet above sea level a hill. But when everything around is flat as a flitter, I guess it's all relative.

So there I was, a stranger surrounded by salt water, in a place infested with no-see-ums, where the highest point was a ship's mast or radio tower. I might have been depressed.

I admit to homesick. I even made up stuff to miss. I mean, when I said "crisp air," the fact was, the rayon mill a few miles east and paper plant a dozen miles west made Crawford air pretty noxious. But I missed it like you miss a fresh tomato in the dead of winter.

After Pat left in November I was so lonesome I made Hank Williams's whippoorwill sound happy. Not simply lonesome—empty is a better word, an emptiness Pat couldn't fill even while he was around. Some days he was simply a scab over a hole, out of which stubborn pain and guilt strove for resurrection.

I'd sit straight up at four in the morning convinced I heard my baby—I couldn't even say him or her—cry. A child I had thrown into a world full of trouble and evil.

Kat tried to teach me to drink but I wasn't even much good at that. Whiskey reminded me of Dick Snipes or my father, either way a brier thicket. The smell of gin made me want to puke. Vodka was okay with orange juice but more than one gave me a hangover. And beer had to be cold enough to freeze before I enjoyed it. I was pitiful.

I tried Bible reading but ran into harlots and pages of thou-shalt-nots. Ladies' magazines weren't much better. So I started reading long novels from the library. *Raintree County*, *The Young Lions*, that kind of thing. Started one called *The Naked and the Dead* but was shocked such language could be printed. Didn't get far there.

One day—about suppertime, only I didn't care—I was in PJ bottoms and one of Pat's undershirts, curled up on the sofa with *The Big Fisherman* and a can of potato chips. Was the knock at the back door Kat? Not sure, I tied my bathrobe and went to the door.

Kat cocked her head and grinned.

"Been pleasuring yourself?"

My neighbor, the foul-mouthed redbird.

"Heavens, no. Just reading. Come on in."

"Let's go to the Boiled Owl. I'm thirsty and slap out of booze."

"The where?"

"This nightclub outside of town."

"I'll just hang around here. You know, eat salt, retain water, read my book."

"What's it about?"

"Saint Peter."

"You ought to be reading about friskier peters than that. C'mon, I promise we won't be out late."

"What if… somebody asks us to dance?"

"We dance, what else? When you feel like dogshit, dancing makes you happy."

"But what about our hubbies?"

"What they don't know won't hurt them—and don't worry. I won't let anything get out of hand. The Boiled Owl is a swinging joint weekends, but tonight should be kinda quiet."

"Why do they call it that?"

"You'll see. Come on, you look like you need some fun."

I stared at my book, then at Kat. "Maybe you're right. I'll get dressed. If you're thirsty, Pat left a couple of beers in the icebox."

"Hell, girl, they'll spoil before he gets back. Put on your best undies and dancing shoes while I wet my whistle."

A bus left us at The Broken Mast, a long, low, concrete block dive with plenty of red and blue neon signs—OPEN, BEER, one off-level BEE. Beside the building sat a skipjack or pungy or anyway small ship with half its mast dangling. The parking lot was paved with white gravel, beer cans, and cigarette butts.

It was also littered with potential suitors, both uniformed and not, who appeared like gnats do after wind calms. When Kat shook out a cigarette one instantly offered a match.

"Thanks. Now, make way, gentlemen."

Light inside was scarce—coming mostly from beer signs. Schlitz, Blatz, Black Label, Hudepohl, you name it. Backlit pinball machines, too, noisy invitations to throw away money. And in one crowded corner long hooded lights hung over two pool tables upholstered in green.

The space was largely dance floor, with booths sprouting like mushrooms around the sides. A small stage in one corner held a battered upright piano, Tucson or Bust painted on its side, a few round-topped stools, and microphone stands resembling chrome-plated wading birds.

A bar stretched across the north wall, with mirrored shelves with wooden gargoyles leering among liquor bottles. Kat pointed to its top, where stood—"leaned" a better word—a stuffed barn owl wearing a rhinestone tiara, plastic beads around its shoulders. If owls have shoulders.

"See why I call it The Boiled Owl?"

"Why 'boiled'?"

"Down home they say 'He's done got drunk as a boiled owl.'"

The smell nearly flummoxed me. Almost too complicated to describe. Stale beer and toilet bowl deodorizer—whiskey and the memory of vomit—hot dogs and cigarette smoke. Peanut shells, cheap perfume—pickled eggs, sulfur matches. Stay ten minutes, your clothes reek for days.

A haystack-sized Seeburg jukebox with enough chrome to make a Dodge sedan grille played Merle Travis, accompanied by clicking billiard balls, jingle-jangling pinball machines, buzzing male conversation. Which lulled immediately, for—except for one floozy at the bar—we were the only women there. We were undressed by no telling how many beer-bleared eyeballs.

As we slid into a booth the bartender brought two bottles of Blatz. "Compliments of the gentlemen."

He nodded toward bar's end, where two men in their forties grinned and lifted half-empty glasses our way. I looked the other direction but Kat swigged her beer and nodded at them.

"Beer's cold. Drink up, Priss. We won't spend a nickel for a buzz tonight."

"Kat, this is weird."

"Nothing to fear, dear. They're just men."

"I know. But I sure don't feel like dancing. Particularly not with them."

"Beer'll help that. Oh look, Priss, this is brand new. Neat-o!"

Our booth had salt and pepper shakers, an empty napkin dispenser, two nearly full metal ashtrays, and a chromed wall box that Kat sidled up to, flipping through the selections. She put in a nickel and punched C-8.

"See, you don't even have to get up to play the jukebox. And you'll love this—Frankie Laine, 'Georgia on My Mind.'"

The men, hats in hand, slid off stools like they'd practiced it. They weren't bad-looking—at least no visible scars or tattoos, neither man limped or stumbled. They wore dark jackets, light shirts, no ties. The taller one wore high-water pants and white socks.

"Might we have the pleasure of your company?" said High Water.

"Me and my friend just got here," said Kat. "We need to let our eyes adjust, you know. Besides, we want to talk a while."

"But we bought you ladies a beer."

"So that gives you all a hunting license?"

"Good one, eh Rick? She's funny, this redhead. Ha. A hunting license."

"Your friend always this hilarious?" Rick asked me.

"Please, just leave us alone."

"Aw, a Garbo, huh? Kid, I just wanted to have a laugh, maybe dance a bit."

Kat took High Water's left hand in hers, which made him grin until he realized she traced a pale circle around his third finger. "Would wifey want to know he bought little Kat a beer?"

When I looked toward Rick's left hand he suddenly needed to scratch behind his neck. "We'll leave y'all alone," he said. "Didn't mean no harm."

They lit cigarettes and faded into the background.

"Maybe that'll keep the flies off for a while," said Kat. "Although there shouldn't be any. I scrubbed my cooter before I left, didn't you?"

"Oh, Kat!" I blushed.

"Priss, what I got to do to get a laugh out of you?"

I sipped my beer. "I don't know. I'm sorry to ruin your evening. I just miss Pat."

"If you're this bad now I'll have your sweet ass to bury before he comes back. Tell you what. Let's just talk. Want to hear exactly where I come from?"

"I'd love to."

"It's a simple story. Might even be some truth to it. I was born in Kentucky, in a place nobody thought enough of to name. We called it The Creek, but it wasn't much of a creek and sure wasn't much of a place. When we went to town it was Combs. Never got to Hazard till I was six and then just for a Saturday afternoon.

"Daddy mined and Mama squirted out babies—seven of us. I was the youngest, I was six when she died. Was raised by my grandmother. Daddy was a good man but didn't know squat about girls. Grandma sent me to that settlement school over in Hindman when I was ten."

"Where's that?"

"On Troublesome Creek. Hell of a name, ain't it? Just to look at it you'd laugh, you can wade it and not get your feet wet, but come a gully-washer it lives up to its handle. The first time I saw that little creek it was dusky dark and as I peered down at it a big old blue heron lifted from it like a haint. I took that bird as a sign I'd be happy there.

"And I was. When I left I could match anybody as far as studies, and I sewed and quilted and canned and made mint candy and I don't know what all.

"I knew better than to hang around Kentucky. I'd seen too many girls get bit by trouser worms and have to marry into a mining clan. Didn't know what I was going to do but I wanted to do it in a city, so soon as I finished school I headed to Cincinnati like the good old Brier I was.

"Right off the bat I met Steve. A Yankee, Catholic to boot. I'd never met one before. He was born in Pennsylvania but thought working on the river sounded good. We soon couldn't live without each other. I mean, he was in my underpants our second date and I was happy as a pig in shit. We got married there—I sure couldn't have brought him home, and I'm kinda glad my grandmother died before she knew—it'd have killed her, me marrying a Yankee mackerel-snapper.

"I'll tell you one thing, Priss, I make Steve wrap that rascal. I'm not going to start having a dang bunch of kids anytime soon. How about you?"

"Motherhood isn't all it's cracked up to be."

"What do you mean?"

"Well… can you keep a secret?"

"I kept my cherry till I was eighteen."

"So did I. But here's the deal—the first time I drank whiskey"—and here I moved in close, despite the jukebox's blare—"I got knocked up."

"Holy kamoley, I gotta hear this. You want another one? Beer, I mean."

"No, thanks."

Then I'll drink for both of us." Kat held two fingers up to the bartender and rummaged in her purse. In a minute two beers appeared.

"The gentlemen over there," said the bartender.

"Tell the gentlemen thanks, but we're in the middle of an important meeting and can't be disturbed. Seriously. Anyway, we're married."

"You're the doctor," he said.

"Priss, sorry about that. Now air your dirty linen."

"I met this boy."

"No shit, Sherlock? I thought you made a kid with some dame. So it wasn't Pat?"

"He was at sea. We were engaged. I was still in school." I began to peel the beer label with a thumbnail.

"Did this boy have a name?"

"Dick."

"Figures." Kat shook salt on the table and slid the shaker back and forth. A slick and gritty noise in time with a Perry Como tune.

"No, really. Dick Snipes. Six-three, dark hair, blue eyes. Ex-Marine—in college. He kinda swept me off my feet."

"Sounds like a dreamboat."

"He was. And so nice."

"They all are till they get what they want."

"No, even after we did it he was nice. Thing was… excuse me."

Two sailors had appeared out of the darkness. The taller one took out a stainless steel Zippo and lit a Camel. "You girls wanna dance?"

Kat triaged them and flashed her left hand. "We told the barkeep to tell you we're married. To Marines with short fuses."

"Sorry to bother you," said the taller. "Joe, let's go."

"I'm going to hang a danged Do Not Disturb sign on our table," said Kat. "Now, get on with it."

"Well, he was fine, like I said. Then I turned up pregnant."

"So he blew town like a scalded hound."

"Pretty much."

"Okay, let's get this straight. Pat's on a ship, you've got one in the oven—I understand, a girl gets horny, makes mistakes. So how'd you keep this from Pat?"

"That's the funny part. I didn't."

"Wait. You mean he *knows*?"

I nodded.

"And married you anyhow?"

"That's right."

"Damn. So where's the kid?" Her eyes widened. "Or did you…"

I had been telling myself a lie for a long time, a perfectly made-up story about my baby, meant for nobody but me. So I was surprised to hear myself try it out on Kat.

"No, no, I had little Millie. I told Pat, but my mother and I kept all that hidden from Daddy—he still doesn't know."

"Girl, this sounds like a fairy tale. How do you hide a baby? In the bullrushes?"

"Daddy works away from home a bunch. I dropped out of school until Millie came. Then took exams and stuff at the end of the summer."

"So you adopted her out?"

I couldn't stop myself.

"Yeah. That was, let me tell you, the hardest thing ever, like pulling off an arm to give to a stranger. The only way I could do it was knowing she went to a good home.

"Millie is so sweet, no trouble at all, five pounds, six ounces, thick coal black hair. She has Dick's eyes. The agency let me pick her family. Her new daddy's a salesman, her mother's a housewife, he's a deacon, she sings in the choir. Little Millie will have a good life."

Kat shook her head slowly.

"What? You don't believe me?"

"Sure I do—we're friends, ain't we? Friends don't lie to each other."

"You just looked…"

"Priss, every tale has its own truth. And I have to believe at least part of it, else why hang around with some forked-tongue bitch? Still, somehow I don't think this tale's finished. Uh oh."

Two more hopefuls, one a sailor, the other a civilian, loomed above the edges of the booth. The sailor was jut-jawed with greasy brown hair, the big-eared civilian wore a pencil stroke mustache and a brown suit a little large for him. "I'm Tom, this is my brother Sid," said the sailor. "You ladies care to dance?"

Kat looked at me and I shook my head. "Sweetie," said Kat, "My sister here needs to go home. She turns into a retroactive virgin when she drinks too much. A plumb retro-damn-active virgin, can you believe it? But I'll dance with both of you—one at a time—before we leave."

The sailor offered his arm to Kat and Brown Suit slid into Kat's side of the booth. "Gee, I'm sorry you're sick," he said. "I didn't hear what your sister said you got, but here's some powders. You know what they say—Snap back with Stanback."

I don't know how I kept from laughing. And he had a nice smile so I thanked him.

"My brother's showing me the ropes. Imagine meeting sisters—small world, ain't it?"

"You don't even know," I said. "Will you please excuse me?"

I was a little confused. I didn't want to get in trouble again but suddenly wanted to dance with this man. And needed to pee.

I headed to the women's room, a mistake. It might have been cleaned during the Hoover administration. There were two stalls, one occupied by the woman who had been at the bar. I could tell by the shoes. I needed to use the toilet but couldn't bear to sit on the other one.

There was more smoke in there than in the bar. I tried to open the transom window but no go. When the jukebox played "Room Full of Roses" the woman began to hum along, off-key, hiccuping. I figured to stay for one more song, to give Kat another dance.

Turned out to be "Slipping Around," which made me imagine Pat wondering where I was and what I was doing. The woman began to cry.

I knocked gently on the stall door, which made her stop.

"Can I help you?"

"Get the damn hell away."

Easy enough. I came out to find Kat in the booth, a man at each side. Brown Suit stood to let me in.

"Feeling rocky?" she asked.

"Not too bad. Maybe one dance, then we better get home. You know how I get."

So Brown Suit, whose name was Fred, and I danced a slow one while Sailor Boy and Kat had another beer apiece. He kept stepping on my feet, which reminded me of Pat, which… well, you know. When we came back to the table I didn't sit.

"Well, fellows, I best take Priss here home before she turns inside-out. That isn't a bit becoming, let me tell you. Enjoyed the dance."

"Can we walk you home?" asked the sailor.

"Not a chance," said Kat. "But maybe we'll see you sometime. Come on, Sis, let's make like a horse turd and hit the dusty trail."

Don't know why I lied to Kat, except I'd been fretting about my baby. What she might look like at three months. I'd decided she must be a girl, Millicent, I'd always loved that name, it sounded classy. I imagined her in a safe, warm home, with loving parents who would give her everything she needed. And she'd grow up to be whatever she wanted to be. A fashion model. A movie star. An airline stewardess.

What harm was it to tell Kat? None, I decided, and it sure made me feel better. Or at least like I had accomplished something besides turning a mistake loose in the world.

But sometimes I worried that the welfare people had given her to a couple of drunks, or worse—maybe to a couple where the man loves to beat wife and baby. You read about men who shake babies to death when they won't stop crying.

Or if not kill her, burn her with a cigarette. Leave her in some restroom. You hear about all kinds of meanness.

Or what if her mother found her dead some morning? Or with a brain-killing fever? My baby, dead or damaged, helpless.

Such thoughts might send me on a half-day crying jag interrupted by staring out the window at someone's washing on the line, wishing I was home, wishing Pat was there, wishing I wasn't so lonesome, wishing I hadn't given poor Millie away.

I probably would have gone nuts if not for Kat. When I was down, she'd make me eat, make me take a bath, go to a movie. When I was good, she and I would go on a picnic or over to Ocean View Park.

Now, that was some place to go.

The town of Ocean View wasn't much—just a long street parallel to the Atlantic, a street that just gave up once it ran out of buildings. But most of the town was a huge amusement park between road and ocean.

The Ocean View boardwalk seemed to go for miles. You could walk in sun or shade, and hundreds of detours might take you to the pavilion or the Tunnel of Fun or a Ferris wheel or any number of roller coasters, including the Rocket, which I was too scared to try. You could ride the Dodgem Cars or the Flying Aeroplane. (I did the first but not the second.) The Penny Arcade was noisy, but a fine place to waste time for not much money. There was a casino, which I never went into, a Test-Your-Strength scene, a shooting gallery, any number of hot dog stands, ice cream vendors, cotton candy, popcorn, peanuts, cupcakes, you name it, somebody sold it.

At the west end, up a level from the promenade, was a dance hall, with a breathtaking ocean view. At night you saw lighthouses, winking lights from ships and buoys, and the sweep of a searchlight at the other end of the park. And every color of light from rides wheeling around in the dark.

Days, ships and planes sailed and flew all over the place. Mostly military during the week, but weekend biplanes towed signs saying Eat At Joe's, or Doumer's Ice Cream Cones. People barnstormed above the beach, stood on airplane wings, parachuted, dangerous stuff.

The dance hall wasn't like the Boiled Owl, which had nothing hopeful about it, just a place to drink yourself into oblivion or get groped or both. I hate to sound like Wanda, but everything there was common and lots of things (except for the owl, which was funny) were downright creepy.

Ocean View's dance hall was well-lit by signs for sodas. Nehi and Cheerwine and I don't know what all else. Lemonade. Ice cream. Candy. For this whole park was what they came to call "Family Entertainment," which meant no alcohol.

Of course, that was wishful thinking. Even though the crowd was younger than, say, at the Boiled Owl—most Ocean View patrons still had futures, some reason to hold their heads up—nobody checked purses or pockets for flasks or bottles, so, if you as much as looked thirsty, someone sidled up to you with a cup of ice and a grin. As Kat put it, "The Lord will provide."

A younger crowd meant louder music, usually live, maybe not great, but you could dance to it. Kat liked fast dancing, and guys stood in line for a turn with her. I didn't care for that at first, but slow dances to good songs were hard to pass up. Only thing, a younger crowd meant young boys tried to convince you they were old enough to drive, or drink, or at least feel your bottom while they danced with you. A fifteen-year-old boy full of hormones and a drink or two is a fearsome thing, and Kat and I slapped our share of them.

Kat and I went to Ocean View several times that fall. It took me that long to pull out of my blues. Knowing Pat would soon be home was good, and, oddly enough, dancing with people my age reinforced my feelings for him. And I started to enjoy fast dancing again when Kat showed me which guys were really good at it. Started to be fun again, but I was careful not to overdo it. I wasn't looking for somebody to replace Pat, certainly. I honestly didn't see myself as two-timing. And I sure knew the difference between a little fun and cheating. Kat helped me with that problem.

Everybody made a big deal out of Christmas. About the middle of December stores hung lights in their windows, the town put out decorations on streetlights, and W. T. Grant's downtown boasted a Santa so kids could sit in his lap. (Like, one day, my Millie.)

The downtown churches alternated hosting a live nativity scene, much more elaborate than when I played the Virgin in Crawford. Tailor-made costumes, lots of real donkeys and sheep. A lighted star atop the Methodist belfry, a Merry Christmas message on the Baptist marquee. I wasn't going to church then—I figured I was too far gone for Jesus to mess with me—but I missed the story.

Got me to thinking about going to church Christmas Day. Kat and I went to Ocean View Christmas Eve, but turned in early, agreeing we needed to be in church, especially when Christmas was on Sunday.

After Kat tamed the woodpecker, we ended up at Sacred Heart Catholic. Fancy inside, all kinds of stained glass and statues. Some of the windows told Bible stories—maybe all, I didn't know. Noah was easy, as was Palm Sunday, and Abraham with that knife raised over his son. Moses and the commandments. Some guy with tablets on his back. Others with several haloed men, their hands up in an Indian greeting, I had no idea about.

Some statues were pretty, like the Virgin Mary by herself or holding the baby Jesus. Others were kind of creepy, especially where Jesus' chest is burst open so you can see his heart. I guess that's supposed to be a comfort, but all it did for me was say "See what you did to me?"

We sat in the back. Kat had converted, so she knew when to kneel and all that. I just sat and tried to make sense of things. I hadn't taken Latin so didn't recognize any mumbo-jumbo except Jesus Christ.

I guess I was looking for a friendly service, but that sure wasn't it. The priest mostly kept his back to us and the music was strange. Seems that Christmas, things shouldn't be too serious. You ought to be happy about Baby Jesus. Maybe if I'd been Catholic and taken the Lord's Supper it would have been different. But I don't see how. It's like they wanted to hide good news behind the hocus-pocus. Baptists might preach hell fire and damnation but at least you can understand it, and at Christmas they ease off a little.

So I came home about as joyful as when I left. Which wasn't much.

Sometimes I think it's human nature to stray. To make promises, then break them. To cheat on loved ones.

I know I did it with Dick Snipes when Pat was first gone. I don't really count the men I danced with on his next tour. I was attracted to a few of them, sure, but by then I knew better than to be alone with them. So I refused "dates," whether for supper or a movie or whatever. Just a dance every now and then.

Maybe I shouldn't have told Pat about them, but I wanted honesty in our relationship. It didn't seem to surprise him and he didn't, at least not in front of me, get all bent out of shape.

I wonder if Steve and Kat are still together. I've lost track of them—years have a way of doing that, especially when the Navy transfers you all over. Last I heard, they were in San Diego, which I imagine Kat loves. She hates cold weather.

To tell the truth, I kind of got scared to hang around with her after that first year. She always had an edge, a wild streak that might pull a girl right down with her.

I quit the dance halls before Pat came home on leave the spring of 1950. Kat kept going, by herself or with other wives. I didn't worry until one morning I hadn't slept worth two cents and stared out the back window at gray dawn. A man left her apartment, stood outside long enough to light a cigarette, looking as proud as a tomcat. Which, I suppose, he was.

Never saw but the one, but always wondered how many boyfriends my buddy Kat had. And whether she was careful. And whether she ever told Steve. I never said anything to her about it.

It dawned on me that, if we're all built that way, what was Walker up to all those months he was gone while I was growing up? Heck, he could have had some shadow family out there somewhere. Another daughter. Some sons, who knew?

For that matter, what about Wanda?

Nah, she's too concerned about appearances to have risked an affair. Besides, she'd have had to lay down her pocketbook.

Pat left the Navy in June 1951. Said he'd had enough cramped quarters and squiggly lines on screens. He wanted to settle down, start a family. Fine with me, especially what you do to begin one. I was tired of dancing with guys I couldn't sleep with.

In July we moved to Newport News. Newport Noise, more like it. More racket, I'd guess, than the middle of Manhattan. All you got there, it seems from television, is car horns and sirens. Newport News has everything.

The Shipyard Apartments on Washington Avenue was a row of four monstrous buildings facing the shipyard, each exactly alike, red brick relieved by concrete details, built during World War I. Not modern, but the best we could do. Each footprint was a five-story C on its side. We lived in the middle of the second C, on the top floor (no elevator, naturally) facing west, so we put up with blazing afternoon sun. Shipyard racket bounced around the courtyard like it was in an amplifier. If you think building ships is quiet work, you got another think coming. And they don't shut down at night.

Then there's the port—ever hear a collier being loaded? If thunder is God bowling in heaven, then that commotion is the devil emptying cinders in hell. Also the train yard, where hundreds of trains, carrying coal and freight and passengers, arrive and depart daily. Then you got sirens and horns from cops and cars. Ambulances. Plus everything on the water from tugs to destroyers has horns and whistles. I mean, this was one loud town. Pat said I'd get used to it, and I suppose I did, but it took a while.

I don't mean to complain. Noise means a certain energy, a kind of excitement you had in the early fifties that I doubt we'll see again. Up and down Washington, people sold about anything you needed—furniture, jewelry, notions. There was Sears and Roebuck, Montgomery Ward, and the biggest department store, Nachman's, where I loved to turn things over. We had several theaters, plus Kresge and Woolworth's, and places to eat galore. Antine's, the Washington Lunch, the Sanitary Restaurant. (Who'd want to eat anywhere else?)

A ton of people clogged the sidewalks, especially around 28th where the buses congregated, always in a hurry—but polite. Men still wore hats and tipped them to ladies, you never worried about some punk snatching your handbag, people held doors open for you.

Not like today.

Pat became assistant manager at Johnson's Music on Washington Avenue, right across from the shipyard, between 37th and 38th Streets. It had been there forever, had survived the Depression, and was taking off again. Musicians were back from the war, the instrument factories no longer made gun parts, and everybody wanted to dance.

Street level they sold pianos and sheet music, harmonicas and band instruments. Upstairs birthed a new division that sold electric guitars, tape recorders, phonographs, amplifiers, microphones, anything that married power and music.

Now, all Pat ever played was the radio. We didn't even have a Victrola. But Uncle Sam had trained him to work on anything with vacuum tubes and wiring.

His first day he sold three guitars—two Epiphones and a Gibson. I remember because he was so proud he went around chanting the brands. Lord knows I didn't know anything about instruments. I was a cheerleader, not a band girl.

Early on, he *was* that department—sales, repairs, buying, advertising, whatever. Soon he became division manager, with two people under him. In 1952 they expanded, moved electric instruments next door, and made Pat a partner.

Meanwhile, our nights were busy, practicing to start a family. Pat said you couldn't do that often enough. I didn't mind, either, and we finally became confident enough about money to quit being careful.

Wasn't three months until I was pregnant. Pat was so proud he didn't know what to do, or, for that matter, who to vote for that fall of 1952. We'd been raised Democrats, but Stevenson was an egghead and Eisenhower, despite being a hero, was military and therefore (Pat said) not trustworthy. Funny, I can't recall who he voted for. (I wasn't twenty-one so couldn't vote.)

I wanted this baby so bad I couldn't stand it, for a million reasons. To fill that awful hole after Millie. To give to Pat to negative my mistake. To give to God a sin offering. To balance the books, to make things right so I could sleep again.

But on a cold, stormy day (a nor'easter like we never had in Crawford) I started spotting. December 10, a Wednesday. I was so scared when the wind howled I nearly went berserk. When Pat got home I had horrible cramps and was afraid I'd lost him. Her. It. Another child I'd not see until eternity.

It was like I was trying to keep it in, and God was trying to pull it out, and God wins that every time.

Pat held me all night while wind and I moaned. The next day we went to the doctor I'd seen after I got pregnant. I liked him okay. Bald, skinny, a little bug-eyed, but nice. I left Pat in the waiting room and walked down the hall with a kind, gentle nurse who held my hand while we waited. She, at least, knew exactly what to do and say.

After the doctor examined me—a humiliation I never have gotten used to—he shook his head and smiled.

"Mrs. Allen, I'm sorry. You had a miscarriage. I'll schedule a D&C for tomorrow."

"What's that?"

"I'll dilate your cervix, then clean out your uterus. It's a routine procedure." Not on me, it wasn't.

"Mrs. Allen, I see no reason you can't have a houseful of children. This isn't your first, you're young, you're healthy. You merely stumbled on the path. Stubbed your toe, so to speak."

If there had been lots of women doctors then, I wouldn't have had to listen to such tripe. Here I was, devastated, again, this time *knowing* my child was down the toilet, God striking me once more for my sin. There the doctor was, his smiling male self having not a cotton-picking idea of what bad shape I was in. This was no stubbed toe.

And Pat said "He's right," as if this baby's death was no big deal. Men just don't know. I must have cried all afternoon. And the next day let that doctor scrape my insides like he was seeding some cantaloupe.

Wind never used to bother me. Now I hate it.

I had to get back in church. Pat and I hadn't been going at all—he worked six days a week and said he'd gone so much as a boy he'd not mess with it again. But Sunday morning's gnawing feeling worsened weekly. Something that said reading the newspaper in bed wasn't right.

With so many service people around, you'd think a church that wouldn't look down at a woman alone wouldn't be hard to find. I mean, thousands of men are deployed at any given time. But the big downtown churches didn't make me feel welcome.

I found a little church northside, one where Pat had sold some audio stuff. He said the music guy played piano and guitar, and didn't sound like a Holy Joe.

It met in a one-story brick building that during the week re-trained veterans. For northside the neighborhood was a little trashy. I saw a calico cat like our old friend Blossom on a stoop, staring at a huge banana peel lying on the sidewalk like it was as natural as the brick underneath.

Inside, the place reminded me of a nightclub—except chairs crowded the dance floor, along with an upright piano that had seen better days, a guitar on a stand, a small amplifier, a drum set.

Nobody dressed fancy. Maybe fifty people, more women than men. A few men looked like they'd slept outdoors, and some didn't smell fresh, but they sistered me to death, *praise Jesus, let's welcome sister Priscilla in the name of the Lord.*

The service embraced more music than preaching. Some songs I knew, like "Blessed Assurance," others were new but easy to learn. I'm not much of a songbird but I can make a joyful noise when I'm in the right mood. They let women stand and read scripture, and the preacher, in a tie but no jacket, seemed not to have sin or hell in his vocabulary.

I returned enough times to realize this preacher never would mention hell. This exchange in what passed for Sunday School pretty well showed this bunch's colors:

"I did something I shouldn't have done."

"Sister, God has forgiven you for whatever it was."

"You don't understand. This was *really* bad."

"Doesn't matter. God has forgiven you."

"That's all there is to it?"

"Sure. You don't even have to ask. Ours is a forgiving and merciful God who accepts you just as you are."

That was my last Lord's Day there. I mean, how do you call yourself a church if you don't say a word about sin?

I went back to First Baptist. It might have been kind of a snooty church but at least the preacher said hell is a real place. As I know from experience. Firsthand.

Back then I had sweaty, heart-hammering, horrible dreams. The kind where you wake not knowing where you are, or, for that matter, who. One dream I sorely dreaded—for it returned many times—featured me and Jesus.

Set in the Holy Land, a scene like they used to print on Bible School cards, colors too bright to be real. A beach with a bunch of bare rocks. Water shimmering in the background. A boat draped with fishing nets. Some sheep, a donkey or two, a cow. Gulls overhead. A rag-tag crowd loitering at the left. Jesus off to the right talking to His disciples.

I kind of barged in and stumbled in front of the crowd. My bewildered face was scarred with something like smallpox. I wore a dark gray robe and an off-white head scarf that matched my no-crying baby's swaddling clothes. Hair not washed in a month. The crowd began to murmur. Men pointed. "It is she," some said.

Around a yellow-robed disciple's neck hung a noose frayed from heavy use. He immediately lurched toward me. Pointy beard, green eyes that bored holes through me. He snatched my baby—I screamed—he leered at me, handed me a silver coin with a coiled snake embossed on it. Ran off behind the rocks, my baby yowling, me screaming "Come back."

The crowd came alive, shouting "Sinner" and "Stone her." Sand and pebbles peppered the large stones. The disciples grabbed me, slapped my face, hauled me before Jesus. Whose hair and robe were whiter than fuller's soap could cleanse. A golden band you could hardly bear to look at surrounded his chest. He held a sickle in his right hand. A dark-skinned man so beautiful he scared me half to death.

He looked at me with eyes full of thunderbolts and flames.

"What hath this woman done?" A great voice, like a trumpet of doom. At its sound the crowd hid behind the rocks.

"She hath sold her man child into bondage, Lord."

He loomed over me like a tall cedar. He smelled dangerous, a mixture of honey, musk, sulfur.

"What sayest thou, woman?"

"Lord, that man in yellow stole my child. What must I do to…"

With his left hand he plucked that silver coin from behind my right ear, then held it up for all to see.

"Satan's bargain," he said, eyes bright with swords of sadness and anger. "She hath committed the unpardonable sin."

He said to Simon Peter, a bulky man with a large rusty key dangling from a leather belt, "Thou knowest what to do. Bind her hand and foot, then cast her into the outer dark."

Like a pack of hungry jackals the disciples immediately surrounded me, while the crowd, hoping I was to be stoned, rose and began to break off shards of flint and chert.

I always woke, scared for my very soul, when I saw the first flung rock.

The details varied—my clothes, the crowd, the animals—but the silver coin and the yellow-robed disciple and the terrible majesty of Jesus were constant. This wasn't the Jesus knocking on the door or suffering little children. This was the One who will return, vanquish Satan, and rule the New Jerusalem. They say flee from the wrath to come, but I had nowhere to hide from His judgment.

I was a mess.

The next couple of years Pat buried himself in the store while I kept house and went to church. About all we did together was eat breakfast and supper, read the morning and evening papers, and practice relations. Oh, for a while I told him I didn't want to try again, but soon enough we got back into rhythm. I needed a child. To fill the chasm Millie left.

I figure I got pregnant over Christmas 1953. Counting back from our daughter's birthday—Tuesday, September 25, 1954—it about had to have been Christmas Day. December was the busiest time at the music store—they stayed open until 11:30 Christmas Eve—then closed on the twenty-fifth. The very next day they held an After-Christmas Sale, which lasted until New Year's.

Christmas morning we slept late, then opened gifts around our little tree, not quite what would be called a Charlie Brown tree, but close. I don't remember what I gave him but I got a record player and two LP records. Bing Crosby's *White Christmas* and *Dean Martin Sings*. From Johnson's, of course. We drank Russian tea and went back to bed—sweet time.

For the whole term I felt fragile and scared. Constantly worried I'd never feel her kick—then that she'd stop turning cartwheels inside me. I didn't feel worthy to have her living in there. Still, unlike with Millie, I took her to church, where, after I began to show, women smiled at me (after checking my left hand) and gave me a shower. That part was nice.

When the nurse handed her to me all swaddled in pink I cried a river. I'd never—and never have since—felt so absurdly happy. Relieved beyond belief. Blessed. Joyful. You name it, I felt it. And I knew I could keep her.

I named her Rosemary Pearl, partly after my sweet aunt, partly because I liked the sound. Had she been the boy Pat had hoped for, we'd have called him Steven Patrick after Pat's uncle. But he was happy with Rosemary, who for a couple of weeks was the sweetest little thing. Slept a lot, ate well, was hardly any trouble. You hardly knew she was on the place.

Marie, Pat's mom, bless her, took two weeks' vacation, hopped on the Greyhound, and came to help. (Wanda would have come except—well—more on that later.) But there wasn't much besides meals and diapers for Marie to do. Pat took her to see the Susan Constant, a replica of a Jamestown ship, one Wednesday afternoon, but otherwise we tended to Rosemary and kept each other company.

Of course, the day after Marie left, six weeks of colic set in. None of us slept worth two cents. We tried the usual remedies—swaddling, putting her on her stomach and rubbing her back, holding her upside down, catnip tea—then took the poor darling to the doctor, who prescribed phenobarbital, but I was afraid to give it to her. Pat took it once, but I threw it out after I had trouble waking him for his turn with the baby.

One evening Pat came home and said "Wrap her good. We're going for a ride."

Mr. Johnson had noticed Pat looking worse than hungover.

"Son, what's the matter?"

Pat explained how when he got home I handed him a fussy baby while I tried to sleep, then all night we tagged in and out, Rosemary alternating between screams and sleep. More of the first than the last.

"Hell, son, is that all? I thought you might have been drinking or tomcatting or worse. Here." He fished in his jacket pocket for a key.

"What's this?" asked Pat.

"The key to my Mercury. Go home, put that kid in a basket, lay her in the backseat and ride her around. She'll sleep as long as she's moving. Keep the car until she outgrows this."

So that evening Rosemary went for a ride beside the river, all the way up to Jamestown and back, two or three times, and she was silent as a stone. We looked at each other in the rearview and grinned. I wasn't far behind Rosemary—I napped beside her.

Of course, the second we cut the motor her eyes sprung open like roller shades, then shut again in an angry squall. But we'd had some rest, and within a month Pat brought Mr. Johnson's car back—full of gasoline, oil changed, greased, new points and plugs, washed, waxed, polished, buffed, and shined. It was the least we could do.

Walker always took the last of December off, and he'd bought a Studebaker coupe he wanted to drive on a trip. So they arranged to come for a week starting Wednesday the twenty-second. "We'll help with the baby, see some sights, it'll be like old times."

What old times? None included Pat or Rosemary. Another of Wanda's weird sayings.

Our apartment had a combination living and kitchen area, a bedroom, and a bath. I decorated the living room—a Christmas tree covered half the front windows, a lit-up Santa sat on the end table, strings of cloth gingerbread men draped themselves around the doorframes. A sofa and easy chair pretty well used up the rest of the room.

The day they arrived it was cold, as only Newport News can be when east wind howls off big water. Battleship clouds but no rain. Pat was off Wednesday afternoon as usual. I needed him there and calm, for wind rattled windows like a plague of locusts. Instead, he paced like a wolf in a zoo. I finally made him sit by the window to look for my parents.

About two Pat saw a green Studebaker. "There they are. Lord, the trunk on that thing is ten feet long. If it's full, we're in trouble." He headed out the door like a man ready to face a firing squad.

Rosemary with her bottle, and I with my hot tea ensconced ourselves on the couch. I wanted my folks to see the ideal mother and child. Perhaps to spite my own mother, I admit.

Footsteps and luggage clattered outside as Pat, pretty well out of breath, opened the door. Stumbling in, bags dangling everywhere, he reminded me of Dagwood after shopping with Blondie. "Folks," he said, "come in and meet your granddaughter."

All smiles, Walker set down his bag and kissed my cheek. He knelt before me and stared at Rosemary. "Look at that," he said. "Sweetheart, she looks just like you did at that age. What a beauty. Just look at that pretty little girl."

"Want to hold her?"

"Heck, I might break her."

"Don't be silly, Daddy. Here."

He sat beside me as Rosemary quietly looked into his eyes and grabbed his heart—hook, line, sinker. Forever.

Wanda's bright smile faded as she looked around. "I thought your place would be bigger," she said. When Pat glanced at me I looked away before we both rolled our eyes.

"It's what we can afford right now, Mother. We're fine here. You and Daddy take our bedroom. We'll sleep in here."

"Wanda, look at this beautiful little girl," said Walker. "Your granddaughter."

She touched Rosemary's cheek. "You forget how soft their skin is. Remember to keep your hand behind her head. Better still, move over, let me have her."

She squeezed onto the couch between me and Daddy. Rosemary took a look at her second new relative in minutes and began to cry. No matter how often Wanda said "I'm your grandma," the baby would not be consoled. Maybe Rosemary was afraid of being shut up in Grandma's pocketbook.

Pat and Walker went on about that car like it was a beautiful woman. A 1951 Starlight, it had a rocket ship for a hood ornament. The wraparound back windows and chrome nose did remind me of a spaceship, and Walker had added a spinning chrome propeller right on its tip. He wanted to take us everywhere. But after a cramped Thursday trip to the Mariner's Museum in a two-door automobile, he backed off. I thought we needed to fill the Studebaker's trunk with all our baby stuff, and Rosemary threw up on his upholstery.

After Rosemary got used to her grandparents, we had as nice a Christmas as you can have when you must sleep on the sofa (me) or the floor (Pat). Christmas Day we woke early, exchanged gifts (Rosemary got more stuff than anyone), had a light breakfast, then packed for a trip to Ocean View. The weather had warmed enough to enjoy the boardwalk, we fooled around until Rosemary started fussing for a nap.

Christmas dinner was canned ham, mashed potatoes, and canned peas and onions. Walker and Pat somehow shared Christmas cheer (nobody was yet bold enough to drink in front of Wanda) and Rosemary slept and it should have been the happiest day since she was born.

I mean, how long since I felt embraced by family? Family? I was for a time outcast from Wanda and, by extension, Walker and Grace. Fallen from grace, you might say. Then I was welcomed by father and sister but sort of tolerated by mother—as if she thought I might suddenly become the wild man from Borneo or something. Now, it was me and Pat and Rosemary and Wanda and Walker (Grace having married and moved to California), and we seemed to love each other. A feeling I have tried to recapture—without, I admit, much success.

Rosemary's first Christmas was happy, and I should have reveled in that feeling.

Except I kept thinking about Millie. Her sixth Christmas. Where was she? Who were her parents? What was she doing? Visions of sugar plums, sure, she was in a warm home with a brother or sister by now, maybe both. Or maybe she was sick. Wasting away with some disease because she hadn't been vaccinated. Or dead.

From embraced to abandoned, back and forth, I felt great after dinner but woke Pat when I cried in the middle of the night. Making him wonder if I was nuts. And maybe I was.

The next morning was cold and bright, with frost on the windowpanes. Our radiators clanked and wheezed like some fiend in the basement was whipping its child. Wanda put on an apron and cooked a big breakfast (have I mentioned I wasn't all that great in the kitchen back then?), ham, eggs, biscuits and gravy. Pat wolfed his like I hadn't fed him in months. Then he and Walker layered up and left for a harbor tour and trip to the navy base. Walker seemed as excited as a six-year-old boy.

Wanda and I washed, dried, and put away dishes while Rosemary napped. I had kind of dreaded being alone with Mama—but a girl can make small talk, especially over coffee.

"Nothing like Eight O'Clock. I'm glad you remembered my favorite brand."

"Mama, how could I forget? You always bought the red bag at the A&P." I stirred some Carnation into mine—Wanda always drank hers black.

"So, daughter. How are things?"

"Fine. Pat likes his job, and Rosemary's a happy baby."

"Have you all talked about moving back home?"

So much for small talk. I got up and sat on the sofa.

"Mama, right now, this *is* home. You mean move to Crawford? No, we haven't." I wasn't sure I liked the direction this was headed. I mean, to live in such a small place after what happened between us?

"I wish you would."

"Pat's doing well—even though I don't see much of him—and he likes it here."

"Do you?"

"It's alright, I guess."

"Such enthusiasm."

"Well, it's okay. I mean, it's too flat to stay here forever. But it's fine for right now."

Rosemary began her little squeak before waking.

"I'll fix her bottle," Wanda said. While she warmed the bottle in a pan of water and tested the temperature on the inside of her wrist, I changed Rosemary and gave her to her grandmother, who began to feed her like she did it every day.

My mother looked almost saintly, a really loving smile on her face. For her part, Rosemary studied Wanda like she was the most wonderful thing she'd seen in her three months. A painter could have sold that scene for a pretty penny.

"She's such a darling," Wanda said. "Reminds me of you at this age."

"Was I that good?"

"Sometimes. But you could raise Cain when you thought you needed to." She shifted the baby slightly and looked at me.

"What, Mama?"

"Oh, nothing, really. I just wonder if you've gotten Pat to go to church with you."

"Well, I go every chance I get. But Pat says he went so much as a kid that he stockpiled it. Thinks he doesn't need it anymore."

"He'll come back to it one of these days."

"I hope so."

"Tell me, daughter. Do you ever think of... you know... your other child?"

"No."

My reply was quick and so was her business look, which I'd not seen in a long time.

"I don't quite believe you."

"It's true. Why should I?"

"Because you're his mother. Truth to tell, I think about him every now and then."

"Okay, Mama, I lied. I do think about her."

"So you had a little girl?"

"I feel sure I did, although I can't know."

"Well, maybe someday we'll meet up yonder, as the saying goes, and then we'll all be happy together."

"Actually, I'd like to meet her before that. Or at least know where she is. That she's okay. That would be enough."

"Sweetheart, this here's your own right-now little girl. She'll have to be enough."

When she handed Rosemary to me she gave us both a little hug. And commenced to pour another cup of coffee.

* * *

We got through the rest of the visit without anyone getting cut or shot. Pat's big After-Christmas sale started Monday, which kept him at the store until close to midnight (or at least he stayed that late), and lasted all week, so he didn't see much more of in-laws. The rest of us went to Jamestown that day, which tired Mama so badly she decreed Tuesday to be a day of rest before their trip home. No shopping. No adult objected, and Rosemary didn't care.

Tuesday was one of those tidewater mornings so wet you could wring the air out like a dishtowel. Temperature around forty, sky battleship gray. (Yes, I know, but that was exactly the color.) Walker must have spent an hour lugging bags down those cold concrete steps to the car. When it was packed, Rosemary and I walked him and Wanda downstairs, where we said our good-byes inside. Too cold to take the baby to the parking lot.

"Sweetheart, when will we see you again?" asked Daddy.

"I don't know. Maybe we can find time to come see you this summer."

"That's too long," said Wanda. "You must move back home so we can see this precious all the time." She kissed Rosemary on the forehead. "And you and Pat, too."

"I can't promise, Mama. But I will talk to him."

When their taillights turned onto Washington Avenue I was glad life would get back to normal, but sad to say good-bye—and to have to think about Wanda's demand. Not anything she'd stay quiet about.

I didn't use to fret much about reward and punishment. Never worried about it, in fact, until after I betrayed Pat. Then I gave up Millie to negate the betrayal, which pleased Pat but deeply scarred me. I sought solace in Pat—who, bless him, never mentioned cheating, abandonment, or, for that matter, my trouble baking angel food cakes. The pure ordinariness of life with him comforted me. I could go a whole month, maybe two, not scared my sins would sneak up and bite me.

Rosemary sure helped. What a dear child, big-eyed and, after that first bout with colic, healthy. Pat fell in love with her, of course, and on good days I actually thought Rosemary negated my giving up Millie. As if such a thing could happen. Instead of balancing things out, such acts accumulate over years like a pile of stones beside a vegetable garden. You can't get rid of them, at least not by yourself—which is what they teach in church.

I didn't know that then. Pat and I talked about making a new life in the Tidewater. Of having a bunch of kids, being happy together forever. But, over a few years, that talk became mere air, and in its place sat an ugly two-headed monster—reward and punishment. Mostly punishment. I had sinned—then given up my first-born—and had to pay.

Walker Lance's heart exploded, so to speak, May 17, 1955. A warm Tuesday. He'd been to his truck before supper. Wanda watched him walk up the driveway, stop suddenly—she later said he looked like he'd swallowed a cat—then fall on his face like a broad-shouldered tree. They said he died before he hit gravel.

My father, gone at forty-five. Far, far too early. At times I had wished my mother out of my hair, but never Walker—not even when he installed bars on my bedroom window. That upset me, sure, but deep down I knew he simply wanted to protect his little girl.

Mama called to tell us and to decree we would come for the funeral—me, Pat, and the baby. Especially Rosemary. No ifs, ands, or buts. I said Pat's work might keep him in Virginia but she insisted we find a way.

Grace, who lived way out in Bakersfield, California with her husband, a potato farmer, said after harvest she'd spend a month with Wanda. Mama was happy with that, for she always had different expectations for us girls. If I'd have lived in Timbuktu, she'd still have demanded my presence.

Wanda calmly said Aunt Pearl would take her to the funeral home to make arrangements. Funeral likely Friday. Walker thought funeral flowers were wasted money, so the obituary would say the in lieu of flowers thing. Some folks would send them anyway, she said, but what can you do? She was so matter-of-fact. Was she on something?

After we hung up I cried enough for both of us. It would have been so nice to say good-bye to Daddy. Had I said anything meaningful to him at Christmas? Probably not.

I wonder if the bond between girls and daddies is different than that between boys and fathers. I know my loss was as sharp as a hat pin and, really, still is. We girls loved him deeply, thoroughly, no room for hesitation, despite his absences. Maybe because of them, who knows?

Pat and Rosemary had watched me like a pair of worried owls. When I hung up and began to cry he found a box of tissues.

"What's wrong, Priss?"

When I opened my mouth nothing came out.

"C'mon, Priss, what?"

I finally blurted Walker's name.

"So he's dead?"

I nodded.

"His heart?"

Again.

"Damn, honey, I'm sorry. Did it happen this evening?"

"Yes."

"When's the funeral?"

"Friday."

"Man, that isn't beans for notice. I hope Fred can cover for me."

He led me to the couch, put Rosemary on the floor, and hugged me. It was sweet how Rosemary, absorbed with her cloth Tess doll, seemed to know not to fuss.

"I'm sorry, Priss. He was really a friend to me."

"I know."

"In the morning I'll see about work. A bus tomorrow can have us there early Thursday."

"Right now just hold me. I can't think. Not yet."

I pulled myself together and, even though it was expensive, called Aunt Pearl. I wanted to know about Wanda. Plus I needed "moral support."

"Aunt Pearl, Mama just called."

"I'm as sorry as I can be, Priss."

"So how did you…?"

"You mean why am I helping Wanda? I'll tell you when you're here. It's okay, though. Really. How are *you* doing?"

"I'm still in shock."

"When will you be here?"

"Probably Thursday morning."

"I'll pick y'all up at the bus station."

"We can catch the P&L into Crawford."

"Nonsense. You'll be tired and hungry. Just let me know what time the bus arrives."

After Pat bought tickets I placed a collect call to Aunt Pearl. The operator asked if she'd accept the charges—in the pause before Aunt Pearl's refusal I said "nine-thirty." Cheaper (and quicker) than a penny postcard.

Wednesday afternoon I was in a fog as we boarded a southbound

Trailways. Passengers, hoping some whiny kid wouldn't sit near them, stared at us as we wedged our way down the aisle. But when the bus got up to speed Rosemary's brown eyes closed in sleep like they obeyed some weird law of motion.

We headed southwest through countless acres of peanuts and soybeans in table-flat Eden-fertile country. Fading sunlight painted trees gold as we neared North Carolina. Before changing for a westbound bus at the Durham station Pat and I ate cheese sandwiches, and Rosemary had a jar of pureed peas. My food was flavored with despair and diesel exhaust.

Thursday morning we climbed down looking like, if not refugees, at least Okies. Wrinkled, smelly. But Aunt Pearl, just the person I needed to see, was there with open arms.

"Aunt Pearl, this is Pat."

"I gathered that. I feel like I already know you, Priss has told me so much."

"She sure thinks a lot of you."

"It's mutual. And, Lord, this must be Rosemary. What a treat to see such a pretty little girl. Sweetie, I'm your Auntie Pearl."

Rosemary, of course, buried her face in my arm.

"Well, come on, let's get in the car."

Aunt Pearl hadn't owned one when I had stayed with her. She'd paid a few hundred dollars to a man tired of fooling with a 1950 Nash Rambler Landau. It was essentially a two-door sedan pretending to be a convertible—its canvas top sort of buttoned over the door and windshield frames. We piled into it, Pat and luggage in the back, me and Rosemary in the front.

"Glad it's not raining. This bucket of bolts leaks."

"We're glad, too. Thanks for getting us."

"Don't mention it. We're stopping at the Tastee Diner. Breakfast's on me."

"Man, I could eat a lifeboat," said Pat.

"You might have to settle for biscuits and gravy," Aunt Pearl said.

"Tell me about Wanda," I said. "How is she doing?"

"She broke down when she called. I just kind of let her cry. Then asked if she wanted me to come over. She paused a while—I almost thought she'd hung up. Then she said 'That would be nice,' so I did. Priss, Sis and I are beginning to talk to each other. Heck, I even took her and Walker's suit to the funeral home yesterday."

"Something good needs to come from this. I was worried. Mama sounded so together—too much so for a woman who just lost her husband."

"She told me she felt all alone—scared. Like for the first time she needed a sister. She asked if I could forgive her. And I said I did. And I even think I might have. Oh, and I brought her some little white pills. That helped."

Breakfast that morning was possibly the best I ever ate. We took up nearly half of that little diner, and kept the waitress hopping. We drank a gallon of coffee and used a bottle of ketchup with our eggs and sausage and potatoes. Pat must have eaten half a dozen biscuits and gravy. If I ate like that every day I'd weigh three hundred.

Full as ticks, we headed west on Sand Hill Road. As we went by the Asheville School lake, Aunt Pearl slapped her forehead.

"Wanda wanted a pack of bobby pins. Where can I stop?"

"There's a store across from the Presbyterian church. Pull in and I'll get them, if you'll mind Rosemary."

"I bet me and Pat can take care of the little doll."

They had exactly what Wanda wanted. As I paid the store lady I noticed a boy behind the counter, playing with one of those United States map jigsaw puzzles.

"Is that your little boy?"

"Yes. His name is Willie Lee."

"How old is he?"

"Six in August."

"He sure is cute."

"Thank you. Willie Lee, say hello to the nice young lady."

He sort of smiled, held up Florida, and said something I didn't really hear. I don't know, I felt kind of weak-kneed. Nerves, maybe. An extremely full tummy about to revolt. Something, anyway. The lady gave me my change.

"Are you okay?"

"Yes. No. I mean, it's not you. I'm sorry. My father died Tuesday, and my mother needed these, and I think I was about to cry."

"I'm sorry for your loss. What was his name?"

"Walker Lance."

"Oh, I remember him! He built a house not far from here—about, gee whiz, maybe thirty years ago."

"He was a fine builder."

"Yes. Again, I'm sorry. If I'd known, I'd have given you the pins."

"That's okay. Thanks. I'll go now."

I kind of collapsed in the Rambler, but was back together when we arrived at Wanda's.

Rogers and Sons straddled a line between solemn and gloomy. Deep-pile carpet, heavy draperies, in browns and golds and greens. High-backed sofas with dark wood trim, pillows with a splash of peach or salmon for relief. Forty-watt bulbs in heavy brass lamps. Walker would have said you'd need a miner's cap to get from one room to the other without running into a door.

That day both viewing rooms were occupied. We had the front one, which looked out on a big, fresh-mowed lawn. Rosemary was delighted by a sparrow visiting a bird feeder beside the picture window.

Walker was laid out in a cherry casket with brass handles, scarred hands at his sides. I didn't want to look closely at his face because they used makeup and wax and who knew what else. I really wanted him to open his deep brown eyes, never to look on me again, at least in this world.

The receiving line had Walker's parents first, then Wanda, me next with Pat, then Walker's sisters and cousins. Aunt Pearl played with Rosemary over in a corner. People filed by for nearly two hours, his friends, his barber, the meat man at the Crawford Super, our postman, anyone who had been part of his life. Wanda's friends, too, wearing muted tones and suitably subtle perfume. Church folks I hadn't seen in a while had grown old.

I couldn't say who said what, but I do remember a gray coat button on the carpet underneath the front pew. Funny what you notice at such times.

Pat drove us home in Walker's old Plymouth, the car we drove to South Carolina to be married. Wanda sat in front and I was in the back-seat with my little girl.

Wanda stretched her legs and straightened her dress.

"Well, that was nice, wasn't it?"

"Yes, Mama. He sure had a lot of friends."

"So do I, Priscilla. They sure are a blessing at a time like this."

"Those folks in the other room ran out of friends and closed up early," said Pat.

"Who was that?" I asked.

"Some woman named Blaine. I looked in, closed casket, nobody around. Felt kinda sorry for her, so I signed the register. I guess they'll wonder who the heck Pat Allen was."

"You *didn't*!"

"Why not?"

"I saw her obituary," said Wanda. "She was Presbyterian."

We had two preachers at the funeral home—one, Methodist, to assure us Walker was with Jesus (how do they *know* that?), the other, Baptist, to exhort us to get right with God. And fans, those old-fashioned cardboard ones with an advertisement for the funeral home on them, for it was in the eighties that afternoon.

We piled into the funeral car and followed the hearse, both black Cadillacs with little boxy tail fins, leading dozens of cars, lights on, bound in procession for the Baptist church.

Moles had been working hard where we had to walk down to the tent beside the flag-draped casket. The Baptist preacher waited until we were settled in the rickety folding chairs, then read the twenty-third psalm. After a salute by Army Reserve marksmen and a bugler, they folded the flag into a tight triangle to give to Wanda. The Methodist preacher prayed. Then Walker was lowered into a rectangular hole surrounded by the sharp odor of carnations, flanked by a pile of red clay covered by a black tarpaulin. At the edge peeked a Miller High Life bottle cap. Then it was over. Three men in the background smoked cigarettes, leaned on shovels, and wondered when we might leave.

I took two flowers, one white, one red, to press, and, later, to put in the teeny cedar chest he'd given me for graduation.

After Walker died I started dreaming dreadful stuff—dreams in which he was in all kinds of trouble and I couldn't do a thing about it. Mixed with a recurrent dream of watching a child get run over by a pickup truck. It was always the same kid, a boy of maybe two in a yellow nightshirt—and the same truck, a liver-colored high-fendered contraption. Sometimes my father drove and sometimes Pat but every now and then I did. I'd wake in a chilly sweat. I wasn't worth shooting for hours afterward.

I kind of sleepwalked through the day and dreaded hitting the pillow at night. But gradually I got better. Pat was patient, bless him. We talked a lot, for one thing, and he said another child might get rid of the dreams. I wanted another little girl, too, but wasn't optimistic he was right. I wasn't sure Rosemary had negated Millie for Pat, because something—God or Satan—gnawed my soul for giving Millie up.

Charles Walker Allen, named for his grandfathers, was born with all necessary gear January 15, 1956. I wasn't really disappointed to have a boy—it was just that I knew how to raise a girl. Pat called him "Chuck," which at first I resisted, then figured it was better than "C.W."

Life was good. The kids kept me busy, and Pat's work was going well—they were talking about a branch store in Norfolk. It seemed natural to think about buying a house and putting down serious roots, even though Wanda often got cranked up about us moving "back home." We always had some excuse, at least until I lost the other anchor in my life.

One Sunday Pat reached for me at dawn—I spooned with him and we made love like hungry teenagers experienced beyond our years. Without waking the kids. Or at least they stayed put. I'm so glad our last time was good. It sometimes dulls the pain a bit, except when the memory of it makes me itch. You can't hardly win.

While I got the kids up, Pat scrambled a dozen eggs and fried a half-pound of bacon and toasted half a loaf of bread, which we four devoured. Nothing but elbows and eyeballs, as Walker used to say. Pat liked bacon crispy but always lifted two "limp" slices early for me. Grape jelly, orange juice, milk, and coffee. We four were happy, pleased to be with each other.

It was October 4, 1959. I had yet to tear off September's page from our Greene's Furniture calendar. When I did, I spoke of Halloween. Chuck wasn't really old enough to get excited but Rosemary said she wanted to be Sleeping Beauty. Pat asked how she'd get trick-or-treats if she was asleep. She said he was a silly goose, he would be Prince Charming.

He herded the kids through bathroom stuff while I washed dishes and browned a small pot roast in our Dutch oven. I added water and a quartered onion and a few peppercorns and set it to simmer. Then I cut up potatoes and carrots in a pan of cold water for Pat to throw in so they'd be done when the children and I returned from church.

I put myself together, then finished dressing the kids. Light jacket weather, sunny, bright. It's a mother's job to make kids wear too many layers.

Rosemary had just turned five and Chuck was a tad past three and a half, so we'd found a little Methodist church that had a good setup for children. It almost didn't matter whether I liked it, but I did, and wished Pat would go too.

But he continued to claim boyhood church years would get him into heaven. I sure hope they did.

I nearly nodded off during the service. I mean, I was tired, and my mind kept wandering back to how the day had started, and the sermon was about money. How they needed larger numbers on that sign on the back wall listing last week's attendance and offering totals. My heart just wasn't in it. So after I fetched the kids and started to walk home I was ready for a slow, happy afternoon with family.

Soon we heard a siren, and as we turned onto Washington Avenue we glimpsed a cruiser several blocks away heading toward us like, as Pat used to say, a bat out of hell. Chuck wanted to watch it go by but I herded them inside and started for the fourth floor. I didn't think much about it until the siren stopped and two sets of leather footsteps careened up the stairs.

"Excuse us, Ma'am," a cop said as he passed. At our landing, our apartment door was wide open, but rubbernecking neighbors blocked our view. Rosemary started running for the door and I missed her collar so she dropped her jacket and barged in and started screaming—this was no "I saw a spider" noise, it tore at my heart like a rusty pitchfork. Still, I picked up her coat like nothing was wrong.

Everything was wrong.

Pat lay in the living room floor in a slough of blood, policemen on either side, one feeling for a pulse, the other calling for an ambulance.

It was like I was falling but had a rapid-fire camera in my mind. The coffee table skewed like Pat had fallen against it. Rags. Newspaper. An overturned bottle of Hoppe's. One of his old pistols—the one Walker had given him at Christmas?—in the floor. The sickening smell of pot roast, solvent, and blood.

I corralled Chuck and hugged Rosemary close, which was like trying to embrace a bundle of shrieking sticks. Some neighbors nudged us away from the door, where the policeman who had checked Pat's pulse found us.

"You're his wife?"

I nodded.

"He's alive, Ma'am. We've called an ambulance."

I had no idea how to calm the kids. Chuck really didn't understand but Rosemary was distraught enough for us all. I was simply gripped by the numbness of disbelief.

Two women took Chuck down the hall a ways, as two more tried to console Rosemary. I stood like a cigar store Indian until attendants came for Pat. One policeman helped me outside after I made sure the kids would be in good hands.

We followed the ambulance down to Mary Immaculata. Back in the Emergency waiting room the cop took out a beaten-up spiral notebook.

"Mrs. Allen, this all looks like an accident. But you'll have to forgive me. I have to ask, do you have any reason to think Mr. Allen had tried to kill himself?"

"No, sir. Of course not. We were happy this morning."

"So you and him weren't arguing?"

"No, sir, we didn't do much of that."

"He was okay with his job?"

"Yes, sir. He was happy there."

"What did he do?"

"Managed Johnson's Music."

"Oh, yeah, back up Washington from here. He ever go to church with you and the kids?"

"He wasn't much for church."

"My partner's back there looking for a note or any other evidence to help us determine if this is an accident. Like I said, it looks like one. But we have to investigate."

"I understand."

He finally put away his spiral notebook. I didn't know whether to keep talking. I knocked around in my purse and offered him a mint. He seemed surprised. Then thanked me and started thumbing through an ancient *Life* magazine.

I hadn't seen a crucifix since I was in the hospital with Millie. At least not that I remembered and certainly not the accusing face of Jesus across from us. My first thought was to throw it outside. What good was a Jesus who would shoot my Pat? Then, ashamed of such thoughts, I prayed to Him—or something, anything, anyone who could make Pat whole again.

After what seemed decades a doctor came out and asked if I was Mrs. Allen. His white coat was stained with gruesome stuff. He looked exhausted. (Later I thought, of course, he had done Saturday night emergency room duty in a shipyard town.) His badge said he was Dr. Anderson. A balding, sad-eyed man of about fifty, who took my hands in his.

"I'm afraid I don't have good news, Mrs. Allen. The bullet entered under his chin and traveled through the part of the brain that controls autonomic functions—like breathing. We can't fix this. We have made him comfortable. He'll be in a room soon, and you can see him then."

"So he's going to die?"

"I'm sorry, Mrs. Allen. But, yes. Perhaps within hours." He gave my hands a slight squeeze. "I'm really sorry."

Somehow I managed to call Mama. And somehow she and Pat's mother and Aunt Pearl showed up red-eyed in that Rambler. I doubt Aunt Pearl had ever driven any farther than Black Mountain, but they drove all night and half a day to the apartment. I had left the kids with a neighbor and instructions to look out for a couple of grandmas and Auntie Pearl. Wanda and Pearl kept the kids so Marie and I could stay with Pat.

He lingered three days, during which we sat beside his metal bed and took turns holding his hand. His room was small and windowless. The usual pitcher of ice water and box of tissues. The accusing face, again, over the headboard. An IV drip on a metal stand. A nightlight on the opposite wall cast weird shadows when the door was closed, which was most of the time. Probably a good thing Pat's bandaged head was mostly in darkness.

When his mother took a break, I talked to him. Told him how we had a great thing, and how much I'd miss him, and would he please tell Walker I miss *him* too. And I said how things weren't fair, and one of these days we'd meet again, and all kinds of craziness, like I was sorry he had to pay for my misdeeds. I don't know if he heard—he never squeezed my hand or smiled or opened his eyes. His steady, shallow breathing never varied. But I felt close to him. When on the third morning I felt his cold hand I knew I was alone in the world with two young children.

Aunt Pearl and Mama drove to North Carolina with the kids. Marie and I accompanied Pat's body on the train to Asheville, where he was met by Rogers & Sons. So a week after Pat died we buried him on the hillside among people he grew up with. I took little comfort from that, for within a year I had buried my father and husband—and, I thought, any hope of happiness.

At first I was numb. There's no better word for it. Deeply, profoundly numb. Your soul is numb, like your jaw at the dentist's, except there you await the itch, the tingle, that announces feeling will return—instead, I wanted to stay deadened forever.

Say what you will, it got me through the first weeks, during which Aunt Pearl and I took a bus to Newport News to clean out the apartment. Still, pain barged in. Although I had endured the shock of death and a funeral, I was so messed up I hadn't really taken in the fact I'd never see Pat again. But when we walked into the apartment, a grim certainty assaulted me. I looked at the floor—still dark where his head had lain—and instantly knew I had been permanently abandoned. I sat in the floor and bawled like an infant left out in the weather by its mother, exposed, that's what the Greeks or Romans, maybe both, called it when they left a baby to die.

Aunt Pearl gave me pills that made me numb again in a little while. But at least I could put one foot in front of the other.

Mr. Johnson, Pat's boss, and his wife showed up with two young guys from the music shop, who packed kitchen gear, bed linens, the kids' toys and clothes, and my clothes and shoes, and shipped them to North Carolina. My church's Clothes Closet was happy to pick up Pat's stuff. The cop who had taken me to the emergency room tried to return Pat's pistol, but Mr. Johnson sold him all of Pat's firearms for fifty dollars. Everything else went to the front steps, where it was quickly scarfed up.

Mr. Johnson gave me five hundred dollars. And Mrs. Johnson, a nurse, gave me advice.

"Honey, you can't do this alone. You're not seeing things normally, and for a while emotions will toss you like a see-saw full of splinters. Find a doctor—or pastor—you can trust."

Aunt Pearl and I headed back to Crawford that evening.

I had no real choice except to live with Wanda, me in my upstairs room, the kids downstairs close to their grandmother. Aunt Pearl had gobs of room, but moving in with her would have been touchy. And Pat's mom, Marie—her mourning was too deep for words. A month after Pat's death she joined him in that burial ground—pills, whiskey, whether suicide or accident nobody knew. We laid her last, unfinished, wreath on her raw grave.

I had my doubts about how my kids and Wanda and I would get along, but things went smoothly. I detected very little bitchiness, if that's a word, in her. Maybe sudden widowhood had knocked it out of her, or Aunt Pearl had softened her, or she was still taking pills. Whatever, it suited me.

After a couple of weeks I came off the rails again. I woke in the middle of the night, crying, frustrated, furious because Pat wasn't in my bed. Like he'd snuck off somewhere. I'd be too angry to get back to sleep.

I mean, here I was, living with Mama, widowed, no part of any plan Pat and I ever cooked up. Made me mad as hops. To think he'd abandon me for some cheap slut! Then I'd realize *I* was the slut who had abandoned *him*. This cycle of guilt and rage went on for weeks.

Wanda tried to take me to church, but I was in no shape to go. For one, it was a while before I had the energy to dress up. For another, I stowed tons of anger in my heart. Against God. Jesus. Church. However you want to say it. Why did God's plan include my Pat's death? Especially such a stupid death.

One morning I had slept late (at least I had slept), bathed, and was at my vanity wondering why I needed all those cosmetics. Wanda came upstairs and tapped on my doorsill.

"Can I come in?"

"Sure."

She sat on my bed as I eyed her image in my mirror.

"I'm worried about you, Priscilla."

"I'm okay."

"No, you're not. You're a mess. Which I don't blame you about, don't get me wrong."

I just stared at her. No sense to deny it.

"I want you to do yourself—and me—a favor."

"What?"

"I want you to look presentable this afternoon at two. We're having a visitor."

"No, Mama, no, I don't want to see anybody."

"It's for your own good. I want you and Reverend Bowman to have a talk."

I didn't reject it outright. He'd been Wanda's pastor a couple of years, after the last Methodist reshuffle. Many thought him the best preacher they'd had in decades. He'd sure helped Wanda when Walker died. And for Mama to seek help from a pastor, well, this might be worth it.

"I'll make coffee," said Wanda. "I baked a pound cake this morning. I'll leave you two in the front room. I promise he won't read the Bible to you."

"Okay, Mama. I'll try. For you."

"No, dear, for you. Trust me."

For the first time since Newport News, I put on a dress. Simple, green, more for comfort than show. Just enough makeup to soften hollow eyes.

Wanda met him at the door as I came downstairs. She practically herded us into the front room, which, except for a dusting, hadn't changed a bit. She brought coffee and cake, then headed to the kitchen.

"Y'all take all the time you want. Let me know if you need anything."

He looked about fifty, a little gray in his temples, kind, brown eyes. Navy blazer, neatly creased khaki trousers, light blue button-down shirt. No tie. Black loafers shined within living memory. We held coffee cups like they were ballast.

"Well, Priscilla, this is sort of awkward. But that's okay. We don't have to talk about anything you don't want to. We can talk about the weather or something."

"Reverend Bowman, let me ask a question."

"Certainly."

"When do I start to feel better?"

"There's no way to predict that. Each of us are different. But eventually you will begin to heal. We weren't made to be miserable."

"That's what I am. I don't know how long I can stand it."

Wanda had put a fresh box of tissues on the coffee table. I took one and began to cry.

He simply let me cry until I pulled myself together. No impatience or judgment.

"Do you feel better now?"

"No. Maybe. I don't know."

"You will. I went into a dark night of the soul when my wife died. It's hard. Hard as hell. But one gets through it."

I immediately liked a preacher who would say "hard as hell." We had weekly talks, five or six, in which I told him more about myself than I had ever told anyone. Except about Millie. But about losing Pat, I *trusted* him. He explained what I was going through. The Numb. The steps that eventually lead to acceptance. Not joyful acceptance, but, *damn it all, this is the way it is and you might as well get used to it.*

It took a long, long time to get there, an up-and-down process that some days would let me think I'd make it, others—well, one night it was so bad I decided to kill myself. I held a single-edge razor blade in my right hand, ready to gash my other wrist, when I heard a man's voice say "Don't." It was so stern and clear and loving I looked all around until I focused on Reverend Bowman's card taped to my vanity mirror. Never mind one in the morning, I went downstairs and called him. Bless him, he talked me through it. Said when Elijah asked God to take his life from him, God sent an angel instead. Reverend Bowman said I had heard either an angel or Jesus. Who gave a commandment. That I kept. And when the sun came up, my kids still had a living mother.

I had Wanda's help caring for Rosemary and Chuck, which helped me gradually improve, but still was often tempted to stay upstairs, covers over my head. Or go to a movie and sit through it two or three times. What I was, was depressed. What I said I was, was tired. How long, O Lord? was my constant question.

I can take or leave alcohol, thank goodness. I could easily, like Pat's mother, have fallen into that pit after he died. I mean, it got me into trouble with what's-his-name, so I was leery of it.

I sure needed something, though. I didn't know which was deeper, the hole in my life after we buried Walker, or the one after we buried Pat, or the one after giving up Millie. Those were days when I was painfully aware of my heart's dark chasms.

Of course, I worried about the kids. Rosemary had seen her bleeding, dying father in the apartment floor. (I never was certain what Chuck had glimpsed.) For a while she cried herself to sleep, and woke from nightmares. She moped a lot that first winter and spring, but by summer seemed better. When she started school it was like a light switch flipped on—she was almost immediately happier. Chuck didn't seem as bothered as his sister. Every now and then he'd ask where Daddy was, and seemed okay when I said heaven.

What I needed was time. Gradually—Lord, it felt like it took years—I quit saying stuff like "if only I hadn't gone to church that morning" and got to where I could say, "Pat, I love you, I'll see you someday in heaven," with some hope that heaven was real.

Pat had saved money from each paycheck, and had a little insurance, once they decided his death was in fact accidental. And I had the money from Mr. Johnson, so didn't have to take any old job, selling candy at the dime store (never again!) or taking tickets at the movie theater.

Wanda and Aunt Pearl were happy to babysit, so I took business courses at Cecil's. Stenography, Fundamentals of the Office, things like that. I had learned to type in high school so was fairly fast and accurate. I wanted a job having nothing to do with food, sewing, or child care.

We were all happy—at least the adults—when I got a job, not long after school started for Rosemary—the fall of 1960. (Kennedy was running for president, so Wanda was convinced the Pope might soon move into the White House.) Our church, Fowler Memorial, needed a part-time secretary. Today I doubt a church would hire its own member, but they likely felt sorry for me, Wanda lobbied hard, and I'm sure Reverend Bowman approved. I answered the phone, kept his calendar, and made sure coffee was fresh and hot—and zipped my mouth. It's amazing what people tell you, in Christian love.

A year after Pat's death things were going well enough, but I needed some space, as they say, and probably so did Wanda. She began to encourage me to get out more—to meet new people. Which I took to mean men.

"Mama, I want no part of that."

"Nonsense. You're young, you need to live."

"I'm fine. I'm living day to day. I have the kids. I'm fine."

"You used to love to dance—why don't you find a square dance team?"

"I quit that years ago, Mama. Besides, who wants to hang around a widow with children?"

"Plenty of men. You'll see. Priscilla Ruth, you're pretty, you're young. I hate to see you so... so..."

"Single? Is that the word you're looking for?"

"No. I just meant you need to have fun before you get old and fat like me."

"Oh, Mama, you're not even fifty, and you're not fat. No more of this."

My job didn't pay enough to let me both move out and feed the children, who had become bottomless pits. I was still looking for a real job and a place to call my own. I had my eye on a little vacant house on Beaverdam Creek, close to water that would sing you to sleep. It was owned by Claude Gray, one of our parishioners.

Mr. Gray was a salaried guy at the rayon plant, way up the corporate ladder. Probably the richest man in our church. He'd gone to school at Duke, but seemed to be a nice man. We became acquainted through my church job, and he was always the soul of politeness.

One evening he became an answer to prayer, stopping at Wanda's on his way home from the rayon mill. Which, come to think of it, by then mostly made nylon.

I'd started supper (fish sticks, coleslaw, baked beans, cornbread) and the kids were sprawled before the TV watching *The Lone Ranger* or *Little Rascals* or something. Wanda greeted him and asked if he'd like some iced tea.

"No, Mrs. Lance, I really can't stay. May I speak to your daughter?"

"She's in the kitchen. Go right in."

I was trying to wipe carrot shreds off my hands and tame a stray hair strand.

"Mrs. Allen, I was wondering if we might talk."

"Of course, Mr. Gray."

A well-barbered sixty, he wore a charcoal suit, a white shirt, and red tie, which I wanted to straighten. Dark bags under his eyes spoke of a bad day.

"Our receptionist is leaving next week. Might you be interested in her job?"

"Mr. Gray, that's kind of you to ask. But I don't have much experience."

"In my opinion, experience is overrated. I know you to be a smart young woman, and you present well. If you can handle our church office, you can do anything. What do you say?"

"Yes. I'd love that, sir. But I'd have to see how much notice Reverend Bowman needs."

"As you are quite aware, I'm in charge of the church's personnel committee. Meet me at the plant's main gate Monday at eight-thirty. Hours will be nine to five, Monday through Friday. You will be the first person a visitor will see, the face of the company. I'm counting on you."

"I'll be there. Thanks so much! Will you stay for supper?"

"No, my wife is expecting me. But thanks."

After he left we decided to celebrate. Fish sticks stayed in the freezer—we cooked a pot of spaghetti sauce.

That was October 1960. The next day Wanda and I picked out two suits at Belk's for me to start work in.

I hadn't asked about salary because I didn't figure women could negotiate that. But when he told me Monday what I'd be bringing home, I could have hugged his neck. A good five times what the church paid me, plus insurance. A week or two later, I had settled in enough to take a deep breath and ask, as he was leaving for lunch at the Lake Club, about his Beaverdam house. He smiled, said it needed work, but he'd take care of that. I could probably move in during December, renting at a bargain.

For the first time since Pat's death I felt hopeful. And thankful. A good job—a place of my own next to living water—and enough money not to have to depend on the kindness of relatives.

Life settled down for a pretty long while. Ten years, in fact, during which my children grew, I became thoroughly rooted in my Beaverdam home (by then I was making house payments instead of rent), and Mama mostly behaved. Church and school, scouts and piano lessons, sleepovers and school dances. Rosemary was gentle until she turned fourteen and began to kick against the rules I insisted on. Chuck had great curiosity, was outwardly happy, awkward as a baby giraffe, and wanted to know everything about cars and motors.

Wanda finally learned to drive, and traded Walker's old heap for a Ford sedan. The first time I rode with her she pulled out in front of a pickup, and if its driver hadn't been on his toes he would have crashed my door like the four horsemen. So I rode with her as little as possible.

I bought a Rambler station wagon. I never used its roof rack, but sure filled the car with groceries and kid equipment. Must have put a million miles on it. I lucked into it, one of those deals you feel guilty about later. It had belonged to Mr. Gray's deceased wife. He wanted to give it to me, but I insisted on paying for it. Fifty was all he'd take. That man was such a dear.

Life wasn't always smooth. For years I had fist fights with depression—nothing bad enough to miss work, but some nights I didn't sleep and some days I thought it would take a crane to lift me out of bed. But somehow I managed.

It was worst on the sixes—August 6, Millie's birthday, and October 6, when Pat died. All year those wounds scabbed over, only to be scraped off again on the sixes. They were different—Pat's death was a known thing, an aching loss that mostly produced tears, while Millie's birth was an unknown thing, causing anxiety, which in a way was worse. I always took Millie's birthday off, for I knew I wouldn't be worth a bean.

See, I never slept a wink the night before. And on her day, my heart raced and I stayed short of breath. Always afraid Millie might wander up. Or wouldn't. Always wondering where she was. What she was doing. Always, always.

IV.

Tears of Shelter

Martha Atkins Blaine

I found another blank book like the one Dr. Jackson gave me in the hospital, for after writing in the first one so long, I needed to continue the story, hoping to make sense of what had happened. Not only to me but also to Henry and our adopted son. It's all twined together, I've figured out by now.

We named him William Lee Blaine. I did, anyhow, Henry didn't care as long as the boy got a middle name. William after my mother's father, who she said was kind and gentle, and Lee, because it sounded nice and, after all, we *are* southerners, even if we live in the mountains.

Henry called him Willie Lee, which stuck.

The first week or so he slept a lot. Well, other things, too.

Henry chuckled.

"He's like a sea gull—Eat, squawk, s***, that's all he does."

He weighed five pounds two ounces at birth, and of course they fall off some. I wondered if he'd ever been held by his natural mother, or anyone, for that matter. I'd have bet not.

He was scrawny, spindly-legged, ski-footed. I'd wake him to feed him. Henry said he'd be fat as a bear before long but I wasn't sure. Wasn't sure of anything, except I didn't much want to show him off yet.

I weighed him on our kitchen scales in a basket, and was happy when the arrow approached six pounds. The formula—which I found in *Good Housekeeping*, Carnation evaporated milk, honey, cod liver oil—worked! When I told Henry his son would soon be ready for company, he reminded me Mama Blaine had complained—like she ever did anything else—she hadn't seen Willie Lee yet. I know, I had vowed never to see the old bag again, but guilt—something, anyhow—led me to say okay.

I regretted it the second the stairs protested. Within seconds of her filling the door I smelled snuff underpinned by a stale coal fire. She caught her breath, looked around, plopped down in Henry's armchair. He came in behind and shut the door.

"Well, let me see the little booger."

Standing outside the nursery with Willie Lee swaddled in a blue blanket, I smiled best I could, unwrapped him, laid him in her lap. In that expanse he looked no bigger than a ground squirrel and not half as stout.

"Lord, Martha, you've brought him home to bury."

"Mama Blaine, what do you mean?"

"Well, look at the little polecat. Is he even strong enough to open his eyes? I'd wager he's liver-growed. Didn't Henry say he was yellow when he was borned?"

"What's 'liver-growed'?"

"Hit's when they don't get no exercise. Their liver and lights stick together. You got to stretch them out. If that don't work you pick them up by the heels and shake them good."

Turning him on his side, she took his right hand, pulled it over his little shoulder, and tried touching it to his right foot—*behind* him! He yowled to rattle the dishes.

"Mama Blaine, give him here before you kill him!"

"Here, take him. Henry, you got anything to feed a pore old woman?"

I took Willie Lee to the nursery for a bottle. I might not have been his natural mother but I knew better than to stretch a wee baby! Like something out of the dark ages. Which, I reckon, is where she came from.

The nursery was pretty, walls robin-egg blue with white trim. On the wall above the crib hung a wooden shoe filled with three boys pointing toward a wooden moon. Wynken, Blynken, and Nod to protect my little boy—a place to sleep untroubled and innocent.

After a while he decided fussing, especially at night, was his calling in life. I got so numb from wakefulness that when I did sleep I descended into a nightmare that troubled me off and on for years. It went like this:

By the night light's glow, two men crept into the nursery. Masked like the Lone Ranger, dressed in black, one held a sack in his left hand, the other grasped a blunt instrument in his right.

The bag man wore a heavy mustache. The other needed a shave and covered his head with a pirate rag. The first opened his sack like an evil Santa while the other reached into the crib like a snake after bird eggs. My baby did not stir when touched or even when lowered into the sack and slung over the first man's shoulder.

When they felt my feet hit the floor and heard me scream and seen my shadow they high-tailed it head-on into a solid wall. They turned, one shielding his face with the sack, the other waving a tire iron, daring me to spring.

Screaming bloody murder, I was hell-bound to grab that sack or die trying. If by then I wasn't awake on my own, Henry waked me, we ran to the nursery to find Willie Lee in the Land of Nod. I leaned against the wall, gasping for air, shaking like a deacon with the D.T.s.

"Come back to bed, baby, it's four o'clock, for crying out loud."

I let him lead me back. Minutes later Willie Lee, starved and wet, cried me awake while Henry sawed logs to beat the band.

*   *   *

A newborn isn't for the faint of heart. It's one thing when you're twenty but quite another when you're kicking forty in the tail. Plus, I hadn't had nine months to get used to the idea. After eleven childless years, in the space of three hours I became a mother with a two-week-old baby, a grinning husband, and enough jumbled joy and nerves to burst, like Jesus said, an old wineskin. But I was dead set to muddle through. Women dumber than me had done it.

After a night when nobody more than catnapped, I fixed Henry's breakfast and shooed him downstairs to the garage. Morning was filled with diapers, bottles, formula, doing it all over. After lunch—Henry came up for a quick sandwich, I had a half-can of tomato soup and three saltines—I sat down and told Willie Lee in our spare time we'd bake a cake.

At five Henry found us both asleep in the rocker. He tried to be quiet but might as well have worn horseshoes. Coming up from deep sleep I had no idea why I held a baby.

"Oh, hi, Henry. How was your afternoon?"

"Not bad. Couldn't wait to see my boy, though."

"Take him. I'll put a cake in the oven, then start supper. "

"Won't argue with that. I missed a piece of something sweet today."

He took Willie Lee and cooed at him. Then he shook his head at me.

"You know, if you two sleep all day you'll get your nights and days so mixed up I'll have to sleep in the yard."

That tongue holder I'd ordered hadn't come yet so I bit my cheek and went to wash my face. Shocked by what I seen in the mirror, dark circles under roadmap eyes.

"Ella Rose was right, there's no rest for the weary."

I scoured icebox and shelves for eggs and sugar and flour and vanilla and such. Mixing the cake perked me up a right smart. Henry laid Willie Lee in his lap and made silly faces. Caused me to pine for a camera we couldn't afford. I poured the batter in a cake pan, began to lick the spatula, and all of a sudden got scared. Something gnawing at me like a mouse worrying a June apple. Focused on Willie Lee.

That feeling didn't go away, even after putting the cake in the oven and fixing a quick supper and putting Willie Lee down and, oddly, after

Henry loved me in the dark. Instead of going right to sleep I laid there for the longest time. Fretting.

"Henry?"

"Mmm?"

"I'm worried."

"What about?"

"Willie Lee."

The covers rustled as Henry turned over.

"Talk to me."

"Well, my father was bad to drink."

"Mm-hmm."

"So was my brother."

"Baby, what's your point?"

"What if... all that is catching? Like measles? And our Willie Lee..."

Henry leaned over on his elbow.

"Baby, I don't know much, but that's blood you're talking. Whatever's in his, he didn't get it from you."

"You sure?"

"Positive."

"Then say he won't pick up anything from your mother, either."

"Lord help, he won't inherit that either. Now get some sleep."

Thirty minutes later Henry snored through Willie Lee's first awakening of the night. Long after the bottle, I held my child and wondered what was in store for him. And what might otherwise have come to pass had another woman adopted him. Or had his mother not given him up. I prayed God to deliver him from the evil of our family curse. I searched for—and found—comfort in my child's warm breath. We were still in the rocker when he awoke again, hungry. He *was* gaining weight, thank the Lord.

Some kids start out sorry—they kind of can't help it. They're defective, like a mixer without a bowl. They turn out to be awful adults.

My Willie Lee, though, was good-natured once he outgrew the colic. The very picture of swaddled innocence. When I laid him on a blanket in the backyard he'd kick, flex his little arms, smile at sunshine and shadow. I'd say funny things, like "Breeze in the leaves in the trees," and he'd laugh right out.

We took him to church as soon as we trusted him not to up and cry with the bellyache. Dressed him up, carried him across the road, as proud as new parents ever were. That was in the old building, where the nursery

166

was stuffed in the back with the choir room—there were so many babies you about had to stack them up like in a Catlick church.

I helped keep the nursery because I couldn't yet stand for Willie Lee to be out of my sight. One Sunday Reverend Dixon stuck his head in to ask if I was okay. That sort of scared me. What in creation had I done?

"When shall we baptize young William?"

"I hadn't thought about it."

"We need to, Mrs. Blaine. Sooner rather than later."

"Oh?"

"Original Sin, Mrs. Blaine. We're born with it, you know, but infant baptism is efficacious. If he dies, perish the thought, he won't go to hell."

"Next Sunday, then?"

"I'll put it in the bulletin."

I hadn't thought of that harsh Presbyterian idea of Original Sin in years—and as I rocked my baby I knew I *used* to believe in it. How could I now? Willie Lee didn't cry because he was sorry, he just had the colic.

That Sunday morning, Henry and I stood before the congregation and promised to bring our son up in the nurture and admonition of the Lord. He was precious in his white christening gown—that Henry didn't want him to wear, said he looked like a girl. But I stuck to my guns. At that age they're just babies.

Eventually he started sleeping all night. Like he chose to straighten up and fly right, like baptism helped him turn a corner. For a while I got up every hour or two just to see if he was breathing.

From bottle to oatmeal to baby food, year one took two shakes of a sheep's tail. From crying to jibber-jabber to "Dada" in a heartbeat. I was happy "Dada" was his first word—Henry got the big head so bad he couldn't hardly get in and out the door. Yet I admit to envy, too. I mean, who changed all those diapers?

At his first birthday he wasn't ready to walk, but scooter-crawled fast as a fence lizard. Many an evening I watched him and Henry down in the floor, chasing, being chased, laughing themselves silly.

Henry taught him to hold up one finger when asked "How old are you?" Like teaching a puppy to sit, but we loved to show off our brilliant baby.

He walked at fourteen months and at two could carry on a conversation, with Henry and me, anyhow. Anyone else grinned, looked at us—what did he just say?

I read to him—about the little engine that could, or Mike Mulligan and his steam shovel. Boy, if I missed a word he'd jump on me like a chicken on a June bug. Words were important, even if he mixed them up a tad. Mike Mulligan, to Willie Lee, was Mike Muggalan. But we knew what he meant.

An important word was "adopted."

Early on, Henry and I had talked about that.

"Baby, we got to tell him now."

"I don't know, Henry, maybe we should wait till he can understand."

"No, he'll find out one way or the other. We'll tell how we didn't want just any silly old baby. We picked him out special, from all the kids in the whole world."

"That's not exactly the way it happened."

"It's how we'll tell it."

"What if he wants to know about his real parents?"

"We *are* his real parents. Besides, we love him enough, that won't be a problem."

So from the time he could listen till he said it for himself, we told him we picked him out from a kabillion babies.

"I'm William Lee Blaine. I'm 'dopted."

Said with a sweet smile, all proud of himself.

I guess if it had been up to me Willie Lee wouldn't have had a haircut until the army got him or he started college, one. I kept his thick brown hair clean and brushed so it shone in the sun like a show dog's coat.

One afternoon in May or June of 1951, a warm Tuesday, anyhow, I'd set up the ironing board behind the sofa, where my worn-out wicker hamper harbored a pile of clothes. That was before I owned a steam iron—my RC bottle had a sprinkler head to shake water on the shirts. I'd know the iron was right if steam hissed when steel pressed damp cloth.

The radio was on WWNC and Willie Lee rode Laura—that's what he called his teddy bear—around in a wooden toy truck when Henry came upstairs. That kid's ears, honestly, were keen as a bat's.

"Mommy, Daddy's here!"

I hadn't heard a thing. But I was glad for a break, for soon I'd switch gears to start supper.

In one motion Henry came in, hugged Willie Lee, and gave me notice my little man was about to get his first haircut.

"Baby, I'm taking Buster Brown here for a ride."

Willie Lee started jumping up and down, holding the front of his pants. I poured a glass of tea and wiped my brow.

"Sweetheart, go to the bathroom before you leave. Where you all off to?"

"Barber shop. It's been two weeks since I had my ears lowered, and I'm tired of looking at that mop on this boy's head."

I oomphed like he'd poked me with a sharp stick.

"Henry, do you have to?"

"If I don't, somebody'll put hair bows on him. He's nearly two, for crying out loud."

"Do you have to *today*?"

Henry didn't use a don't-argue look often, but there it was. I snipped a lock of Willie Lee's hair to save in my Bible and shooed them out, tears ponding. When they drove off I bawled like somebody had died. My boy wasn't a baby anymore.

I'd never been inside the barber shop, but I guessed it was dark and tinged with brown, a place where men lied about women, deer, and fish. I didn't want my son in there, but wasn't much to do about that. I had two hours to finish the clothes and cut up a fryer.

I'd just popped the last piece of chicken in the skillet when Willie Lee scampered up the stairs and busted into the kitchen. He looked like he wore messy lipstick, and the loop of a lollipop handle stuck out the corner of his mouth.

He *was* cute. Skin white around ears and neck, hair slicked down on top except for a wispy cowlick disobeying the tonic. Nobody would mistake him for a girl anymore.

I knelt and hugged him.

"How'd he do, Henry?"

"Cal flew him up on the crossboard like he was on an airplane. Willie Lee's eyes got great big when he wrapped his neck and pinned the cloth up behind, but Cal talked to him, kinda like gentling a horse. They were great friends after he let him pick what color sucker he wanted."

Willie Lee showed me its remains.

"Mommy, sucker."

"That better not have ruined your supper. "

My little boy smelled like a trollop. Talcum, hair tonic, cigars, cigarettes rolled into one worldly odor. "After supper it's into the tub with you, young man."

"Aw, Mommy."

"Don't 'Aw Mommy' me. I mean it."

Somehow that smell on my little boy conjured meanness I meant to shelter him from. So I scrubbed him pink with Ivory soap. Late that night I realized the barbershop odor reminded me of my brother Jacob. Made me shudder.

Next afternoon he begged his daddy for another haircut. Cute.

Willie Lee and I had an afternoon routine—I'd lay down with a book after lunch and he'd crawl up on the bed, I'd read to him, we'd take a nap. One Sunday—he'd just turned four—instead of snuggling up he unleashed those brown eyes to bore through my soul.

"Mama, what's a bastard?"

You could have knocked me over with a broom straw.

"Where did you hear that word?"

"At church."

"Did somebody call you that?"

"Tommy."

"Darling, I'm sorry."

I hugged my boy and tried to figure out what to say—and how to keep from crying.

"That's a bad word, honey. You must never say it."

"Like Daddy's bad words?"

"Well, kind of."

"What is it?"

"It means a person whose mommy and daddy aren't married."

"Why's that a bad word?"

"It just is. It's ugly. And hurtful. Promise me you won't ever say it."

He raised his right hand, put his left on his chest.

"I promise. Don't cry."

I couldn't help it—a combination of rage that some little—well, bastard—would call my precious son that, not to mention the hurt I feared he had felt. I wanted to shoulder that pain for him. Tears of shelter, you might say.

Henry got mad as hops when I told him.

"Tommy whomuch?"

"Bob and Nell Joyner's boy."

"That little fart heard that in his own house, I'd bet. I'll have a prayer meeting with Joyner in the morning."

"Lord, don't get into a fight."

"Don't worry, Baby. I can handle myself."

The way Henry told it, he told Mr. Joyner—by the way, an elder in our church—that he held him personally responsible for anything his runt of a boy might say. That if Tommy called Willie Lee a bastard again he would personally beat the stuffing out of Mr. Joyner. Only I doubt he said stuffing. Wasn't the last time Joyner gave us trouble, though.

Mike and Marcia Capps were fellow Presbyterians, younger than Henry and me by about ten years. You wouldn't think we'd have much in common. Henry and I were, well, frumpy, while they were handsome, he tall and broad-shouldered, she tall and sunny as she could be.

But in 1954 they adopted a boy who had been in several foster homes, a five-year-old, same age as Willie Lee. Our kids became best friends.

This took a fair amount of what Henry called guts, for Mike and Marcia were white, and the boy—we all called him Scooter, even though his name was Bob (no middle name, like Henry)—was of mixed-race parentage. He wasn't all that dark-skinned, for his mother, they said, was light-colored and his father was white. Still, this was 1954 in the mountain South. But Mike was a Marine machine gunner-turned-deputy sheriff, and Marcia was a school nurse. They weren't afraid of anything.

I'd like to say Scooter's skin color never caused problems, but I *am* proud to say the six of us might as well have been family, and tried not to let such things bother us. It's hard, though. People can be ugly.

Willie Lee was a whiz at memory work. A good thing, for they loaded him with it at both school and church. He had to recite little poems in first grade, but that was easy—he'd spouted nursery rhymes forever. In church he'd been saying baby Bible verses—John 3:16, the Twenty-third Psalm, things like that.

When he was promoted to the Primary Department, the Sunday School gave him a little pink catechism. The children had something like two years to memorize it—nearly a hundred and fifty questions.

Our Presbyterian kids spout catechism like they guzzle Kool-Aid. I did it in my time, so I knew all that stuff, automatic as breathing. But after Willie Lee I realized Presbyterians, down deep, don't really trust predestination or election. Little ones still have to be baptized and keep the right answers on the tips of their tongues, understood or not.

Question One: *Who made you?* Answer: *God.* I agree, with my whole heart. But the last one is: *What is heaven?* Answer: *A glorious and happy place, where the righteous shall be forever with the Lord.* The first part is surely right, but the older I get the more I wonder about the second. Who *are* the righteous? I certainly don't know—and David says there's none righteous, not one. But maybe little children can sort the righteous from the not.

Anyhow, it's cute to hear fifteen young'uns put their sweet little hearts into it. Belief with no grain of complication.

"Who made you?"

"God."

"What else did God make?"

"God made all things."

"Why did God make you and all things?"

"For His own glory."

"How can you glorify God?"

"By loving Him and doing what He commands."

"Why ought you to glorify God?"

"Because He made me and takes care of me."

Train up a child in the way he should go: and when he is old, he will not depart from it. Another thing I believed before Willie Lee. Solomon may have been the wisest man ever, but I got news for him.

The last two days I have stared at my journal, no idea of what to write next. Dr. Jackson used to say sometimes your brain needs a break. So this morning I decided to bake a cake instead of scribbling.

It's a comfort when you mix things and they come out right. It'll happen most every time in the kitchen. Like that pie I call Simple Simon. Easiest thing in the world. Melt three-fourths of a stick of butter in a pie pan. Mix three-fourths cup of flour, same amount of sugar, same of milk, until it's good and ready. Pour it into the center of the dish. Then add blackberries or peaches or other fruit. Do not stir. Bake for an hour at three-hundred and fifty. Comes out perfect every time.

We did everything to make Willie Lee a decent, Christian boy. And he was. But something happened. Nothing big and sudden, like racket will make a cake fall. A series of somethings, I guess, that you don't even notice. And that's what I have to unravel.

*   *   *

Willie Lee was quiet, stayed in his room a lot during cold weather, spent summers out in the woods as much as I'd let him, down where I'd played when I was a girl. He fiddled around the wading pond and the place he called Schlitz Mountain, where Mr. Whisnant and Miss Elder's brother got my brother drunk. By then those old sots had gone on to their reward—you'd think they'd have died of liver disease, but Mister Whisnant had a stroke and Miss Elder's brother walked out in front of a transfer truck, some said on purpose.

Our side yard wasn't very big, but Willie Lee about wore it out playing football and baseball and basketball. By himself, and with Scooter. He wasn't much good, but he got plenty of exercise and fresh air. Went out for Little League when he was old enough, but didn't make the cut. I wouldn't let him play football—he wasn't big enough anyhow. He'd have gotten smeared, as the kids say.

He suffered the usual childhood diseases—chickenpox, measles, mumps. We avoided polio, thank Jesus, with those new shots—and he never had whooping cough. But he had earaches. I used to warm eardrops—put the glass bottle in a saucepan of water on the stove. I'd soak a cotton ball with them. Made me cry to hear him cry.

When he was five our doctor said to have his tonsils out.

"Does that mean the hospital?"

"Yes, for the operation. He'll have to stay a night or two, depending on how it goes."

"I'll stay with him."

"They won't let you. It's against policy."

"They'll just have to change their policy, then."

But no amount of stubborn, foot-stomping, or whining moved that mountain. The night before his surgery they chased me out at seven. He was laying in bed holding Laura Bear and smiling.

"Be fine."

Which had been something he had said since before he was two. I almost lost it when Henry finally laid a hand on my shoulder and said let's go.

I didn't sleep a wink, worrying about him all scared and hollering for his mother.

Next morning he went to surgery first thing—they wouldn't let us in until two. I didn't know what to expect, but here was Willie Lee laying in bed with a cup of ice cream, grinning like a man who just won the lottery.

"Mama, they put me in a bed with wheels and we rode on an elevator."

"Do tell. What else do you remember?"

"They told me to count backwards from twenty, then they put this yellow thing over my nose and mouth. I made it to sixteen. Then I was back in my room."

"How do you feel?"

"Throat's a little sore. Ice cream helps. They say I can have all I want."

So much for worry. And, you know, he never had another earache.

Mama Blaine keeled over from something—blood clot, or heart attack, or meanness. They didn't find her for a while, which made even me sorry. Nobody deserves to lay dead for days. But Henry's sister noticed she hadn't complained in a while, went over, found her in the kitchen floor, chicken leg in hand. I didn't ask about the smell.

We dressed Willie Lee like for church and went for the visitation at Rogers and Sons. Her casket sat in the big old house's south room, high-ceilinged, floor lamps pointing upwards, heavy velvet curtains with tassels and balls. And the sickening smell of carnations. Which I suppose is better than the odor of a decaying body. I hoped that closed casket was really, really sealed.

There wasn't much snuffling into handkerchiefs, and the whole thing took only a half hour or so. Henry and his family lined up in front of the coffin, shook hands with most, hugged some, glanced at the box every now and then to see if she might knock on the top, demanding release.

Willie Lee shied from cousins and uncles and aunts, but kept coming back to his grandmother's casket. He didn't cry, just looked at it like this whole experience was the most interesting thing he'd ever seen.

I knelt and asked what he was thinking about.

"The last time I saw her."

"What happened then?"

"She called me a shit-ass."

"William Lee Blaine, watch your mouth. What had you done?"

"Nothing."

"She'll not do it again, honey."

He touched the shiny handle at the end of her casket, looked at me like *can we go now?* If he grieved I didn't see it. Of course, Henry, her blood child, didn't much either. It was like a burden lifted.

But you know what they say about still waters. No telling what churned in his little mind.

My boy loved to climb trees. Even when little he'd stand under low limbs and stretch his arms up. I'd lift him and he'd suddenly vanish like some no-tailed squirrel. Absolutely fearless. Henry said Willie Lee was so hard-headed he wouldn't get hurt if he fell. I didn't know so good about that.

I was bad to read women's magazines. Always looking for something to prevent problems with kids. And one year they all had articles about enemas making healthy children. One summer day—he was maybe eight, I called him to come get his enema. I'd given him one back in the spring—he didn't like it, but I didn't think it was a big deal. He'd always been good about coming pronto, but that day he high-tailed it across the road, hid in the woods. I seen his shirt tail disappear like a bird nest in a windstorm.

I scoured the woods for an hour, knew he was up a tree, quiet as a napping owl. So I went home and stewed, waited for Henry to finish what he was doing in the garage.

"Why's the hot water bottle out? You sick or something?"

"I was going to give Willie Lee an enema but he ran off."

"Why, is he sick?"

"It's just a precaution. Kind of like a car. Changing the oil, you know."

"Lord, Baby, he ain't no dang car. No wonder he's hid out. You got to promise never to do that again."

"But it's for his health."

"It ain't healthy for a boy to hide from his mama. Feed him extra prunes or something."

We headed across the road. Down behind Mr. Whisnant's house Henry started calling.

"Come on down, boy. She ain't going to do it again."

Nothing.

"You better say it, too, Baby."

So I yelled I was sorry. We beat through the woods for another ten minutes before Henry stopped.

"Willie Lee, I see you. We come in peace. Come on down, son."

"Darling, I'm sorry. I won't do it again. Where is he?"

Henry pointed into the trees. "Up that pine."

"How'd he get up there? There isn't a limb for forty feet."

"Must have shinnied up that maple, then jumped. He never wanted you to see him."

In 1956, Willie Lee turned seven and Reverend Dixon finally retired. Our new pastor, Reverend Sam Winters, was young and energetic, and I'd say, if we had been Baptist, he revived us. That resulted in a new Educational Building. Classrooms, Reverend Winters's office and a library downstairs, kitchen, fellowship hall upstairs.

Ours was a neighborhood church—many folks walked to it in good weather. We had not only the Elder and Whistnant families but what you might call common people too, car salesmen and factory workers and postmen. Not all Presbyterians are starchy—about half our men wore no neckties. A plumber taught Sunday school next door to a class taught by a lawyer. A good mix, you might think.

It was a friendly place, where Sunday afternoons our boys loved playing dodgeball, softball, basketball, you name it. During summer, Montreat Assembly sponsored programs combining missions and hiking and swimming and such. Willie Lee and Scooter loved going there for a week at a time.

But something tainted the air after 1954. Oh, I know it was bad in Arkansas and Mississippi, but even in our little mountain town we saw troubles. Which touched Scooter, who had become my second son.

I'll not detail it here, except to say that Reverend Winters put together a communicants' class in 1960 that included Scooter. This offended a few old white men, particularly Mr. Joyner that Henry had told off some time before. It ended well—Scooter became a member of our church—but these were tense times. I prayed a lot in those days.

Early in 1961 Henry's arms and legs began to bruise, great big blue-black spots, took forever to go away. I said go to the doctor but he said he wasn't sick—just tired.

The plant's clinic was good—full-time doctor and nurse, several part-timers. They sewed up wounds, pulled fish bones out of throats, set broken bones, did insurance exams, whatever was needed. In a plant working thousands of people they seen anything from infections to cut-off hands, gave anything from tetanus shots to transfusions. I made sure the doctor would see Henry even though he didn't work there anymore, then nagged until Henry seen that doctor.

Home from his appointment he set his cap on the counter and looked at me.

"Doc Brewton says I got to see a fancy doctor. Says I'm a nemic—I don't have enough red blood. When I asked him about Geritol he just laughed."

"Have you made an appointment?"

"Lord, Martha, I got to think about it."

"Think about it, my foot. Tell me who he says to see and I'll get you there."

"Just let me rest a minute, I'll do it."

I ended up making arrangements and marching him to town. I went because I was scared—and to make sure he really went. He was as scared of a needle as a horse is of a rattlesnake.

Dr. Smith's office was in the New Medical Building. People had been calling it that for nearly forty years. A squarish red brick building downtown at the corner of Market and Walnut, it looked big from the street but the lobby made you think you were in a small high-ceilinged box.

As we watched the elevator arrow arc toward us I squeezed Henry's hand, which was cold and wet as a trout.

I itched to disinfect the doctor's waiting room. No telling what you might catch. But before long a clipboard-carrying nurse, she couldn't have been five feet tall, called Henry's name.

They weighed him, took temperature and blood pressure, led us into a small room. Cold, like every doctor's room I've ever been in. Henry sat on the edge of the examination table and looked around like a puppy about to pee in the floor.

"Looks like a torture chamber."

"Henry, don't be silly. This is where you start getting better."

Dr. Smith was a moon-faced man with round glasses and dark, slicked-back hair. I seen right off he knew what he was doing. He asked Henry a hundred questions while prodding here and poking there. Every now and then he'd say *I see* or *Mmh* or *Uh huh.*

"Mister Blaine, I want a blood sample. Also stool and urine. Bring those by the lab downstairs first thing tomorrow. Stop this afternoon to let my nurse take blood."

"What do you think's wrong, Doctor?"

"Mrs. Blaine, anything today would be a shot in the dark. Dr. Brewton is correct, Mr. Blaine is anemic. Figuring out why necessitates lab work. Anemia has hundreds of causes, some trivial, some quite serious. So I want those samples pronto. I'll see you Friday."

July 14, 1961 Dr. Smith ran late. He'd done emergency surgery that morning, they said. But he'd be with us soon. Henry and I went to the window for the view of Beaucatcher Mountain.

"Sure is a pretty day."

"Shame to spend it cooped up in here. You know he ain't going to have nothing good to tell us."

"Now, it's likely something they have pills for."

"No, I got this feeling I ain't long for the world."

"Quit talking foolishness, hear?"

About a quarter till five the nurse came out.

"The doctor will see you now."

He stood in the conference room holding a sheaf of papers.

"Please sit down."

He sat across from us at this shiny mahogany table. Took off his glasses, rubbed his eyes.

"Long day, huh?"

He put his glasses back on, looked at Henry, then me, smiled a little.

"Yes, Mr. Blaine. And it isn't nearly over. But I want to spend as much time with you as is needful. I'm afraid I don't have good news."

I grabbed a handkerchief, took a deep breath, held Henry's hand. It was like we'd been pushed off a cliff and were waiting to fall.

"Leukemia. Acute granulocytic leukemia. An aggressive kind, far into its work. There isn't much I can do. I'm sorry."

It was like right after we fell, God dropped anvils on our heads. I mean, one minute you're anxious, but hopeful, then the next you feel like the world has turned mean on you. Like Jesus went to hell with no return ticket.

"Are you sure?"

He stacked those papers like he hoped something might jump out at him.

"I am certain, Mrs. Blaine. Had we caught it earlier, we might have had a chance. A combination of radiation and arsenic has been known to effect remission. A drug called 6-mercaptopurine shows promise, but never after a late diagnosis. If it were a tumor I could excise it, irradiate

178

the site, and he would have a decent chance. But this is cancer of the blood, specifically of the bone marrow, and we can't remove that, clean it, and replace it so it won't produce cancer cells. I'm truly sorry."

Henry took a real slow, deliberate, deep breath.

"How long, Doc?"

He stood and looked out the window.

"Only God knows for certain, Mr. Blaine. Two or three months. Maybe longer, maybe shorter."

"I don't want nothing to do with a hospital."

"The VA would be free."

"It ain't money, Doc. I just don't want nobody poking and prodding me all the time. You can't rest in a hospital."

"Mrs. Blaine, do you feel you can care for him at home?"

"Of course, Dr. Smith. I'd do anything for Henry."

"It's not a question of 'would.' It's a question of 'could.'"

"Dr. Smith, I've been taking care of people all my life. I'll give Henry what he needs."

"Good. For my part, I will try my best to keep you out of the hospital."

By that time I was crying and Henry's arm cradled my shoulders. Dr. Smith turned and put his hairy hands on ours.

"I'm sorry, folks. I will stay as long as you like. To answer any questions."

"That's all right, Doc. Thanks. Just let her and me be by ourselves."

"Certainly. I'll be around for another hour."

And with that he left us—two penguins on a melting iceberg—alone.

We didn't stay long. What was the good in it? We had parked on Spruce Street, and the Plymouth was hot as blazes inside. We were in West Asheville before it was comfortable in there. I'd sweated through my blouse and jacket and looked awful. Probably didn't smell fresh, either. And somehow I had to be brave.

I remembered our bus ride the day he came home from the service, how happy we were, how excited to be close to each other. 1945. This was 1961. We'd been married nearly thirty years, except for the war, happy times, about to end. I tried not to cry but no use.

He pulled the car to the curb and put his arm around me.

"Baby, don't cry. It'll be all right."

"How can you say that?"

"My uncle had about the same thing. He went quick, with no pain."

"So what?"

"Could be worse."

"Henry Blaine, can you mean that's what you want?"

"It's a sight better than the bloody gravel. Or that stuff where they cut your legs off a foot at a time. I'd a heap rather be dead. Besides, over there—I never told this—I seen men blown apart—and the funny thing, they were kind of lucky. Worse was men with guts ripped out, pleading for their buddies to shoot them between the eyes. At least this way I won't suffer."

"But you're not even fifty. You got to fight this."

"Don't go nowhere. I'll be back in a minute."

He left me in a pile of tears, came back with vanilla ice cream cones.

"Here, baby. This'll make us feel better."

The man has known less than an hour he might be dead by October and he's buying me ice cream?

Reverend Winters was a thick-shouldered man, not all that tall, but stocky, like he'd played football. Which he did, come to think of it, at Davidson College. He wore dark suits and white shirts and was thoughtful in the pulpit, not one to scare you into faith.

Everybody liked his preaching but he would rather read in his study than glad-hand people in the hall. His wife, Peg, on the other hand, just bubbled. Maybe five feet tall, she loved to host circle meetings, sing in the choir, work with the youth. They didn't have children, but she loved them. She seemed closer to Willie Lee than to other kids, maybe because he was adopted.

The day after the diagnosis, Henry and I went on some errand or another. We hadn't been home ten minutes before Reverend Winters knocked.

"I came as soon as I heard."

"Thanks, preacher. It's been a long day. We're still trying to make sense out of things."

"How about cake and coffee?"

"Martha, no thanks. I'm trying to stay at playing weight. Henry, say it's been a rough day?"

"You bet. We've been running from one thing to another, and I don't have much spunk these days."

"Did I understand correctly? Leukemia?"

"Yep. A bad kind. You'll bury me before Christmas."

"Don't say that, Henry. Nothing is impossible with God. How are you all holding up?"

"How would you think? This is awful."

"Martha, it must be. What can I do for you all?"

"If you got pull with the man upstairs, it's time to use it."

"Henry, nothing special. But I pray for you all every day. And will be happy to pray with you this afternoon."

"That would be a comfort, preacher."

His prayer asked for strength and healing, mercy and grace, forgiveness and love. I sat, eyes closed, holding Henry's hand, thinking *this is just words, he means well but it's just words, God can't heal my Henry with just human words.* And then *it can't hurt, maybe words will do some good, it's all we got, is each other and words.*

"I guess your son knows?"

"We figured to tell him today. He'll be home directly."

Like he was on cue, Willie Lee clomped up the stairs. I swear, sometimes he sounded like he rode a Great Dane in steel-toed boots.

"Mom, I'm home!"

He tore into the living room like an awkward calf. He wore a plaid shirt, blue jeans with rolled-up cuffs, one tennis shoe unlaced, ball cap flopped at an angle. Still my goofy little boy—for a few minutes yet.

He nodded at me and Henry, then looked kind of confused at Reverend Winters.

"Hello, Willie Lee. Good to see you."

"What's wrong?"

Henry's smile was bittersweet.

"Son, we got to tell you something. Come, take off your hat and set by your old man."

He glanced at the preacher, then sat on the couch beside Henry, who took a deep breath.

"Willie Lee, there ain't a good way to tell you this. I wish there was. But there ain't."

"Are you sick, Dad?"

We looked at each other. So he knew. Henry nodded, tears puddling in his eyes.

"How bad?"

"Pretty bad, son. I have leukemia."

"What's that?"

"A kind of blood cancer."

"They can give you medicine, can't they?"

Henry shook his head.

"'Fraid it's too far gone for that."

Doubt, fear, anger darted from his eyes like birds ambushed by a prowling cat.

"I don't believe it."

He stood between me and Henry.

"It isn't so. It can't be. Mom, say it isn't so."

I held out my arms but he wouldn't come to me.

"It'll be all right, son. Please. It'll be all right."

He looked at Reverend Winters like he'd been betrayed.

"You said Jesus said if you pray you can move mountains."

The preacher looked like he wished he was somewhere else. Which, I guess, we all did.

"Willie Lee, I did. We pray, but sometimes we don't get the answers we want."

"But the other Sunday you said Jesus said a father wouldn't give his kid a snake if he asked for a fish. And if he's so big and powerful, won't he heal my dad? Or was all that just Sunday morning crap?"

"Son, watch your mouth. My sickness is just a part of God's plan."

"God aims to kill you?"

Reverend Winters started to answer.

"No, son, it's not…"

Willie Lee ran to the door and flung it open.

"If that's how God works, I hate him!"

Slammed the door, ran downstairs crying. I watched him rush across the road into the woods, going to his places. Like I did years ago, only now I had nowhere to hide.

The only way I got through that time was with the help of Boots, Marcia, Peg, and prayer. Which might all be the same thing, I don't know.

It was hard. Besides a dying husband I had what was beginning to be a rebellious boy. We didn't talk much. I fed him, washed his clothes, in return, maybe, he didn't talk back much. Not like after Henry was gone. For Henry hated backsass worse than sweet potatoes.

Peg took the boy under her wing. He started going to the manse every now and then. Really, I didn't mind. Peg was sweet, and I had my hands full taking care of Henry. No, that isn't right—at first, he took right good care of himself. I was simply trying to be brave. Boots and Marcia were my ever present help, while somehow Peg blunted Willie

Lee's anger. And I'm sure she said to spend as much time as he could with Henry, for they grew closer during his illness.

Which I kept praying about. *Let this cup pass. Let me be the sick one. I'd happily swap my health with Henry. You did miracles in the old days, Lord. One more, please. Let this cup pass.* Many a night I went to sleep to that verse. Next morning, nothing new. Phooey, nothing new was a good day. New was always worse.

We did lots of errands, Henry and me. Had his suit dry-cleaned. Bought him a fresh necktie. Went to the Veterans' Commission about death benefits. Henry had burial insurance, so we visited Rogers and Sons. It had been around forever, in a brick two-story house in West Asheville you were sure harbored a family of attic ghosts. The Rogerses had recently added a chapel that promised to be lighter, more cheerful. Right. It had a round stained glass window in the middle of which was a harp with wings.

Bill Rogers, the daddy rabbit, took us into his office, a dark room stacked with cloth-bound double-entry ledgers. He jotted facts about Henry into a spiral notebook—for the obituary. Then we creaked upstairs to pick out a casket.

"Bill, nothing fancy. Pine will do."

He stopped beside a plain wooden-handled box and a white silk liner.

"Henry, this would give you good value."

I couldn't hardly keep from crying. I walked over to an oak casket with brass handles and an off-white liner with embossed flowers.

"Henry, this one's much more substantial."

Henry looked at Mr. Rogers and shook his head.

"No, it's *my* casket. I want pine. And this box will not be open. I don't want nobody gawking at me and saying 'Don't he look natural?' Meaning no disrespect, Bill, but I never seen a natural-looking corpse, not even one you worked on."

Mister Rogers smiled. He'd heard that before.

"But what about the family?"

"Let 'em come see me now. Especially them that owe me money."

There were a hundred things to do, some that really weren't needful. Like Henry had our mechanic mothball our car—said he'd do it himself but was afraid if he barked his knuckles on something he'd bleed to death.

"I don't drive, remember."

"Willie Lee'll be sixteen before you know it and proud to drive this old Plymouth. I'll turn in the tag, cancel the insurance, you can keep it covered up on blocks out back."

Henry's doings about drove me to drink, to tell the truth. I mean, for years I had my routine. Then suddenly I had Henry home, underfoot, getting ready to die. I was forced out of my habits and made to face his death, and I didn't like either one. They say anger is normal after a death. Well, I had it beforehand. I admit it.

On a bad day I asked him if he wanted to go to the hospital.

"Baby, don't put me in any dang hospital. Maybe I'll just go off like an old broke-down dog. Or rent me a back room at Rogers. That way they wouldn't have to drive out here to get me."

"Henry, don't! This isn't funny."

"Didn't mean it to be. Listen, Baby, I'm trying to make this easier on you."

"There's no way for that."

"Sure there is. I got this road map."

"What are you talking about?"

"My uncle Tom gave it to me. See, my father's people got cancer—liver, lung, prostate, kidney—the ones that eat you alive with pain for years, then kill you. Except for Uncle Tom, who had the same thing I've got. See, the doctor said they could do this or that. He didn't want no this or that. He just went to bed in broad daylight. Quit eating, wouldn't hardly drink nothing. Two or three weeks, gone. No pain that he ever let on about. That's a good way to go. So I know how to get where I'm going."

"And where exactly is that?"

"Remember when I studied to be a deacon? The *Confession* says you immediately go to the highest heaven, where you behold the face of God. I reckon Jesus'll be there too. And you know something?"

"What, Honey?"

"I bet me and him will go fishing."

All I'll do if I get to heaven is give Jesus a good talking-to. Which means I likely won't end up there.

*　　　*　　　*

One Friday putting up laundry I found a knife in Willie Lee's dresser. Blade about six inches long, sharp enough to shave with. Leather sheath, dangling from its end a length of shoestring lanyard.

Didn't want to bother Henry with it, but…

"Know anything about a knife in Willie Lee's room?"

"About this long? Leather scabbard?"

I nodded.

"Baby, I carried that thing all over Europe, I wanted him to have it."

"He'll cut his leg off."

"No, he won't. I showed him how to handle it, gave him a good whetstone."

"He's not old enough for that."

"Sure he is. I had worse at his age."

I didn't see that doing anybody a bit of good.

October was warm, and the leaves turned as pretty as I'd ever seen. Nice days Henry'd take his cane—which he said he didn't need but made him feel safer—shuffle downstairs and park himself in a plastic-webbed lawn chair in front of the store. Warm himself in sunshine and wait for the 3:30 whistle, prelude to traffic from the plant. Henry waved at everyone, his friends honked their horns. Sometimes they stopped to chat but as he got weaker they didn't so often. Thinking, I'm sure, that soon he'd not be there. And then they'd not feel guilty for driving on.

Sometimes I'd leave Mary Anne in charge of the store and sit with him and soak up sun like an old cat. Willie Lee too, soon as he got home from school. Boots, too, her shift permitting. But as leaves left and weather got cold he stopped. His blood was thin, he couldn't stay warm.

November 27, 1961, the Monday after Thanksgiving, I woke to bright sun through the kitchen window. Kind of scared me, because I never slept that late. Looked out the window—frost all over, like a picture postcard.

Thanksgiving? A day I tried to be cheerful, but it was a put-on disguised with cranberry sauce. Henry, the color of a discarded winter squash, sat in his recliner, splotches on the backs of his hands, head kind of tilted like he heard something we didn't. We had a house full—Puss and Boots and Tommy and Amelia, Mike and Marcia and Scooter, and us. I'd have settled for a saltine, but they all brought turkey and trimmings. Henry ate one bite of pumpkin pie—his last solid food. The preacher and Peg came that afternoon, but not even Peg could make Willie Lee laugh. We watched football on television, something Henry relished, but he dozed, sort of in and out.

After the game we moved him back into the bedroom. I tried to give him water but he smiled, squeezed my hand, dozed off. He'd not drink again.

I stayed home Sunday, worried he might go during church, which Boots laid out of to be with me. Willie Lee called after church, wanting to spend the night at the manse. I said fine but talked him into coming by to hug his father beforehand. At which Henry smiled again.

I was thankful Henry seemed free of pain.

Anyhow, when I opened the bedroom door Monday morning Henry's face was to the wall and his shoulder was cold. Not stiff. Just cold. He'd gone to be with Jesus.

I didn't cry right off. After all, I'd had a little time to prepare, and his struggle was over. I sat with him a while. When it rushed over me like a lead apron that I'd let him die alone, I lost it.

I called the manse and told Peg Henry was gone.

"I'll tell Will to come right home. He's finishing breakfast."

Not five minutes later he trudged up the stairs like they were quicksand. When he opened the door I held out my arms.

"Son, come give your mother a hug."

"He's dead, isn't he?"

"Yes."

We embraced in the middle of the kitchen and cried a while. Then we stood at the foot of the bed and stared.

"Were you with him… when…"

"No, son. I was asleep on the sofa."

"So he died by himself."

I started crying again. I guess Peg called Boots, for she started up the stairs as Willie Lee touched my shoulder.

"Have you called Rogers?"

"No, son, I wanted you here first."

"I'll call them."

"The number's on the refrigerator."

And, you know, he called Mr. Rogers, then the school to say he'd be out a few days, then sat with me and Boots through maybe the longest morning of my life. It was sweet—but every now and then I'd catch him looking at me like he wondered what kind of person I was.

We had visitation and the service at the funeral home because I couldn't bear every Sunday to remember Henry's casket in front of our pulpit.

Tuesday the family gathered for a private viewing. Henry didn't want that but I told Mr. Rogers I needed a last look. There weren't many— Scooter's family, two of Henry's brothers and their kids, his sister Inez, a few cousins, me and Willie Lee.

"You want to see your father?"

"Whatever's in there isn't my father."

"So you won't tell him goodbye?"

"He's dead. He won't hear me."

"Honey, don't say that. He's with Jesus."

That look, which I seen a lot in the following years, like I didn't have a brain in my head.

I spent a few minutes, handkerchief in one hand, a twist of Henry's hair in the other, Boots's arm around me. After I kissed his cold, powdered cheek, I sat, and the funeral men closed him up. Until the trumpet sounds.

In the chapel underneath that stained glass harp Henry's casket was surrounded by flower arrangements. Willie Lee and I stood in front of it, while Henry's brothers and sisters lined up past us. For an hour and a half, people clutching handkerchiefs filed by, shaking hands, hugging. Folks from the plant, customers, church people, neighbors. Lots of "Sorry for your loss" and "We're praying or you" and, to Willie Lee, "Son, I'm sorry" and "Look how you've grown."

Folks exiting the receiving line sat in pews and talked softly, some pointing at Henry's people and asking who they were, others content to visit with people they hadn't seen in a while. No more interested in leaving than a cat in a sunbeam.

When the Rogers family made themselves obvious, people began to go home. Mr. Rogers asked if I wanted to take some flowers but I shook my head. After Boots drove us home I had to have another bath, for I smelled of every woman's perfume, every man's stale cigarettes. A kind of neighborhood roadmap for the nose. Willie Lee went to his room and shut the door.

To be honest I don't remember much about the funeral except Willie Lee didn't cry at first. Sort of stared straight ahead, like he was watching a movie ten miles away. Scooter and his parents sat with us. Reverend Winters read the twenty-third psalm and the saying in John about many mansions and a choir lady sang "Peace in the Valley." During the chorus a shaft of light lit up that stained glass harp right pretty. I almost smiled, for if Henry was with Jesus he was still joking—I can hear him yet.

"Lord, Baby, it would bore me to death to fly around with a dang harp for eternity."

It was nippy at the graveside—nice sun but a steady coat-tightening breeze. Enough air stirring so you missed the graveyard smell of boxwood. They'd spread a fake grass rug over the mound but missed some red clay clods.

While Reverend Winters talked about dust to dust and the new heaven and new earth and the new Jerusalem and death shall be no more, I wanted to scream at God for taking my Henry.

Then it was over and Mr. Rogers handed Willie Lee the tight triangle of American flag that had draped his father's casket. Then the boy broke down and cried a river.

Boots stayed at the house during the funeral, because even back then thieves read the obituaries. When we came home she hugged us both, shooed me off to rest, fed Willie Lee and Scooter from the mountain of food people had brought, everything from baked ham to Swedish meatballs, green beans to scalloped potatoes, apple pie to coconut cake. Enough for a month for two normal people—or a few days for twelve-year-olds.

I couldn't eat a thing that night but I confess, after Willie Lee went to his room, Peg and Boots and Marcia and I shared a bottle of wine. I don't remember what kind, but it came cold and pink out of a brown ceramic bottle and I slept all night. Without a dream.

Bless these women, they stayed close. I guess they knew fireworks would happen between a widow and her adopted son. I had no idea what to expect. They did.

V.

Call Me Will

William Lee Blaine

Will Blaine. Not William, per birth certificate, or Willie Lee, which Mom and nearly everybody she knows used to call me. Sounds hick, doesn't it? Right out of these backasswards North Carolina mountains. People, call me Will.

Born a bastard, I became a Blaine when Henry and Martha Blaine, Dad and Mom, adopted me. I was two weeks old, they say. I don't remember, myself. But it's the kind of deal where you think you remember stuff even though you're too little when it happened but maybe you saw a picture or heard a story so often you think you remember. I mean, when I was two some kid called me a bastard at church. If I'd known what that meant I'd have whopped him and said I was a bastard for only two weeks. Mom said I couldn't possibly remember that but I do.

Anyhow, I don't remember not knowing I'm adopted. They must have told me before I had my own words.

Don't know much about my adoptive family. Mom kept a store, The Top of the Hill Grocery and Garage, because her dad started it way back when. Her mom was a housewife, I guess. I never knew those grandparents. Dad was chief mechanic at The Top of the Hill. Before that he worked at the rayon plant. His dad was a farmer. I never knew him, but Mama Blaine I remember. She called me a shit-ass. At least she didn't call me a bastard. That would have hurt.

Mom didn't much like Mama Blaine. Really, nobody did. She was what Mom called a pill, I guess because you just had to swallow her. That's the trouble with family, adoptive or blood, if somebody's a pain in the ass you can't divorce them. Which is something I had to learn.

See, I tried to split up with Mom, so to speak. Just thinking about that is pretty weird. Like a broken arm that didn't heal right. After years you kinda get used to it but it still aggravates hell out of you.

I wouldn't exactly call Mom a pessimist, but she is a world-class worry wart. The kind who, when you go for Sunday afternoon ice cream, instead of looking forward to a treat, worries that the glove compartment might fly open. So imagine how she flipped out after Dad died and she had to finish raising me. Nearly damn drove me bonkers and in fact landed her in the nuthouse. That's a story for later. Right now, Dad's on my mind.

When I was a baby Dad "bearded" me, rubbing stubbly chin on my face and belly. I swear I vividly remember him picking me up with callused hands, smelling of Chesterfields and motor oil and outdoors.

The rayon plant he worked at back then had hedges and flower beds and a baseball diamond to maintain, plus about a million acres to mow, not to mention dikes. See, in the nineteen-twenties a bunch of Dutchmen stuck the plant along the banks of Hominy Creek. They built dikes, like beavers build dams—they can't help it. Flat tops, no sweat, but steep sides made Dad have to figure how to mow the dikes without injury to his crews.

He could have been an engineer or something. He fixed anything, lawn mowers, cars, whatever. If he'd never seen it he'd take it apart to see what made it tick—or not—and when reassembled it usually ran again. I used to "help" him, fetch wrenches or sockets and stuff. He'd tinker for hours with a clock, or two-cycle engine, or some valve with a hundred teeny parts. He was patient as a spider.

He taught me how to fish. When I wasn't big as a pup he turned over a shovelful of garden dirt and let me fill a baby food jar with redworms and nightcrawlers. We looked for grubs and beetles under rocks or downed limbs, flushed grasshoppers and crickets from dry grass. Hoppers were my favorites because they spit what he called tobacco juice on your fingers.

We fished down at Mr. Crowder's pond, where I caught bream and bluegills and bass and catfish and once even landed a crappie. There were turtles and water snakes and dragonflies and kingfishers and swallows and herons and bats and frogs galore. I don't think I've ever been happier than when fishing there with Dad.

His real love was trout fishing. He was crazy enough over trout to spend stray Saturdays at the hatcheries at Balsam or Pisgah Forest. Thousands of fish eager to be fed swirled that cold clear water, from fingerlings to teen-aged fish to adult rainbows busting to eat insects and mice and whatever instead of boring old pellets. Mom went with us once, and kept telling me not to fall in, like I wanted to hang out in icy water with a bunch of trout. Dad could contemplate those fish for hours, imagining one holding in a stream where he'd lay a fly in front of its snout. Mom said he was like her mother, who could stare at chickens for hours. Dad said there was a hell of a difference between a bull trout and a stupid chicken.

Dad took me to Davidson River before he got sick, so I learned to stand on slick rocks and cast without hooking a laurel bush, but I never was good at it. He wanted us to hike into the Nantahala Forest and camp. I have pictures of him there after a day's fishing, grinning over a stringer of forty fat trout—you can't find fish like that anymore. Probably my biggest regret—except for what I did to Mom—is that he never showed me that wild water.

In the spring he'd stay a week and return smelling like woodsmoke and ramps and something wild, which I realized later was alcohol. Not on his breath but from his skin, like some folks smell of garlic or paprika He never drank at home. Mom wouldn't stand for it, what with her boozehound brother. But fishing trips changed the rules.

One time he came home late. Mom was worried as hell, having expected him about lunchtime. As she paced I tried not to act nervous so she wouldn't freak. She listened to the radio to see if World War III had started over in Graham County, shuffled from window to window to look for car lights. Finally about nine the old Plymouth rumbled in.

When he bumped up the steps Mom opened the door with a "Where Have You Been?" and he grinned and set that cooler down like it held half of Fort Knox. Finger to lips, he opened it.

That red metal Coca-Cola cooler held a block of ice and a two-foot rainbow, the biggest trout I'd ever seen. Still had a bunch of color. Funny, I have no memory of eating that monster, although we must have, because we never had it mounted.

Fishing wasn't his only religion. Brought up Methodist in Haywood County, Dad met Presbyterian Mom. Something had to give, so he joined Harmony Presbyterian, the little church across from the store.

When I was about ten they elected Dad a deacon and gave him two little books, a blue catechism and a black *Book of Church Order*. Now, Dad read the newspaper, and every now and then a piece in *The Reader's Digest* or *Field and Stream*, but aside from the Bible I never saw him read a book. So it was odd to do homework on one side of the kitchen table and watch him worry those books on the other side.

"They'll make you take a test?"

"Sure thing, son. I better pass it."

He spent about three months making notes about election and predestination and foreknowledge and foreordination, weird ideas I took for granted as a kid. When he was ordained deacon Mom was as proud as if he'd won a county fair ribbon. Maybe more.

My best friend as a kid was Scooter Capps. His real name was Bob. Not Robert, just Bob, given in one of his crummy foster homes. Along the way somebody had called him "Scooter," which stuck.

Mike and Marcia Capps, Mom and Dad's church friends, rescued Scooter from the child welfare system in 1954. The year of *Brown vs. Board.*

Scooter and I hit it off immediately. Maybe by five you can make friends without worry over who has what toys. Of course, it didn't hurt that we were both adopted. Us against the wedlock-born world, you know.

It took guts for Mike and Marcia to adopt Scooter, because in mountain North Carolina they were white and he was Black. But Scooter and I played together, went to church together, spent the night together. Nobody who knew us made a whit of difference between us, and, truth to tell, there wasn't much except hair. His birth mom was fairly light-skinned and his father was white. Wearing a cap, Scooter could pass for a Florida-tanned white guy.

My first brush with Jim Crow was the next year, when we started school. I got to walk to the all-white Sand Hill school, while Mike had to drive Scooter all the way over town to a Black school. It was what white people called separate but equal. It made me and Scooter cry, too, but that was the way things were back then.

You'd think church would be different. We sang "Jesus loves the little children, all the little children of the world, red and yellow black and white they are precious in his sight," which we kids believed—but did Harmony Church?

Mountain churches weren't exactly enlightened about race, although the Presbyterian assembly at Montreat desegregated in 1960. By then Scooter and I went to summer programs and snuck out after midnight to ring the campus bell and rush back before getting caught. Or trekked on predawn hikes up Graybeard to watch the sunrise and sing hymns to Jesus.

But four years earlier, when Reverend Sam Winters became Harmony's pastor, things were different. He replaced a guy named Dixon I don't much remember except he was ladder tall in gray suits with a gold key dangling on a chain. For all I knew he wore that while tending the manse's rosebushes. He preached with such zeal that even somebody wired on coffee zoned out for a nap.

Rev. W showed up when we were seven. He was pretty cool, drove a black '49 shoebox Ford, had played baseball at Davidson College. He wasn't the kind to stand in solidarity with the Little Rock Nine, but was kind, and cared for his flock.

Dad and Mom and I were at Mike and Marcia's when he first visited them. Marcia poured coffee and Mom gave out pound cake and Scooter and I sat beside each other, having been warned to behave. After about six years of small talk he looked at us boys.

"I trust both youngsters have been baptized."

Dad looked at Mike.

"Willie Lee was sprinkled as a baby."

Mike sat his coffee cup down.

"We can't say what happened in the welfare system, but since Scooter's been with us he hasn't. Reverend Forbes never mentioned it."

"Good grief, that's... well... oh my, what if he had choked to death on a fishbone? We'll fix that this minute."

Standing, he took Scooter's hand.

"Marcia, lead us into the kitchen."

Like the people followed Moses we circled the sink while Rev. W sat Scooter on the counter. He made the faucet trickle into his right hand, laid his left on Scooter's shoulder, and dripped water on his head.

"Bob Capps, I baptize you in the name of the Father, the Son, and the Holy Ghost, Amen."

We said Amen and clapped and congratulated Scooter, who best I remember looked kind of bewildered. But at least if he died he'd go to heaven.

For the next five years Rev. W preached us through weddings and funerals and hospitals and new babies and Bible School summers and kid's catechisms and childhood diseases and hundreds of fellowship suppers.

Mrs. W was no wallflower either. More of her later. It's enough now to say she took me and Scooter under her wing. Plus she loved Rev. Forbes's rosebushes.

When we turned eleven Rev. W urged four of us to make professions of faith. Three white kids—one girl, two boys—and Scooter. The way this worked, you took a communicants' class, about beliefs and stuff, then answered questions before the Session, seven old white guys who said whether you got in or not.

Rev. W was no dummy. He knew this fight might cost him his job. He met with Dad and Mike, both deacons. Not that they had any clout. See, deacon and elder were very different. Elders safeguarded what the books called "spiritual government" while Deacons mowed the cemetery and cleaned out gutters. Elders wore suits to meetings, deacons shirt-sleeves. But Rev. W needed Dad's and Mike's go-ahead.

"I'll poll the Session about this. In private."

"Reverend Winters, with all due respect, why not in public? Then they can't change their minds without losing face."

"Henry, if they say no in private I'll have opportunity to convince them otherwise."

"You ain't going to change their minds about that, Preacher."

"Mike, I must try. Unless you all want to avoid the question altogether."

"And tell Scooter his church says he's not welcome?"

"I wasn't saying that at all."

"Oh, hey, I know. Listen, Preacher. You got seven elders, right? They've watched Scooter grow up, he's never, that I know of, been called an ugly name, he's always been welcome, especially with the blue-haired set. But without naming anybody—one or two of those old boys would blackball Jesus because he was a Jew. Does the vote have to be unanimous?"

"No. Simple majority."

"Then unless that Alabama bus burning the other day gets everybody riled up, your worst case is 5-2 in favor. That's worth the risk. They know Scooter ain't no Freedom Rider."

"I still want to talk to them individually. I just wanted to let you all know beforehand."

So he did. Before next Sunday's sermon—on that deal in Galatians about no Jew or Greek, slave or free—he made an announcement.

"Friends, this afternoon at four we begin a communicants' class for all interested in making a profession of faith. Four of our youth have enrolled, and anyone else serious about a decision is welcome."

Six straight Sunday afternoons we studied about predestination and all that junk, a kind of *How to Be a Presbyterian* class. Deacons, elders, presbyteries, synods, all that. We learned there's not one word in catechism or confession about race. Rev. W also coached us on four questions speaking to our particular situation. Which, of course, meant Scooter. Toward the end of June Rev. W pronounced us ready.

The Session holed up in the oldest part of the church, in a one-window room facing the cemetery. No place people our age hung out. The elders sat behind a long wooden table that looked beat up enough to have belonged to John Calvin. That rainy afternoon the room was gloomy as an undertakers' convention.

They brought in a dozen metal folding chairs—the kind that put your ass to sleep in fifteen minutes—for four sets of parents and a curious deacon or two. The room smelled like a bunch of wet, slightly perfumed dogs. They made our class wait in the hall while they started the meeting—late, of course.

Rev. W sat in the middle, flanked by elders who, Dad and Mike said, looked like they had just caught a whiff of rotten squirrel. The preacher called them to order, then prayed.

"Father, your servants are in your house to do your business. Guide and direct us by your Holy Ghost. Keep us mindful to listen to your still, small voice, of reason, of justice, of love. In Jesus' name, Amen."

All muttered "amen"—or at least something.

"Mister Moderator, I have a question."

This from Dad's best friend Puss, that day in shirtsleeves and a necktie.

"Yes, Howard?"

"Do we take the kids all at once or one at a time?"

"Together, Howard. That's the quick and fair way."

"Mister Moderator, I move we consider the candidates one at a time." This from a childless elder, a secret drinker suspected of torturing cats.

Rev. W peered over his cheater glasses and scanned the table.

"Do I hear a second?"

After about half a breath he declared the motion dead for lack.

"Bring in the candidates."

We stood before them, nervous as steers at a stock market.

"Okay, people, relax. This isn't the Spanish Inquisition. You know the five questions."

He led us to agree we were sinners and to pledge to be governed by the church and all that other stuff. Easy enough. Then he sat back in his chair and looked at us. Asked us about election and effectual calling and all that stuff. We sounded pretty good for a bunch of kids.

"Are there other questions for these candidates?" asked Rev. W.

My knees knocked about as hard as rain on the windowpane.

"Then those in favor of admitting these candidates to membership say aye."

There were six.

"Any opposed?"

The nay came from the suspect elder, who never once looked at Scooter or me.

"The ayes have it. Congratulations, folks. You will appear before the congregation next Sunday. I expect no opposition to this vote. A formality, really. This meeting will adjourn after prayer."

Afterward the nay tried to shake Mike's hand.

"Nothing personal, Mr. Capps. A man has to vote his convictions."

Mike stared at the hand like it was a copperhead in a leaf pile.

"Tell my son that, sir, not me."

196

The elder put on hat and raincoat and left.

Rev. W was wrong. That week the disgruntled elder called all the deacons except Dad and Mike and thought he drummed up enough support to go to Rev. W and demand either he postpone presenting all of us together or leave Scooter out. Either way, there would be no trouble.

"What kind of trouble are you threatening me with?"

"We can take this to Presbytery."

"Ah. A grievance. All because I choose to follow Jesus."

"No sir, because you value your own agenda over those of the faithful."

"I see."

"I don't think you do. Preacher, you're messing with a way of life that's worked for generations."

"Sir, that may be. But times are changing. We need at long last to do what is right. I'm sorry, but I'll present all four Sunday as, by the way, your board directed me to do."

"You'll regret this."

"I'll take that chance."

Sunday morning Mike covered the front sanctuary door, Dad the back, giving out bulletins and greeting everyone. The pews were fuller than usual, with several butts we never saw except at Christmas and Easter. Mom, never much of a songbird, sat in the choir beside Marcia to look the crowd in the eye.

After announcements and prayer and the Apostles' Creed we sang number fifty-four, "There's a Wideness in God's Mercy," which says God's mind is a heck of a lot bigger than ours. Then Rev. W asked us four to stand in front of the communion table. I looked that bunch over. You could tell who was against Scooter—they looked everywhere but at us.

Rev. W asked questions, we answered in unison.

"My friends, I present these to you as candidates for full membership in this church and the Church Universal."

"One at a time!" Someone I'd never seen before yelled.

Rev. W looked him straight on.

"This is a worship service, not a business meeting. The Session voted to instruct the church to accept all. Now, what say ye?"

After a silent moment several loud, male, old voices said nay. Like rusty horses.

Then most of the congregation stood, choir first. Mom and Marcia led them down to offer us, as they say, the right hand of fellowship. Behind them all except the nays lined up. We shook hands for five minutes, during which I saw eight or ten soreheads head to the front door. Good riddance, as far as I was concerned. They missed a good sermon.

I didn't start out to be a mechanic. It just kind of happened. I mean, Dad was always teaching me something. First, I guess, was in the garden. I'd "help" by putting bean seeds in the rows he'd lay off. Then he'd let me cover them with a hoe. I thought I was hot shit when he let me run rows with the layoff plow.

Then he brought home this second-hand tiller. Lord, he was proud of that machine. Best I remember it was green, with a horse-and-a-half Briggs motor. The crossbar was kind of gray with Choremaster in raised yellow letters. You started it with a crank rope. Throttle on the left handlebar, clutch lever on the right.

Delightfully loud, it had four sets of front tines and a metal bar on the back meant to be a layoff deal but only kept it from pitching backward. Thing would bog down in heavy dirt and just plain stop if it hit a sizeable rock.

He took a couple of laps with it, grinning except when it tried to throw him to one side. I jumped up and down, dying to run it by myself, so he got behind me and "helped" steer. I wasn't yet strong enough to manage it by myself.

But I learned, when we put it to bed for the winter, to drain the gas and change its oil and clean the air filter and replace the spark plug. I could gap a plug at the age of six. He noticed that.

I kind of shifted from garden in the summer to garage in winter. When I was little I fetched tools while he worked on cars. Learned which weight ball peen hammer to whack a ratchet handle to loosen a reluctant nut, learned the difference in metric and English sockets (the rayon plant was Dutch, so a few metric tools migrated to The Top of the Hill), learned where he kept a flywheel puller. He taught me how internal combustion happens. And one day—I think I was nine—he brought home a dead lawn mower.

He set it on the workbench and looked at me like he'd given me the keys to Fort Knox.

"Make it run, son. Make it run again."

That thing looked like a cooter. Rusty, bent in weird places, wobbly wheels. I spent many weekends taking the motor apart, cleaning everything, putting it back together. Cleaned the carburetor, put a new kit in it. New gaskets and all. New Champion J-8.

It cranked right up, but ran a little lean. Adjusted that with a screwdriver. By that time Dad had heard the motor and stood outside the garage door with a look on his face that made me as proud as a prizefighter with greasy fingerprints.

"Son, you can fix that, you can fix anything."

So he taught me about points and plugs. Grease fittings. How to open a radiator without scalding myself. Later, how to change out belts, how to fix a carburetor. Bleeding brake lines, replacing lining. Changing bulbs and fuses. By eleven or twelve I could pretty much fix anything having to do with a car.

Then there was diagnosis. Like your motor makes a weird noise, runs a little rough? Put the flat end of a crowbar on the running motor, lay your ear to the crook, and you can hear a bearing about to go. A busted valve spring. A ring about to ruin a block. As good as a stethoscope. Eventually I got good at it.

Then Dad got sick.

That's when I quit believing in God.

See, the God I don't believe in has nothing better to do than sit on his ass and "plan" everything. Like one day he sees Henry Blaine and says *I'll give him leukemia.* Or, worse, from the beginning of time he knows this good man will die way too early and doesn't or won't or can't change that. Crap, any way you cut it.

God works in mysterious ways. Right. The mystery is how anybody believes in a God who says *Ask and it shall be answered* then pays no attention to constant prayers like Mom and I offered. Oh, we prayed, out loud, in church, silently, at home, under our breath, in school, I was poster kid for *Pray without Ceasing.* Didn't do a damn bit of good.

It happened so quickly. I mean, he was diagnosed in July and died right after Thanksgiving. That isn't right.

The day Dad told me how sick he was, I blew up at Rev. W about God and everything. I stormed out for the woods, pissed off, scared, not knowing what the hell to do. After an hour I found myself on Sand Hill Road at the manse, where Mrs. W was working in her flowers.

"Will, what's wrong?"

"It's Dad."

In a second I went from fury to heart-shattering desolation. She took off her gloves and ran over and hugged me.

"Whatever this is, Will, we'll get through it together."

See, maybe because they didn't have children or something, Mrs. W and I were close. Nothing weird. It was like she knew what I was thinking and I could talk about it. And she called me Will.

So she held me while I cried like a faucet. She was short and even at twelve I leaned down into her warm hug and in a few minutes my cry turned to hiccups.

"Damn it, I'm sorry."

"Don't worry, Will. What is Henry's trouble?"

"He's about to die."

"Oh, dear. What…"

"Leukemia. A bad kind."

"Lord, son, here, sit on the porch. You want to talk about it?"

I shook my head.

"Then we'll be quiet together. You shouldn't be by yourself right now."

For a couple of hours I doubt we said a dozen words, just watched bees and hummingbirds work her zinnias and black-eyed Susans, and followed birds at the feeder and cars and trucks going by.

Rev. W drove up and waved and went to the back door. If he had shown, I'd have apologized, but I guess he decided to let her handle me.

By suppertime I was okay to go home. I don't remember what Mom fixed, but, too raw to talk, we ate in silence.

That was Friday, July 14, 1961. He died Monday, November 27. A hundred and thirty-six days. I just wanted to hang out with him, but he made a list of stuff to do and divided it among the three of us. I mean, anything from draining the Plymouth and putting it on blocks to choosing a damn casket.

It about drove Mom up the wall, and me too, sometimes. See, we couldn't be upbeat. No *It's a good day, let's have a picnic.* He didn't allow sadness, either. Even-steven, no matter how we felt. Because, he said, either he'd beat cancer or be with Jesus. Either way, a winner.

One Saturday morning he poured a cup of coffee—he liked it black and strong—and told me to get a root beer from the fridge. Mom was working on something in their room. We sat at the kitchen table. I tried to smile. See, this was after we all knew he'd not beat it.

He looked at me through coffee steam.

"Rough stuff, huh, son?"

I nodded, afraid to speak for fear I'd break down.

"Nobody ever said life is fair. It ain't in the Bible, anyhow. For what it's worth, you're bearing up."

I took a swig and nodded.

"Son, I want you to do two things. One, take care of your mother. Can you do that? Not let anything happen to her?"

"Yes, sir."

"And two, go to college. Make something besides a wrench jockey out of yourself."

"But Dad, I like to work on cars and stuff."

He raised his index finger, which always shut off protest.

"We're promising here, son. Cross your heart?"

We made the sign. He set his cup down with a shaky hand and smiled.

"Okay, bud, we're pledged. If you don't do what you say I'll haunt hell out of you. Understand?"

Mom came out and looked at us.

"What are you two up to?"

"Martha, the boy and I are just sealing a pact."

And that was the end of that.

It wasn't just the three of us. Puss and Boots helped with the list, and Rev. & Mrs. W visited a lot and I had Scooter, of course. He kept me sort of focused on schoolwork and on weekends we played one-on-one basketball or just walked through the woods.

Mom used to tell how when she was a girl a hundred years ago there were all these paths through the woods where she walked without seeing a soul unless she wanted to. By 1961 you couldn't go a hundred yards without stumbling on a house being built. Scooter and I didn't mind, because we loved playing on heavy equipment parked for the night. We even started a yellow dozer one afternoon but got chased off by some wet blanket adult. We always came home with pockets full of nails and screws and other neat stuff.

And we carried BB guns. We really wanted to kill a crow. That never happened—if you had a rifle they wouldn't show, and if you didn't they crowed at us. They're pretty smart.

Those woods are almost gone now. We didn't know we were seeing their destruction. But those trips got me away from the crap at home.

The garage kept me from going totally nuts. Getting lost in an engine got me through October. By then we had worked through that crazy list. If anyone was ever ready to die, it was Dad. He'd go out a winner. And leave me and Mom losers. Complete bummer.

I spent the night he died at the manse. I should have stayed home, but Mrs. W offered and Mom was too sad to insist I hang around. It was the Sunday after Thanksgiving so we didn't sing "Come Ye Thankful People Come" or any of that crap. I called Mom from the church office and she said okay but come see your father first.

For a day or two Dad had mostly slept. I stopped by to change clothes. "How is he?"

"About the same. Kiss him goodnight. He'll like that."

He lay in the middle bedroom. Dim light, cloudy day, untouched water glass on the bedside table, the sickbed smell of stale breath and disinfectant and yellow mums.

I bent down and touched his shoulder, cold under his pajamas.

"I'll be at the manse, Dad. Good night. I love you."

When I kissed his clammy forehead he gave the tiniest smile, then stopped breathing. I thought *Jesus he just died* but in a few seconds he inhaled, really shallow, but alive. I choked up and hugged Mom and got the hell out.

Did I know it was the last time I'd see him alive? Probably. I mean, at the manse we grilled hamburgers and watched Ed Sullivan and played Chinese checkers and I slept like a damn rock but I kinda had to know.

Monday morning as I brushed my teeth the phone rang.

"Will, it's your mother."

So I knew who and what and why and Mrs. W drove me home. I was kind of numb. I mean, I didn't cry that day. In fact, after I hugged Mom I called the funeral home folks and the school. Aunt Boots had shown up to fix breakfast, and I started to step into the next couple of days like he'd have wanted.

Like I said, I'd renounced God but a combination of Mrs. W and the garden gnawed at my infant atheism. She kept showing me little things she said were God's blessings. Flowers, birds, all that. And being in a garden makes you at least mindful that some force makes things obey the *be fruitful and multiply* deal.

But the visitation was full of *He's in a Better Place* and *You'll see him again* and *You'll understand by and by* and it was all I could do not to laugh in their Presbyterian faces. I guess they really believe that malarkey. Not me. I mean, I saw him that morning, dead as a flatiron, and his face didn't say he'd seen Jesus or some bright light. It was like, damn, what have I stepped into?

Mom wanted me to look at him laid out in the casket but I wouldn't. At the funeral I insisted Scooter sit with the family. I didn't cry until it was over and Mr. Rogers handed me the flag that had draped his coffin. I suddenly knew the next years were just Mom and me. Oh, Jesus.

This stuff is still hard to talk about. I mean, all that happened years ago, when I was twelve and had no more idea of who I was than my cat Sally. No, Sally knows she is on earth to take naps, suck the heat out of the room, and eat cat food. Me, I didn't know beans.

With Dad they buried the boy I'd never be again. Mom wanted me to stay twelve forever, yet depended on me for grown-up things. I felt stretched on some medieval rack, torn between child and adult. Which I didn't like worth a flip. I was stuck.

I guess in the nineteenth century a boy could haul off and raft down the Mississippi, but 1961? I wouldn't be free until I drove, after enduring four long years. And then Mom would have to give me the keys.

Stuck. With an unlucky woman, surrounded from birth by a family of lushes. Her dad drank himself to death and her brother hustled down the same road before his kid killed him. (My cousin, the murderer, another story.) She adored a man whose mother became a cross to bear for decades. She likely thought children would make all that okay, but no go. Then I turned out not exactly a comfort, especially after Dad's early death.

Winners at life—like President Clinton—say people make their own luck. But I severely doubt Martha Blaine made hers. Who would conjure all that up?

Others say luck, phooey, it's all God's will. Mom is in that camp. She somehow believes in God's providence. Whatever.

Still, she is superstitious. She will not leave a building by a different door than where she entered. Will not give gloves or knives as presents. Believes a bird in the house means a death will come pretty darn soon. She's a pessimist who takes pains (ha!) to ward off bad luck.

Dad was an optimist who carried a buckeye (to ward off rheumatism, not that he lived long enough to get it). He picked up sidewalk pennies only if Lincoln stared at him. He planted beans and cut toenails by the signs, all that weird stuff. Would not lay a hat on a bed. Kept a lucky buffalo nickel in his wallet. Said a man can't be too careful.

So if I'm a bona fide mess, I came by it honest, an inheritance from adoptive parents that included a ton of mountain superstitions and warped ideas about how God and luck and the world work. And for all I knew, my bio parents were even stranger than Mom and Dad. That nature vs. nurture stuff? I had plenty of nurture, and eventually needed to find out about nature. But not immediately.

The first couple of years weren't awful. Aunt Boots continued to prop Mom up. She drove, so when Uncle Puss rode the bus to work she saw that Mom got around. Aunt Boots made sure I remembered Mom's birthday, and helped Mom in ways I probably couldn't even think of. Uncle Puss took me bowling, and tried to teach me eightball until Mom figured out that was best done at a poolroom.

And Mom had a network of maybe a dozen neighbor women who stopped by at least once a week. They refused to let her pine away.

On my side, Mrs. W kept pointing me toward the light in the world.

She and I, well, that's hard to unravel. Looking back I see I was a little in love with her. Not that I said or did anything about that—she was my pastor's wife and I was a kid. But she was pretty, and pleasant, and the only adult female who didn't threaten to remake me. She didn't smother. She heard and accepted my anger toward God.

Besides that she was a hell of a teacher. She loved Bible stories, and kept me reading them even after I'd rejected Jesus. She taught the senior high girls' Sunday School class—this was before women taught older boys—and at times she and I read and talked about David or Samson or Jacob. Mom would hardly have let me drop out of church, but at least Mrs. W kept me interested in going.

Then they damn moved.

I suppose I should have expected that. After the Harmony Four deal, several families moved their membership. But the suspect elder felt called to make Rev. W's life as miserable as possible. He couldn't chair a Session meeting without a fight over something—from participating in the community Thanksgiving service to ordering a new range for the fellowship hall. The old bastard never got enough traction to bring a grievance to the Presbytery but he flat knew how to devil a fellow enough to make him want to shoot him.

Not that Rev. W packed heat. He was as forgiving a person as I ever met. But I expect a time came when he thought *screw this, I'm looking for another church.*

See, Methodists shuffled preachers around every four years, so folks didn't get too attached to them. But Presbyterian pastors tended to hang around a long time. Except when they didn't. Trouble is, they never announced leaving until on the verge of it. And they never move to a smaller or poorer church. It's the old story:

Pastor comes home, sets briefcase down.

"Honey, I've been offered the pulpit at First Wherever."

"Dear, that's wonderful. You'll take it, of course."

"Well, I have to pray about it."

She disappears into the bedroom. He follows. She has opened a suitcase.

"What's this?"

"You pray, I'll pack."

I doubt it went down at the manse that simply. Still, I felt betrayed. My best adult friend, here one Sunday, gone the next. I never saw her again.

When your first real love is your pastor's wife... well, that's best left unexplored.

Thirteen that summer, about to enter seventh grade, I hadn't had much truck with girls. I mean, I didn't officially like them until sixth grade, when Dad got sick and I searched for comfort anywhere. Before that it was mostly No Girls Allowed. We boys shot marbles at recess, or, when teachers' backs were turned, played stretch with pocket knives. Shoved each other around, told bad jokes, that kind of thing.

But in fourth grade my teacher's daughter, also a fourth-grader, came daily after school to our room to wait before going home. June's hazel eyes and brownish bangs and lovely long neck were suddenly powerful enough to make some dorky kid, namely me, volunteer to clean blackboards and dust erasers.

Our cloakroom, a dark high-ceilinged narrow hall connected to the neighboring classroom, had coat pegs and a bench where we took off galoshes. In winter it stayed crammed with jackets and toboggan caps and all the earmuffs and crap mothers made us wear. A perfect hiding place.

June's mom chased us out of there several times. Not that we were doing anything much besides tickling each other and giggling but I remember in the midst of wet wool and mildew, her sweet lilac hair. Sometimes I dream we're no longer fourth-graders and her hair smells so fresh—but I always wake before we kiss. Really pisses me off.

In sixth grade I fell for a new girl, Lynn, who wore impossibly dark hair in a ponytail. Her skin hinted of Cherokee. I dogged those deep brown eyes like some pitiful pup. I mean, I could have broken my face running into a post or something.

Harmony Presbyterian held a hayride that October, because a deacon had a tractor, trailer, and spare hay. I invited Lynn, who, to my delight, accepted. The air, tinged with woodsmoke, was cold enough to be what Puss called "scrooching weather." When Lynn and I paired up in loose hay I laid my head in her lap while she played with my hair. I thought I'd died and gone to the softest heaven.

After Dad died Lynn's father was promoted again and she vanished as quickly as she had appeared. I moped for weeks, and decided not to fall for another girl who came from off.

I mean, Sand Hill kids' parents worked at the mill or sold cars or something. Nobody got transferred, for Pete's sake.

The next fall some Harmony wet blanket—perhaps the pain-in-the-ass elder—decreed we'd ride on bales, not loose hay. Scratchy, upright, in the wind, in sight. Which sucked.

The pinnacle of elementary education was the Great Big Eighth Grade Party. Because some of us were kind of backward—I mean, this *was* the mountains in 1963, when people still killed hogs and squirrel-hunted—they decided we must learn to dance. This teacher from town came to do some serious hillbilly improvement. Tall and thin, he dressed like a fairy and brought a fancy record player and a bunch of footwork charts. For several weeks after school we learned foxtrot and waltz and cha-cha. At least we could touch girls without getting whopped.

My first date was a big deal. New scratchy suit, dark socks, shined shoes, corsage for Diana, just about the sweetest girl there. She had a turned-up nose and cute freckles and sandy hair. I couldn't now say what she wore, but surely patent leather was part of it. Aunt Boots and Mom drove us to the school, where we danced and sweated and drank punch made from lime sherbet and ginger ale. I expect we ate crustless white bread chicken salad sandwich quarters, too. On the way back I desperately wanted to hold hands with my date but Mom kept turning around to ask dumb questions, which Diana cheerfully answered while ignoring me.

The first girl I really kissed was Teresa. Talk about cute—you could hide in her dimples. Her crooked little smile tore me to pieces, and if you didn't grin when she laughed you were seriously ill.

By ninth grade I was embarrassed to have to ride a bike, but it did provide freedom. I made a circuit around Sand Hill on my red and chrome two-speed Schwinn, prowling back roads and what was left of the old woods Mom loved.

Teresa's house was on my route. If Mom had known, she wouldn't have let me go within six miles of it. Her mom was divorced, for starters, and drank beer. Not that she offered us any, but... They had a color TV and a stereo with cool records and a rec room, where Teresa and I danced, alone, lit only by the TV.

She taught me the twist and watusi and all, but she especially enjoyed a slow dance to Ricky Nelson's version of "Unchained Melody." I say "dance" but it was mostly swaying around and holding each other for dear life. She enthusiastically taught me all kinds of kissing niceties. For a glorious summer every chance I got I rode down there after supper to talk and dance and make out, after which I'd ride home for a hot date with Minnie Fingers.

I'd had my own room forever. My nursery had been next to Mom and Dad's bedroom, kind of in the middle of the place, then after they decided (I guess) not to adopt another kid, they moved me into the end room on the south side. I loved having two windows.

It used to be Mama Blaine's room. I think Mom was afraid to move me there but Dad convinced her there'd be no cooties or bad vibes. I'm sure she scrubbed it to the bone and repainted before I moved in. A kind of Presbyterian exorcism.

I pretty much kept the windows open unless it was a downpour or cold as whiz. Kept me healthy—hardly ever took a cold. Long term? Well, between what the rayon plant and the paper mill in Canton spewed into the air, our window screens rusted away every couple of years. But, so far, so good.

I guess it was a typical boy's room. An old metal bed painted blue under the window on the west wall, a bookcase on the north wall, desk to one side of the south window, dresser and wardrobe on the east wall. Next to the door on the north wall was a terrarium on a wooden table. Depending on the season and what I was into, it housed a toad or snake or something. Plus snails. Beside the bookcase Mickey Mantle grinned at me from a poster.

The bookcase held a Bible, Dad's old *Book of Church Order* and *Westminster Confession*, a Boy Scout manual, a *World Almanac*. I had a couple of model airplanes, a football, a baseball and fielder's glove, two arrowheads, and a chunk of milky quartz the size of a tennis ball.

I didn't hide much in there, for Mom was, well, nosy. I kept three or four dollar bills in the *Almanac*, and, after seventh grade, two rubbers in an old wallet in a jacket I seldom wore.

By then I'd mostly figured out the sex thing except how in the fire you put together a willing girl and privacy.

I mean, you heard about sex young, even back then. One day in the third-grade lunch line, Kate, who had a big brother and therefore access to filth, whispered in my ear.

"Know what 'fuck' means?"

I mostly heard breath.

"What did you say?"

Again, about the same.

"Spell that."

"F-U-C-K."

"No, I don't."

"It's when a man and woman go naked in front of each other."

"Why?"

I was Presbyterian, and lacked imagination.

Kate giggled her skinny ass off, likely thinking me dumb beyond redemption.

I guess then I figured sex had to be a little more complicated than that, and maybe a lot more fun. But over time you hear jokes and see an occasional *Playboy* picture and you got a decent idea of what to do with your increasingly unruly pecker.

Wasn't long after Dad passed—that next summer, I guess, when one night I was reading Zane Grey—I was really into westerns in those days. I heard this gentle tap, tap as Mom opened my door a little.

"May I come in?"

"Sure."

She had this funny look on her face. Anxious. Still wearing her supper apron, and worrying a piece of Kleenex to death.

"Son, can we talk?"

This was weird.

"Sure. What about?"

"Well, you know… about how babies happen."

She sat on the edge of the bed, still giving that tissue hell. I figured to let her off the hook.

"I'm pretty sure I know about that, Mom."

"Well, good. Because, well, you're getting older… I guess I really want to know... do you know how to keep from it?"

"From...?"

"Having babies."

"Mom, it would be pretty gross if I had a baby."

She crammed tissue crumbs into her pocket.

"That wasn't what I meant, and you know it."

"I think I know how to be safe, if that's what you mean."

"You better do more than *think* you know, young man. It's so easy to lose yourself and, well, next thing you know you've got a girl in trouble and both your lives are ruined."

"We could just get married."

"Willie Lee, it's not that simple. A child changes everything. Forever."

I couldn't help what I said next.

"So I ruined two people's lives?"

"No, no, not at all. I've told you, your birth mother knew she couldn't provide for you, and loved you enough to give you up for adoption. That was hard to do, but she knew it was best."

"So she wasn't glad to get rid of me."

"Heavens, no. she sacrificed her feelings as a mother so you could be cared for."

"How do you know all that?"

"Your case worker told us a little about your mother."

"Like what?"

"Like that she was eighteen or nineteen, had a high school education, that's about it."

"So you kinda made the sacrifice thing up."

"Son, you put two and two together. You put yourself in her place. And there are things women just *know*."

"What about my... bio father?"

"He had some college. That's about all I know."

"So he knocked her up..."

"Willie Lee, please don't be so crude."

"So he split, right? Got out of Dodge?"

"I suppose."

"So do you know where she is? My bio mother?"

"No idea. Listen, son, this isn't why I came in here. I've said before, you're the best thing that ever happened to your dad and me. God wanted you to be our little boy. But you're not so little anymore, and I just needed to talk about the birds and the bees."

I scooted over and put my arm around her.

"Come on, Mom. I don't even *have* a girlfriend."

She hugged me and stood, tears about to spill. She resurrected another tissue and wiped her eyes.

"Willie Lee, I love you."

"I love you too. But I'd love you even more if you'd call me Will."

"I'll try. Will."

"See, it's not so hard."

She smiled and left. I'm certain we were both glad that was over.

Laura James, my first serious girlfriend, was a grade behind me. A freshman with cat-green eyes and a sweet smile and great curves, she wasn't much for flashy earrings or charm bracelets. Oh, she wore what we called a virgin pin—a silver circle about the size of a fifty-cent piece—and a thin silver necklace with a cross I envied because of where it got to hang out. But, really, she didn't need decoration.

Laura's dad was an engineer at the plant, where they made a big deal between hourly production employees, like Dad had been, and salaried office types, like Mr. James. A status thing. (Kind of like the difference between elder and deacon.) Some hourly guys rented one-story houses on teeny lots in the mill village, just across the road—they walked to work. Salaried people got two-story homes on the hilltop—none of them hoofed it to the office. (The houses on the lake, where muckety-mucks like vander Kaaden and Moritz lived, were even bigger and sat on a half acre.)

Mom actually supported my getting a drivers license, to free Aunt Boots from so many errands. Whatever. I'd take that if I escaped the house on weekends. I wasn't hopeful. But after I took Dad's Plymouth out of mothballs, Mom actually let me go out on dates. Maybe the next few years wouldn't be so bad.

I loved that old car, a 1949 four-door sedan. It originally had a six-cylinder motor and three on the column. Green, somewhere between olive and moss, except the right rear fender was gray primer. Dad bought it new but soon swapped the motor for a V-8 with a four-barrel and three on the floor. It was pretty easy on fuel until you romped it, which sucked gasoline like flushing a commode. I mean, that car would mortally fly. I tied a squirrel tail on the antenna and ordered chrome exhaust pipe extenders from J.C. Whitney and, for the hell of it, a big Wild Woodpecker decal—basically Woody with a cigar clenched in his teeth, like birds have teeth—for the rear deck. Cost five dollars and eight cents with postage, but worth every penny. (The squirrel tail was free.) I called it the Streak. Sure, it was redneck as hell, but a machine to put fear into the hearts of any girl's parents, for the backseat was big enough for a ping pong match. Or whatever.

I had no real hope Laura would go out with me. I mean, there was the car thing, and the social class deal, too. Not as bad as those love-across-the-tracks songs like "Patches" or "Dawn," where either the girl or the boy was too poor to hang with, but it was real, so it took a month or more to screw up my courage to ask her out. I was working Saturdays at the garage, so it took a whole day's scrubbing to make my fingernails presentable.

I guess she had seen me coming, so to speak, because when I invited her to the game she didn't say she'd have to ask her mom or anything. Within three months I asked her to go steady, and she said yes. I was amazed.

Not that we went anywhere much except school and her house, one of the big brick ones at the crest of the village. Its entry had a piece with coat hooks and a long mirror. Beside it sat an umbrella stand. My first time there, Laura showed me three framed paintings, or prints, or what-ever on the opposite wall. One I kinda recognized, a lah-di-dah blue-suited boy. Laura nudged me in the ribs.

"You like them?"

"I guess. Tell me about them."

"Well, the first is by Gainsborough. Beside it is one of Monet's water lily studies."

"Looks like he needed glasses."

She laughed and held my hand.

"He was an Impressionist. They all broke away from Realism."

"What's this dark one?"

"The pair over there is Don Quixote and Sancho Panza. You know that story?"

"Windmills, right?"

"That's part of it. *Don Quixote* is Mother's favorite book, by the way."

"What's that in front of them?"

"A dead mule."

"Why?"

"It's a scene from the book. Don't ask me how it died. Daumier painted it."

"Your mom must have a weird sense of humor."

"Shh. She's in the kitchen. I'll introduce you."

Which wasn't too intense. She was nice, certainly not the kind to let a fifteen-year-old girl run loose. She was cool, though, with us hanging out in the den, where if we were too quiet she brought us a plate of cookies. They had this big-assed sofa where we spent lots of Saturday nights watching TV and smooching and talking. Laura was more into the talking part, but, hell, she wore a hint of Wind Song and had the smoothest skin and I didn't mind a bit. I was in love.

My first Saturday evening there we were making out, not watching *The Lawrence Welk Show*, when she corralled my hands and settled into the couch beside me, her wonderful eyes searching mine.

"Let's just talk. I want to know all about you."

"Like, what? I mean, you know what I do at school and all."

"No, I need to know *who* you are. What you're thinking. What you believe."

"Oh. Well, I think you're really cool."

"Silly. I mean *really*."

"I can tell you what I don't believe."

"Okay."

"I don't believe in God."

She looked at our hands with a flicker of doubt. Pouted those pretty lips.

"But *I* do."

"It's a free country."

"And I'm pretty sure you do, too."

"Why?"

"Because you have this huge need for love. Look at how you hold me. You're like a big thirsty sponge."

"You don't seem to mind."

"I don't, if you keep your hands under control."

"So what does this have to do with God?"

"God is love, right? Really, what you're looking for is God, not me."

"So you're saying I don't want a steady girl?"

"I'm saying all real love is interconnected. What we ache for in each other is tied up with a search for meaning. It's not all physical, although that's part of it. It's to find God. To find what we are here for. To discover *who* we are in relation to all the world and heaven too."

"You kill me, girl. I've never met anybody like you."

She was deep like that—always connecting stuff I'd never have put together. I mean, what sixteen-year-old boy uses Sunday School language to talk about the ache in his pants?

Starting tenth grade I'd barely thought about life beyond high school, except to feel guilty because I'd rather be a mechanic than go to college. But when Laura and I talked about college, I saw she was eager, and if I had a chance with her I needed to be, too. Plus it would make Dad's ghost ease off.

"So, where do you want to go to college?"

"Girl, I don't know. Somewhere pretty far from here."

"Why?"

"So Mom won't breathe down my back."

"She's not that bad, is she?"

"Wait till you meet her."

"I want to go to Wake Forest."

"Isn't that really expensive?"

"Dad says I can probably get a scholarship."

"What do you want to study?"

"I'd like to do pre-med. I want to be a doctor, except I might have to settle for nursing."

"You could practice on me, either way."

"Silly. I just meant the deck is stacked against me because I'm a girl."

"You sure are. It's the main thing that attracted me."

"Cut that out. I'm trying to be serious."

"So am I. Listen, If you want to be a doctor, who'll stand in your way? I sure won't. You might find a cure for cancer or something neat like that."

"It's not that easy, Will."

"I bet you'll make it. You're smarter than any guy I know."

"But what about you? What will you major in at your far-away college?"

"I don't know. I'm not much good at math. I kind of like history, but I don't know what you do with a degree in that."

"Oh, any number of things. Teaching, for example."

"Like I want chalk dust on my clothes for forty years."

"Okay, you could be a journalist, like Upton Sinclair. Or you could be a lawyer."

"After you become a doctor, could I be your lawyer?"

"Sure, Will. I'd like that."

Hell, law school sounded pretty good, and if it held Laura's interest I'd keep talking it up. Why not? It was a hell of a long time until senior year.

*   *   *

"Why don't you invite your girlfriend to church, then she can eat Sunday dinner with us. That would be nice."

I didn't know so well about that, but Mom's "why don't you" was a command. My job, I knew, was to be calm and, at least for the moment, not mention atheism or anything.

Unless you count a hot dog at the football game, it would be my first meal with Laura. For all I knew, her folks ate porterhouse steaks every night. Or went out. She talked about many things, but food wasn't foremost.

In a light drizzle I picked her up at ten-thirty. The time suited me, because I didn't have to go to Sunday School. Laura was lovely, as usual, in an ice blue dress and navy raincoat. I wore my suit, a brownish tweed thing that itched me to death if I had to wear it more than an hour.

"You don't carry an umbrella in your car?"

Dang. I wasn't sure if we even owned one.

"Here, Will, we'll take this one."

A green ceramic barrel by the door held three or four. So I got Laura to the car without messing up her hair, which looked, well, kind of stiff, but I didn't mention that.

Mom had been cooking since last night, so wasn't at church. But the blue-haired set oohed and aahed over Laura, and I felt proud to sit beside such a beauty. The preacher—Rev. Barnes, who had succeeded Rev. W—was his usual boring self, but Laura smiled at his lame jokes and seemed interested in the sermon, which, for all I knew, was about some big yellow dog. I might have been proud, but was also flat nervous.

Fortunately, it had stopped raining when we got out, so I didn't have to do the Sir Walter Raleigh thing. After we crossed the road I walked up the stairs behind her and reached around her soft shoulder and opened the door. We were pretty much assaulted by the warm smell of baked ham and yeast rolls.

"Please come in. Willie Lee, don't stand around like a knot on a log, take her coat and let her make herself comfortable."

Mom was wearing her company apron—instead of her stained everyday deal this one was mostly white, with navy rick-rack around the edges—and she wore no hairnet.

"Mrs. Blaine, I'm Laura James. It's a pleasure—I've heard a lot about you."

Mom had that "I bet" look for just a second, but recovered well.

"Willie Lee talks about you all the time. I think he might like you."

Laura blushed and made sure her hair was in place.

"What can I help you do, Mrs. Blaine?"

"Not a thing. You two wash your hands, then sit down. It's about ready."

Man, was it ever. The centerpiece was a Hostess ham with some kind of brown sugar glaze. She had scored a diamond pattern all over it, with a clove in each diamond, with pineapple slices on top. There was a big bowl of lima beans, a Corningware dish of baked candied sweet potatoes topped with little marshmallows. A dish of baked macaroni and cheese, a bowl of stewed okra and tomatoes. Beside each plate sat a pear salad garnished with grated Velveeta and Duke's mayonnaise. Plus a basket of rolls, and all the butter and jelly and pickles and iced tea you could hold. I had to give it to Mom, she knew how to lay a feast on you.

She made me pray over it, which didn't take long, but it took a good five minutes to pass things around the table. Between *oh that looks scrumptious* and *I haven't had this since forever* and *my mother never serves this* we were kind of watching each other. Mom didn't like how I loaded my plate, but didn't squawk. Laura was careful not to take too much but I could tell she liked mac and cheese more than lima beans, and she didn't know so well about one dish.

"Mrs. Blaine, this… sure is colorful."

"Why, child, that's okra and tomatoes. You must never have it at your house."

"No, Ma'am. I think I've seen it at the S&W, though."

"They put sugar in theirs. This is better."

So she took a serving.

While we ate, Mom asked about the sermon (it was about the lost coin), and asked if Mrs.Cole was well enough to come back to worship (she apparently wasn't). She asked about Laura's sisters (one, a senior, kind of put up with me, and the other was in college so I hadn't met her), about their dog (Fluffy, some white pain-in-the-ass pug-nosed thing), about what books she liked (everything from Poe's poems to *Silent Spring*), that kind of thing. Every now and then Mom got up and refilled a bowl, and kind of stared at Laura's plate, in which a small untouched serving of okra and tomatoes was half-hidden by a wall of marshmallows.

Laura was watching me, too, which I realized after I had loaded a hot yeast roll with half a pat of butter. You can't bite into such as that without a serious outbreak of melted liquid so I put it down and let most of it mingle with the limas and stuff before attempting to eat it. I managed not to embarrass myself too badly.

As if we weren't full as a bunch of ticks, Mom had baked a chocolate cake and Aunt Boots had contributed an apple pie. We had to eat some of both—plus ice cream. After that, Laura offered to help with the dishes. That scored points, I could tell. Mom protested, but only a little, and gave her a clean apron so not to ruin her blue dress. I hung around to dry, just to make sure the conversation didn't get out of hand.

When we finally got in the car Laura scooted close to me.

"Your mother is so sweet to have me over like this."

"She just wanted to look you over, that's all."

"So did I pass the test?"

"I guess. Heck, I don't know the rules. It's a first time for me, too. I'll let you know in the next day or two."

"I won't eat for a week."

"Bet you will."

"No, seriously, Will, slow down. You don't want me to throw up in your car."

So I did, and she didn't, and that night I called to see how she was feeling. And to apologize for stealing her umbrella.

That October Laura's mom let her go with me and Scooter to a church music thing at the Presbyterian assembly in Montreat. Turned out, it was one of those Sundays when you can't stand to be indoors. When Scooter and I pulled up at Laura's house she came out, hair gleaming in the sunshine, and waved to her mother. At first she rode shotgun in the Streak, but I stopped at the school to rearrange her and Scooter in the front seat. I wanted to brush her leg, accidentally, of course, as I shifted gears.

That lovely leg was wrapped in white jeans, the rest of her in a light blue Oxford cloth blouse and a kind of tan cashmere sweater. I thought I was the luckiest guy in the country.

We headed east, windows down, engine exhaust in the air, radio blasting the Stones's "Satisfaction." At the end of the expressway I laid down on the horn in the tunnel and roared out US 70, slowing at the highway patrol station and speeding by the VA hospital and gas stations with Indian head chenille bedspreads hung out to attract all the Yankee leafers heading our way, tourists bent on spending money in the mountains. Soon we passed the old red hotel in Black Mountain and turned left toward Montreat.

I toned things down as we neared the campus gate, for Montreat didn't care for loud. We drove by a bunch of big dark cedar-shake-sided houses and circled Lake Susan with its PLEASE DON'T WALK ON THE WATER sign and parked down by the auditorium. Inside, people were setting up a choir platform on stage while bunches of chaperoned kids wanted to be most anywhere else. We picked up programs to prove to parents where we'd been. I had no idea what to do but it didn't include two hours of indoor church crap.

The oldest campus buildings, like the campus gate, were faced with local creek rocks, making them dark and, well, knobby. Cut stone on the new stuff tried to blend in but pretty much missed. Laura's green eyes fell for the campus. It didn't hurt that red and gold leaves floated to the ground like spangles, and the creek made a beautiful racket. She was happy to plop down on the rock wall beside it and listen. Somehow I thought better than to pop out my transistor radio—I just sat beside her. I figured if we got too moony on Scooter he'd take a walk or something.

"Don't you love the music of tumbling water?"

"Yeah, it's cool."

"Our rector calls this living water. He says this sound is why Jesus was baptized in a river. It's the only thing Baptists got right."

"Ha! I was sprinkled. Scoot was too. Man, tell her where you were baptized."

"In our kitchen sink."

"You're kidding."

"Serious as a switchblade."

"Why?"

"It was the closest water, unless you counted the bathroom."

"I don't understand."

Scooter kind of grinned and examined his knuckles.

"Well, I was adopted when I was five, right?"

Laura nodded.

"Nobody had bothered to baptize me. When the new Rev came to visit he kind of freaked about that so sprinkled me in the kitchen."

"That is so fascinating, Scooter. Tell me more."

"That's about it."

Scooter's eyes said he was about to have some fun.

"Man, you told her yet?"

"Told me *what*?"

I shook my head. Some kind of chorale ended and applause floated over the creek's noise.

"I've been meaning to, but haven't…"

She grabbed my hand.

"What, Will? I'm dying to know."

"Sweetheart, I was adopted too."

She glanced from one faceful of brown eyes to the other like *were we for real?*

"Wow, that explains why you don't look like your mother. I just figured you took after your dad's side of the family. This is so, so cool."

"Really?"

"Sure. Think of it, you both might have a whole 'nother family. People who look like you. A shadow family, right? You know, that sort of goes about its business not aware of you at all. No, that's not right, your mother has to wonder where you are, what you're up to. Maybe your dad, too. I mean, your mom might have married and have a family so you have brothers, sisters, cousins, aunts and uncles, too. Ever wonder about that?"

"I got plenty of family, thanks. How about you, Scoot?"

"Well, if I found out my old man was rich or something…"

"Do either of you know where your mother is?"

We shrugged our shoulders.

"What if they lived around here? I mean, you might run into your mother at the A&P! Or this summer you might have played a pickup game with your brother. You can't mean you never wonder about that."

"So you could be my half sister?"

She shoved my shoulder.

"That's sick. I'm serious, Will."

"Well, yeah, I think about it, but not enough to do anything about it."

"You will one of these days. Until then, this family will be waiting for light to hit them. Gee, I wonder where they are. Someday you *have* to find your birth mom."

"Well, not right now. I mean, I'm not Oliver Twist or anything. Mom's a pain in the ass but she's not mean. Besides, she wouldn't understand."

"Do you think that would hurt her?"

"I *know* it would. Don't you, hombre?"

"Definitely. Mrs. B, she's, like, nervous."

"How about your parents, Scooter?"

"Mike and Marcia have offered to find them, but if they didn't care enough to raise me, to hell with them. I got plenty of what I need at home. Will here knows Mike's good at finding people when the time comes, right, dude?"

"Yeah. But who knows, I may never need him."

This knowing look crept onto her face.

"I bet when you have children you'll find her. You'll want to know what kind of history you'll pass on to your family."

"Maybe. But right now I'm fine."

Was I? Today I remember her soft voice and sunlight on her downy skin and music and falling leaves floating in the air—then the music stopped and we headed back. But I also remember sweet Laura naming something I'd vaguely wrestled with for years. A shadow family. A piece of myself, yet unknown.

Don't know who I inherited my temper from, or how far back it went. But I remember when I was two or three Dad picked my sorry ass off the pew during a hissy fit in church. I still remember that spanking, outside, at a merciful remove from open windows. Back then spankings (a gentle-sounding word) were common as colds and done in public. Now, they'd probably lock Dad up and re-adopt me. Anyway, I'm calmer now, but, especially right after Dad died, Mom and I were forever screaming at each other, then making up, after one of us apologized.

I always knew when Mom was about to rag on me. I'd be at the kitchen table and she'd stand at the sink or counter, her back to me. Except for running water or scrape of spoon in bowl she'd be silent as snow. Like animals sense when a kinghell storm's coming, I'd know something was about to boil over.

LBJ decorated my notebooks and stuff—Laura Bethany James, a mouthful of music, nothing to do with our louse of a president. I was saving for a Christmas present—because she loved to write, a silver pen and pencil set. Yes, I had it bad.

One afternoon I piddled with algebra or some dumb thing. Mom silently washed vegetables like they'd never come clean. I doodled Laura's initials once more, and figured we might as well get it over with.

"Mom, what's wrong?"

"Nothing."

She started chopping onions while I waited. She wore a hairnet, and one apron string dangled. She was getting stoop-shouldered, like she carried some burden. Not the first time I had noticed her getting older.

"Mom, c'mon. Say what's eating you."

She switched from onions to carrots—the pressure cooker was on the counter so we'd probably have beef stew. After a minute she looked out the window, attacked a stain or something on it with her left hand, sighed and turned around, knife in her right hand.

"Willie Lee, I'm worried about you."

"What now?"

"That girl you're seeing."

"Laura? What's wrong with Laura?"

"Well, for one thing, she's too young. Can't you find somebody your own age?"

"Mom, we kind of found each other. She likes me and I like her—a lot."

"Willie Lee, you mustn't get serious about a girl like that."

She had to know she was crossing an edge, because my face turns red when I'm pissed.

"Like what?"

"Son, her father's a professional man."

"So?"

She pointed the knife at me like teachers brandish a yardstick to show the whole class your stupid mistake on the blackboard.

"So they live in a nice brick house, not over a store. They have a new car, not a jalopy. Son, you can't keep up with those Joneses."

"Aw, Mom, if they were snooty they'd send Laura to private school. Besides, the Streak is a cool car. What you said is a crock of crap."

"Don't use that word around me, young man. I've taught you better."

"I'll say it if I want to. Because that's what this is, a load of crap. Would you rather I said 'shit'?"

"That'll do, son. Go to your room."

"I'll go where I damn want to."

I swear I threw my yellow number two straight at the floor but somehow it broke on the cabinet beside her head. I snatched jacket and keys and slammed the door behind me, not sure if I heard her scream "William Lee Blaine, come back this second" or just knew that's what she yelled as I peeled out, bound for I didn't know where.

I ended up at Scooter's, whose Mom convinced me to haul my carcass back and apologize to Mom—with flowers.

I tiptoed up the stairs and listened at the door. Nothing. Inside, the kitchen felt abandoned and the pressure cooker sat on a cold stove eye. Its weight was on the counter. The table was set for supper. In a second Mom came out of the bathroom, having I guess fixed her face after a cry. She looked doubtful. Of me, of everything.

"Mom, I'm sorry. Really sorry."

I held out three red zinnias, about all Mrs. C had left in her flower garden. Lord, how Mom looked at me, sorrow and hope and anger and love all balled together. Finally, after a tight smile she put the flowers in a green glass vase.

"Willie Lee, you could have put my eye out."

"I know, Mom. I'm really sorry. I won't do that again."

"You better not. You know your father would have whipped you good."

"Like, I said I was sorry."

She walked over and hugged me.

"I'll start the stew. Want a glass of lemonade?"

The storm was always over when she offered food and drink. I finished my homework, we ate supper, did dishes, watched *Rawhide* or *Wyatt Earp* or some shoot-em-up, and went to our rooms. Peace, at least for a while.

One damp February Tuesday Laura and I headed home from a basketball game. Sand Hill had lost big-time to Pisgah, which wasn't supposed to happen, and one of our cheerleaders had turned an ankle. Laura was stewing over something, maybe the game. She sat close until the heater kicked in, then moved toward her door. As we pulled into her driveway she stared straight ahead when I tried to put my arm around her.

"Will, we need to talk."

I have always hated to hear that.

"Can you come in for a few minutes? Not long, it's a school night."

"Sure. Sweetheart, what's wrong?"

"We need to talk, that's all. If we stay here my folks will fret."

So we went in and took off our coats and told Mrs. J about the game. She gave us a pot of Russian tea and fruitcake cookies and settled us in the den with a look that said not to stay long.

Mr. J's fire needed attention. Laura pulled the screen aside and fed it a stick of wood. It popped sparks into the room so she put the screen back in a hurry and sat beside me, arms folded across her lovely chest.

"Will, I've been thinking."

I looked to the mantel for an anchor while her pouf of a dog parked his ass beside her and eyed the cookies on the coffee table. I found a picture of Laura in a Girl Scout uniform, cute enough to melt a brick.

"About what?"

"That we should start seeing other people."

Well, goddamn.

"You tired of me?"

"No, of course not. Not at all. I just… well… you know…"

"No, I don't. Laura, honey, what's wrong?"

She took my hands and turned the greens on me like headlights on a deer.

"It's just that I'm worried. I say I love you—and I do—but you're my first real boyfriend. How do I know you're the one if I have no other experience?"

I didn't know what kind of wood she had laid in the fireplace but it flamed up fast, then set in for a slow death. Kind of like my ego.

"So somebody has asked you out?"

"No."

She had to feel my hands shaking.

"Then it's your mom, right? She wants me to get lost."

"No, she likes you, although she did say the Christmas gift was extravagant, and warned me not to get serious."

"So, just like that, you're dumping me."

"No, silly. Just don't assume because there's a game I'll go with you. Ask me, don't take me for granted."

"I can do that. You sure no one else is hiding behind the curtain?"

"No. Well, Susan did say somebody asked her how steady we were."

"Who? I'll teach the jerk a lesson."

"Will, that's enough."

She let go of my hands and raked a strand of hair from her forehead. "Do we understand each other?"

"Laura, I don't understand a damn thing. Fifteen minutes ago I thought we were happy as kittens in a yarn basket, and now… I mean, I love you, I love you a lot."

"I love you, too. But slow down. There's a lot of life ahead. If I'm going to spend it with one person, I have to be absolutely certain. Ask other girls out. I'll date other boys. But I'm not kicking you off the team, you're too good a kisser."

She hugged me and buried her face in my shoulder. I kissed her hair, which, as usual, smelled of clean, healthy girl. On the coffee table our tea and cookies were cold and untouched, and the fireplace was full of embers. I didn't know whether to cry or stomp so I simply held her. Soon she broke away and handed me my jacket and smiled.

"No hard feelings?"

Afraid of what I might say, I shook my head.

"See you tomorrow."

"Night."

Outside I found no comfort in the sky, only low clouds and a sharp breeze. That lucky bastard of a hopeful dog would probably get a cookie and crawl in bed with Laura. Meantime, I sat in the Streak, started the motor, and turned off the radio, for I couldn't stand to hear Chuck Berry or the Beatles. Hell, as it was, I cried a lapful on the way home.

Who knows exactly what went down when Mom and I had our big set-to? I mean, nobody else was around. I remember weird details, like the dishtowel draped over her left shoulder, the back door bell hitting the floor after I slammed the door. But what actively happened between coming home from school and cutting out in an absolute rage I can't honestly say. Maybe I don't want to remember, I don't know.

I mean, it was like some humongous sack of shit attacked me that morning. A zit as big as a Chrysler hubcap bloomed on my nose's end. A disaster of a quiz popped up in Earth Science. Then Laura was hanging out with Ronnie Pressley, the jerk, in the lunchroom. He wedged his tall, sorry self between us.

"Buzz off, Blaine. She's my date tonight."

She sort of smiled as he laid a hand on her soft shoulder like he was so damn cool. I guess I'm glad I don't pack a switchblade.

If we'd had a cat I'd have kicked the bastard when I got home. I threw my books on the table and grabbed a Coke from the fridge. Then I was stupid enough to pick a fight with Mom when she was about to fix my favorite supper. She wore a frumpy apron over her store dress and had that dumb dishtowel slung on her shoulder. A bowl half full of hamburger meat sat on the counter waiting for egg, bread, salt and pepper, Worcestershire and ketchup. Meat loaf time.

"What's wrong, son?"

She made sure the egg wouldn't jump off the counter, then turned to eyeball me. I told her about Laura, hoping like hell for sympathy. Instead, she lectured me about how Laura and I were never meant to be, ground she'd plowed a million times. I started to yell at her. She shouted back. I kind of lost it. After that my memory gets as fuzzy as moldy bread.

Next thing I'm certain about is scratching off in the Streak and heading I didn't give a tinker's damn where. I no longer had the Coke but my hands were sticky. A chest-constricting dread hit me. Had I told her to go to hell? Or said she wasn't my real mother? Had I shoved or hit her? Who knew? But I couldn't go back. Not just then.

I rode around forever, most of the damn time with the radio off so I wouldn't have to listen to songs about love gone bad. I didn't head to Tunnel Road, where I'd probably run into that son of a bitch with my girl. I finally found a familiar parking lot and cut the motor.

The Mountain View was a long, low, windowless concrete-block building. Except for neon beer signs it might have been chicken house, adult bookstore, or roadside church. A place of refuge—and education— for a kid with a car. Plenty of commerce flowed between gravel parking lot and bar. Underage guys paid some sketchy half-lit bozo a dollar for a fifty-cent beer. I always backed in on the west side, to see the law in time to leave discreetly, and never hung out there when I knew Scooter's dad was on duty.

After several cold tallboys I woke next morning in a turnout halfway up Mount Pisgah, no idea how I got there. My cashless wallet lay in the backseat, but at least my license was still there. Some stupid bird hell-bent on aggravation sang its ass off about ten feet above my head. Whoever tended the campfire I smelled had probably filched my two remaining dollars, but I doubted he'd cough them up.

Dread returned, in spades. When I tried to put things together, nothing worked. I roached around under the seat for a quarter, then drove down to the phone booth at O'Kelly's store and called the house. No answer. Headed home, snuck upstairs. No police tape. Kitchen floor clean, no blood, meatloaf makings in the fridge. Bell reinstalled. Mom's coat, gone.

I didn't see much way not to ask downstairs, where Mary Anne had opened the store. I stood at the door a while as she straightened the cash register area and ignored hell out of me.

"Where's Mom?"

"You don't know?"

"No."

"She's in the hospital. Boots took her last night. Mike Capps is hunting for you."

"So what happened?"

"You really don't know?"

"Listen… how much trouble am I in?"

"Deputy Capps can tell you that. Meantime I have customers. Go see Mrs. Blaine. And apologize like you mean it. She's like a mother to me."

The one empty parking space at St. Joseph's Hospital was smack in the middle of the steep hill in front. I didn't trust my emergency brake, so circled around, left the Streak at the Ford dealer, and hoofed it up to the entrance.

The smell of a hospital gives me the creeps. It's too clean—like somebody's about to yell at you for dirtying things up. The desk lady didn't have a record of Mom being there. She said to ask back at the emergency room, and showed me the way. A nurse went back into a side room, where she and a kinda dried-up nun whispered in my direction. Soon the nun came out.

"You're looking for Mrs. Blaine?"

"Yes, ma'am."

"Who exactly are you?"

"I'm Will Blaine... her son."

"I thought maybe so. Come with me."

You could hear her squeaky shoes and starch a mile away. Our elevator opened on the fifth floor into a cramped waiting area next to a nurses' station. The cracked vinyl furniture looked as tired and anxious as I was.

"Wait here."

I was about to sit when I spied the crucifix below the clock. Time for Jesus. Or maybe time for me to split. But a restroom door opened, and there was Aunt Boots, out of uniform, closing her purse and looking around, birdlike.

"Child, where have you been?"

"I'm sorry, Aunt Boots. How is she?"

"I don't know exactly. They're going to keep her for observation. She's —sort of in and out. What happened yesterday?"

I told her what I remembered.

"Well, either you hit her or she fell. She's got a big pump knot on her head. The doctor says it's too early to say if amnesia is permanent. She's at least had a concussion. You don't remember hitting her?"

"Aunt Boots, I just don't know."

"Well, she loves you more than anything, so I doubt she'll file assault charges. Mike might, if he ever finds you. Have you talked to him?"

"No."

"Let's try to call him from the nurses' station. So where did you spend the night?"

"In my car. I had some beers."

"Really? I could have sworn you smelled like Shalimar."

She looked at me over her glasses like I was some insect.

"Why do men do this? You all do, even as young as you. It's exasperating."

The nun came back from down the hall.

"She's asleep. She mustn't have company. And she may be here a while. Hello, Mrs. Franklin. Good to see you again. Now, son, do you need me for anything?"

"If I could use the phone…"

I left word at the sheriff's office for Mike that I was heading home with Aunt Boots, who looked me up and down and straightened my collar.

"You're a mess. You carry a comb? No? Well, you'll stay with Howard and me for now. Let's pray she makes it through this—for the good of us all."

Aunt Boots tailed the Streak like a female Paul Drake. This home stop was for clothes and stuff, but when I saw Scooter's car and a deputy's cruiser in the parking area, I said "Oh shit." Too late to head for high timber.

Turned out to be a big deal. The Capps family—Mike, Marcia, and Scooter—were upstairs, along with Uncle Howard and Mary Anne—and Laura! Everybody around the dining table, one seat empty, across from Mike, next to Marcia. I wanted a hug from Laura but her face said no.

Mike's uniform looked as tired and unhappy as he was.

"Sit down, boy. Gimme your keys."

He pointed to the table. I laid them down and wondered if I'd ever see them again.

"Spare set?"

I nodded.

"Get 'em."

I handed them over and sat back down. Everyone but Mike stared at the table top or anywhere but me. Mike cleared his throat.

"Okay, people. We're here because of this hard-headed kid. Will, do you know how much pain you've caused in the last twenty-four hours?"

I sort of shrugged, looked around for comfort, but even the cookie jar seemed ominous. I felt like a movie guy under a hot lamp, about to be beaten with a rubber hose.

"A dang lot. And do you know the trouble you'll be in if your mother, perish the thought, dies, or is permanently damaged? Look at me, kid. What can you say for yourself?"

"Just that I'm really sorry."

"Sorry doesn't cut it. How about telling us exactly what happened yesterday?"

"I don't really remember."

"Son, I'm no lawyer but I'd love to get your scrawny ass under oath. Let's start with what you did when you got home from school."

"I came inside—Mom was over there at the counter. She was getting ready to fix supper."

"And?"

I looked at Laura, wondering why in hell he'd dragged her to this inquisition.

"I told her... I'd had a lousy day. We started arguing..."

"Dang it, Will, that's nothing to wrangle about. What really triggered the argument?"

No help for it.

"Laura."

All eyes shifted her way. She blushed like a red rubber ball.

"Miss James, can you shed any light here?"

"I... well, Will knew I was going out with another boy. He didn't like that, I guess."

"What say you, young Will?"

"She's right."

"So let me see if I have this straight. When you got ticked off because your girl decided variety was the spice of life, you assaulted your mother?"

"Now, wait..."

"No, you wait. I mean to find out about yesterday."

"I really don't remember."

"Okay, listen up. Boots found your mom and called me. Boots was here because Mary Anne heard racket upstairs, saw you flee the scene, and called her.

"When I got here Boots had Martha up in a chair—the one you're in, in fact—Martha held crushed ice in a dishtowel to the side of her head, which had a knot on it consistent with being whacked with a Coke bottle. Which is in an evidence bag. I expect your prints are all over it.

"The floor was sticky. The doorbell was in the floor, like the door had been slammed too hard by a certain someone."

He sighed, like he wanted this to be over. Or to wring my neck, one.

"Experience says three witnesses to a crime will tell four versions of what happened. So it's all muddled. Martha maintained she didn't—or didn't want to—remember what happened. That she might have fallen. Might have hit her head on the door frame. Right, Boots?"

"Yes. She kept repeating *I can't remember* and *He didn't mean it.* That part over and over. *He didn't mean it.* Will, what *did* you say to her?"

That tightness in my chest ratcheted another half turn.

"I don't remember. Really, I don't."

Mike stood and looked down at me.

"The only witnesses say they don't remember. So let me take a stab at it. Maybe she told you not to put yourself out over Miss James. Maybe she told you not to see the girl again. Any of that ring a bell?"

"Maybe."

"Scooter, any of that sound right?"

"Yes, sir. Last summer Will told me Mrs. B wanted them to quit dating. He was ticked."

"Okay. So, Will, you were P.O.ed about all that so you told Martha to mind her own business. She said since you're her son, you *are* her business. And—I don't think I'm reaching here—you told her to go to hell. Or maybe said something about being adopted. That maybe she wasn't your real mother. Am I making myself clear?"

"Yes, sir."

"Then you busted your mom upside the head with a Coke bottle. Or you just knocked the bottle over when you shoved her into the door-frame as you stormed out. Or you didn't touch her and she slipped in the spilled drink. That's three versions.

"Any way you cut it, you're why Martha's in the hospital. And that makes us pretty dang mad."

"I'm sorry."

Marcia gave my hand a squeeze.

"Will, listen. We all love Martha. And we all love you. That's what makes me so sad—that yesterday happened.

"You've got much soul-searching ahead—not to mention apologizing and making up. And I think we all want to help with that. In whatever way we can. Even Mike. We all love you."

Mike pocketed my keys and laid his meaty hands on the table.

"Okay, kid. This love-fest is over. You're grounded until further notice. You're going to stay with Pu... Howard and Boots until we see what's what with Martha. And you better pray she gets better—fast. Got that?"

"Yes, sir."

"Scooter, take the young lady home. Marcia, come with me. Will, go with the Franklins."

"Can I have a minute with Laura?"

Mike was a runner, so carried a stopwatch.

"Sure. I'll be outside. You got sixty seconds."

The soundtrack behind my time with Laura was the Streak starting, its motor gunned a couple of times, then its hood popped, after which (I was sure) Mike pocketed the distributor cap. Hood down. Boom.

I broke down when Laura hugged me. Tears, heaves, the whole deal. Repeating *I'm sorry*. I wanted the smell of her to be with me forever.

She finally held me at arms' length.

"Whatever happened, I love you. But it'll be a while before we see each other again."

"Why…"

"You're grounded, silly. Until that's over, I'm not walking to the movies. When your mom comes through, we'll face the future. Right now, she's the important thing. And don't worry about Ronnie—he's history."

After I blew my nose and wiped my eyes she kissed me on the forehead and left. Uncle Howard stuck his head in the door.

"Get your stuff, son. We're going home."

Home turned out to be their son Tommy's old room in their brick rancher, one of those long deals with a breezeway and sunken living room. Tommy, off in the Air Force in Vietnam, was about ten years older than me. Uncle Howard and Aunt Boots were really proud of him.

Aunt Boots had boxed up all his ball trophies and stuff, so it didn't feel like a museum. I had my own bathroom across the hall and free range in the kitchen. But I still felt like a prisoner. I couldn't go anywhere but school and church, and couldn't stay after school or go to a ball game.

It was weeks before I got to see Mom. Which, at first, was fine. I mean, I was scared she'd be all different or something. Not that different would be bad, if it meant less clingy. But Aunt Boots said Mom wasn't getting better. A lot of time she was not exactly asleep but not awake either. Some days she barely talked and had strange twitches and jerks.

Aunt Boots mentioned catatonia, which I guess was nurse talk for some weird mental state.

One Thursday afternoon I was doing homework—algebra or something—at the kitchen table. Aunt Boots came home, laid her keys down, and adjusted her glasses.

"Will, Martha needs to go to another hospital."

"What do you mean?"

"A mental hospital. They'll send her to Broughton tomorrow morning."

"So what will they do to her?"

She sat across from me and lit a cigarette. She was upset, because she only smoked when worrying with much bigger things than supper.

"Electroshock. It's like jump-starting her brain. Electricity can restore a normal path of thinking."

"So is she… crazy or something?"

She flicked an ash into an amber ashtray shaped like North Carolina and looked at me over her specs.

"Will, she's sick. Her brain isn't working right. This treatment is usually successful, so it's well worth a try."

"How long will she be there?"

"Who knows? At least a month. Maybe longer."

I must have looked worried.

"Will, we're not going to throw you out on the street."

"Has she… asked… about me?"

"We'll know she's getting better when she does. Remember that, son. She loves you more than anything."

The week after Mom went to Broughton, Aunt Boots came in after work and laid her purse on the kitchen table. She looked official in her nurse's outfit, and, as usual, I searched her face for news. Instead of bad news or the lecture I dreaded, she smiled.

"Will, your mother asked for you today. We'll see her Saturday."

I closed my U.S. history textbook, in which at the rate we were going we weren't going to get as far as the Mexican War.

"That's great. Do we have to wait until then?"

"You're in school, young man."

I rolled my eyes and twirled my yellow number two Eagle.

"Isn't Mom more important than this stuff?"

"Maybe, but we'll wait until this weekend."

"When will she come home?"

"They're not saying."

"Did you *talk* to her?"

"No, it was a Dr. Jackson. He says she's making progress, but slowly. And we shouldn't stay long. But her seeing you is important."

She took a pack of ground beef from the fridge. A bottle of ketchup. Lifted an onion out of the bin.

"Meatloaf okay for supper?"

I grinned.

"Well, I'm not as good a cook as Martha, but I'll put it together after I change clothes."

I knew then I was, if not all the way restored with Aunt Boots, at least back over the mountain. They'll have meatloaf in heaven, or I'm not going.

That was Tuesday. I spent the next few days torn between happy and anxious. Looking forward to seeing her—or worried that something bad would happen. I really couldn't concentrate much, and couldn't see Laura, and didn't talk to Puss or Boots. I was a mess.

But Saturday morning Puss & Boots and I piled into his car, a big-motor yellow 1965 Olds 98 that I really wanted to drive, but knew better than to ask. There was room enough in there, I swear, for a football team. The backseat was all mine except for iced drinks in a cooler on the floorboard behind the driver, and a small box of fruit for Mom—oranges, apples, bananas.

The ride was so mushy a backseat guy could almost get carsick. I sat in the middle and kept my eye on the spearlike chrome strip running down the middle of the hood. Around even a middling curve I had to brace myself to keep from sliding into a door. Between that and ears popping, I sure was glad to get to the foot of Old Fort Mountain.

About thirty minutes later we parked in front of a chunky brick building, five stories with dormers on the top floor and a three-level front porch with a crazy bunch of white columns flanking central doorways. Like balconies a dictator would address his people from.

Outside it seemed there were enough windows to let the light get in, but when we walked inside even the light felt dark.

The receptionist led us down the hall to a waiting room and said she would ring for Dr. Jackson. Aunt Boots was impressed he worked on a weekend.

"Bootsie, people stay crazy on Saturdays. Why wouldn't a doctor be here?"

"Howard Franklin, just hush. Physicians think they need the weekends to play golf—they know nurses will handle things while they're gone."

Because of high ceilings and marble floors you'd expect to hear a doctor from a long way off, but he sort of appeared, in white coat like you'd expect, but high-top sneakers, like he'd play basketball after lunch.

"Good morning, folks. I'm Dr. Jackson."

He made a little bow to Aunt Boots.

"You must be Mrs. Franklin. And this would have to be Mr. Franklin. That means you are Mrs. Blaine's son, Willie Lee."

His hand was callused and strong, like he did something besides doctoring.

"I'm Will, actually. Good to meet you."

"Sorry. She calls you Willie Lee. I am very happy you came. Before I take you all upstairs, I want to tell you a few things."

He might have been forty—short-cut hair a little gray at the sideburns, horn-rimmed glasses, half a dozen pens in a pocket protector. A good smile—I liked him right off.

He pulled up a wing chair, sat on seat's edge, put elbows on legs, and clasped his hands.

"Mrs. Blaine is improving, slowly. She's had a number of electroshock treatments, and after each she bounces back a little more quickly. When brought to us, she was semi-responsive, but now she has some appetite, pays attention to her appearance, and talks more freely with me and the nurses. Eventually we hope she'll be okay. It's just going to take a while.

"Whatever trauma she suffered has fixed itself. She's hale, physically. She's not yet as mentally strong as we'd like her to be, so I want this visit to be brief. I wouldn't bring up anything unpleasant. Tell her she looks well. Answer questions, if she has any, but it's okay to be evasive if she asks something that might arouse anguish."

"We brought fresh fruit. Can she have it?"

"No, Mrs. Franklin. Policy, you know. She's in a six-bed ward, and there might be some, well, jealousy. Not everyone here gets visits, you see."

"Can I tell her I'm sorry? For whatever I did?"

He didn't look at me like I was a worm.

"Certainly. But no detail. 'I'm sorry' is a healing phrase. 'I love you' is too. 'I won't hurt you again' at this stage might not be. Understand?"

"Yes, sir."

"Mrs. Franklin, do I understand you are a nurse?"

"That's right, Doctor."

"Do you have any particular questions?"

"Is she still amnesic?"

"Yes, especially as to immediate matters. Part of that is the electro-shock, part might still be due to her trauma. We're working on her memory. It's my theory that memory is best sneaked up on, so to speak, from behind. So she's keeping a journal. I have encouraged her to tell her own story from first memories on—I hope she will find some healing there."

"I've never known Martha to write anything except a recipe or letter to Henry overseas."

"She thought at first she couldn't do it, but the last day or two she has taken the journal voluntarily. I'm hopeful. Would you all like to go up now?"

We rode a huge elevator with a bunch of padding on the walls to the top floor. Its black operator, whom Dr. J called Miss Emma—they seemed really easy with each other—knew what she was doing. No stomach-churning when the driver jerks the car up and down to find the floor. That stuff drives me nuts.

This area didn't feel as dark as downstairs, although the hall laddered with ward doors wasn't too inviting. I had to think disinfectant smells better than what it masked.

They had wheeled Mom out toward the front of the building, into a small visiting parlor. You know, a few upholstered chairs, a small table with a vase of artificial flowers, a floor lamp with an underpowered bulb. An oval hooked rug on the floor.

I was really jumpy by then. I mean, I didn't know what to expect. Arms strapped to the chair? Tubes coming out of her arms? Shaved and scorched scalp?

None of that, although she wore a weird little gray knit cap. She looked, well, like Mom. A little tired, but otherwise the woman I remembered. She was in a kind of greenish gown with a gray blanket over her lap.

"Mrs. Blaine, I believe you know these people."

Aunt Boots hugged her and kissed her forehead.

"Martha, how *are* you?"

"I think I'm going to be fine. Hello, Howard."

He hugged her too, then stood behind the wheelchair, revealing me in my nerve-wracked awkwardness.

"Willie Lee, thank the Lord, come here."

I hugged her and we both started crying and Dr. J shoved a handkerchief between us and poked me on the arm, a cue.

"I love you, Mom."

"Oh, son, I love you too. It's so very good to see you. So very good. Just let me feel you for a minute. You still smell like Prell. And my little boy."

Embarrassed, I knelt beside her chair like some guy in one of those old church paintings.

"Martha, you really look well."

Aunt Boots, I suppose, figured somebody had to break this spell or we'd be there all day.

"She sure don't look like a sick woman to me."

Dr. J glared at Puss for that remark.

"Folks, Mrs. Blaine needs to be back in time for lunch. Let's say good-byes. I'm sure you all will return soon."

I stood, still holding her hands. Rather, she still gripping mine.

"I love you, Mom."

She smiled and closed her eyes, long enough so I worried she might be tripping out on us. But she squeezed my hands.

"I know you do, son. I know you do. And I love you."

Dr. J himself wheeled her to the ward door, where an orderly took over. It was hard to see her go back in there, but I was glad to have seen that she likely would be okay.

Downstairs, Dr. J thanked us for coming.

"Will, you did fine. Mrs. Franklin, I'll keep you posted on her progress. I hope this visit will hasten the day you can take her home."

Outside, Puss looked at me.

"You hungry, kid?"

"Yes, sir."

"I know a little place downtown that serves great pan-fried trout. Then, if you behave, I might let you drive back home."

"Really?"

"Don't get mushy on me, boy, or it won't happen. Let's have lunch first."

And we did. And he did—let me drive that big old Detroit boat— while he and Aunt Boots sat in the back like teenagers on their way to the prom. He only yelled at me once, when I goosed that 4-barrel 455 to get around a transfer truck before the grade got steep.

"Do that again and you can fill this dang tank."

I grinned at him in the rearview. He grinned back. Life seemed to have turned a corner.

*   *   *

The day we sprung Mom, nothing would do but for Puss to get up before God and head to Morganton in that big Oldsmobile. Darker than a nightmare outside. Aunt Boots knocked on my door, opened it, and turned the light on.

"Wake up, sleepyhead. Today's a big day."

I put on a T-shirt and jeans but she sent me back for what she called proper clothing. We rushed through breakfast—oatmeal with raisins—then headed out.

Puss and Boots sat in front, while I laid down in the backseat and tried to sleep. The ride was smooth but he had to have the radio on, and after WWNC faded to a scratch, the only clear channel was the Christian station in Ridgecrest or wherever. Even Puss wouldn't listen to that. Bunch of sunshine pumpers that time of morning.

I probably couldn't have slept anyway. Nerves. I knew that coming back, Mom would be with us and there was no road map that I knew of—at least not for me. I had no idea how well Dr.J had fixed her—or if they had just taped up the cracks and hoped she'd hold together.

Puss had to slow the heck down for fog at the Divide—it was like trying to drive through Velveeta. We ran out of that about halfway down the mountain, into a gray dawn spattered with house lights of farmers or somebody.

It was daylight when we pulled into the hospital grounds. The main building's front looked sleepy, although lights showed elsewhere. The front door was locked until eight. So we had an hour to kill.

"I swear, Howard, when you die I'll start your funeral a half-hour early. You always have to be anywhere way before you need to."

"Boots, you never know what'll happen to make you late. I wouldn't want to miss out on nothing."

A mockingbird in a magnolia next to the main building was a good deal more cheerful than I was. You didn't need a jacket at that elevation, and it was turning into a pretty day. We walked in circles like clover leaves, each of us going out and coming back counterclockwise in some hope another fifteen minutes had passed.

Inside, the receptionist said Dr. J would have to discharge Mom, and he wouldn't be in until ten. But at least we could wait inside, and they had several magazines to prowl in.

When Dr. J showed up he got a nurse to take Puss and Boots up to Mom's floor, then led me into a conference room.

"Will, I want to speak to you a minute."

"Sure."

"I just wanted to say we may not be giving you the same mother you had before."

"What do you mean?"

"Well, she's been through a lot. She'll probably be more fragile than formerly. She's been very anxious for a long while about many things— her health, your attitude, what will become of her when you go to col- lege—all sorts of anxieties. I'd like to think we have helped with that. Her medications might make her more passive than you have seen. I just didn't want you to walk into your new life blindly."

"So, is she probably still going to keep me on a tight leash?"

He smiled like I'd shown him something he'd been looking for.

"Maybe. Maybe not. That might depend more on you than her."

"How so?"

"Will, you're, what, going on seventeen? I remember that time. It's hard enough to make your own body obey reason, much less take responsibility for another person. But I can say that your mother has made remarkable progress. She came in broken, no self-esteem at all. She leaves as someone who is discovering—perhaps for the first time—who she really is. She may be a little frightened by that. But she needs to keep discovering this new person, and you can help."

"How?"

"One thing she's learned here is to write. About herself. About what's around her. About relationships. Whatever you do, Will, don't make fun of her. Don't discourage her. Never give her even a hint you might snoop in her journal. Got that?"

"Yes, sir."

"And if she wants to talk about what happened, let her. And don't lie to her about anything. I have an idea she would know if you were."

"Does she know… what happened?"

"Between you and her?"

"Yes, sir."

"I have an idea she does. She hasn't said much, but she knows more than she lets on. Never avoid that if she wants to talk. Don't bring it up, but don't skirt it either. Got that?"

"I think so."

"Good. Here's my card. Don't hesitate to call or write with any con- cerns. I wish you and your mother nothing but the best."

Out in the hall, Mom and Puss and Boots were talking to a nurse. Mom looked good—maybe a little stooped, but otherwise okay. She wore a church dress, all pink and soft, and held a book across her chest, a ledger bound in blue cloth like she was taking a business course. She hugged me with one arm and held on to the book with the other.

Her cloth bag and stuff went into the trunk and she and Puss sat up front and Boots and I sat in the back.

"You ready to ride, Martha?"

She looked straight ahead.

"Take me home, Howard. I need to breathe some mountain air."

She kept twisting a strand of hair with her left hand, something I had never noticed her doing. Not worrying it like she wanted to pull it out, but absently, like you'd scratch your head or something. Absently, but steadily.

The fog was gone and the day was about as pretty as you could wish for. About halfway up the mountain she pointed toward the hillside.

"Look. The leaves are changing color. Aren't they beautiful?"

I hadn't even noticed. And the higher we drove the brighter they got. At the gap she closed her eyes and smiled.

"Lord, it's great to be heading home."

At The Top of the Hill Puss pulled the land yacht into the parking lot. Mom sat, smiling, making no move to get out. Puss jerked his head toward me—*get out and open her dang door*. So I did. She emerged from the car and just stood there. Took in the store building, the brick church across the road, the long view toward Pisgah, took a deep breath, and pronounced it good.

"You all don't know how good it is to be here again. I belong here. I really do."

Mary Anne ran out and hugged her. Paid me no attention. Puss and I lugged Mom's stuff upstairs. Boots left Mom and Mary Anne to catch up on things, came upstairs, and began to heat a pot of vegetable soup she'd made yesterday.

"Will, this is lunch today, and you can reheat it for at least one more meal. It's good soup—I made it with marrow bones. Look out and see if Martha's ready to come up."

She was coming up the stairs, that blue ledger clutched to her chest, the left hand twisting a strand of hair.

"Will, I want you to do something for me."

"Sure, Mom, what?"

"After I change clothes and have a bite to eat, I want you to move that little table and chair next to the mantel—the one I pay bills at—into my bedroom under the window, okay? It'll be a private place to journal in."

"I can do that. Anything else?"

She hugged me.

"Just keep the boogerman away, okay?"

"I'll try."

Whatever that meant.

After lunch, Puss and Boots left and Mom and I talked a while. She seemed calm. Happy. Tired. Not too nosy. Wanted to know what was happening in church, which I didn't much care or know about. Asked about my grades, which were okay. Asked if I'd heard from Dad's people.

"What are people saying about why I was gone?"

"Nothing that I've heard."

"Well, you know they're talking. They always do."

"Let 'em talk. That's no worry of yours."

"Maybe you're right. I'm going to my pensive citadel now. For a nap. You hang around a while, okay?"

"Sure. You can count on me."

Pensive citadel? When did Mom start reading poetry? I only knew it because our English teacher read it to us the week before, something by Wordsworth or Coleridge or one of those guys about nuns in their cells. Was Mom turning Catholic?

Marcia and Scooter dropped by about four with a coconut cake. Mom made a pot of coffee and we sat around the dining table and had about as normal a conversation as four humans ever had. It was right on, really.

"Martha, you look great. And what's more, you sound great."

"Marcia, I feel better than I have in years. One of the things I have to work on is taking care of myself. I was pretty lousy at that."

"I think most women are."

"You may be right, but I was worse than most. I haven't worried about who I am since I was a kid and had to drop out of school. I've been taking care of people my whole life. Now all I have to worry with is me and Will, and we're going to be okay, right, son?"

"Sure, Mom."

"Scooter, how's school?"

"Okay."

"Is that all, just okay?"

"I'll put it this way. I'm looking forward to college. This separate but equal thing is, well, you know."

"A pack of lies?"

"You got that right."

"So are you and Will going to WCC together?"

"We hope so."

"Good. What I have to do is find the gumption, I think that's the word, to stay here by myself while you boys fly out of the nest."

"We'll take care of each other, Martha."

"I know. And that makes me glad."

"Okay, Marcia, we got to go."

Mike stood and gave me a small paper bag I'd noticed when they came in.

"Here. I reckon since Martha's back I don't have jurisdiction anymore. Be careful, Will."

"I will, sir. Thanks."

In it was the Streak's distributor cap. No longer grounded.

So they did fix Mom. Would it be permanent? Who knew? But for the time being, things were fine. I'd try to get out of the house after church the next day and see Laura. That would tell me something.

Lord, it felt fine to hear that sweet motor rumble again. Even finer to head to Laura's house in the Streak. Something about squealing tires on a curvy two-lane makes my blood flow in the right direction.

I hadn't seen her except at school since my inquisition. We parted friends then, and she'd been cordial at school, but I still didn't know what to expect. She met me at the door with a hug that kind of made me melt—soft, insistent, I don't know, you can't really put that into words. It just *was*.

She peeled me away from her sweet self, smiled, and kissed the tip of my nose.

"I'm really glad to see you."

"Me too."

"C'mon in."

The dining room table was set for two. The sideboard held enough for a half dozen. Little sandwiches, a pot of chili, dishes of fresh vegetables. pickles, olives, a bowl of chips, a pitcher of lemonade.

"Man, are you trying to fatten me up for the kill?"

"Just a welcome-back lunch. I've missed you."

"Girl, I've missed you, too. But I'm not sure which is better-looking, this spread or you."

She started to speak but I put my finger to my lips. "You, of course. It was a joke."

"Well, dig in. The food, I mean."

We filled our plates and sat. I went heavy on the sandwich side, she loaded up with rabbit food. Like a goofball I started to eat, while she bowed her head, then picked up a celery stick.

"So how's your mother?"

"Pretty well. I think she's going to be fine."

"Is she... different?"

"Yeah, she's writing, keeping a journal."

"She's never done that?"

"Not that I ever knew about. It's part of her therapy or whatever. I know I've been given strict orders not to snoop."

"Heavens, I hope you wouldn't. I know I'd not want anybody seeing mine."

"You keep a journal?"

"More like a diary. But sometimes I write some pretty private things. It helps me think things out."

"I kinda do that when I'm driving."

"Sounds dangerous."

"Not really. I keep my eyes on the road. I just think clearer when I hear a motor running smooth. Can I have some more chili?"

"Sure, help yourself."

Such food needs bowls, not cups.

"Will, I'm sorry."

"About what?"

"Whatever part I played in your mom's... illness."

"You didn't have anything to do with that."

"That wasn't my impression the day Mr. Capps pulled us all together."

"Mike can get a little excited."

"He had good reason, Will. Nobody knew where you were. We were worried sick."

"Sweetheart, I'm sorry. I really am. But it's over, Mom's better. You and me, we can go on like before."

"Can we?"

"Can't we?"

"I don't know. Will, I'd love to. I mean, I do love you. But I've had lots of time to think."

She hadn't eaten a bite, and this conversation was beginning to run off the rails. Was this my last meal with Laura?

"And?"

"I don't know. It's just that you're so… hungry. You have this huge hole in your soul."

"You help fill it."

"Yes, but I worry. You have a great, kind spirit—but you also have a big capacity to hurt. Like with your mom. I know you didn't mean to, but you did. I don't want that to happen to me."

"Laura, I'd never hurt you."

"Not intentionally, I know. But sometimes you're a little scary."

"What do you mean?"

"All I'm saying is, you aren't complete. And it doesn't have much to do with me. It's that you lost your dad when you did. Remember? That was the first story you told me about yourself. Also, you don't know about your birth parents. Those things make for big holes."

"You're probably right. I'm not so sure about the bio parent deal, but there's not a day passes I don't think about Dad."

"See? You're still angry at him for dying like he did. And until you deal with that—and until you find out about your shadow family—your temper will keep on getting you in trouble. There. I'll quit preaching. Have some strawberry shortcake."

Which was berries and whipped cream over angel food cake, not biscuit halves like at home.

"Thanks. Both for the preaching and the spread. I do love you."

"And I, you. Always. No matter what happens when you go off to college."

I had enough to think about without rising to that bait. My love and I finished dessert and spent a quiet afternoon working a jigsaw puzzle, one of those thousand-piece deals, a picture of Paris or Copenhagen or some damn where. Any reason to be near her. I made up my mind to worry about college later.

I never had been what you'd call academic, although I always tested into college prep instead of "diversified occupations," which, given my garage job, I should have tracked into. I mean, I liked to read, and could write okay, but math was something other people were good at. Except fractions, which I learned early, matching bolts with wrenches.

I really hadn't worried until I held an SAT book at an unfamiliar desk with a number-two yellow in my shaking hand, my heart about to slam out of my chest. I did pretty well on verbal—I could bullshit through an essay, and reading comp was good. But math, wow, I was fine with geometry but some other stuff—calculus I guess—looked like Arabic or something. I did well enough overall to get in some schools, but not in engineering or anything.

Western North Carolina wasn't exactly eaten up with universities, and my scores wouldn't get me into Chapel Hill or State, and we sure couldn't afford out-of-state. That left App State, Western Carolina, and Asheville-Biltmore College. Scratched the last off immediately—I couldn't stand another year at home.

Mom didn't see it that way—living with her, I'd save the price of room and board, and she'd make sure I ate right and did homework. Plus I could keep looking out for her. Not exactly my idea of "the college experience." The question was, how to afford it?

Our guidance counselor looked old enough to have advised Teddy Roosevelt to go to Harvard, but when she found out I was the only child of a deceased veteran, she made me an appointment with the NC Veteran's Commission. They might have a scholarship.

So I met with Richard A. Snipes in the courthouse. Four o'clock on a Thursday, room 409. Like a Chevy. A number I remembered without writing it on the back of my hand.

It was one of those drafty days after a rain when wind goes right through you, especially if you wear church clothes. Clouds scudded like madmen, their ground shadows racing fast as crows. Even shook the Streak, a heavy machine. I parked in front of City Hall, where folks scurried in and out, paying water bills and parking fines and whatever.

Even on a bright day the courthouse looked clad in defeated Confederate gray. From the elevator on the fourth floor I found Mr. S's office around the left-hand corridor. I had expected him to have a secretary, but the door was open and he sat behind the only desk.

"Come in, Mr. Blaine. Please have a seat."

I'd bet Mr. S kept his three-piece suit on all day. An Elk's lapel pin, a pocket pouf to match the tie, Brylcreem or something to tame thinning hair. He smelled of something fruity, although you could tell he wasn't a fairy or anything. I mean, he wore a gold wedding band. Broad shoulders, good posture, a bit of five-o'clock shadow.

"So, Mr. Blaine, I gather you want an education."

"Yes, sir. It's okay to call me Will."

He smiled, leaned forward, and took me in with piercing blue eyes.

"Well, sir, then I will, Will. Your father was ETO, Third Army armored, I believe."

"How do you remember that? It's been six years."

"I never forget a face, and have a fine filing system. I might not remember who won the Series last year—the Orioles, right?—but I remember people."

He looked through the folder.

"Blaine, Henry. A shame he passed on so early. Is your mother still living?"

"Yes, sir."

"And you are the only child?"

"Yes, sir."

He straightened his tie and fished forms from a drawer.

"I think we can help, Will. Fill these out in duplicate. The scholarship committee is interested in personal motivation for college, so emphasize that in your essay. I need these hand-delivered back here in two days. I'll see that the committee gets them in a timely manner."

He sat back in his swivel chair and put index fingers together under his chin. Kind of a little smile.

"Son, I believe we can award you some money. Even a few hundred would help. Tuition is crazy these days. UNC is about five hundred a semester."

"Yes, sir. I appreciate your help."

"Will, promise me something."

"Yes, sir?"

"When you turn eighteen, don't neglect to register with Selective Service."

"No, sir, I won't."

"Good. I can't stand to hear of boys who go to Canada to avoid serving their country. We have to stop the global spread of Communism. I was a Marine, you know. If I thought a son of mine was a draft-dodger, I'd disown him. I guess it's good I don't have children."

"I'll be sure to register."

His face turned cloudy, like he'd just smelled a fart.

"Will, you will likely be given a IV-A classification. A deferment because you're a sole surviving son. You'll be pretty undraftable. Unless, of course, you feel called to serve your country. Especially in the Corps."

"Yes, sir. I'll remember that."

"See that you do."

He stood and shook my hand.

"Be sure to return those forms ASAP, son."

"Yes, sir, I will. Thanks again."

I left feeling weird, like he stared a hole through my back. Yet when I turned around, his door was shut and no shadow paced behind the pebbled glass.

The summer between high school and college passed as fast as a salted slug. If not for Laura, I would have gone bonkers, for Mom had a list, and nothing to do except work through it. Slowly. At least we didn't have to choose a casket.

Mom and I visited Wachovia Bank—the one downtown with the cool stone faces over the first floor windows. Inside was all old-fashioned dark wood and polished brass, like this place had been secure as hell since the Crimean War. The snooty guy who helped us called it a perfect place to keep money. So we opened a one-hundred-dollar checking account. *For emergencies.* I wasn't eighteen, so it had to be in both our names. Like, she couldn't wait six or eight weeks, she had to embarrass me right off the bat.

Mom insisted I needed new clothes, especially a suit for church and football games. Like I planned to attend church. Aunt Boots offered to take us downtown, where we parked in the big lot at Sears on Coxe Avenue. Threading through the loamy garden center, we fought the crowd to the men's department for socks and drawers and some wash-and-wear shirts. We stowed these in Aunt Boots's trunk, then trudged to Battery Park for khaki pants and blue jeans at Penny's. Everyone who wasn't at Sears was there. You shopped either store amid a tangle of cash register bells, jangling phones, and the rolling monotony of escalators.

Then down Patton Avenue to The Man Store, in an old building with a high, stamped-tin ceiling. Inside felt like a church, soft music and muted talk and the clean gray smell of fabric. With a piece of white chalk and a yellow measuring tape, Alf Diamond, a white-haired guy in dark pinstripes, measured me for a scratchy three-piece wool suit. He wasn't simply selling clothes—he was providing something holy—dignity, or at least some class. He threw in a dress shirt and paisley necktie either because he liked Mom or felt sorry for us—maybe both.

At the Square, Uncle Sam's Loan Office carried at least one of everything. Piles of army surplus—boots, socks, canteens, ammo boxes, knives—more military stuff than Patton Avenue's Army Store—piled on every flat surface. Mom bought a metal footlocker. Anybody could jimmy it—but it seemed to suit her. Aunt Boots and Mom headed to Sears for the car. I put our bags and packages in my new footlocker, then stood it on its end on the sidewalk, and leaned on it. I lit a cigarette and looked the Square over, like a gangster in some old movie.

I tried to look like old Thomas Wolfe leaving for New York. Even wished for a rakish fedora. I knew something was happening but I didn't know what it was. A little short of breath, legs tingly. I thought I was ready to leave Buncombe County in the broad daylight for a land with no hovering women.

Aunt Boots snapped me out of that daydream by tapping twice on her horn. At least it didn't say aaaa-oooo-gaah.

The footlocker held enough clothes for all quarter without a trip to the laundromat. I had a Webster's Seventh, and a Bible, my graduation present from Harmony Presbyterian. A brand-new windbreaker into which Mom had sewn name labels ordered from the back of some women's magazine. Like anybody finding a warm jacket on a blustery day might give a shit about William Lee Blaine. A framed eight-by-ten of Laura, signed "Love Always." A box of yellow number twos, another of Bic pens. Blue ink. A pack of Bicycle cards. Towels and stuff. An umbrella. A picture of my uniformed dad. I loaded a couple of packs of Trojans and Dad's army knife into his knapsack and snuck that in, too.

Mom added stamps and postcards and stationery, with more than a hint to write to her, but I'd direct most of that toward Laura. Toothpaste and deo. An *Upper Room* I'd never open. A pair of fleece-lined gloves she made me pay her a penny for. (Did I mention she was superstitious?) An imitation leather Elmer Fudd cap I wouldn't be caught dead in. And, at the last minute, a tin of chocolate chip cookies. Amazingly, the trunk barely bulged.

I'll say one thing for Mom. This cost a wad, but she never complained. I guess she was glad to spend her nest egg on me.

* * *

Scooter and I had mailed our applications the same day. I'd gotten my acceptance on a Friday, but his came five days later, days during which we didn't mention what we both thought—that even though his grades were as good as mine, his color might keep him out.

He brought it over, shit-eating grin plastered all over his face.

"Dude, I got in."

"Congrats, man. So—want to room together?"

"Well, if I got to stay with some honky, it might as well be you."

"Right on, dude. This is pretty cool."

The housing people no doubt wanted no trouble placing the dozen or so Black students, so we got our preference—308 Buchanan Hall.

Mike Capps, like me, was a gearhead. Car freak. Loved to work on them, sell, buy, trade, drive them. That summer he unloaded a souped-up '39 Ford and a motorless '56 T-Bird on some midlife crisis guy. In return Mike got a dark blue '65 Country Squire, one of those deals with fake wood sides and tailgate. 390, automatic. It even had front seat belts. That thing had room for all our stuff in the back (except for a couple of duffel bags lashed to the roof rack).

Of course, he had modified the motor—bored and stroked, new camshaft, glasspack mufflers—so I heard them coming about a quarter mile down the road. It was about six on one of those cloudy mornings that amplify sound like it was coming across a river.

Mom and I sat at the kitchen table. She cradled a cup of coffee like its sole purpose was to keep her hands from wringing. Neither of us had slept much—because of excitement or dread. I looked toward the Ford's loping rumble and smiled.

"Here they come. I'll go help load."

She made a mess of a smile.

"I'll be down in a minute, son."

At the car I found Mike and Marcia outside, him smoking a Camel, her rearranging herself with her compact. Scooter had the back door open, so we loaded my footlocker and suit bag and some grocery bags full of snacks and stuff. Didn't take long.

Mom likely spent that time in the bathroom fixing her face. She came downstairs carrying her pocketbook like Queen Elizabeth, head held high and resolute.

"Well, Martha, today's the big day. We get rid of these hungry boys."

"I'd not put it that way, Mike. We're just loaning them out for a while."

"Hell, I'm giving mine away. I can't afford to feed the big mooch anymore."

So we pulled out, Mike and Marcia and Mom in the front, me and Scooter in back, speeding west on US 19-23 toward Cullowhee. Or going as fast as a two-lane allowed. Mike wouldn't drive on the new interstate, said it put him to sleep. Besides, we had to stop at Clyde's for breakfast.

"It's why we left so early. There's a chocolate pie and pancake magnet in there, I swear. I can't go within twenty miles of it without pulling into that parking lot."

So a little after seven we began an hour of food and coffee and talk, laden with the smell of cigarettes and bacon and laced with concurrent conversations of truckers and locals.

The food was great—I had three eggs and biscuits and bacon and hash browns—but the conversation was like wading a swamp without boots. Do you think it'll rain, did you pack your umbrella, I bet that bunch two booths down is heading for WCC, is there enough gas to get back, when do you think it'll turn cold, reckon the cat will miss you, will we have good fall color this year, Lord, I thought my head would explode. I just wanted the merciful Jesus I no longer believed in to get me to school, away from this sea of anxiety band-aided by trivial words.

When we pulled into campus about ten, a crowd of fresh-faced do-gooders mobbed us to ask where we were headed. They stuck a Buchanan Hall card under our wiper blade and pointed us up the hill, the top of which was concealed by a cloud, like it might pour any second.

Buchanan looked like an architect had thrown a chaos of bricks and windows and handrails against the side of the hill until the various levels stuck. It, too, was full of student types who installed us in 308 in a half hour. Made sure we each had a campus map, a dining hall coupon for coffee, and a purple-and-gold beanie to wear on campus. All year.

So there the five of us stood, looking at bunks and desks and closets, watching the window for rain, wondering what next.

Mike put his arm around Scooter.

"Son, I'm proud of you. Study hard, hear?"

"I will, Dad."

Marcia took a deep breath and kissed Scooter on the cheek and gave him a big old hug.

"We love you, son. Do your best."

And the Capps family walked out the door.

Mom was doing well with the goodbye thing. At least she wasn't bawling.

"Son, the summer just flew by. Seems like you graduated yesterday."

Depended on your viewpoint. She took both my hands in hers.

"Willie Lee—I mean Will—I'll miss you."

"Me too, Mom."

"Study hard, now."

"I will. Listen, I'll see you Thanksgiving."

"You don't know how much I'll look forward to that. Meanwhile you be careful."

She leaned to me and kissed my forehead.

"I love you, son."

We walked outside, she dabbing her eyes with a handkerchief, me praying not to be embarrassed. But she hugged me again and slid into the backseat of the Country Squire and waved. I bet before they were out of sight she broke down and bawled.

To tell the truth, I had a lump in my throat. But not for long. Scooter and I, college men, put on those stupid beanies and headed for the Union.

VI.

Turn These Notes to Cheerful

Martha Atkins Blaine

Me again, back to this journal, trying to make sense of things. To see if there's any pattern to what has happened, especially between Willie Lee—Will, I mean—and me. How did we end up this way? Where did we go wrong? For that matter, where did he? Might be something I never know. But I'm trying.

I admit I'm a worry wart. And, when Henry died, I was pretty well flattened. Now, a grief-stricken worry wart is an evil spirit, especially hovering over a twelve-year-old boy. I see now, I wanted Will to step into Henry's shoes (which was impossible), and I was so afraid of being alone, of *abandonment*, that I hung myself around Will's neck like an albatross.

Who is more anxious, "natural" mothers or adoptive moms? No telling, but I was older and had wanted a kid forever, so I probably worried more than average. I'm sure that's how Will saw it.

Anyhow, after you've fretted your kid through everything from potty training to first day of school—mumps and measles to tonsils and broken bones—here bounds his way a whole 'nother gang of temptations. A dedicated worrier can't relax even one hour.

For example, at fourteen Will took up smoking. He didn't say a word, just went to school one morning with a pack of Camels in his shirt pocket like he was all grown up. We sold them downstairs, so it was easy to swipe a pack when Mary Anne or I wasn't looking.

I always thought tobacco was nasty, but back then many folks smoked, from punk kids to teachers and preachers. (Rev. Winters used maple-flavored tobacco.) Magazine ads said NINE OUT OF TEN DOCTORS PREFER CAMELS. Nobody feared they'd cause lung disease, not even the government, which put Lucky Strikes in Henry's war rations. "Couldn't be bad for you," he said, "or Uncle Sam wouldn't do that."

So, what could I say? Will's father, former pastor, and teachers, people he looked up to, smoked. I simply wrung my hands and told him not to steal them. After all, they were only nineteen cents a pack.

Then there were girls. He visited girlfriends all over the neighborhood on a red, white, and chrome bicycle he traded somebody out of. His favorite female seemed to be Teresa, about a mile down Oak Street. She was cute as a bug's ear. One summer Will took off on that bike like lightning to her house every night after supper. I didn't much worry until he started coming home after dark, shirts all wrinkled, smelling like Wind Song. I grounded him a while, which didn't please either of us much.

Sixteen was a dreaded milestone, for he had taken Henry's old Plymouth out of what he called mothballs. Will couldn't wait to drive that thing. Scared me to pieces, for it was fast and loud. I just knew he'd wrap it around a tree. At least for several weeks his attention shifted away from girls. Some nights I sat with him in the garage, talking and listening to those awful Beatles on the radio.

After he got his license, he went out of his way to be nice. *Can I take you downtown? Drive you to Spartanburg to see Aunt Ardie?* And, you know, he didn't scare me a single time. He was a good mechanic—and an excellent driver.

Still, I spent countless hours at the window, waiting for his headlights. One Friday after a ball game his curfew was eleven. Eleven-fifteen, no Will, every light in the house burning, me pacing a hole in the floor, almost wishing for a cigarette. Eleven-thirty, no Will. I cut the lights off, more easily to see headlights. Picked up the receiver to make sure the phone wasn't dead. Wishing it to ring, a living Will's voice on the other end saying things were fine. Dreading it to ring, a law officer with horrible news.

About twelve-fifteen that old car rumbled up. Will got out and shut the door and I came out on the landing in my robe. He took the stairs two at a time and put his arm around me.

"Mom, I'm okay, don't worry."

"I can't help it, son. Where in the world have you been?"

"Riding around. I guess I lost track of time. I'm sorry."

At least he smelled sober, alcohol being another evil to fret about.

"Willie Lee, don't ever do that again. I was worried sick."

"It's Will, Mom. And I won't."

The next morning a dent with white paint had bloomed on the rear fender. A story I didn't want to hear. And, of course, last night's promise soon evaporated.

It's one thing if your sixteen-year-old drives a Simca. But a hot rod? Yet I didn't demand we trade for something sensible. It was a direct connection with his dad, and besides, he would have souped up a safer car. You can't win.

He soon had a new girlfriend, daughter of an exec at the plant. I seen right off that wouldn't work. They were Episcopalians. I mean, how could a proper young lady let herself be seen in that jalopy? He'd even tied a squirrel tail on the radio antenna.

Laura James was a nice girl, a year younger than Will, cute in an upper-crust kind of way. Perky. Happy, deep brown eyes. Good manners, nice clothes, the perfect person for your son, in the right circumstances.

Marcia said let it flame out on its own. Boots agreed. You'll only make him furious, she said. So for a long time I kept quiet, even when they started "going steady."

My nerves weren't all that strong, and got weaker as his senior year loomed. I still hated to be alone, and dreaded his graduation and college, which would leave me twiddling my miserable thumbs. I see now, he too was scared—that when he left, Laura would find another. We were both as insecure as tadpoles in an ocean.

One day he came home in a perfect snit. Gave off a don't-tread-on-me aura I should have recognized. Instead I told him he and Laura wouldn't work. He said—or at least I thought he did—he was going to marry her. I said I'd never give my blessing.

He exploded. Next thing I knew, I woke in a hospital ward with five other women. Through a high window I saw dawn begin to break. My feet were cold under a cotton blanket. We were in metal beds with side restraints like jail bars. The bare walls were maybe beige, still too dark to tell. Soft snores from the beds. The smell of disinfectant and floor polish. A faint electric buzz.

On the night table beside my bed stood a card, GET WELL. *From what?* I wondered. *Where in the world am I?* I wasn't scared. I felt calm, quiet, like a snowfall in the night. Not strong. Not happy. Yet, not anxious, bruised, or bothered. What had I become?

I was in the state asylum in Morganton. They said at St. Joseph's Hospital I was mostly out of my head or didn't remember anything, so they did bunches of tests, found I wasn't much damaged physically, and sent me to Broughton Hospital for electroshock to make my poor old brain return to normal.

I have to say, my weeks there weren't all unpleasant. They fed me regularly (and pretty well, except the hospital gardener must have planted six acres in zucchini). Besides electroshock, I had sewing therapy, every afternoon embroidering little pink and blue and yellow flowers on pillowcases. Napkins. Tablecloths.

I also had plenty of time to read the Bible and write in my journal.

Which was the nicest thing. Dr. Jackson convinced me my life was worth writing about. I might even find out what has made me what I am. Which is a woman beginning to see she is a child of God, slowly—but surely—getting better all the time.

When I got home Will and I had a contest to see who might walk on more eggs without breaking them. But we eventually knew where to travel safely and comfortably. He was into everything a high school senior does—my task was to make plans to be lonely.

Re-reading this story, I'm struck by how painfully little happiness it contains. It's probably time to turn these notes to cheerful—or at least happier. My life hasn't been totally miserable.

I knew I needed company when Will left for school. The store provided plenty during the day, but late at night a big old place gets lonely as it creaks and pops and breathes. I figured to keep writing in my journal. Or praying. Which, I have learned, can be much the same.

One evening Mary Anne and I were closing the store. We'd checked up—cash drawer and daybook matched to the penny, after only two attempts! Lights out, key in the door. Around the corner trembled a furry shape. Spaniel and something, probably several somethings. Droop-eared, brown-eyed, brown and white with auburn patches. Making little eeky sounds. Mary Anne held out her hand and found he loved to be petted.

"There's a collar, but no tag. I wonder where he came from."

"Should we feed him?"

"If we do, he'll stay."

"If we don't, he might starve. He's thin as a fence rail."

He practically inhaled a can of Alpo. A bouncy dog, but no pee-in-the-floor puppy.

"Now you've had supper. Go home."

At this point I was determined not to be responsible for any critter except Will.

"Mrs. B, I don't think he'll leave now."

"Well, you go home, then. Will and me can take it from here."

The dog didn't follow Mary Anne, for he'd seen me open his food. He bounded up to the landing and sat with me, head cocked, like he knew not to ruin my hose.

"Go home!"

The little devil, I swear, grinned at me. *I'm here, lady.*

"Well, you're not coming inside."

Will, who had been working on sets for the senior play, drove up, gunned the motor, and cut it off. He stopped halfway up the steps, balanced schoolbooks on his hip, and smiled.

"Hey Mom, who's your friend?"

"He just showed up. I've said *Go home* but he doesn't seem to understand."

"Hey, Go Home. Good boy."

When I seen Will skritch the dog's ears, I hoped the pooch would stay. "You're a cool mutt, Go Home."

"What kind of name is that?"

"It's his name. Don't you like it, boy? We are going to keep him, right?"

"He has a collar. He belongs to somebody."

"I bet somebody put him out. Look how matted his fur is. You need a bath, Go Home. Don't you, boy?"

So Will bathed him with flea soap and brushed him good. He looked pretty shiny not to be a purebred. That night we fixed him a bed on the landing, but he whimpered, so I got up and let him in. Tried to make him sleep beside my bed. That lasted about a minute. After Go Home settled around my feet and sighed, I knew I'd not be shy of company after Will left.

As I fell asleep I thought about predestination. Or was it foreordination? Presbyterian words, anyway, learned as a child and barely understood but somehow known to be right, at least in my mind. Somehow God predestined me and Go Home to meet—or God foreordained Go Home to be abandoned at my place, simply because God, who knows everything, knew I needed future comfort.

We made only a feeble effort to find the dog's former owner.

I've heard it said, it's only half a life without a dog. I don't know about that, but I can say that Go Home sure made a difference in mine, which was about to change drastically—from a high schooler's mom to a college man's mother. Will joked once about taking Go Home with him to Western. That was enough. I'd sooner let him take my right arm.

It helped that his senior year was busy. School play, senior picnic, prom (he took Laura), pictures, ball games, annuals. The summer before school started we shopped downtown a lot. Clothes, school supplies, an umbrella. And a metal footlocker for his dorm room. I had a pang when I seen that footlocker on its end on the Pack Square sidewalk, Will leaning on it, smoking a cigarette, trying to look "cool."

That night we laid out his stuff—sheets, a blanket, towels—in a trial run to see how much room we had. He was quiet. (Go Home stood just outside Will's bedroom door, question marks in his eyes.)

"Will, honey, what's wrong?"

"I don't know. Nothing."

"No, come on. You're too quiet. I thought you'd be chomping at the bit to leave."

"Well, I have mixed feelings."

"Want to talk about it?"

"Not really. It's just that…"

I sat on his bed and waited.

"Are you afraid of something?"

He sat on the corner of his desk like he didn't want it to fly away.

"I guess. I mean, what if I can't hack it?"

"Nonsense. You're a smart boy."

"No, remember that aptitude test? I was cut out to be a farmer or miner or something."

"Those things aren't reliable."

He looked at Laura's picture, a glossy eight-by-ten signed "Love Always, Laura." So that was at least part of it.

"Will, if you and her are meant to be, a year apart won't hurt."

He gave a sad smile. "It'll be longer than a year. She's a sight smarter than me. She wants to go to Wake Forest or Duke or Virginia. She even turns up her nose at Carolina. And she's beautiful. Some guy'll snatch her up quick."

"You don't know that, son."

"Well, I can hope. But she wants to be a doctor. Why would she keep hanging out with a grease monkey?"

"Will, don't say that. You're going to make something out of yourself. You won't be fixing cars forever."

"Maybe that's what I *want* to do, Mom."

I stood and took a deep breath. "You have a scholarship. You have your whole life in front of you. Nobody in our family had this chance. You're going, young man. You hear?"

A year ago I would have pleaded for him to stay home with me.

"Even if it means leaving you by yourself?"

"I have Boots and Pearl and Go Home and Mary Anne, not to mention church. I'll be fine. You and Scooter will make your own way. Now, hand me those towels."

*   *   *

Other days I wasn't so brave. The one step forward, two back routine. But I found that when I was back two steps on my left heel, I went forward by paying attention to my Bible. I don't know if you'd call it meditation or absorption or what, but reading a passage enough times led to another explaining what I had puzzled over. Not that I heard voices or anything, but my mind seemed directed. Guided. Shepherded. I don't know the right word.

The Christmas before Will left, our Sunday School class was reading Isaiah's prediction of Jesus' suffering. "A man of sorrows, and acquainted with grief" kept ringing in my mind. That sure described me after Henry died, except "acquainted" might be too weak a word.

Did this Old Testament Jesus take grief away? As my mind went over and over this passage, I suddenly went straight to Matthew: "Come unto me, all ye that labor and are heavy laden, and I will give you rest."

What about this burden I've carried for years?

"Take my yoke upon you, and learn of me: for I am meek and lowly in heart: and ye shall find rest unto your souls. For my yoke is easy, and my burden is light."

I don't know how such things work, but from that Christmas I felt my burden lighten, I felt closer both to Jesus and my need to let Will go.

I don't know who was a bigger fan of meat loaf, Will or Go Home. I always fixed it on Will's birthday, and several times a year besides. He'd have asked for it Thanksgiving and Christmas if I'd have let him get away with that. So our last supper before he left was meat loaf, mashed potatoes, string beans, a nice green salad, dinner rolls. Coconut cake for dessert. We had a pleasant, quiet supper. But when I tried to talk Will into helping with the dishes, he wanted to say goodbye to his car. I knew freshmen couldn't have cars, but you'd think it had feelings or something.

Well, so did I. After Go Home and I finished the dishes, I went to the garage. The hood was up, Will's bottom the only thing I could see from my vantage.

"You're not spending your last night here in this garage. Whether you like it or not, we're going to have a good evening. Together."

I stomped upstairs. In a few minutes I smelled lanolin hand soap as he walked into the kitchen. I had turned on the stove and gotten a Jiffy Pop, a salt shaker, and two bowls. "We're going to have popcorn, drink ginger ale, and talk."

He smiled at me. "Okay, Mom, it's your party. But please don't make us play Uno."

"I won't. Remember when you were little, we used TV Time popcorn?"

"Sure. It had a blob of gunk in one side. You let me squeeze it into the pot."

"That was oil. This is lots more convenient." The corn began to pop, like little firecrackers, which made the aluminum foil expand into a ball. Will poured Canada Dry while I let steam escape from the pouch. We went to the living room, Will and I on the couch, hopeful Go Home on the floor, tail going fifty miles an hour, especially if Will flipped him a piece of corn.

My son was kind of in-between. Old enough to buy beer (horrors!) but not yet shaving every day. I urged him to keep his face clean, but he still had his share of pimples. He had a kind of crooked smile, for we couldn't afford braces. His way of cocking his head when listening to you reminded me so much of Henry. I loved that boy to pieces.

"So, Mom, what do you want to talk about?"

"Something pleasant. Did you see Laura this afternoon? You didn't mention her at supper."

"Yeah. But... she cried when I left."

"Isn't that better than seeing her jump for joy?"

"I guess."

"So are you looking forward to tomorrow?"

"Sure." He flipped Go Home another kernel. Lord, that dog was patient.

"That's all? 'Sure'?"

"What should I say? I *am* a little scared, you know."

"Will, there's nothing to be frightened about. This will open so many doors, so many opportunities. I'm proud of you."

"Well, we'll see what the first quarter brings. It *will* be kind of fun. Except I never have liked purple. And they'll make us wear some stupid beanie."

"You'll get used to it. Listen. I love you more than you know. Despite our troubles, I love you more than anything. You will go tomorrow into this new world. Whenever you feel anxious, know that I pray for you every minute.

"I'll mail you care packages. Cookies to share with Scooter and all your friends. I'll write every few days. And when you come home for break I'll fix you a meatloaf.

"So make me proud, William Lee Blaine. I'm counting on you."

"But what if I…"

"Don't even think about it. More popcorn?"

"No, thanks. I think I'll turn in early. Tomorrow's a big day."

"At least let's watch a little television."

So we watched *Hogan's Heroes*. The nine o'clock movie was *Fail Safe* but neither of us much cared for that.

Will walked Go Home, then gave me a hug. "I'll try my best, Mom."

"I know you will, son. Sweet dreams."

"You, too."

I went to my room to write for a little while. I tried not to hear him tiptoe downstairs. Then there was scratchy music through the floor-boards, and the occasional knock of a tool.

I had hoped for a more cheerful time, but at least he wasn't out gallivanting. The next night I'd have no idea of where or what. With that thought, I began a good cry. It was my party—I'd cry if I wanted to.

The big day turned out not to hurt so bad. I was up way before daylight reading about Pentecost, praying for tongues of fire to light on my son's head. I perked coffee, took a quick bath. Dressed and waited for the racket of Mike and Marcia's new (to them) station wagon.

Once everything was in the back or tied to the roof rack, we looked like the Beverly Hillbillies, except in a bigger car. Mike stopped at that restaurant in Hazelwood, Clyde's I think it is, so that took a while. I couldn't eat a bite, but Will and Mike and Scooter made up for that. Mike joked about getting rid of Scooter, but Mike's a big baby underneath that sheriff swagger. He was having a tough time, too. Marcia and I mostly kept quiet.

When we left the kids at the dormitory it was threatening to rain. Not much was said, but nary an eye was dry as we hugged and headed to the empty car. Little talk on the way back, except to wonder when leaves would turn and if we'd have a cold winter.

Go Home was happy to see me, but kept peering into Will's room like *where is he?*, then looking at me like *what have you done with him?* So the dog and I had the first of many long chats—about Will, the state of the world, and whatever else was on his doggy mind.

I've always been able to find plenty to do, but that fall I became a one-woman make-work program. Extra promotions for The Top of the

Hill, cookies for Will, embroidery (my Broughton stay opened some craft door in my brain), reading, writing, cleaning. I even painted the kitchen one weekend. Anything to keep worriment at bay.

So it wasn't long, really, until Will came home for break. Then pretty quickly the first quarter was over. (His grades? B in English, some Cs—a D in Zoology, so he wouldn't make a doctor—and an F in Spanish.) Then Thanksgiving. By Christmas I was, if not used to him being gone, at least tolerating it. He needed me, for he trailed tons of dirty laundry behind him.

I needn't have done all that worrying about Laura. A pretty, bright high school senior, of course she had found a new boyfriend before September was over. She wrote Will what they call a "Dear John" letter. He shrugged it off, but you could tell he was hurt. He said he wasn't dating at school.

"I don't have time, what with all the reading. Besides, I haven't seen a girl I'd like to hang out with."

"It'll happen, son."

"Whatever." A word he seemed to use a lot.

By winter quarter he'd gotten a weekend job at a filling station in Sylva. I wasn't happy about that, but what could I do? At least he was enthusiastic.

"How do you get to work?"

"I got a bicycle."

"How far is it from campus?"

"I dunno, maybe four miles."

"But what about ball games? Don't you want a social life?"

"Mom, the games are a pain in the drain—and besides, the few people who hang around weekends are either schoolies or drunks. I'd rather keep my hands busy and make a little money."

"Isn't your scholarship enough?"

"Sure, but that's not the point. Making a customer happy is worth a lot."

His grades came up a bit next quarter, but he'd never be on the Dean's List, and he still hadn't passed a language. Fine, I figured, as long as he got a diploma. I didn't know the foreign language was a requirement.

At the end of his sophomore year he came home, books, footlocker, dirty clothes and all. Perfectly normal. So I washed everything and was putting it away until, I thought, late August.

I carried his long-sleeved shirts into his room to hang in the wardrobe. "These will be ready for you to take back to school."

He was at his desk, staring out the window. Maybe watching a squirrel, I thought, like Go Home likes to do.

"I'm not going back, Mom."

If this had been a soap opera I would have dropped the shirts and fainted. As it was, I took a deep breath, hung up the shirts, and sat on the bed corner.

"Whatever do you mean, son?"

"Mom, I'm nearly twenty-one. And, believe me, I know what I need to do."

I didn't know what to say.

"Mom, don't cry. Listen. I've spent two years spinning my wheels. Nothing in the classroom has caught me except a couple of English courses—and you can't do anything with that. The only time I'm like really happy is at work. So, I'm asking for my job back. We can be partners in The Top of the Hill. What do you say?"

Somehow this didn't seem bad, although a voice inside said to tell him he was crazy. "Son, are you sure?"

"Plenty sure. I need to get on with things. Find out who I am. Make myself useful. That kind of stuff. Plus, I can't graduate without a language. It isn't worth it."

"Can't you take a leave of absence so they'll keep your place? I mean, let's think about all this."

"I've already told them I won't be back. They can give my seat to somebody else."

"What about your scholarship?"

"I wrote to that Snipes fellow. It'll save the state some money."

"Will, I can't bless this without thinking about it."

"Sure. I'm sorry to disappoint you. But like I said, I'm pretty near miserable except when I'm at work."

"Well, at least you're not running off to California to find yourself."

"Not into that scene. I might not know who I am, but I sure know *where* I am. I belong right here. How about it? Will you hire me?"

"If you're dead set, we'll work out something. But our mechanic, Mr. Lewis… I can't just get rid of him on short notice."

"You don't need to. See, here's how I figure it."

At the kitchen table Will outlined a path for us. He'd start as Mr. Lewis's assistant, and Mr. Lewis would move on, or not. Either way, Will would be happy fixing cars and expanding into "performance" mechanics, maybe set up a race car. Sell chrome lug nuts, fancy valve covers, Continental kits, cutouts. Become an inspection station, for apparently there's money in that. By the time I needed to start supper, I knew I'd eventually agree. I would absorb another disappointment—that he'd not graduate—but I had weathered his sharp rejection, so could do anything, and this had a bright side. Working with my son over the long haul had its attraction.

I've known women who washed clothes on Monday. Even in the middle of a frog-strangler. Their lives were hitched to a routine: Monday, wash; Tuesday, iron; Wednesday, scrub; Thursday, mend; Friday, sweep; Saturday, bake; Sunday, go to church (if any energy is left). Like Scripture, didn't vary a jot or a tittle.

I didn't grow up that way, because Ella Rose was "delicate." I did most of the washing Mondays if that worked out—or when I got around to it. After Papa died, I inherited the store, so had enough work for two women. Washing happened when it happened. Period.

Will didn't complain about helping with laundry. He hung it outdoors in good weather, then brought it in after supper to be folded, ironed, and put up. (In bad weather a forest of folding racks filled the living room.)

That often became a time when Will and I talked, even if the TV was on. Mostly small stuff when he was in high school, how was your day, did you pass your algebra test, that kind of thing. But after he dropped out of school I thought it might be time for him to think about his birth parents. If for no other reason than to quiet *my* mind a little.

See, I was sometimes awakened by Will's voice yelling *You're not my real mother*. It happened so often that I realized he likely did say that before I landed in the hospital. And I feared that once coaxed from its cave, that voice would never leave until Will and I aired it out.

One evening—a Monday, because *Gunsmoke* was on—Will folded sheets and towels while I ironed blue jeans (he kept telling me not to, but they looked so much better on him). I figured I might as well jump in.

"Will, can I ask you something?"

"Sure, Mom."

"Do you still wonder about... your birth mother?"

He picked up another towel. Sniffed it, as I had taught him, to smell the sunshine.

"I guess."

So this was going to be like pulling teeth.

"Either you do or you don't."

"Well, sure. I mean, not all the time or anything."

After folding the last towel he started sorting white from black socks like he hoped that would be a big problem. Go Home raised his head like he didn't want to miss anything.

I sprinkled the jeans and took after the right leg with the iron.

"I've told you what little I know. She was in high school. Brown eyes. Medium height. That's about it."

He slowed down so he wouldn't run out of socks.

"Will, would you like to know more about her?"

Red crept from his shirt collar to his cheeks like a little tide.

"Sure. I guess. Like, did she live around here?"

"Maybe, because you were born at St. Joseph's. But many girls in trouble went to different cities to have their children. And even if she was from here, that's been a long time. She could be anywhere."

"Why are you telling me this?"

I folded his jeans, keenly aware of their warmth and my racing heart.

"I keep having this dream... nightmare, really, where you scream: *You're not my real mother.*"

"Damn, did I tell you that?"

"Watch your language, son. All I can say is I've wakened to that voice enough that I think you must have."

"Mom, I'm sorry. If I said that I sure didn't mean it."

"Yes, you did. In the fury of the moment, you meant it. So I have two things to say. One, I forgive you. Two, if you want to try to find your birth mother, I won't stand in your way. I think I can take it."

It had been a long time since he had let me see him cry.

"Mom, I'm sorry."

Our tears wet each other's shoulders for a minute or two.

"There, son, I've said it. And I mean it."

"Mom, thanks. I'll take you up on that one of these days."

"Just let me know beforehand. I've had enough surprises for two life-times. I've lost parents, a brother, a husband. I don't think I could stand to lose you, Will. I love you more than anything."

"Don't worry, Mom."

"Ha! That's what mothers do. We worry."

We finished the laundry, Marshall Dillon got his man (as I knew he would, it being rerun season), and we put things up. When Will took Go Home for a walk I looked at the ceiling and said a thank-you prayer, because that had gone pretty well.

VII.

Discovery

William Lee Blaine

The kindest thing to say about me and college is we weren't compatible. I didn't hate it—some courses were really cool. But I didn't love it. I toughed it out for two years, until it was apparent I'd never graduate. See, back then they had requirements, and I flunked Spanish. No language, no diploma.

Campus life? Well, I'm no jock, although through Scooter I knew some of those guys. I had no enthusiasm for intramural sports. My musical abilities ended at dialing in a radio station. I might have gone to three or four Catamount games. If there was ever a panty raid I didn't hear about it. I guess you could say I wasn't much of a joiner.

I read a lot. Enjoyed English classes, even composition, where my instructor was not much older than me, with wild hair and a worried look. Spent a lot of time in the library with Steinbeck, Hemingway. Went on a Wolfe kick, although my professors didn't think much of his work. A time or two I was immersed in some story and forgot to show up for a quiz. That kind of thing doesn't do wonders for your GPA.

Maybe my deal had something to do with the legislature that year changing Western Carolina College to Western Carolina University. Like a bunch of old men in suits will suddenly make higher education… well, *higher*. I couldn't tell my particular place in the chain of being was elevated a particle by their decree.

Or maybe (here's true confession) I never cared enough to get with the program. I wasn't lazy—unless I didn't like the subject. I aced Modern American Novel, but zoology? They lost me at simple genetics. I mean, who gives a shit about a fruit fly? And I proved I had no bent for languages. Way down deep, I knew I'd never work on Peugeots. Alfa Romeos. Volkswagens.

It didn't help that WCC/U was a suitcase college. Come Friday afternoon the campus was as deserted as a moon crater. People scattered like roaches when you turn on a light. Freshmen couldn't have cars, so bummed rides to get hell out of Dodge.

I mean, there was nothing to do weekends. Back then the legal age for beer or wine was eighteen, but nobody legit sold it anywhere near campus. You might talk a senior into bringing you a bottle from Waynesville, but I didn't know any of them my first year and couldn't afford liquor anyway. It was either study all weekend or listen to crickets sound mournful when the Saturday sun set behind the mountains. And whoever heard of a mournful cricket?

I would have been happy to catch rides to Sand Hill, except fresh into first quarter this letter came from Laura. She'd dated some jerk a couple of times and said I was therefore free to see college girls. Like any of them hung around weekends. So I stowed her picture in my footlocker. (I saw her a couple more times over winter and spring breaks, but she was off to Wake Forest the next fall. Then med school. She's now an OB/GYN, married to a radiologist. I'm an auto mechanic. Who's happier? Who knows?)

Anyway, I borrowed a bike and (after tightening and lubing the fool thing) pedaled to Sylva and got a job at a garage. Saturdays, 8-3, $1.25 an hour, plus the owner slipped me six Blue Ribbons every couple of weeks. Kept me from going bonkers.

So I beat on, like that Gatsby boat thing, for two years. Mom knew I wasn't going to graduate—they sent grades to your parents unless you were married or something. So she wasn't too surprised when I said I'd not go back. Disappointed, yes. But not shocked.

Actually, I came home with more than a tad of excitement, for I got my job back at The Top of the Hill. There's fine satisfaction when some doofus drops off an ill-running car and a day or two later you give it back, engine purring like a kitten. And then he pays you money to boot.

So then. Home. With a job. No particular responsibilities except to get along with Mom. About to turn twenty-one. And it wasn't long before I met Tina Green, who pretty quickly became a serious girlfriend. I mean, she threatened to make me very happy. As they said back then, I had it made in the shade. Still, I was troubled.

Part of that was keen remembrance of my promise to Dad. To "make something out of myself." I worried that somehow, somewhere, he was watching, and thinking I was pissing it away. Even though I was following in his footsteps. Enough to give a guy a headache.

Another part was wondering where I had come from. Who were my bio parents? Where were they? Still alive? Other children? Did they wonder about me?

See, I had pondered such questions for a long time, but one night freshman year they got focused. I was in a bull session in Buchanan. This guy from South Carolina listened to some of my story, then looked at me like I had walked in from downtown Hanoi or somewhere.

"You an orphan, or what?"

"No, man, I'm an adoptee, not an orphan."

"What's the diff?"

I think he finally understood when I said David Copperfield but when I started in about adoption I got tangled up. Back in the room I decided to look that stuff up. Again.

Here I was, a stranger in what you might call the middle of damn nowhere, my dictionary in a pool of yellow light, smoke squiggling from a cigarette in my overflowing ashtray, and guess what? "Adoptee" wasn't in my *New Collegiate*. The beatenest thing. What I was, wasn't in the damn dictionary. So maybe I didn't exist. Which might mean I didn't have to keep going to Spanish class.

About that time Scooter came home and laid his stuff on his desk.

"So what's happening?"

"I just found out I don't exist."

"Cool. First time you realized that?"

"What do you mean?"

"Shit, man, I've known that forever. And I'm happy, because non-existent no-minds don't make racket, and I need my beauty sleep."

And with that he jumped to the top bunk and faced the wall.

So I quietly cobbled my own definition from "Adopt": an adoptee is "a child taken by other than biological parents as their own." The adoptee therefore has full rights of inheritance and all that crap. Legally same as if we'd been born to them. Which gives us stability, comfort, peace of mind. At least that's what the law said. I was supposed to feel all warm and fuzzy because Henry and Martha Blaine adopted me.

But there's also something of the orphan about an adoptee. An orphan is "a child bereaved by death of both father and mother; or, less commonly, of either parent." Well, "bereaved" means "deprived." An orphan, for example, survives a car wreck in which her mom and dad are killed. But is the degree of bereavement far less when you have been given up? (Some of us say "abandoned." Like a dog you get for Christmas and didn't like so put an ad in the paper, Free To Good Home.)

Sure, I thought, I'm an adoptee, but there's a decent chance I'm an orphan, too. That my bio mom is dead and my bio dad, well, he might as well be, for they usually run like hell when they get the news. And Henry's dead and Martha ain't in great shape, so I might soon be both adoptee and orphan, abandoned by four different people.

Heavy territory.

That night I decided to find out who the people who conceived me and gave me up were. I had to know how much of a mongrel I was. I lay a long time listening to Scooter snore and wondering about the next step.

*   *   *

After I left school it didn't take long for routine to set in. Work at the garage six, off one. Lunch in the back room on wet days, on a front bench when nice. Supper upstairs with Mom most evenings. A little TV with her, although since I'd learned to read at WCC/U I preferred a good book. Except when *Hee Haw* was on. (The jokes were awful but the girls were great.) Maybe a game of Rook or Hearts. Or popcorn and a soft drink. Sleep, then do it again.

Mom was better. I still walked on eggs around her, but she had quit twisting her hair and staring off into some place only she knew about. Sometimes I'd catch her looking at me like she wasn't quite sure I was real. But she never once fussed about me dropping out of college, and really seemed to enjoy working with me at The Top of the Hill. We got along well.

One night—this was in July—she was putting up laundry and I was watching *Bonanza*—no, that came on Sunday nights, and she never washed clothes on Sunday, so forget Hoss and Little Joe. Anyway, the TV was on.

She folded a towel and laid it on the coffee table.

"Will, I've been studying."

"What, Mom?"

"Are you still… curious about your birth mother?"

"Sure."

"Well, I've given you all I know. She was in high school, medium height, brown eyes. That was all the county would tell me."

"I remember that."

"Well, I've been thinking. I'm pretty sure that before—you know, before the hospital—you told me I wasn't your real mother."

God, there it was, flopped out on the table like a huge cold fish.

"I said that? Lord, I'm sorry. I didn't mean it."

"I can't be perfectly sure, but you have said it many times in my nightmares. So you must have said it. Or at least thought it. And you did too mean it, by your hateful tone of voice."

You bet I was looking for a hole to crawl into.

"I'm sorry, Mom."

"And I accept that. Like I said, I've been thinking. If you want to find your birth parents, I won't maybe much like it, but I won't stand in your way."

"You mean that?"

"Yes, son. Both of us have holes in our hearts. My big ones are for Henry and you. Yours is for Henry and your... curiosity. Now that you're here, part of mine is starting to fill back up. To heal. And that feels good. I would be selfish to deny you a chance to fill one of yours."

We shared a big old hug and cried on each other's shoulders.

"I'm sorry, Mom. I won't hurt you again."

She wiped her eyes and shook her head.

"See that you don't. Now, I've got laundry to deal with."

So, suddenly—and without asking—I had permission—however reluctant—to find Dick and Jane, or whoever the heck they might turn out to be. That felt kind of like getting into a roller coaster car—about to be thrilled and frightened at the same time.

I'd poked around enough to know North Carolina seals original records when a kid is adopted, so there's no legal way in hell to find bio parents. But I took a day off and went to the courthouse anyway, because if I browsed in the birth records something might jump at me. Some kid born the same day's mother might have been in a ward with mine, you know?

I parked the Streak in front of City Hall and looked up the hill toward Pack Square. Bright sunshine after last night's rain made it look clean for a change, and pretty lively for nine-thirty. Lawyers heading to court, people delivering bread and bags of onions to lunch joints, men smoking in front of the pool hall, shoppers in and out of the drug store. A mist of diesel exhaust and coffee and yeast rolls and stale beer hung at nose level. *Patton* was playing at the Plaza.

In the courthouse lobby I stopped to look around, when this lady popped out of a dark hallway.

"You look lost. What can I do for you?"

"I've come to find a birth record."

"They're in the Register of Deeds office. This way."

She opened the heavy brass door and led me past several kind of like ticket windows, where women messed with deeds and money and wedding licenses. We ended up in a side room where tons of ledger books huddled on shelves.

"What year?"

"1949."

She gave me the once-over and a blue-eyed smile.

"Let me guess. The year you were born?"

"Maybe."

She pulled one down and set it on a long wooden table.

"Have at it, son. Anything else I can do for you?"

"I guess not."

"Well, if I can be of service, let me know."

As she left I thanked her and got out a pencil and eyeballed that ledger.

It was covered in light blue raveldy fabric, corners trimmed with metal. An old-fashioned deal with steel pegs. To expand it you screw off the cap and screw in another inch worth of peg and cap it back. This one was about six inches thick.

The room wasn't exactly noisy but high ceilings reflected low-grade racket from leather heels with metal taps, squeak from desk chairs, the shuffle of paper, the crash of date stamps. A quarter hit the stone floor and rolled half a mile before coming to a stop.

The ledger went by month so I opened it in the middle and kept on to August 6. Six born that day, four girls, two boys. I skipped the girls. The last record was covered with a piece of pink paper with a faded blue note on top: To SBPW, Raleigh. A piece of yellowed tape held the edges. My God, I thought. Some slack-assed clerk screwed up, and forgot to pull this. I'm about to find out who I really am.

Man, my heart tripped fast as a dog kicking fleas. I looked around, afraid some deed guy might hoist me by my collar and toss me out. But the coast was clear. A typewriter in the distance, a siren outside. Otherwise calm.

When I edged the gray paper up the brittle tape came loose to reveal a birth certificate:

BABY LANCE, born 3:37 A.M., five pounds two ounces
Delivered by Frank A Thomas, MD at St. Joseph's Hospital.

Then lines I read about a million times:

Mother: Priscilla Ruth Lance, unmarried, age 18
Father: NONE NAMED

I had seen a copy of my adoption order, indexed at the State Board of Public Welfare—SBPW. So this had to be me and her.

I figured somebody might hear me rip it out of the book and I couldn't risk showing Dad's knife so I fished the notebook out and copied all the dope down, although I about broke a pencil I was shaking so bad.

Priscilla Ruth Lance. Nice name. Could she still be in Buncombe County? She'd be about thirty-seven. She wouldn't rat on her boyfriend, so she had nerve, which was cool. Who was he and is he still around?

I slid the ledger back in its space even though tons of signs said not to re-shelve stuff. I didn't want anybody to see where I'd prowled, at least until I was well outside.

Would the library have her high school annual? Worth a try.

Pack Library was a diagonal walk across the Square from the court house. Halfway there I felt light-headed so stopped at a bench and hoped Pay Days would tide me over until supper. I had three or four dollars but if I didn't buy lunch I'd have plenty of beer and cigarette money.

The Square was scattered with people, some heads down in a hurry, others lollygagging, tourists probably, rubbernecking Governor Vance's phallic symbol, wondering which greasy spoon to eat lunch at. A wispy-haired man in a seersucker suit and panama hat bounced by carrying a leather briefcase. A middle-aged farmer leaned on a lamppost, hands jammed in overall pockets. He puffed a cigar and watched a ragged woman in a fright wig mutter as she rummaged a trash can. Nary a hippie in sight—you had to go to Chapel Hill to find one back then.

A bit of breeze on my back kept bus fumes mostly at bay so except having to shoo a yellow jacket a couple of times I enjoyed my nutritious lunch—salt, peanuts, caramel, whatever that gooey stuff is.

I tossed their wrappers and trucked over to the library. You came into a dark room with a card catalog and circulation desk. A band around the top of the wall showed chariots and Greeks or Romans or somebody with lances and stuff. I told the librarian what I was after, and she pointed me upstairs to the North Carolina collection.

From shadowy stairs you came into a big room with bookshelves all around, some glassed in, most open, and enough windows so even on a dark day you didn't need much electric light. A bunch of long tables with plenty of room to walk around, and several clots of people using them. An older lady wearing a big bracelet to match her throat thing, what do you call it, a brooch, looked like she ran a tight ship.

"What may I help you find, young man?"

"A high school annual. 1948 or 1949, I think."

"We have Lee Edwards and Crawford High yearbooks for those years. Which school?"

"Could be either one."

She laid 1948 and 1949 for both on this long wooden table with thick carved legs.

"Look at these all you want. I'll re-shelve them when you're through."

"This table sure is fancy."

"It used to be a square grand piano, a kind popular in the 1890s. Minus the works, of course. What's left is the legs, soundboard, and top. These pegs are where the top was hinged. Brazilian rosewood, it is. I like to think Thomas Wolfe studied at this table—at the old library, of course. You know about Thomas Wolfe?"

I nodded, although I didn't know much. I wanted to tear into those yearbooks, not hear a lecture about some dead writer.

"If I can help, please let me know."

The room was so quiet I was aware of my heart. I started to crack my knuckles to relax but that might rile her up. I picked up one of those wheel bubblegum colored erasers with a cheap plastic brush and threw it in my knapsack. You never know when you'll need something like that.

The Lee Edwards *Hillbilly* was kind of moss green with gold letters and smelled like an old library dog. Priscilla Ruth Lance wasn't in either volume so I was up shit creek if the Crawford *Wildcat* didn't come through. It was faded maroon with black letters. Past pictures of teachers and all, I found the senior class. Suddenly, page thirty-two, toward the bottom, there she was, Priscilla Ruth Lance at seventeen or eighteen, looking to the left of the camera like she's sharing a secret. She had a nice mouth and dark eyes and like every girl wore a strand of imitation pearls. All pictures came with a little quotation. Hers? "Full of sweet dreams, and health, and quiet breathing." Like everybody else nose-whistled or something.

I glimmed that black-and-white picture for a long time, looking for ironclad proof she was my mother. Dark eyes. Cheekbones maybe. High forehead. The shape of the face. Maybe hair the same color, but hers was thick, nothing like mine turned out to be.

When I looked up everybody stared at me like I was a madman and the librarian was headed my way.

"Son, are you all right?"

"I think so. Why?"

"You had your head down and sounded distressed."

"I didn't mean to."

I wiped my nose with the back of my hand and looked around. People suddenly bookwormed again.

"Is it something you found?"

She pointed to the book.

"Could I get a copy of this page? Then I'll leave."

"Stay as long as we're open. I'll be right back."

They had this copier about the size of a hay baler—you almost expected it to have a steam whistle. She returned with a copy, a question mark plastered all over her face.

"My mother."

"I thought maybe so. Copies are a quarter, but this one's on me."

"Thanks."

I eased it into my pack like it was part of an old Bible or something and headed for the Streak. Which, amazingly, didn't have a parking ticket. I'd forgotten to feed the meter. I cranked it up and headed home, where Mom was sure to want to know what I was up to. I hadn't said much about my trip, just that I'd be home for supper. So I had twenty or thirty minutes to figure out what to say. She'd given permission, but, still, I didn't know if I could be straight up with her yet.

I parked, ran the steps, and unlocked the door. So Mom was downstairs in the store. I laid Priscilla's picture on my desk, studied it a minute, then put it in the drawer.

Mom had left a pot of spaghetti sauce on a low simmer and a note asking me to stir it if I got home early. It smelled great but my stomach would have to calm down before I could eat.

I tried to nap but nothing doing. My mind surged like a Redstone rocket. I got up and poured a ginger ale and smoked a cigarette and stared at Priscilla's picture. Could she still be around? Did she, like Laura had said, have another family? Was she even still alive? How to find out? Mike Capps, of course. He kind of knew everybody. Or could find them. I was about to call him when Mom came upstairs.

"Will, are you okay?"

I guess I looked a little weird. I sure felt that way.

"Sure."

"Well, I'm glad you're here early. Mary Anne had to go home sick, and I'm expecting a delivery any minute. Can you fill in for her?"

"Sure. I'll be right down."

So I shelved Mike Capps for the time being. I hadn't known for twenty-one years, so what was another day or two?

Supper was great. I'd calmed enough to eat two platefuls plus a salad and a piece of chocolate cake. For a change, Mom wasn't too nosy. We watched TV and she went to bed early.

About two A.M. I took a commode-hugging fit, one of those where you look for your toenails because you're turning inside out. I lay with head on cold porcelain and wondered if I'd ever feel right again.

Of course, the dry heaves woke Mom, who helped me sit up and cleaned my face with a cold, damp towel. Like she'd done when I was a little kid.

"You'll be okay, son. You're getting color back in your face. Can you stand up yet?"

"I don't know. Mom, I'm sorry."

"Shh."

She felt my forehead.

"Does your stomach hurt?"

"Not now."

"You don't have a fever, thank God. If it was food poisoning, I'd be right beside you, because you said you didn't eat lunch in town."

She looked at me sideways.

"You found her, didn't you? Or at least learned something about her."

Mom would have made a good private eye. I nodded and knew I couldn't start lying now. Spread out on the bathroom floor smelling like puke was bad enough.

"I learned her name."

"Do you know where she is?"

I shook my head.

"Anything besides her name?"

"Not really."

"Alright, then, let's see if you can get back to bed. Tomorrow—or today, really, is another day. We'll talk later."

And we did. And she seemed okay, even interested in Priscilla's high school picture.

"A pretty girl. You favor her from the eyes up. I hope she's kind."

So far, so good.

With Mom's green light, I went Saturday afternoon to see Mike Capps. I figured he'd know how to find most anyone—and anyway I hadn't seen much of Scooter since I left school. He was working in his uncle's radiator shop ("The Best Place in Town to Take a Leak!") that summer.

I found Mike and Scooter on what Scooter's mom called the patio, a slab of concrete the back door gave onto. Not awninged or umbrellaed, it enjoyed shade early morning and late afternoon. Four plastic-webbed lawn chairs clustered around an upturned telephone cable spool, upon which Scooter's mom sat a tray holding homemade chocolate chip cookies and sweet tea and four ex-jelly jars.

Scooter's dad in sleeveless undershirt and aviator sunglasses reminded me of Brando in *On the Waterfront*, not the old fat one you see now. Scooter's mom had been gardening and her hair was tied up in a blue bandana. For an older lady she had a nice neck.

"Have some cookies, boys."

"Thanks, Mrs. C."

"Well, Will Blaine, is this a purely social visit, or do you have a request?" asked Mike.

"Mr. C, now that you ask, I found my bio mother's name."

"Well. Congratulations. I guess."

He sounded like he'd dislodged a rock in his throat.

"I was wondering... if you might, you know... help me find her."

Mrs. C looked quickly from Mr. C to me.

"So do you want to meet her, dear?"

"Yes, Ma'am. That would be cool."

Mr. C smiled sideways at Mrs. C. like maybe I was dumb as a bag of hammers. He cleared his throat and shook his head.

"'Cool' ain't the best word when you're opening a number ten can of worms, Buster."

"What do you mean?"

"Son, finding is one thing. Meeting is another. Look here."

He spit in the yard and started to count fingers on his right hand.

"One, twenty-one years ago she gave you up thinking to make a screwup, no offense, halfway right. Two, North Carolina certified her to be safe from the likes of you. So with time she feels better, or at least protected from having to own, no offense, some stray kid. Who, by the way, lurks in her head. She probably dreams about him, right, Marcia?"

"That's right. Listen, Will, your poor birth mother certainly has to feel guilty over giving you up and at the same time be curious about who and where you are—and those fight forever in her mind."

This was not exactly what I expected. Scooter rolled his eyes and I looked from Mrs. C to Mr. C, who still held up stubby fingers.

"Three, if she married and has kids, she ain't got time to fret about you showing up. So, four, when you do, she ain't going to think you're God's gift, see what I mean? Five, what about her husband, for God's sake. *She* had a what? What else has she not told me? Six, her children. Now some damn lousy kid says he's my brother. Who in Christ's name does he think he is?"

"Mike, mind your language."

"Marcia, the boy's legal, he needs to hear this. Will, I can probably find her. In fact, I bet a month's pay on it. But if I give her up, this might mean a heap of unpleasantness. Understand?"

"Yes, sir. I don't want trouble. But, like, I have to know."

"Will, don't get me wrong. I know you think you must find this woman. And maybe you do. Just understand, this is serious business."

"Yes, sir."

He looked at Mrs. C and shrugged.

"Marcia, what do you think?"

She eyeballed me like a hawk spies a snake.

"Mike, I'm thinking of two women. There's the, as you say, Will, 'bio mom,' who we don't know a thing about. She might be at peace or a nervous wreck. Or, for that matter, dead of a heart attack. Then there's Martha, who, bless her, has seen enough trouble for two lifetimes. She's the other side of this coin. Like me, she would do anything to protect her son from harm. You were, I can testify, the most wonderful thing in her life, the answer to years and years of prayer. You were almost a little messiah to her, born to save her from childlessness, barrenness, sorrow, and loss. So she's the one I'm concerned about. Have you thought what this might do to her?"

"Actually, Mom knows I'm looking for... you know."

"Really! You have told Martha you're trying to find your Bio Mom?"

"Yeah."

"And she's alright with that?"

"Well, what she said was, she won't stand in my way."

"So you don't have her blessing yet. Okay, son, listen. She ended up in the hospital because of I don't know what you said or did, but that's at your feet. I know she says she has forgiven you, but that's what moms do. But I can't condone anything that might endanger her mental state. Another trip to Broughton might just kill her."

She looked all three of us in the eye.

"Although I expect you guys will do whatever you want."

She stood and brushed a crumb or two of dirt from her jeans.

"End of lecture. I have to start supper. Will, can I set a place for you?"

"Thanks, Mrs. C, but I'll go home and look after things."

"See that you do, son. Give my best to Martha."

"I will."

For a while we guys looked at anything but each other. I studied a robin perched on a power line. Scooter whistled through his teeth. The robin flew when a crow's shadow skimmed the patio. Mr. C finally cleared his throat.

"So, Will, what do you think?"

"Whether I meet her or not, I want to know where she is."

He shook his head and sat back in his chair.

"Shit, why shouldn't you follow every other lost soul? Okay, kid, show me what you got."

I took the yearbook page from my back pocket.

"Ten-four, son, this is perfect. Library, right? Okay, go back and make a list of her classmates. Crawford High would have had, what, sixty or seventy? They'd be in their mid to late thirties, so ain't many died on us. Bring that and I'll see what I can dig up. Tell you what—just list the boys. They don't change names on you."

"Thanks, Mr. C."

"Save that until you see how deep a shit pile you're about to step in. "

I took him the list Monday evening—Wednesday morning he called.

"You still sure you want this info?"

"Yes, sir."

"Well, I ain't responsible for whatever this causes. Got that?"

"Mr. C, I wouldn't blame you for a thing."

"That's good, because I've fed your scrawny ass for years. Wouldn't have such a dog turn around and bite me."

"Don't worry."

"Ready? Here goes. Fall 1949, not long after you were hatched, Priscilla Ruth Lance married a jock named Patrick Allen, a class ahead of her at Crawford High. He's a Navy man, or was. They moved to Newport News. Lived on Washington Avenue. They had a kid, Rosemary Pearl, September 25, 1954. Another one, Charles Patrick, January 15, 1956. This Allen guy was honorably discharged in 1952, worked a while at Johnson Music on Washington Avenue. He died October 7, 1959. Don't know what of, Virginia is stingy with death certificates. Likely an accident, he wasn't but twenty-six. Or maybe somebody shot him, you never know."

My heart was doing a Richard Petty thing while he rustled paper like he was unfolding a road map.

"Is that all?"

"No, kid, get this. Your old lady moved back to Crawford. 257 Beaverdam Road."

"God, that's..."

"Yeah, ain't that some shit? She lives maybe ten miles away."

I scribbled so fast I wondered if any of this would be legible.

"What else?"

"Your grandma, Wanda Lance, Priscilla's mother, lives in Crawford, over by the Baptist church. Your grandpa died in 1960. Heart attack. So you likely need to quit them coffin nails."

"Is there more?"

"Here's your mom's phone number. She works at American Enka. Receptionist at the front gate. I've checked her out. You look like your old lady, for what that's worth."

"You actually saw her?"

"Yeah. She looks all right."

"What else?"

"Ain't that enough?"

"Sure. Mr. C. How did you find all this?"

"Professional secret, kid."

"What do I owe you?"

"Not a thing, except maybe to keep your name out of the paper. I don't want to see some headline like *Crawford Woman Drops Dead after Man Claims to be Her Son.*"

"That shouldn't be a problem."

"You don't know people like I do. My advice, Will, is to lay off this for at least a week. Let it sink in, study the best way to deal with it. The quietest way. Promise me that?"

"Yes, sir. I will."

"Good. Ten forty-two, son."

He hung up and left me to stare at the key that might unlock the door to who I was. Or get it slammed in my face. Either way, I'd deal with it.

I had to drive by her house. I left The Top of the Hill one sunny afternoon about two-thirty. Beaverdam Road started—or stopped, if you count how the creek flows—just to the left of the first of beautiful downtown Crawford's twin bridges. After about a mile I found her house on the left, one of those one-story deals from the twenties, front porch crowded by boxwoods. Wood siding, dark shingles. Lots of trees. A black-and-white cat napped on the porch rail. A cotton mop hung from a clothesline to the right just past a side porch. A power mower waited for somebody either to start it or steal it. A boy's bicycle leaned against the building like a forgotten promise.

The house was set back about a hundred feet from the road, which quickly curved to the left. If I drove back and forth she might call the law, so I parked beside the creek just past the curve for a partial view of the back of the building.

One of those folding lounge chairs that threaten to eat you when you sit up was draped with a towel like she might sunbathe or take a nap. She had a small garden with a row of droopy sunflowers and a couple of kooky blue snowball bushes. A squirrel helped itself to whatever stocked a bird feeder hanging from a limb.

There wasn't a garage and no car sat in the driveway so I waited. I didn't know if receptionists left at shift change or stayed until five. Not much traffic so I had time to think.

I decided not to call her, because she might say go to hell and hang up. I would ring the doorbell or knock. Write her a note first? Nah, that would give her leave to reject me. She'd have to shoot me down face to face.

An hour revealed no sign of life except the cat, which came around back to study the bird feeder and riled a jay bird. By then enough cars had seen me to call the law. So I got hell out of Dodge. I had plenty of time.

Saturday morning I headed back to Crawford with binoculars I borrowed from John Lewis, the older mechanic at The Top of the Hill. A car sat in Priscilla's driveway, a '62 Chevy Biscayne, white, a dent in the left rear quarter panel. I parked around the curve and settled in to see my mother.

It was a cloudy morning, a bit of breeze, quiet except for Beaverdam Branch, noisy because it had rained in the night. I cranked the passenger window up so I could concentrate. Truth was, I was nervous, afraid I'd get caught, afraid to see her, afraid I wouldn't. Your basic mess.

The two-door sedan had a red interior, automatic tranny, big white-walls. No crossed flags on the front quarter, so it wasn't a hot-rod 409 or anything. The license plate was one of those new green on white jobs I hadn't gotten used to seeing.

Didn't see the cat, but made out a birdcage inside the back window of the house. Probably a parakeet, or I'd have seen a flash of yellow. The flag was up on her mailbox, so I had missed her—or whoever—coming out to put mail inside. A sort of terrier dog wandered through, sniffed the back porch, moved on.

A car slowed and turned into her driveway. A Ford with a Foster Memorial UMC front plate, a 1958 Fairlane, dark blue, a woman driving. She stopped like she wasn't used to the brakes. She primped in the rearview, then headed to the front porch. She wore a pale yellow dress and a big purse dangled from her arm. Bulletproof light-colored hair. No doubt, my grandmother. If she decided to whop you with that handbag, you'd be a goner.

In a few minutes the yellow dress appeared at the birdcage window, someone in dark colors beside her. I was afraid they'd seen me but couldn't leave, not yet.

Soon three people walked to the Ford, the woman with the pocketbook, a burr-headed kid, and a woman who had to be Priscilla. Like Mr. C said, she wasn't bad-looking for that age. Pleasant-looking, too, like she might be approached.

The kid climbed into the back, the women got in the front, and they backed out and headed the other way. So I had seen my mother, my grandmother, and my little brother and I was shaking like some kind of madman. I guess my little sis was somewhere else.

I guess because of the creek I didn't hear a cruiser pull up behind me. I about freaked out when I heard the door shut and saw a sheriff's uniform in the side mirror.

"Will, what in hell do you think you're doing?"

I had never been so grateful to hear that rocky voice.

"Mr. C, thank God it's you."

He looked the interior over like I might have a bale of weed or something in there.

"You're a mighty lucky boy. I just happened to be in the area when the ten sixty-six came. How do you feel that your own grandmom called the cops on you?"

"Really?"

He patted my arm, kind of hard, like he meant to make an impression.

"Yes, really. Now go home. Stay hell away from here unless you plan to introduce yourself properly. And when you do—because I see you will, come hell or high water—take a bath, get a haircut, wear a suit, look like you stepped out of a Sunday School graduation. These people are pretty straight, if you catch my drift."

"Yes, sir."

I started the Streak and turned around in the first driveway. As I drove by Mr. C's cruiser he wrote on a clipboard propped on the steering wheel. I guess some kind of report, like maybe I had a police record now.

VIII.

Planets Playing Tricks

Priscilla Lance Allen

Millie's birthday in 1970 was a Thursday, hot and muggy, but you still felt fall was around the corner—walnut leaves were turning gold. Starlings had begun to bunch up to head south. When I went out for the paper the air smelled damp, like tidewater air without dead fish. Rosemary's leaky old black cat Fiddlesticks rubbed my legs and eyed the door—I had banished her to the yard a while back, but the beast was forever sneaking in. A musical wren in the dogwood seemed to know the old girl's birding days were past.

I read the obits to make sure I wasn't there, then my horoscope. "Get busy with small but important duties in the morning," it said. "The planets are playing tricks to see how you handle situations. Show that you are a sensitive person."

Small is easier than important, so after breakfast I piddled. Straightened a picture here, fluffed a pillow there, swept the kitchen, dusted the mantel, looked out the window for the mailman. And those planetary tricks.

Tomato soup and half a grilled cheese sandwich, in honor of Wanda, was lunch. I'd have listened to Helen Trent too, but that radio program was long gone. So I opened the paper, read Billy Graham's column. Today's Chuckle. Noticed that the Tourists lost. Tried the comics but couldn't concentrate, even on *Blondie*.

I washed and dried dishes and was putting the bowl back in the cupboard when—bing, bong—the doorbell exploded right above my head. I jumped halfway to the ceiling, my heart leapfrogged, I caught the bowl before it shattered. Then dropped it anyway. It broke almost perfectly in two.

Millie? No, it had to be the mailman—but he'd already been by—maybe the Fuller Brush man or a neighbor needing a cup of sugar, a Jehovah's Witness.

I laid the broken bowl in the sink, hung up the dishtowel, and headed for the door, fretting I'd left some lunch on my face. I stood at the door, took a deep breath, and opened it.

There stood a young man some six feet tall, with light brown Beatle-cut hair. Needed a shave. And, merciful God, he had deep blue eyes. This couldn't be my Millie. He's probably working his way through college selling magazines.

He certainly wasn't Mormon, for I smelled cigarettes and a whiff of stale beer. He wore a light blue short-sleeved shirt and blue jeans. A loosely-knotted red and blue striped necktie. Ragged low-top, likely stinky tennis shoes. A smile nervous enough to fracture his face.

"Mrs. Allen?"

Dear Jesus, he knows my name. But, wait, it's on the mailbox. "Yes?"

"I—my name is William Blaine. I... well... I... was born in St. Joseph's Hospital twenty-one years ago today. 1949. I was adopted soon after. If you... please excuse me, like, I'm pretty nervous here... if you are Priscilla Ruth Lance—or were—you might be my mother."

Boom. Time for a radio soap opera's crashing minor chord.

Let's open the cliché drawer. Ton of bricks. Took my breath away. Rug from under my feet. Rang my chimes. My life, forever changed. Planetary tricks, indeed.

"Say your name again?"

"William Blaine. William Lee Blaine." He swept hair from his eyes. Those eyes. "I go by Will."

He had mine and Wanda's skin. "And you turn twenty-one today?"

"Yes, Ma'am."

We both shook like lab rats shocked by some mad scientist behind the boxwoods.

"You're sure you were born at St. Joseph's?"

"Yes, Ma'am. I found my birth certificate." He pulled a folded piece of steno paper from his shirt pocket. Its story? Boy Lance, five pounds, two ounces (I never knew that), born at St. Joseph's Hospital 3:37 A.M. (Didn't know the time either) August 6, 1949. Delivered by Dr. Frank Thomas (so that was the rude man's name). Mother, Priscilla Ruth Lance. Father, some guy called None Named.

Once on *Mickey Mouse Club* they showed a science experiment. They had a room with about a thousand mousetraps set with ping pong balls. Some guy in a white coat tossed a single white ball into the room, which sprang every one of them, balls bouncing every which way. My mind felt like that.

"Where... how...?"

"At the courthouse. Downtown."

"This was to be sealed. Forever."

In his smile a hint of Aunt Pearl. "Maybe so, but some lazy clerk scotch-taped a pink piece of paper over mine."

I began to cry. Joy, grief, who knew? Then a shaky moan that had to have summoned at least one witness to each neighboring window.

He was scared of a wailing woman. And I hardly knew what to do with a long-lost son.

"Please, Ma'am, like, don't cry."

"I can't help it. And don't call me Ma'am. Call me... please... call me Priscilla." I held my arms out to him. "Here, son. Yes, Lord have mercy, I'm..."

When we hugged he broke down, too. "God, you really are…"

"Don't talk. Just let me hold you. Please believe this. I never saw you. Never heard you cry. Never touched you, never smelled your newborn skin. Oh God, Will, forgive me."

We fit together like jigsaw-puzzle pieces—wet ones, for we were crying like babies.

"So now what?" asked my new-found son after I recovered enough sense to invite him in. I booted Fiddlesticks out, made coffee, put a plate of chocolate chip cookies on the kitchen table.

Good question. Stuff bounced around body and mind like a kazillion hopped-up hamsters. I mean, in my kitchen sat a very real child my other very real children knew nothing about. And I had so many questions. Where was he staying? What did he want? Who was he, anyway? For that matter, now that I had seen this resurrected child, who might I become? Would we see each other again? It was all I could do not to explode.

He touched the back of my hand. "Priscilla?"

"Oh, sorry. It's just that I don't know 'now what'? I mean, here you are in my kitchen and my kids—my other kids—don't know a thing about you. For that matter, neither do I. Where do you live, for example?"

"Sand Hill."

"You're kidding."

"Not a bit. You know The Top of the Hill? I grew up there. Mom—that's what I call her—runs the store."

"What, five or six miles from here, if that? You mean… wait a minute. The bus to town used to stop there, right?"

He nodded.

"Lord, I used to watch a skinny kid in the side yard kick a football across the yard and run after it like he was knocking down a whole team to get to it. He thought he was Choo Choo Justice or somebody. Sometimes he had a light-skinned Black kid with him."

"That was me. The white one. Scooter's my best friend. He's adopted, too."

"So I watched my own son and didn't know it?"

"I guess."

"Why didn't some kind of instinct kick in? I mean, I was watching my child!"

He dug a wrinkled Camel pack from his jeans pocket. "Blows your mind, doesn't it? Can I smoke? Like, I sure need one."

"Not in the house. If you must, let's move to the side porch."

A screaking screen door spring ushered us onto a messy porch. Gardening shoes and trowels in the corner, frayed Lions Club broom against the wall, cat food dish on the floor. With flies in it. A dangling dishrag on a makeshift clothesline.

The western sky was the color of a sprained ankle. As if my news wasn't enough to make me sweat, the mercury crept toward eighty-five and the air was as still as a snake watching a bird. Prelude to a thunderstorm,

On the rail sat a clay saucer I meant to put under a potted coleus. I took the straight chair and Millie—Willie—Will—leaned against the rail and lit his cigarette.

"You said 'other kids.' Tell me about them."

"I have two, Rosemary Pearl and Charles Patrick. Rosemary's nearly sixteen, Chuck is thirteen. Thank God they're at church camp, home tomorrow."

"So they're my half-sister and half-brother. I've always been an only child, so that's going to take some getting used to."

"There's a lot of that going around. Tell me about yourself."

"Not much to tell. Like I said, I grew up at the store. Mom ran it, Dad was our mechanic. He taught me all about cars and stuff. He died when I was twelve."

"What happened?"

"He had some kind of leukemia. Killed him pretty fast."

"Do you go to church?"

He kind of looked at me sideways, like he didn't know quite how to answer that.

"Not anymore. Mom's a Presbyterian, and I guess I am, too, but haven't been to church in a few years. I don't believe in that stuff anymore."

"We're Baptists. Will, you have to believe in something."

"Let's not get into that."

"Fair enough. Tell me about your mother. What's her name, what's she like? I mean, I think I remember seeing her in the store, but I…"

"Martha Blaine. Like, after Dad died I was… you know, she expected me to do all that stuff he did. And I wasn't but twelve. We got along okay for a while but when I started dating, and talking about school, well, she ended up in the mental hospital. She thought I was going to leave her forever or something."

"Will, I know that feeling. Only too well. My husband died when I wasn't even thirty."

"Oh, wow, what of?"

"He was cleaning a pistol. It went off."

"Man, I'm sorry."

"So did your mom—Martha—is she alright now?"

"Yeah, she's okay. A little what you might call fragile. But we get along. Now, anyway."

"So there was a time you didn't?"

He put out his cigarette, shook out another, and tamped it on his lighter. "Okay, confession time. We had this fight. I think I told her she wasn't my real mother. It put her in the hospital."

This sounded like truth. "Will, listen. I may be your 'real' mother. But all I did was have you. Your *real* mother—what's her name again?"

"Martha."

I found a handkerchief in my apron pocket and dabbed sweat from my upper lip. "Martha changed all those diapers. She nursed you through Lord knows how many sick times. Bandaged your skint knees. Martha's your *real* mother, got that?"

He lit another and looked toward the creek. "Sure. I know that now. But back then it was a different story."

"So you'll not hurt her again?"

"Not intentionally, anyway."

"Does she know you're here?"

"Yes. I'm being out front with this."

"Good. So, did you go to school?"

"A couple of years, at Western. But I wasn't cut out for that. See, Dad taught me all about cars, I'd helped him work on them since I was a kid. I dropped out and came back home. I'm a mechanic at The Top of the Hill."

"My Chuck loves cars. I bet you and him would get along fine."

"So do I get to meet your kids?"

"Lord, Will, let's take this slow. I haven't known you thirty minutes yet. Yes, I expect that will happen. But how? I can't digest this all at once. I mean, here's my firstborn on my back porch, talking to me for the first time. I scarce can take it in."

"That's cool. Like, we both live here. It's not like I'm from somewhere like Wisconsin and have to leave tomorrow. But I have one important question today."

"What?"

"Who is my father?"

Hadn't spoken his name in nearly two decades. In fact, until I saw Will's eyes I thought I'd blotted him from memory.

"His name is… Dick Snipes. He'd be, let's see, about forty-two now, if he's still alive. I haven't seen him since I told him I was pregnant—he flat out disappeared."

"Ran away fast as trout water, huh?"

"Something like that."

"So you have no idea where he might be?"

"For all I know he's in Timbuktu."

"What was he doing when you met him?"

"Said he was a student at Warren Wilson. He'd also worked for the railroad."

"Mind if I hunt for him?"

"You found me, why should he be any different?"

I stood too fast, and had to grab the porch rail. He reached for me, then stopped.

"Are you, like, okay?"

I smoothed the wrinkles in my apron. "I'm just… Will, you have no idea. I've never felt like this. I'm torn between happy to have seen you—ecstatic really—and frightened that you might hang around and upset all of our lives, yours, mine, Martha's, my kids' or that you might leave again. It's complicated. I want to get to know you, and I want them to, too, but I have to figure out how to tell them. Like they say, what's a mother to do?"

He laughed, stubbed his cigarette in the saucer, and touched my shoulder. "Priscilla—wow, just calling you that is so cool—Priscilla, don't worry. I won't blow your cover. Here's my phone number. Call when the coast is clear."

We walked around the house, his eyes on the ground, mine darting about, looking for neighbors, Fiddlesticks, squirrels, stray children, whatever else might dart across my path. I had an urge to hold Will's hand but somehow couldn't. On the front porch I turned to him and laughed.

"What?"

"You know, it's funny. All these years I dreamed of you. I imagined what you might look like at three, or seven, or whatever. Whether your hair was brown or blond. What color your eyes were. How you were doing in school. But all that time, I knew you were a girl."

"No kidding?"

"In my mind I named you Millie. I dreamed a whole world for you.

And now look, here's my Millie, a big strapping boy. A man, really, of age today."

"Millie rhymes with Willie."

We laughed, cried a little, hugged, and said goodbye. As I watched him bounce down the hill I felt faint. I sat on the front step for what seemed an hour, blowing my nose and wiping tears, whether happy or pained I couldn't say. I went to the kitchen, glued the broken bowl back together, then dealt with the back porch's mess. Except I forgot those darn cigarette butts.

We never had a thunderstorm. I guess God figured I'd had enough excitement for one day.

IX.

Don't Know What You're Talking About

William Lee Blaine

So my old man's name was Dick Snipes. Sounded familiar somehow. Friday morning I headed downtown to ask the nice library lady how, if he was still around, I might find him. She showed me how to use the City Directory.

Last year, a Richard A. Snipes and his wife lived in West Asheville. He worked at the Veterans Administration Hospital—she was a house-wife. I checked backward until I found him working for the North Carolina Veterans' Commission. Bingo! The dandy at the courthouse. The guy with the pocket pouf who helped me get my scholarship. Man, I thought, the world gets real small sometimes.

On my way home I checked out his house, one of those bungalow deals like all over West Asheville. Neat, trim, good yard, shade trees. No dog. If anybody was home, they didn't show. A perfectly normal house with front porch and mailbox and all.

I dropped by Mike Capps's house, hoping he was home. The cruiser was in the driveway, so I knocked.

"Well, if it isn't my favorite college dropout. Come in, son, what's on your mind?"

"Can you check out a guy named Richard A. Snipes? He works at the VA Hospital."

"What's got you curious about him? Most VA types are pretty clean."

"I think he might be my father."

"Wow, you step in deep puddles. Okay, give me a day or two."

He called the next day.

"Hey, Will. Your guy's clean as a whistle. Nothing to interest the law. He seems not to have any kids. That he admits to, anyhow. I suppose you plan to see about that."

"Yeah, I guess."

"Be careful. Men can get violent when they're cornered."

"I just want to see if he'll talk to me. I mean, I don't want to freak him out or anything."

"Just a word of caution. If he has no kids, his first thought will be *Oh Hell, what does this sumbitch want? Blackmail money?* That might drown any inclination he might have to talk."

"I'll be careful."

"10-4, son. Holler if you need backup."

So I headed east. The VA hospital in those days was in a bunch of different buildings, on a hill in Oteen. Stately old stuff, yellow stucco, porches on the ends of the residential and patient buildings. Kind of run-down, but you could tell it once was hot stuff. I parked the Streak in a visitor space in front of the A building and went in.

A receptionist buzzed his secretary, then led me down a hallway. Man, his girl was a looker—a bit older than me, red hair, nice body, dimples. Made me wish I'd worn a decent jacket.

"Young gentleman to see Mr. Snipes, Sarah."

"Come in. I'll see if he's busy. Your name?"

"Will Blaine."

"What is your business?"

"I just want to talk to him."

Sarah looked at me like *yeah, right, another guy looking for a soft government job.* She buzzed his office.

"A Mr. Blaine to see you, sir."

"Who?"

"Mr. Will Blaine, sir."

"Send him in."

He wore what looked like the same tailored suit the last time I saw him, except he'd gained in the middle. Lost some hair, too. His desk was clean except for one stack of triplicate-form papers. He looked at me over those half-frame glasses guys wear after forty and smiled.

"Mr. Blaine."

He stood and shook my hand as Sarah closed the door. Man, she smelled good. Snipes pointed to a chair off to the side. He sat across from me and looked me over.

"Young man, you seem to be doing well. Are you still at Western?"

"No, sir. School and I didn't mesh gears. I'm a mechanic at mine and Mom's gas station."

"Sometimes we go to college to find out we don't need to be there. Happened to me, in fact. So. What can I do for you?"

I put hands on knees, mostly to keep them anchored to something.

"Mr. Snipes, I have something to ask you. Or tell you. Anyway, it's pretty personal. Do we have a few minutes?"

"Certainly."

He buzzed Sarah and asked her to hold his calls. I'd never heard anyone do that except on television. His eyes, the same blue as mine, seemed amused.

"Now. We have all day."

"Okay. I was born in August 1949 to a senior at Crawford High. She gave me up for adoption. I have recently found her. Priscilla Lance. Priscilla Ruth Lance."

The smile had mostly vanished, while, I thought, he was doing some quick arithmetic.

"Will, why are you telling me this?"

"When I talked to her, naturally, I asked who my father was."

He leaned forward and looked me level in the eye.

"And let me guess, she said I was your father."

"Yes, sir. Well, she said Dick Snipes. She said you were in college and you had worked for the railroad. Or at least that you told her that."

"Son, do you know how many men are named Dick Snipes?"

"Only one around here, sir. I looked in the City Directory. Far back enough to learn you worked for Southern Railway a year before..."

He interrupted me with something between a laugh and a snort.

"Let me ask a question. Assuming for a moment—and that's *all* we're doing, assuming—that I am that same Dick Snipes, what would you want from him?"

"Nothing, sir. Nothing past maybe getting to know each other."

"Really? You bothered to hunt me down. What is it? Money?"

"No, sir. Honest. I'm just trying to find out who I am. Where I come from. That's all."

He studied me for probably ten seconds, maybe more. Enough to freak me out a little. He sat back and seemed to relax.

"I'm sorry. I don't know what you're talking about. Now, if you don't mind, I have papers to process."

I stood, trying not to shove the man I now figured was my father— and a lying bastard. At the door I turned around.

"If you change your mind, I'm at The Top of the Hill. I'm a good mechanic."

I never saw him again. I guess if you have two moms, that's enough.

X.

No Big Deal

Priscilla Lance Allen

Saturday breakfast was usually fix-your-own, cold cereal and fruit or oatmeal, but the Saturday after Will showed up I fried bacon and potatoes, scrambled eggs, baked biscuits—even broke out a fresh jar of grape jelly. Rosemary and Chuck ate with relish, but eyed me suspiciously while Tweety the canary chirped his dumb little head off.

The kids take after Pat—tall and skinny. That morning they could nearly have passed for slouchy twins, in pajama pants, T-shirts, and socks. Only Rosemary's long hair would tell them apart from the back.

Knowing about Will only made these two characters dearer to my heart—and I had to tell them about their brother. I finally took a deep breath and smiled.

"Kids, I have something to say. It's pretty important."

They were silent. For what seemed forever. Finally Chuck looked at me.

"Are you going to let us get that cat?"

Rosemary rolled her eyes and dismissed him with a wave of her hand.

"C'mon, Mom, out with it."

We had a set of ceramic owl salt and pepper shakers. I started sliding the salt shaker back and forth between my hands.

"You guys have a brother. An older brother."

Chuck started to laugh until he realized I was serious. Rosemary got That Look.

"You mean…"

"Yes. Before I married your father, I… made a mistake. I had a baby. I gave him up for adoption the day he was born. Thing is, he showed up a few days ago."

If we'd been in a comic strip, a lightbulb would have gone on over Chuck's head.

"Does he smoke cigarettes?"

"Yes."

"So you fibbed about those butts I found."

"I'm sorry, son. You caught me off guard, and I had no idea whether I'd see him again."

"What's his name?"

"Will. William Lee Blaine."

That Look, which I was getting used to on Rosemary's face, had grown to something between disbelief and horror.

What's the matter, darling?"

"*What's the matter?* You have to ask?"

"I'm sorry, Rosemary. It was a pretty big shock for me, too."

"Shock? It's awful. I can't even start…"

She whacked her spoon on the table, ran into her room, and slammed the door. I imagined cartoon steam blasting from her ears. Chuck was silent as a stump. I got up to hug him but he sensed what was coming and darted to his bedroom and shut the door.

I looked at Tweety, who wouldn't talk, either. All I could do was sit at the table and cry, hoping that in gaining a son I wasn't losing two other kids.

Next day, Sunday, we piled in the car and headed to church with, I sensed, no particular sense of joy or hope. If I was looking for something uplifting or helpful or even non-threatening in the sermon, I didn't find it. Daniel and the end of time or something. My lambs sat silently beside me. We came home for lunch—spaghetti and meat sauce with a salad, during which I tried to make small talk. That didn't work well, either.

When I began to take up the dishes I announced we were going to Have a Talk. Which had only gotten started when Rosemary took off to her room with "I'm not ready for all this."

At least Chuck didn't bolt.

"Are you upset too?"

He stared at the table a while.

"Dunno. Does he live around here?"

"Yes."

"So will he… why did he… bust into your life?"

I sat across from him and started the salt shaker game again.

"He wanted to find out about me. Us, really. He wanted to know where he came from, I guess."

"So do we have to do anything?"

"Like what?"

"Like… I dunno. Take him in or something?"

"Chuck, he has a family. He has a place to live. It's not like he's a stray dog."

"Is he nice?"

"Yes. Very nice."

"Does he look like you?"

"Maybe a little. Why?"

"You're sure… he's telling the truth?"

"Yes, son, I'm sure of that."

"Why'd you tell us? I mean, couldn't he have stayed a secret?"

"That didn't feel right, Chuck. I'd like you and your sister to meet him."

He glanced down the hall.

"She's crying."

I walked behind his chair and massaged his skinny shoulders.

"Chuck, I love you two more than anything. Please don't worry. Will won't change my love for you. That's not going to happen. I'd hoped this would bring us all closer together."

He stood and gave me a hug.

"This is really weird. But I love you, Mom."

"Thanks, son. I'm sure you'll have questions. Don't be afraid to ask."

He sat back down and looked at Tweety, who had, for the first time in his daylight life, gone silent.

"Did... Dad know?"

"Yes, son, he did."

"And he was cool with it?"

"Yes. Well, not at first. But he eventually forgave me."

"That's weird."

"Maybe. But your father loved me in spite of things. And he loved you two very, very much. Now, if you don't mind, let me tend to your sister. You okay?"

"I guess."

I mussed his hair.

"You'll get used to this, I promise. Go shoot some baskets or something. By the way, this is between you and me and Rosemary. Your grandmother doesn't know yet."

"She doesn't know you had a... another kid?"

"She knows, but has no idea he's stepped out of the woodwork. I'll have to figure out how to tell her."

"Good luck with that."

Tweety chirped in agreement.

I headed down the hall, air thick with tension. I knocked on Rosemary's door.

"Rosemary, honey, can I come in? Please?

"It isn't locked."

As usual, her room was almost messy. No clothes in the floor, for she used her small club chair for a clothes rack. She sat on her bed, back to the headboard, eyes red, a pout on her face.

"What can I say, Rosemary? I'm sorry."

"So that makes everything fine?"

"No, honey, but it's a start. What else can I say?"

"Did you think all that would stay in the past?"

"They told me his birth certificate would be sealed. He'd not be able to find me. I had no reason to think… until he showed up here."

"So you'd never have told us if he hadn't."

"I don't know. Probably. When you came of age."

"So we could have grown up without knowing we had a brother."

"Maybe. But please don't hold that against me. It was… hard… to go through all that."

If that made her sympathetic I couldn't tell.

"Are you sure he's your kid?"

"Yes. He has his father's eyes. Too many details match up. I'm sure."

"What does he want?"

"To get to know me. Us. It's kind of a find-out-where-he-came-from thing. And—can I sit on the bed?"

"Sure."

"You might not believe this, but every August sixth, his birthday, I have gotten anxious. Wondering where he was, what he was doing. Except I thought he was a girl."

"How could you not know that?"

"I was drugged or something. I remember very little of that day."

"Did Grandma know?"

"Yes."

Her expression began to move into neutral territory.

"I bet she had a cow when she found out you were… you know."

"Well, she wasn't happy. And I dread telling her about Will."

"Do you have to?"

"If he is going to become part of my… our life, I have to."

"Did Dad know?"

"Yes. The wonderful thing was, he still loved me."

"So you're saying Dad—boy, I don't know the words here—forgave you?"

"Yes. Your father was a special man."

"Did he know the baby's father?"

"He never asked, and I never told."

"So who *was* this other guy?"

"Doesn't matter. He's been out of my life for twenty-one years. I don't know where he is or even if he's still living."

She stared out the window like she wondered if the past 1 lurked behind our oak tree. At least she didn't seem ready to heave a paperweight at me or burst out crying.

"Anything else I can tell you?"

"This is about enough for now."

"Rosemary?"

She finally looked at me.

"You know I love you and Chuck more than anything, don't you?"

She nodded. Slowly.

"I'll not push Will on you. I want you to meet him, but not until you're ready. Whether we end up being a family, I don't know. I'm just happy to know he turned out well. Promise me you'll try to keep an open mind."

"I guess."

"Good."

Rosemary was slower to come around than Chuck. I had to remind myself that a fourteen-year-old girl's body fights with her brain enough to confuse the brightest. Adding "Surprise, you've got a big brother" makes for a king-sized struggle to make sense of things.

She and I had several talks—some I planned, others off the cuff. One Saturday I was getting ready to fix supper. I had cabbage and carrots on the counter, ready to make slaw, which she normally helped with. That day she hung in the doorway like she needed to be hinged to something.

"Rosemary, what's the matter?"

"Nothing."

I opened the refrigerator and got out two green bottles, 7-up, her favorite. I set them on the kitchen table with an opener.

"Here, daughter. I know better than that. Let's talk."

She looked at me, and for a second I feared she'd say something ugly and run for her room. But she opened our drinks and sat across from me.

"It's this whole Will thing."

"What can I say or do to help?"

"I just can't believe it—not that you had a baby, but… remember when we had that talk about babies and stuff?"

"Sure."

"That would have been the perfect time to tell me. Like, you know, *Rosemary, I know how easy it is to get pregnant, because it happened to me.*"

"I started to. No, really, I did. But I couldn't."

"Why not?"

"I don't know. Embarrassed, I guess."

"But you had to know we'd find out sooner or later."

"No, they promised I'd never know anything and neither would he." She finished her drink and looked sideways at me.

"What?" I asked.

"Just wondering. What else have you not told us?"

I laughed, I hoped not too quickly. "Child, I don't know. But I can tell you, there's no more kids out there anywhere."

Another day she was doing homework at the kitchen table. I turned from the sink to see her stare out the window while doodling on notebook paper.

"Penny for your thoughts."

"Nothing, Mom. Just… nothing."

"I don't believe there's nothing in that pretty head of yours."

She laid her number two yellow down and looked at me.

"So—if this Will becomes part of the family—what am I going to tell my friends?"

"You could start with the truth."

"No, like, I mean… they're going to put two and two together, that my mother, you know, before she was married…"

So, she'd figured her own mother to be a wayward woman. Which, of course, I had been.

"Rosemary, that's nothing to make them think any less of you. Besides, you can come at it from the positive side. *Like, guys, wow, I have a big brother. Isn't that cool?*"

"Well, maybe. But who said I wanted another brother? Chuck's enough of a pain as it is."

"Yes, but a big brother is different."

"You never had one."

"There were times I wish I had. I think it would have made it easier to be a big sister to Grace."

"Wow, I hadn't thought to ask. Did Aunt Grace know about… Will?"

"Yes. Your grandmother and Grace knew. Aunt Pearl. Plus a doctor and some nurses. And the welfare lady. That was all. We women kept it from my father."

"So Grandpa was gone before you showed—and you had the kid before he got home?"

"That's right."

"This story is kinda unbelievable, you know."

"I didn't make it up."

"I can believe that."

"What else can I tell you?"

"Maybe something later. I'm still trying to understand all this, deal with it, however you want to say it."

I had to be patient. Rosemary had a new kind of grief to get through. She'd had an identity—Priscilla Allen's daughter, boss of her brother, stable kid, healed a bit from her father's death. Then here shows up an intruder. An interloper. I'm not the oldest anymore. Is Will my boss now? What is all this going to look like? Do I even want to meet him? If I do, will I like him?

Chuck was easier. Maybe boys are less sensitive about unplanned pregnancies. Maybe he was just a tad too young at twelve to realize what all this meant to us females. Or maybe he wanted a big brother. Maybe all that was true. Whatever, he was at least easier to talk to than his sister.

"Son, what do you want to know?" I asked him after school one afternoon.

"About what's-his-name? Will?"

I nodded.

"I'm mixed up. I mean, you said Dad was gone, right?"

"He was on a ship."

"How long had he been gone?"

"I don't remember. A couple of months, I guess."

"So you missed him?"

"I sure did."

"Then why…"

I grabbed his hand.

"You'll make more sense of it when you're older. I just somehow met this boy and he took me out dancing. I was pretty blue. He cheered me up."

"Dancing. Okay. So I've got this—what do you call him? Half-brother, who has nothing to do with Dad? That's weird. I mean, I barely remember Dad. Or do I remember him from his pictures? And how do I even talk to a brother who doesn't relate to Dad?"

"I don't know, son. That's something you'll have to work out for yourself. I do think you'll like Will."

"You said he and his mom run The Top of the Hill?"

"Yes, Chuck. You know that place?"

"There's a car there that's really cool. A '49 Plymouth. Souped up. Is that his?"

"I think so. I know it's loud, anyway, rumbly. Dark green with a kind of gray back fender."

"That's it. You think he'd take me for a ride?"

"I'm sure he would."

"Well, that part might be kind of cool."

The next Saturday Chuck spent the night with a friend. After supper, Rosemary and I settled in to watch TV. Except it turned into another Conversation.

"So, Mom, can I ask a personal question?"

"Don't know how much more personal they can get, but go ahead."

"Like, who was the guy you... made this mistake with?"

"Rosemary, that doesn't make any difference. He and I were a couple for maybe two months. I told him I was... you know... and pfft, he was gone. I have no idea if he's still alive—and don't care."

"Wow, you only hung out six or eight weeks?"

"That's right."

"He must have been... pretty attractive, right?"

"He was handsome, yes, and a great dancer."

"So what was his name?"

"I don't see why that's important."

"Because, Mom, details. They make the story real."

"I had almost forgotten it until Will jarred my memory. His name was Snipes. Dick Snipes."

"There's a Tina Snipes in my class, but her dad's name is Tom or something. Was this Dick Snipes from around here?"

"Lord, I don't... no,... seems like he said he was from the eastern part of the state."

"How old was he?"

"Maybe four or five years older than me."

"What did he do? For work, I mean."

"He said he was a student. I think at Warren Wilson College. On the GI Bill. He'd been in the Marines in the war. Had worked for the railroad."

"Did you know anything about his parents?"

"Just what he said. His father was Army, and he didn't much like him. I don't remember a thing he said about his mother. Rosemary, the fact is, I never knew whether he was telling the truth or not. He could have been from Kalamazoo for all I knew."

"There's a lot of 'he saids' here. That means you didn't know him long, or very well, yet... you let..."

"Rosemary, don't be too harsh on your mother. I was young—your father was at sea—I was lonesome—and when it came down to brass tacks, I didn't know how to say 'no.' I just hope that... that you'll be stronger than I was."

"Don't worry about me, Mom."

I lifted an eyebrow. "That's what I told your grandmother. And I'm your mom, which means I'll worry about you no matter what you say."

"Speaking of Grandma, when are you going to tell her?"

"After you and your brother are okay with it. Actually, I'd like you all to meet him first."

"I'll let you know. This is still pretty overwhelming."

Will had shown up August sixth. It was nearly Halloween before the kids broke routine to huddle in Rosemary's room. They were in there with door shut for an eternity—a half hour or more. And quiet. Me in the living room, TV on, Tweety in the dining room, rattling his cuttlebone like it was his archenemy.

When Rosemary's door opened I didn't know whether to be afraid or startled or what. The kids came in, turned the TV down, and sat on the sofa.

"Mom, we think we're ready," Chuck said.

"For what?"

"To meet Will, what else?" said Rosemary.

"Are you sure?"

"We've talked about it, a lot. And we've decided it's best. Like, you want us to, right?"

"Of course. But this is a life-changing thing. I want you to be certain."

They smiled at each other, without any weirdness I could detect.

"We are. So you think he could come over soon?"

"I'll call him. Is Saturday okay?"

They looked at each other and shrugged.

"I guess," said Rosemary. "I don't have anything to do except homework."

"Don't guess. I want a good decision here."

"Saturday's fine, Mom."

"You'll have to clean up your rooms."

"Aw, Mom," in unison.

"Don't 'Aw, Mom' me. Go do it. I'll call Will and let you know."

"The garage closes at noon on Saturdays. He said give him an hour to eat a sandwich and clean up. He should be here anytime," I said to Chuck, who watched every car come up the road like it was the last in existence. "But you'll wear the paint off that windowsill before he shows up." It was a quarter after one.

The house was clean. Kitchen and bath mopped, floors vacuumed, flat surfaces dusted, fresh newspaper in Tweety's cage. That was stuff you do for any expected company. But how do you dress to meet your brother for the first time? I had told the kids not to wear church clothes, but nothing hole-y either. Chuck wore clean jeans, a UNC sweatshirt, and a fairly new pair of Converse sneakers. Rosemary had been in her room for nearly an hour. She wasn't much to primp, so I wondered what was going on in there.

"He's here," Chuck shouted, and, yes, a motor rumbled into the driveway, accompanied by the rachet of the emergency brake, then quiet. Too quiet. I mean, even the bird was still.

I opened the door to Will, who carried a potted yellow chrysanthemum in one hand and a carton of ginger snaps in the other. "Hi, Priscilla."

"Come in, Will. There are people in here who want to meet you."

He smelled of Brut, cigarettes, and hand cleaner. We paused for a quick hug, then I took the flowers and led him into the living room. "Will, this is your—this is Chuck. Chuck, meet Will."

Chuck hadn't moved from the window except to turn toward his new brother.

"Hi."

"Hi. It's great to meet you."

Chuck nodded and smiled sheepishly.

"Here, let's make ourselves at home." I motioned to the sofa and chairs. "Rosemary, we have company," I said to her still-shut door.

As Will sat in what I thought of as my chair—Lord, he could sit anywhere he wanted as far as I was concerned—Rosemary came into the living room slowly, eyes toward the floor.

She looked freshly scrubbed, in jeans and a white blouse and nice brown flats. She had put her hair into a ponytail, which I always thought was cute. Will stood as she came in and put out his hand a little high for a handshake but not high enough for a hug.

"Hi, I'm Will. Great to meet you."

She kind of plucked his hand out of the air with hers.

"Rosemary."

"Pretty name."

So we sat, Chuck and I on the sofa, Will and Rosemary in chairs opposite, the plant on the table between us.

"Aren't these lovely flowers?" I said.

Everybody nodded. The canary broke the silence.

"I guess Tweety says hi, too," I said.

"Is Tweety a girl or boy?" Will asked.

"Everybody knows Tweety's a girl," said Chuck. "And Sylvester is a boy."

"Well, who always wins in Looney Tunes?"

"Tweety," said Chuck.

"What does that tell you?" Will asked, with a wink toward Rosemary.

"That girls are smarter?" she asked.

"You bet," he said. "At least that's been my experience."

She smiled but didn't commit teeth to it—at least not yet. But he had pushed the right button.

Will slouched on his end of the sofa until, I guess, he noticed my "straighten your shoulders" look. He sat up and smiled.

"It's great to be here, no kidding. Like, what do y'all want to know?"

"Do you like basketball?" asked Chuck.

"Sure, I mean, to watch. I'm not much of an athlete."

"Tar Heels?"

"They're okay. I like Carolina blue better than Catamount purple, anyway."

"Ever play HORSE?"

"Is that a challenge?"

Chuck smiled crookedly. "Might be."

"You're on—later." He looked at Rosemary, eyebrow lifted.

"Do you like to read?" she asked.

"I do. If I'd stayed in school I probably would have majored in English. How 'bout you?"

"It's okay."

"I like Hemingway. Who do you like?"

"I don't know. Emily Dickinson's pretty cool."

"How about Thomas Wolfe? You read *Look Homeward, Angel* yet?"

"Our teacher says he's old-fashioned."

"Try him sometime. His descriptions are kind of wild."

I stood and smiled. "Okay, children—ha, listen to what I just said. You're all my children, aren't you? So let's go to the dining room. Will, bring those cookies if you don't care."

Our dining set was a round oak table with ladderback chairs and a china cabinet. I laid out four dessert plates and brought out the cake saver, in which was a lemon pound cake I'd baked yesterday. "Rosemary, take drink orders. We're going to celebrate."

So we sat, the four of us, me with a cup of coffee, Chuck with a glass of milk, Rosemary and Will each with a 7-Up. Will had laid a cookie on each plate like something you'd see in church, and I followed by breaking slices of pound cake in two and giving each plate a half. Then I lifted my coffee.

"Family, here's to us. May our relationship be good and last long."

Glasses and cup clinked, which began an afternoon of getting to know each other. I don't know if it was sugar or what, but after we ate a quarter of that cake and all the ginger snaps we spilled into the backyard. It was one of those fall days when you *have* to be outside. No clouds, high in the sixties, a little breeze.

At first we just sat under the oak tree and talked. At one point I asked Will what was the most important thing that had ever happened to him.

"Well, aside from being born and getting adopted, for me it was Dad's death."

Both Rosemary and Chuck snapped to attention.

"Your father died? So did ours," said Rosemary. "Tell us about yours."

"I was twelve. Sixth grade. Like you, Chuck. It was like, Dad was okay one day and dying the next. I mean, he had some evil leukemia thing, diagnosed in July, dead in November. I'm still not over it."

Both Rosemary and Chuck's eyes were full, and I was pawing a pocket for a handkerchief. Will had been looking at his shoetops but turned his attention to his siblings. "Priscilla told me about your dad. That must have been real tough for y'all."

"It was," said Rosemary. "Like you said, it still is. I still have night-mares about it."

"Me too," said Will, and got up and hugged both kids. Not a dry eye under that shade tree. "We three got a lot in common," Will said. "Let's help each other through whatever else is left of the pain."

They decided to ease off on emotional stuff and pass the football. Then they played HORSE while I sat in a lawn chair and positively beamed. I had not felt such soul warmth since Pat was alive. And it felt pretty darn good. Well overdue.

I had asked Will not to sneak off to smoke, and he didn't. I expect the poor boy was about to scream for a cigarette, but maybe that would be good for him. Maybe he would quit soon.

We fixed supper, Will grilling hot dogs and the rest of us heating pork and beans and making slaw and opening a bag of barbecue potato chips and putting mustard and such on the table. After the supper dishes were done and put away, Will took us all for a ride in what he called The Streak. I sat up front with clenched jaw. The kids had a ball in the back. Will said he hadn't had such fun in a very long time and, when he left, way after dark, hugged us all. "I'll be as much a part of your lives as you'll let me," he said.

"Do we get to meet your... Mom?" asked Rosemary.

"Sure. Eventually. But that needs to be slow. She's kinda fragile."

"We have time," I said. "We have time, and each other. It'll be okay."

"Wait," said Rosemary. "Will, what do you mean by 'fragile'?"

"Mom's been in the hospital."

"I'm sorry. What was wrong?"

"She kind of had a nervous breakdown. But she's getting better."

"That doesn't sound like much fun."

"It wasn't. But she's a little stronger every day. I expect it won't be long before she's okay to meet Priscilla. Then y'all. One step at a time."

I had to tell Wanda. My mother, who had said ugly things about me and this baby. Who had vowed it to be no grandchild of hers, or words to that effect.

I had forgiven her years ago, but forgiving and forgetting are vastly different, at least for me. Mama had mellowed, especially after Daddy died—she'd lost some of her edge. Still, I had no idea how she'd react. Would this stir up those old feelings? Get her back up on that old "How Would That Look?" high horse of hers?

She usually came for Sunday supper. Her church didn't do Sunday night worship, and I wasn't that kind of Baptist anymore. She brought leftovers to combine with ours, not that two teenagers left great quantities. If there wasn't much, we'd have frozen pizza or chicken pot pie.

The day after Will came, she brought half an apple pie and a box of

Kentucky Fried Chicken. I mashed potatoes and cooked frozen peas, so we actually had a decent supper.

I'd asked the kids to let me break the news, but halfway through the meal they were about to burst.

"Mom, can we tell her?" Rosemary asked.

Wanda smiled. "Tell me what, darling?"

I gave up and nodded at my daughter, who suddenly seemed the most knowledgeable person in the world. "We have a brother, Grandma. His name is Will and he's cool."

Wanda had been about to attack a chicken leg but laid it on her plate. Her face showed a good deal more blush than usual. She looked at Rosemary, then at me.

"Whatever do you all mean?"

"She means what she said, Mama. He showed up here back in August. August sixth, to be exact."

"You mean…"

"Yes. And these two know the story. And yesterday they met him."

She squirmed in her chair. "So he had turned… twenty-one the day he showed up."

"That's right."

"Grandma, what's wrong?" asked Chuck.

"Well, dear, this is a huge surprise." She looked at me, eyes brimming. "How did he find you? I thought…"

"So did I. But he found me, no matter how, and I'm so glad he did."

"He's really cool, Grandma. You'd like him."

Wanda put her hand on mine and bit her lower lip. "You'll have to excuse me. I… I have to go."

She got up, picked up coat and pocketbook from the living room, and headed to her car. I left the kids with eyes full of disbelief, and followed her outside. When she rolled down the window I put my hands on the doorframe.

"Mama, you can't just run away from this."

"You can't think I'd just sit there calmly, do you?"

"What's to be afraid of?"

"What do you mean? You've let this… this person into your life without even finding out who he is? You don't know a thing about him."

"Mama, I don't need to hire Joe Mannix to investigate him. He's who he says he is."

"He could be a con artist, Priscilla. Out to take advantage of a woman like you."

"What's 'a woman like me' supposed to mean?"

"You know, without a husband to protect you. Oh, Priscilla, I didn't mean it to sound harsh. I just don't want you to be hurt again, that's all."

"Listen, Mama. He's bona fide. He has the right birthday. He has my hair and coloring. His father's eyes. The stories match. Plus, he's seen his original birth certificate—with my name on it."

"So you intend to... stay in touch with him."

"Yes. You need to let him in, too."

"I have to think about that."

"So go home and think. When you find it in your heart to do the right thing, let me know." She began to crank the window shut so I turned and walked to the front porch. Watched her drive down the road, faster than usual. Shook my head. Heard the kids scoot away from the front window, where they'd been watching us. Went back inside.

"Okay, gang, let's finish supper."

"Is Grandma okay?" asked Chuck.

"She will be."

"What did she say?" asked Rosemary.

"Nothing that needs repeating. Grandma is, well,... remember when you first heard, how it was a shock? She's got to get over that, too, just like you did. And I expect there's still some shame to deal with."

"Mom," said Rosemary, "what do you mean? Is she ashamed of Will or something?"

"Not exactly."

"So, what?"

"Well, your grandmother's a generation older than me. Back in 1949, having a baby before a girl was married was something to hide, to be ashamed of."

"I don't get it. There's a girl two classes ahead of me who had a baby. She's still in school, her mom and grandmom keep it during the day. It's really not a big deal."

"Well, this is 1970. A lot has changed. We might have to give Grandma some time with this. It took a while for you guys to get ready to meet him, remember? Now, eat your supper."

She called the next morning. Wanted to know Will's name, where he lived, all that. Said someone at her church could be trusted to find out if he had "spots" on his name.

"What's this all about, Mama?"

"I want to make sure we're not making a horrible mistake."

"We?"

"Well, aren't we all in this together, now that you've let him into the family?"

"Well, I suppose so. But I hope that will be a happy thing."

"We'll see."

Two days later she called. "Priscilla, can I come over?"

"Sure."

"I'll be there in a little while."

So I put on another pot of coffee and found some cookies. Tidied up the kitchen. Wondered what she'd come up with.

After settling in at the kitchen table, she took a deep breath. "Well, your young man is who he says he is."

"That's good to know."

"He is apparently a top-notch mechanic. That would have pleased your father."

"Does this mean you're okay to meet Will?"

"I'm thinking about it. I just don't know how to tell people about— all this."

"What do you mean?"

She put her coffee cup in its saucer and put her hands on either side of the cookie plate like it might head for the hills.

"Well, to say, you know, that I have this what you might call extra grandson, makes me sound pretty dumb. To say I knew you had a baby and gave him up but never told it sounds, I don't know, mean, or uncaring, or something. I don't know what to do."

"Just tell the truth, Mama. That's always okay. Trust me. He's an easy boy to love."

She looked over her glasses at me and sighed.

"Priscilla, this is hard for me, so don't interrupt. I've done a lot of thinking about what I said to you when I learned you were in trouble. I said some pretty hurtful things. I just want you to know that all that was said out of anger and whatever, and I apologize. I probably meant it then, but that's been a long time. I'm sorry."

I reached across the table for her hand.

"It's okay, Mama. I accept your apology. And we won't speak of it again."

"You're sure?"

"Yes. Now, listen. I'm having him over Thanksgiving. You need to meet him before that. How about Saturday? I feel sure, by the way, that after being around him a while, all your questions will kind of evaporate. You'll be proud of him. You'll own him, so to speak."

"What about his mother? Or other mother. Mrs. Blaine? Will she not want him at her table that day? By the way, she's Presbyterian."

I laughed. "You don't change much, do you, Mama? He might have to eat two turkey dinners. We'll work that out soon. Then one of these days we all might be thankful together."

She finally relaxed enough to eat a cookie.

"You know, this is really strange. I've stopped at The Top of the Hill before. For gas. He might have filled up my car. I might have met his... mother, too. You'd think there'd be some kind of, I don't know, electricity or something between people so close to each other."

"I've thought the same thing, Mama. It's weird, you're right."

"The kids okay with this?"

"They were upset at first. Had loads of questions. I think they felt like I had lied to them about Will. Now, they're just miffed I didn't tell them a long time ago. They really like him."

"Well, if they do, and you too, I'm sure I will. You think he'll like me?"

"If you behave yourself."

"Touché. I deserved that."

So, thanks to Will, I found out who I was. A widow. A mother. Of *three* children. *All of whom knew and liked each other.* I was so happy he found me.

Widow, not by choice, for sure. I'll always miss Pat. His voice has faded a bit, but sometimes in dreams he asks me to join him. I have to believe he's in heaven, wherever and whatever that is, and that I will see him there—but not yet.

My friends used to try to set me up with men, but no thanks. My social life is church and bridge club. Crawford Baptist suits me fine—those loving people accept me exactly where I am. The bridge club judges me not by clothes or car or looks, but card sense. I have a fair amount of that, inherited from Walker Lance. So, another man? Forget it. It was too hard to lose Pat.

A mother, for sure. Why want to be anything else? I have a deep, abiding love for my younger ones, Rosemary and Chuck. But I always listened for word of the oldest, as lost to me as someone in outer darkness.

My make-believe Millie, as ignorant of me as I was of her, boats in parallel currents, never to bump into each other.

Then, like a gift, Will showed up. I suppose some birth mothers would think that a thing to run away from, fast as a cheetah. They've put all that behind them and want no reminders. But my mythical Millie became a real, live, good-looking young man, hugging me on my front porch! To use a new word, we "bonded" immediately.

So, yes, I'm a widow, and a mother—of *three*. Who is fairly well-adjusted for the first time since I was a little girl. A mother about to need help with two teenagers, one of whom, Rosemary, sometimes thinks I'm the second dumbest person in the world (Chuck being ahead of me by a cat hair). Both kids need an older guy to look up to. He's a sweet boy, this young man, and I am so happy he came into our lives. Priscilla Lance Allen, this April Fool, is well-blessed, at last.

XI.

Glazed Donuts

Martha Atkins Blaine

I shouldn't have fretted about Will's re-entry into The Top of the Hill. He threw himself into the work like he was created for it. And not just car repair. He jumped into our whole business—store and garage—with an eye toward making it more efficient—and more profitable.

One of his first customers was Sand Hill's lawyer, a man of large appetite and little patience with what he called fools. Who, best I could tell, were all Democrats. But Papa always told me Republican money spent just like Democratic money, a lesson I passed on to Will.

When the lawyer got his bill, he blustered a while, invoked the Lord's name in vain. Said he didn't have that kind of money to put into an old car. (A '65 Bonneville about a mile long.)

Will smiled. "Sir, I don't set the prices for quality parts. And I'm sure you wouldn't want me to use cruddy stuff. Want to do some trading?"

"Son, what do you have in mind?"

"Mom never incorporated our business. She doesn't have a will, either. Neither do I, for that matter."

"Will Blaine, you got yourself a deal. What say I become your business attorney? Just trade brakes and gas and such for legal work and advice?"

"Fine with me."

"I'll draw up articles of incorporation tomorrow. Say, who does your bookkeeping?"

"Mom and Mary Anne keep the books. They have a guy who does their taxes."

"I have a crackerjack young man in my firm who could do all that for you. He's up to date, if you know what I mean."

"I'll ask Mom. Meanwhile, let's do the articles and wills."

"You won't be sorry if you let Sutton Law handle the whole ball of wax."

"Like I said, I'll ask."

I didn't think much of Mr. Sutton's idea at first. Trading for wills and such was fine, but the financial part was sticky, mainly because of Mary Anne.

Back during the war I hired her to take care of the store when I was fooling with Henry's awful mother and mine too, pretty near a full-time job. Mary Anne was a teenager then, not the smartest girl, but good at stocking shelves, chatting up customers, and, best of all, honest to a fault.

After the war she and I kept what amounted to ledgers on brown paper bags. A man at my church offered to do our taxes, so we found out what he wanted at the end of the year, and gave that to him. Quirky, but so was he, and all was well for a long time.

Then Will came back. By that time, "my girl" Mary Anne was in her mid-forties and, not that I wasn't, set in her ways. When I told her about Will, she barely nodded.

"He's going to work in the garage," I said.

"Fine."

"He'll also help with management. We need to catch up with the times."

The flash in her dark eyes said trouble.

"Mary Anne, I know you don't much like Will. But he's my son. We'll make room for him."

"What about the books?"

"He'll need to see them. Likely you'll have to explain how we take care of things."

"I don't know if I can do that, Mrs. B."

"He's not stupid, Mary Anne. He just doesn't know beans about accounting."

"I didn't mean that. I meant… well, I don't know if I can work closely with him. Not after he hurt you so bad."

"That's in the past. I have forgiven him. I take it you haven't."

"Not really."

"Well, you'll have to decide. I'd hate to lose you. But I'll understand if you can't work with my son."

"Let me think about it."

"Take all the time you need."

A couple of days later she came to work looking like she hadn't slept a wink. "Mrs. B., I'm giving my notice. I'll be leaving at the end of the month."

"Mary Anne, please don't. We've been together a long time."

"I know. But my mind's made up."

"Is it Will?"

She looked at her shoetops and nodded. "I think he's taking us—you—in the wrong direction."

I started to tell her she could leave right then, but if I fired her she could collect unemployment on our account. Such a thing had never happened to The Top of the Hill. So I gave her a hug.

"I wish you the best. Do you have another job lined up?"

"I'm working on it."

"Well, the ice deliveryman is outside. Go take care of that while I tidy up around the register."

"Yes, Ma'am."

I didn't know John Lewis, our mechanic, all that well. He was in his mid-fifties, had served in the Navy in the war, Pacific duty, best I remember. Destroyer or something. He kept his graying hair short, and was shaped kind of like a pear. Wore white coveralls, which I thought odd for someone who works with grease and oil. But it suited him, and if he was happy, so was I.

I had no idea how he'd react to Will. How would a man past middle age, used to working alone, take to having a kid barely legal for a boss?

Turned out not to be a problem. Will deferred to John about tools and repairs. Will consulted with him even if he knew good and well how to fix whatever ailed the motor.

They had a word in common: performance. They talked about it for hours. I finally figured it had something to do with making cars go faster. There was all manner of talk about bores and strokes and injectors and camshafts and lifters and I don't know what all. Man talk.

Next thing I knew, an old car showed up behind the garage. Reminded me of something you'd see before the war.

"Will, why is that rattletrap back there?"

"John bought it a while back. We're going to fix it up."

"What is it?"

"A '39 Ford. It'll make a cool modified."

"A what?"

"Modified. That's a class of race car."

"Lord, child, don't tell me you plan to…"

"John and I will set it up. His son will drive. Part of the new Top of the Hill look."

"New look?"

"Yeah, it'll be cool. Instead of just gas and groceries we'll be a speed shop too. We'll probably never be as successful as Banjo Matthews or Toy Jones, but it'll be fun to race with those guys."

"Just make sure it pays for itself. And that you don't drive it. Scares me to death."

*   *   *

Will convinced me to try Lawyer Sutton's tax guy. Mr. Levi, a pasty-faced man in a gray suit and brown shoes, came over one afternoon to see our books. By then, for receipts, we had a day book—for expenses, a folder with check stubs. A cash drawer. A folder with paid invoices. Another with pending bills. Same difference with the garage's books.

"And you've been keeping this business on the rails for how long?" asked Mr. Levi.

"I started in 1930 or so. I was just a girl when my father died."

He shook his head. "This is all?"

"What else should we have?"

"A general ledger, for starters. Separate accounts receivable and accounts payable journals. You don't even seem to have a chart of accounts."

"You can help us with that?"

"Certainly."

He pushed his glasses back up his nose, took out a yellowed handkerchief, and mopped his brow.

"I can make order out of all this. It's probably not as bad as it looks. Do you want me to write payroll as well?"

"We don't have but three employees. I can handle that."

"How do you figure payroll taxes?"

"I write paychecks based on these charts." I pulled them out of a grease-stained folder. He looked at them like they might be contagious.

"These are out of date. I'll bring current ones before Friday. You're sure we can't do payroll for you?"

"I can handle it, Mr. Levi. I want to control at least part of this business."

"Fine. I'll work up a chart of accounts and we can go from there."

We shook hands. As he left, I looked at Will.

"I almost expected to see chalk dust blowing off his back."

"He'll take a load off your shoulders. Give you more time to think about making new things happen."

Which they began to do, soon enough. As Will upgraded from fan belts and spark plugs to wheel covers and chrome shifters, I began to stock new things—Capri Sun, Tic Tacs, Gatorade. Nerf balls. I'd always stocked plain chips but began to keep Pringles and Doritos. Irish Spring went beside old Ivory bars. You know what I couldn't keep? Hot Wheels. Those little things flew off the counter beside the cash register.

We started to sell magazines, too. I was afraid women wouldn't buy them, but was wrong. Not just *Life* and *People* but *Cosmopolitan* and *Vogue*. We also sold *Popular Science* and *Popular Mechanics*, mostly to men and boys. Will talked me into *Rolling Stone* and tried, half jokingly, to push *Playboy*. Nothing doing with that.

One day Will said we needed to have a meeting about the future. He got a Coke and I poured a cup of coffee and we sat in the space between garage and store, a kind of waiting area for car repair customers.

"So, son, what's on your mind?"

"We need to sell beer and wine."

"I don't think so."

"I do. Mom, this is 1970. There's a new term for what we're doing here—convenience store. Mr. Levi says the really successful ones sell booze. The profit margins are unreal."

"Wouldn't that draw a bad crowd?"

"The world has changed since Grandpa started this store. Remember you told me about the old men who snuck away from their wives and drank here of a night? That's not who hangs around a convenience store. People stop for a six-pack or bottle and take it home. It's convenient. So what if it costs a dollar more than somewhere else? It's what Mr. L calls a profit center. Double the cooler space and stock half with beer. Keep some cold white wine. We would make some serious money."

"I don't know. I've seen what alcohol can do to a family. I'd hate to play a part in that."

"They're going to buy it one place or another. We might as well get our share."

"Well, I'll think about it. What else is on your mind?"

"That's about it. I'm off to tune up the old Chevy in there."

"Will, wait a second. I want you to think about something, too."

"What, Mom?"

"You and John divide the labor on your side. I don't have anyone since Mary Anne left. I can't do this by myself anymore. I'm fifty-seven, you know."

"Did you have someone in mind?"

"No, but I need to tell you I'm looking."

He hugged me. "Sure, Mom. I should have thought of that. I'll be on the lookout, too."

*   *   *

Meantime, Will was blooming. Put on a little weight, which he needed, for I doubt he had eaten two square meals at college. He was happier, too. Still, as usual, I found grounds to worry.

He had picked up a fondness for beer at Western—some weekends his boss had paid him in Pabst Blue Ribbon. I wanted him to quit drinking, but Mike and Howard said let him keep a little around. But if I found signs—and, Lord knows, I knew them—they'd put the quietus on that. So I got used to counting Blue Ribbons in the fridge. (Part, of course, of my reluctance to sell it in the store. That was an argument I'd eventually lose, but for a while I stuck to my guns.)

I also regretted he'd quit church. I tried to coax him into coming back, but he said if he had only one day off, he wasn't spending it there. But when he began to date Tina Green, that changed in a hurry.

She was Will's age, a tall, dark-haired, brown-eyed girl I'd describe as pretty, in a country kind of way. She didn't wear jewelry, and you had to look close to detect makeup. Not a girl who trailed a cloud of smell-good. A teetotaling Methodist, she lived way up South Hominy. Descendant of old Uriah Davis, she was kin to everybody up there. Some of those folks, I'd heard, were right ornery.

Not that Tina was hard to get along with. I found her to be sweet and kind. She baked cakes and cooked meals that didn't involve a box of shells and cheese. She played softball for the Piney Mountain Methodist Church. And she was good for Will.

She was a teller at our bank, so it didn't take long for him to notice her. Asked her out a couple of weeks after they met, and neither of them, as far as I know, even thought about looking at another. She latched on to him like she'd won an Oscar, and he didn't mind a bit. It wasn't hardly any time before he brought her to the house, and she had introduced him to her family. Anyone with half a brain knew this was getting serious, fast. Maybe too fast.

One night after supper I sat him down in the living room.

"Will, I'm happy you're seeing Tina. You two are… careful, I hope."

"C'mon, Mom, that's pretty personal."

"Well, I know not many couples wait until they are married, like in my day."

"Don't worry about that. But you need to know I told her I'm adopted."

"Sure you did. Not to would be unfair to her."

"Well, she thinks I need… you know… to find out about my birth parents. To know, as she puts it, what's in my 'genetic soup.'"

"Do you agree?"

"Sure. You said to warn you. I think this is it."

"You really love this girl?"

"I do."

"Then give me a while to pray about it."

"Thanks, Mom. I don't want to hurt you anymore."

"I likely can stand it."

It didn't make me mad when he started going to Piney Mountain with her. At first, he'd meet her at eleven for worship. Took a month or so for him to go to Sunday School too. And one day he came downstairs without a pack of cigarettes in his pocket.

"What's new, Will," I asked, pointing to his shirt.

"Oh. Tina asked me to quit. Says she doesn't like how I smell."

"Well, I hope you stay quit. I know it's hard to do."

"She's worth it, Mom."

And I couldn't help but notice he never touched those four Blue Ribbons in the fridge. Bless her.

It didn't take him long to decide to search for his "bio mom," as he put it. One rainy evening after supper he sat in the living room with Go Home in front of him, itching for Will to skritch him behind the ears.

"Mom, can I have tomorrow off?"

"Sure. What do you need to do?"

"I'm going to the courthouse."

Which sent a little shiver down my back.

"What's there, son?"

"They have birth records, right?"

"Yes, but they won't have yours. At least not your original. That was sealed and sent to Raleigh."

"But I figure if I can find out who was born that day there might be a way to talk to their mothers. One might remember my bio mom."

"Not likely. But, you're right, it's a place to start."

"You okay with that?"

"I said I was—and I am—and glad not to be surprised by all this."

"Good. Wish me luck."

What else could I say? I just smiled and turned my attention to the television. Couldn't tell you what was on, though.

*   *   *

The next day, he returned with his mother's name—Priscilla Lance—and high school yearbook picture. He was so nervous that he spent a good part of that night throwing up his toenails. I nursed him like when he was little.

Mike Capps found this woman—living in Crawford! (Seriously—you can't make this stuff up.) A widow with a daughter and son, she worked at the plant.

After Mike called, Will and I sat on the landing with Go Home. There was a nice breeze, in which crickets and katydids chorused about the upcoming fall.

"So now what?"

"Mom, I have to meet her. It's like, too weird where she's living. What, maybe six miles away? I mean, I might have seen her a zillion times and not known it."

"How about writing her a letter?"

"But what if that spooks her? I mean, if she didn't want to see me, that would be too easy for her to ignore, or write back and say 'buzz off.'"

"I've tried to put myself in her shoes. I think, especially since there's no husband to confess to, she might be open to a meeting. You never know. So do you just walk up and introduce yourself?"

"Maybe. I'm going to check out what she does on weekends. Maybe I can find a time I know she'll be by herself."

"Your birthday's coming up. That might be an emotional day, maybe she'd be more receptive to a visit."

"You think that's a good idea?"

"Lord, son, who knows? I'm new at this. I can say that, on a child's birthday, any woman with a heart thinks about him or her. What did Mike say?"

"About what you'd expect." Will let his voice get gravelly. "Don't. But if you do, wear a suit, get a haircut."

I had to smile. "Sounds like him. And you'll likely ignore it. Now, let's see. Do you know how old her kids are?"

"Rosemary's nearly sixteen. Charles is fourteen."

"If she accepts you, she'll have to tell them. But mind you, she might be too ashamed. She might kick you out to keep her secret."

"How can I know?"

"Call her?"

"But what if she says she doesn't know what I'm talking about and hangs up?"

"Then write as persuasive a letter as you can, explain why you called, say you want nothing except information about who in her family died of what, and leave it at that."

"I sure don't want to screw this up."

"Just go slow. And plan to be disappointed. That way, if she accepts you, you'll be as happy as a clam. This will work itself out, Will. One way or another."

In a couple of weeks—on his twenty-first birthday, in fact—he met the "bio mom." And, I have to say, my world didn't end. It didn't even rain, although I'd expected a storm all afternoon. He came home about four, smiling, said she was nice, open to getting to know him, nervous, nice, didn't know how to tell her kids about him, didn't smoke, did he mention she was nice? Said she'd probably met me years ago at The Top of the Hill. And I fixed meat loaf for his birthday and pretended everything was perfectly normal.

So they were going to have a relationship, as they say. Which meant a realignment of entanglements with everyone, me included. Funny, though, that didn't feel too bad. Will was happy, which pleased me, and by then I was secure enough with him in our business that I wasn't afraid of losing him. Of course, I was nervous about meeting her. But I figured to get through that, too.

Here, toward the end of my third journal—would you believe I have written that many volumes?—I am having trouble with words. See, Will scheduled me to meet his "bio mom," who I almost called his mother, which, of course, she is, or at least was. Now, if she's "bio mom," I'm "adoptive mom," which is also to say I'm his mother. And I myself witnessed the "bio mom" telling Will I was his "real mom." If that sounds swimmy-headed, all this relationship stuff is enough to make a body dizzy.

Anyhow, we met, and I survived. No, that's far too negative a word. I came out of that meeting with relief, sure, but also a sense of hope, hope that one day Will and Priscilla Allen and I might be friends. Priscilla, whatever you call her, is a nice young woman. A tad preachy, perhaps, but pleasant. They favor each other—she'd have to own him if pressed.

She has a way of turning her listening head exactly like Will, which I have said before also reminds me of Henry. Nature or Nurture? Who knows?

Will arranged us to meet at our church, because he thought I'd be more comfortable in a familiar place. I suppose that made more sense than meeting in, say, a bowling alley or restaurant.

A church—one that's been around a while, anyway—has a certain smell, like a hospital but friendlier. Certainly more complicated. Chalk dust and carnations. Leather bibles and floor wax. Diaper pails and Kool-Aid. Mothballs and spaghetti sauce. And the real or remembered seasonal odor of poinsettias and lilies.

Our pastor's secretary opened the back door for us. Walking in, I was flooded by memories. The morning Will was baptized, sunshine streaming like the touch of God's hand. Will, in worship, reciting the catechism with his little friends. The dark time that wretched Joyner man tried to blackball Scooter. All that rushed to my head like when you stand up too fast—I got kind of fluttery.

"Mrs. Blaine, are you okay?" she asked.

"Sure. I just need to sit down."

She led us into the conference room off the pastor's study, a room with four dark blue wing chairs surrounding a blonde wood coffee table holding a Bible, a box of tissues, and some dog-eared *Presbyterian Journals*.

"Will, it's stuffy in here. Open those drapes and crack the window a bit."

"You sure?"

"Yes. That's how the light gets in."

The window, on the east wall, faced a patch of woods like those that used to cradle each neighborhood house. Opening curtain and window was like hanging a breezy, chirping picture of my childhood.

I sat my nerves in a chair and told Will to keep an eye peeled for Mrs. Allen. (What to call her?) I made sure my blouse was buttoned and hose intact. I mean, how do you dress when meeting your only son's mother?

A pot of coffee sat on the corner table beside a box of wonderful West Asheville Krispy Kreme Donuts—my particular weakness. I can turn down a piece of pie, even with whipped cream on top, but you could lure me into an occupied tiger cage with a fresh glazed donut. As long as I tasted warm sugar I wouldn't mind hearing the latch snap shut.

Soon I heard car wheels on gravel—a car door shut—faint voices. After the back door opened, footsteps down the hall said she wore sensible shoes. My heart began to go rabbity.

She was dressed what I'd call professional, smart suit, satin blouse buttoned at the neck, low heels. A bosomy woman who, for this event, did not flaunt that. Her smile—and three sunflowers—put me immediately at ease.

"Mrs. Blaine, there's one for each of us. I grew them myself."

"Will, see if there's a vase in that cabinet. Oh, good, a Mason jar is perfect. Now put some water in with these beautiful flowers. Mrs. Allen, thanks so much."

"Please, I'm Priscilla."

"Then I'm Martha."

"A pleasure to meet you."

"Me too."

Awkwardness threatened to settle between us like a wet, smelly dog. She sat in the chair beside mine, started to open her pocketbook, then noticed the box of tissues.

"I better take one. I've been close to tears all morning."

So we sat there, mothers holding Kleenex, son too nervous to sit, eyes darting from one mom to another. He knelt between our chairs.

"Please don't cry. I just want us to get to know each other. Like, I'm super happy to have found you."

He grasped her hand in his, which stabbed my heart a bit. Then he gave me that smile I never could resist and took my hand, too.

"Mom… like, wow, I'm just realizing this, look, I'm the link between y'all. I'm literally what has brought you together. I hope we will make a cool triangle."

With free hands we women reached for tissues.

Priscilla recovered first.

"Will, I was right the other day. Call me Priscilla. When you say 'Mom' to Martha, it sounds so natural and proper. She *is* your mom, no matter who gave birth to you. So never call me 'Mother' or anything like that. Are we clear?"

"Sure… Priscilla."

"Martha, this is from my heart. I wouldn't hurt you for the world. So if you want this to be the only time you lay eyes on me, I will hug you both and disappear best I can."

"Thank you, Priscilla… but… Will needed to find you, and did it with my permission. So, no, let's get to know each other."

Will held our hands again. I feared his smile might break his face.

"Mom, are you sure?"

"Yes, son. See, I've always wondered about your... Priscilla. What was she like? Where was she? Did she have other kids? A raft of questions. Now we'll have answers."

When a sunflower suddenly listed to the left, Priscilla disengaged herself to right it.

"You know, Martha, it's funny you say that, because I've always wondered who got my baby. Did it wind up in a good home? What did you and your husband do? All that. And I have to laugh. See, I made up a story. I called my baby Millie. Especially on August sixth I wondered what she was doing, where she was. I had a private birthday party for her in my heart."

"You thought Will was a girl?"

"I was sure of it."

"So you never saw this guy?"

"No. I don't remember much after I got to the hospital. I expect they gave me knockout drops or something."

"That's cruel, you know? To have a baby and not..."

"I expect they do that so you won't renege on your agreement."

Open and honest, we talked the morning away. Finished the coffee and most of the donuts. Traded hugs in the parking lot. Will and I waved to Priscilla as she drove down the hill—then we crossed the road and went upstairs.

To start a new era, a stretch that, so far, has been smooth. Will and I have big plans for The Top of the Hill, which now flies a checkered flag beside our usual American one. In the next five years we want to tear down the building my father built and replace it with a new setup with a beer and wine section. Will and Tina are, I think, getting ready to announce their engagement. I've hired a young person to learn the ropes with an eye toward relieving me of store management. I'm thinking about retirement.

I'm a far cry from where I was when Dr. Jackson gave me my first blank journal. Back then I had no idea who I was or what was wrong. Now, I have something like a normal life. Dare I finally take Psalm thirty-seven to heart: "Fret not"? Dare I hope it will last?

After all I've been through—and I think Dr. Jackson would be proud of me for saying this—I choose to hope.

Thanks

This novel, some six years in the writing, is a work of love and hope.

Autobiography? No. Autobiographical? Well, with Thomas Wolfe, I have "used the clay of life" vouchsafed me. An adoptee handed to his adoptive parents at some six weeks old, I was always told I was adopted, and thought that perfectly normal. No "abandonment issues," no bad-mouthing my birth mother. I was raised by parents who loved me probably beyond what I deserved.

I have many to thank—and apologize to those I have forgotten. (It's been a long time since I began this book.) Chief to thank are three of the four folks who call themselves the Holden Beach Writers' Conference. I have been Holden Forth ocean-side for some two decades with Mary Caldwell, and Guy and Anita Sayles. Many scenes from this story were read (by me) and improved and appreciated (by them). My sister Debbie Burden, who had no idea she had an older brother until 2016, read the typescript with much interest and empathy. My sister-in-law Kathryn Long told of a visit to a home for "unwed mothers" she endured as a Baptist teenager. Chaplain Dorri Sherrill told me a story of a cat interrupting a sermon. June Fuchs, whom I met years ago at a literary event in Rugby, Tennessee, told me about Ocean View, Virginia, near where she grew up. Erica Abrams Locklear, mountain friend one ridge over, thinks I am a pretty decent writer. I am indebted to all y'all.

Most of all, I thank Mary, attentive and insightful reader, best friend, wife, who believed in this book from the beginning. I couldn't have written it without her.

About the Author

Wayne Caldwell is the author of two novels, *Cataloochee* (2007) and *Requiem by Fire* (2010; reissued 2020), and two volumes of poems, *Woodsmoke* (2021) and *River Road* (2024). He has won the Thomas Wolfe Memorial Literary Award from the WNC Historical Association and the James Still Award from the Fellowship of Southern Writers.

www.ingramcontent.com/pod-product-compliance
Lightning Source LLC
Chambersburg PA
CBHW011642010726
47495CB00011B/2866

* 9 7 8 1 9 6 3 6 9 5 1 3 7 *